BOOKS BY

Carrie Carr
=====================

Destiny's Bridge

Faith's Crossing

Hope's Path

Love's Journey

Strength of the Heart

The Way Things Should Be

Something to Be Thankful For

Diving Into the Turn

To Hold Forever

Carrie Carr

Yellow Rose Books

Nederland, Texas

ISBN 978-1-932300-21-5
1-932300-21-X

First Printing 2008

9 8 7 6 5 4 3 2 1

Cover design by Donna Pawlowski

Published by:

Regal Crest Enterprises, LLC
4700 Highway 365, Suite A, PMB 210
Port Arthur, Texas 77642

Find us on the World Wide Web at
http://www.regalcrest.biz

Printed in the United States of America

Acknowledgements:

There were storylines in this book which were new and definitely out of my comfort zone, and I had a lot of help along the way. Some of the best ideas came from my wife, Jan, who never complained about all my questions about pregnancy. I'd like to thank Judy for being my technical advisor for child development. My deep appreciation goes to my beta reader Tena, who trudged through the first draft bravely. My editor, Ruta, who seems to know the characters better than I do — it was a true pleasure working with you. Kudos to the artistic talent of Donna Pawlowski whose covers rock. And, as always, thank you to Cathy who never complains when Lex and Amanda "tap" me on the shoulder.

To my mom, who has unceasingly cheered me on—thank you! I wouldn't be where I am today without you.

And, most of all, to my greatest supporter and best friend, my wife, Jan. Thank you for always being there for me. Forever and always, my love.

Chapter
One

HEAVY STEPS ON the back porch echoed loudly. The thick, wooden door opened and quickly shut behind Lexington Walters. Rain water dripped from her drenched black hat and duster as she struggled to remove the soaked items.

At the sound of rapidly moving feet Lex looked up in time to intercept a damp, naked toddler. "Hold on there, lil' bit. Give me a chance to catch my breath."

"Me want up!" the tiny dynamo demanded, raising her arms.

Lex hung her hat up next to the coat and squatted to the child's level. She scooped her up in her arms and kissed her dark head. "Where's everyone?"

"Lorrie, come back here. You know better than—" Amanda Cauble-Walters stood outside the doorway to the downstairs bathroom, fluffy towel in hand. "Looks like you could use one of these, too."

"Yep. It's coming down in buckets out there." The late-July downpour had been a surprise, but not an unwelcome one. The ranch hadn't fully recovered from the previous year's drought. Lex shifted Lorrie until she was able to prop her on one hip. She took the towel from her partner and wrapped it around the squirming child. "Stay still, kiddo. I'll be done in a minute, then you can get down and terrorize the house some more."

A little over two and a half, Lorrie ran everywhere, keeping both aunts busier than they expected. Her mother, Amanda's sister Jeannie, had gone to a rehabilitation clinic in Austin to regain her strength not long after Lorrie was born. She'd actually started in a smaller place in Somerville but didn't feel she was making enough progress, so she moved. They had agreed to keep the baby with them so that Jeannie could concentrate on recovering from the stroke that incapacitated her after Lorrie's birth.

Lorrie pulled Lex's wet hair. "Uck." Now that she had greeted Lex, she leaned as far as she could toward Amanda. "Manny," Lorrie grunted, as she stretched her short arms out.

"I see how I rate." Lex handed her cargo to Amanda. "How was your day, besides busy?" She followed Amanda to the bathroom and watched her struggle to put Lorrie in pajamas.

"That's pretty much it. I don't think I was ever this worn out, even when I worked late at the office." Amanda was on leave of absence from Sunflower Realty, where she was the office manager. "This little dynamo ran me ragged today." Her job finished, Amanda tickled Lorrie's foot.

The child giggled and squirmed until Amanda set her on the floor. She immediately held her arms in the air. "Wex, up!"

Lex rolled her eyes, but dutifully grasped the toddler under the armpits and lifted her high in the air. "Is this what you wanted, kiddo?" A high-pitched squeal answered her, so Lex spun in a slow circle, while holding Lorrie over her head.

"If you get her stirred up, you have to try to put her to bed," Amanda threatened. It was after seven in the evening, which was about the time their young charge went down for the night.

"Ossie, Wex. Ossie!" Lorrie commanded. Her wish was granted when her aunt placed her behind her head, with Lorrie's chubby legs draped to each side of her neck. She grabbed a handful of Lex's damp hair and kicked her feet. "Go!"

Lex galloped to the stairs, using both hands to hold Lorrie close. "Hang on. We're heading to bed, Lorrie." She took the stairs slowly, bouncing a little on each step much to the child's delight.

Martha stepped out of the kitchen when she heard the noise. She shook her head at Lex's antics. "I swear, I don't know which one is the bigger kid."

"I know what you mean. I had no idea Lex would enjoy having a child in the house as much as she does. She's so good with Lorrie." Amanda's voice softened. "I want to give her that, Martha. I know she loves Lorrie, but I want to give her a baby of our own."

"Maybe the next time will be the charm, honey."

"Possibly. Two failures aren't the end of the world. We've got an appointment next week, this time in Dallas. I didn't like the doctor in Austin. He was so impersonal, and I thought Lex was going to deck him when he kept asking where my husband was."

Martha put her arm around Amanda's waist. "It's going to work out. I have a good feeling about this one."

Amanda leaned into Martha, until her head was on the other woman's shoulder. "I hope so. I don't think I can handle much more disappointment. I didn't want to tell Lex, but I got a phone call today from my sister. She's coming for a visit this weekend, and I'm afraid she'll want to take Lorrie with her."

"Did she specifically say? Although I know she hasn't been out to the ranch since she's been in rehab, I can't see her wanting to take Lorrie away."

"Not in so many words, no. She did tell me she had a surprise to share, and seemed very excited about it." Amanda could still hear Lex and Lorrie upstairs. "Great. Now it sounds like they're singing. We'll never get her to sleep at this rate." She started for the stairway, until she was stopped by Martha's gentle grasp of her arm. "What?"

"No sense in borrowing trouble. Let's wait and see what your sister has to say before we get all riled over nothing. Maybe she's decided to move to Somerville."

Amanda closed her eyes and took a deep breath, releasing it slowly. "You're right. I'm afraid of what losing Lorrie would do to Lex. And to me."

The housekeeper let go of Amanda. "Forgive me for saying so, but I don't think Jeannie wants to be tied down with a child. She's been well enough for over a year to take that baby, and she hasn't done it. I believe she's more than happy with the arrangement you have."

"As far as I'm concerned, Lorrie *is* our daughter. She doesn't even know who her mother is. The few times we've taken her to see Jeannie, my sister is so detached from her. She's never bonded with Lorrie, and hasn't held her since she was an infant." Amanda started up the steps. "I'll tell Lex tonight about the phone call. I don't want her to be blindsided by Jeannie's visit."

AMANDA STOOD IN the doorway of the former guestroom, which had been converted to a nursery. It was directly across the hall from the master suite, and Lex had spared no expense in decorating it for their niece. A colorful strip of cartoon characters ran across the middle of the walls, accenting their pale yellow color. The crib was made of light oak, as was the matching rocker, chest of drawers, and changing table.

Lex sat in the rocker, singing softly to Lorrie. She had changed into boxer shorts and a tee shirt, although her hair was still damp. The little girl's eyes were closed, yet her right foot kicked, almost in time to the song. Upon feeling Amanda's presence, Lex looked up with a tender smile on her face. "Hey, there." Her voice was low and she never stopped her rocking.

"Hi." Amanda stepped farther into the room, her gaze never leaving her lover's. "Looks like you finally got her to sleep."

"Yep. Although the hardest part is letting her go and putting her in her crib." Lex looked down at the child in her arms. "She's adorable, isn't she?"

Amanda nodded, too choked up to answer. The thought of losing the toddler to an indifferent Jeannie was almost too much to bear.

"What's the matter?"

"Nothing. I can't believe how much she's grown. It won't be long before she'll need a real bed." Amanda walked over and lightly played with Lorrie's hair. She couldn't get over how much the child resembled Lex, although her eyes were gray instead of dark blue.

Lex lifted the toddler so Amanda could hold her. "It seems like only yesterday she was a tiny baby. Where does the time go?" She watched as Amanda kissed the tot's forehead and laid her in her crib. "Why are you crying?"

"I heard from Jeannie today. She's planning on visiting this weekend."

"Really? That's great. She's okay, isn't she?" Lex stood and moved next to the crib.

Amanda put one arm around her lover and placed her head on Lex's chest. "She's fine. She told me she had a surprise, and I'm worried about what it could be."

"You're afraid she's coming for Lorrie, aren't you?" Lex wrapped her arms around Amanda. "She hasn't cared so far. I don't see any reason for her to change."

"My mind tells me you're right, but my heart is saying another thing altogether." Amanda sniffled when she felt a light kiss on the top of her head. "I couldn't stand it if we lost her, Lex. She's too precious to me."

Lex rubbed Amanda's back in a soothing pattern. "We can't think that way. We'll end up going crazy if we do." She tugged her lover away from the sleeping child. "Let's go. I think we could both use a snuggle."

LEX CURSED AS she slipped through the mud. In the short walk from the jeep to the corral she had almost fallen several times. There was a small part of her that wanted it to be raining so she could stay inside with Amanda and Lorrie. Her partner was still worried about her sister's upcoming visit, and nothing Lex did made her feel any better.

"Hey, boss." Roy Wilson, foreman of the Rocking W Ranch, waved from the corral fence. "You're just in time. Chet's about to bring out that new little filly he's been working with."

Lex stood beside him. She mirrored his stance, crossing her arms over the top rail and propping her chin on her hands. "Is she turning out to be half as good as she looks?"

"I think you'll be pleased with the results." Roy pushed his western hat up on the back of his head and rubbed where the band had been. "You made a real good deal with Chuck Bice, offering Thunder's services for one of the foals. I don't think that stud will throw any bad ones." He noticed that his employer was unusually quiet. "Is something bothering you, Lex?" She was silent for so long, he wasn't sure she would answer.

"I don't know." Waiting for Chet and the horse to arrive, she turned her head, resting her cheek on her arms. "Do you ever wonder if there's more to life than what you're doing?"

He gave the question serious thought. "You mean, like doing something else?"

"Yeah."

"Well, sure. I think we all have, at one time or another."

"What would you do, if you weren't foreman here?"

Roy scratched his jaw. "You'll probably think it's funny."

Lex raised her head, so that her complete attention was now on him. "Try me."

"You know I've spent nearly my whole adult life here on the ranch." At her nod, he continued. "It's always been a dream of mine to have my own little spread. Nothing on this scale, just a few dozen head of cattle, and a decent place to hang my hat."

Lex leaned against the corral, draping one arm over the top rail. "Why haven't you said something before?"

He dropped his gaze and kicked at the drying mud. "Like I said, it's only a dream. I could never afford something like that."

To give Roy time to get his feelings under control, Lex returned to her previous position. "Don't give up your dreams, my friend."

Roy looked up at her profile. She seemed sad. "I...I won't."

They both stood silent as the ranch hand led the dark horse into the corral. She was saddled and appeared comfortable with the extra weight on her back. Lex ducked between the rails. She slowly moved toward the animal until she was standing next to Chet. "You've done a nice job with her, Chet."

"Thanks, Lex. She was one of the easiest horses to saddle train I've ever worked with." He patted the animal's neck. "Why don't you climb up? I think she's ready for a test run."

For the first time since she left the house that morning, Lex smiled. "I think I will." She gathered up the reins and swung herself up onto the saddle. The horse stepped sideways, but was quickly brought under control by its rider. "Whoa, girl. Take it easy." Lex waited until the filly stilled. She lightly touched her heels to the horse's flank, and used her legs to guide her forward. "That's it. Nice and slow."

Chet climbed through the wooden slats to stand next to Roy. They both quietly watched as Lex put the new horse through its paces.

Chapter
Two

AMANDA PACED ANXIOUSLY around the living room. Jeannie called earlier to say she was on her way, but she still gave no clue about her reason for coming. She alluded once again to her surprise. The uncertainty of it all kept Amanda on pins and needles.

"It's going to be fine." Lex hated seeing her so upset. Truth be told, her own fears had kept her awake the previous night. She had no idea what Jeannie had to say, and the ball of worry in the pit of her stomach had turned into a boulder. "Why don't you come sit next to me? You're going to wear yourself out."

"I can't. I'm afraid if I get too still, I'll throw up." Amanda paused long enough to peek through the curtains in the front windows. "Finally! There's a car coming down the driveway." She readjusted the material and headed for the hallway. Moments later, Lex was by her side, opening the front door.

Lex was momentarily stunned when she came face-to-face with a man, who stood next to a beaming Jeannie. "Uh, hello."

Jeannie linked her arm with his. The large smile that graced her delicate features spoke of her happiness. "Well? Are we going to stand on the porch all day, or are you letting us in?"

"I'm sorry. Of course." Lex stepped back and held the door open wider. "Why don't we all go into the den?" She exchanged looks with Amanda as the newcomers walked ahead of them.

Amanda recovered from her shock at seeing her sister so intimate with a man she'd never seen before. "Would you like some coffee? I believe there's a fresh pot in the kitchen."

He shook his head and spoke for the first time. "Actually, we'll both take juice, if you have some."

"Sure." Lex patted Amanda on the back. "Sweetheart?"

"Coffee, please." Amanda waited until Lex left the room before taking a spot on the dark leather sofa.

The three maintained an uncomfortable silence until Lex returned with a tray. "I hope apple juice is okay. It's Lorrie's favorite at the moment, so it's all we have."

"That's great." Jeannie took both glasses from the tray and

handed one to the man next to her. She watched as her sister-in-law shakily placed the tray on the coffee table. "I'm sorry, I don't know where my manners are. Guys, this is Rodney Crews. He's a doctor at the rehabilitation center. Rodney, this is my sister, Amanda and her partner, Lex."

Rodney nodded to the couple. "It's great to finally meet you. Jeannie's told me so much about you, I feel as if I know you already."

"I hope it wasn't all bad." Lex couldn't help but rib Jeannie. Their relationship had always been based on mutual affection, with a large dose of teasing tossed in.

Jeannie laughed and shook her finger at Lex. "No, not all of it. I didn't want to scare Rodney off before he got a chance to meet you."

Rodney squeezed her hand. "Nothing to worry about there. Anyone related to you can't be bad, darling."

The endearment caught Amanda off guard. She was ready to find out more about this mystery man. "So, sis. What brings you out here? I thought we were going to go see you next week."

"I know. But I couldn't wait any longer. Rodney and I have wonderful news." She turned and gazed at him for a long moment. "We're engaged."

Amanda's jaw dropped. "Engaged? I didn't know you were even seeing anyone."

"Actually, we've been together for several months. Last week Rodney asked me to marry him."

Lex was about to say something, but a small cry coming from the nearby baby monitor caught her attention. She stood immediately. "If you folks will excuse me, I'll be back in a minute." She stepped from the room without another word.

"Aren't you happy for us, Mandy?" Jeannie took a sip from her glass. "After all, wasn't it you who told me I needed to get on with my life?" She remembered all too clearly her sister's comments from the year before. "You were right, you know. I would have never gotten better if it hadn't been for that."

The coffee table was suddenly quite interesting to Amanda. She had trouble meeting her sister's eyes. Now that Jeannie had found someone to spend her life with, Amanda was afraid she'd want her daughter, too. "Of course. I'm thrilled for you." She looked up, but focused on a point over Jeannie's head. "Congratulations."

Childlike chattering brought everyone's attention to the doorway. Lex walked into the room, with Lorrie sitting on her shoulders. "Sorry about that, everyone. Somebody woke up from her nap." She cringed when the toddler pulled her hair. "Lorrie, cut that out." She sat next to Amanda, who relieved her of her burden.

"Come here, you." Amanda kissed Lorrie's cheek.

Rodney's eyes widened. "Is that her?" he asked his fiancée.

"Yes." Jeannie handed him her glass and got to her feet. She went to stand in front of Amanda, and held out her arms. "Come to mama, sweetie."

Lorrie immediately locked her arms around Amanda's neck in a stranglehold. She had never gotten used to Jeannie, even though she'd visited her at the rehabilitation center a few times. "No." When Jeannie tried to pull her away, she screamed and held on tighter. "Manny!"

"What's the matter with her? She's acting like a spoiled brat." Jeannie gave up the battle, stepping back and placing her hands on her hips. "What have you been teaching my daughter, Amanda? Have you been telling her bad things about me?"

Lex rubbed the child's back with one hand, while she placed her closest arm around Amanda. "That's ridiculous. She just woke up, and she's not very comfortable around strangers."

"Strangers? For God's sake, Lex. She's *my* daughter." Jeannie took a step forward, which caused Lorrie to whimper again.

"Leave her alone, Jeannie. There's no sense in tormenting the child," Rodney interjected.

Jeannie returned to her seat. "But I'm her mother. There's no good reason to act like that."

Amanda ran her fingers through Lorrie's wispy hair, which further settled the child down. "You may have given birth to her, but you've never shown an interest in her, and she knows that."

"Well, she needs to get used to me. Especially since —"

"Wex." Lorrie leaned over and grabbed Lex's shirt. "Mine."

Lex allowed the young girl to climb into her lap. "That's right, kiddo. I'm yours." She glanced over Lorrie's head at the couple on the loveseat. "Especially since what?"

Jeannie looked at Rodney, who nodded. "Especially since I'm three months along with her little brother or sister."

"You're what?" Amanda stood. "But you've never had anything to do with your daughter. I didn't think you were even interested in children."

"I know." Jeannie rubbed her belly. "But Rodney and I are looking forward to our family. That's another reason I wanted to talk to you today."

Amanda imagined the unspoken words. Her greatest fear was coming true. Jeannie had returned to take Lorrie away from them. As tears welled up in her eyes, Amanda spun and raced from the room.

Lex put her arms around Lorrie and stood. "I'll be right back."

"Would you like to leave her with us? I'd love to get acquainted with her." Rodney put his arm around his fiancé. "I'm pretty good with children."

Before Lex could even take a step, Lorrie started to cry. "Want Manny."

"I think Lorrie and I will both go check on Amanda. Excuse us." Lex carried Lorrie from the room.

THE SOUND OF SLAMMING cabinets led Lex to the kitchen. Even with Amanda's back to her she could tell her lover was crying. "Amanda?"

"I can't do it." Amanda turned away from the counter. Tears fell freely from her eyes. "There's no way I can sit in there and listen to my sister brag about what a wonderful mother she's going to be. What's to say she'll treat this baby any better than Lorrie? My God, Lex. She's never shown an interest in this precious little girl. How could she be so callous?"

Lex brought Lorrie closer. The toddler sleepily reached for Amanda, who immediately took her into her arms. "I don't know, sweetheart. Maybe being pregnant again has brought out maternal feelings in her."

"But she acts like she wants Lorrie. How can we allow that?" Amanda rocked side to side, holding the child close.

"She hasn't said she wants Lorrie. Only that she's engaged and expecting another baby. Maybe that's all she's here for."

Amanda's expression hardened. "I'll fight her, Lex. There's no way I'm giving up this sweet child to someone who's never loved her."

"Let's hope it doesn't come to that."

"Comes to what?" Jeannie asked from the doorway.

Lex turned and tried to give her a reassuring smile. "Nothing. We were on our way to the den." She glanced over her shoulder. "Right?"

"Sure." Amanda forced a calmer look onto her face. "How long will you be staying in town, Jeannie?"

"We were planning on stopping in to see dad, and Gramma and Grandpa. We'll probably be staying with them."

"Good," Amanda muttered under her breath.

"What?"

Amanda inhaled deeply. "I said, good. I know they'll love to see you." She glared at Lex, daring her to say differently.

Jeannie followed them. "There is something else I'd like to discuss."

"Oh?" Amanda fought to keep control of her emotions. She didn't want to upset Lorrie, who was playing with her necklace.

Rodney stood as they entered. "Is everything all right?"

"I was about to talk to Lex and Amanda about Lorrie." Jeannie went and put her arm around his. She waited until the two women were seated. "Seeing her makes what I have to say much easier."

Lex swallowed the heavy lump in her throat. "And what is it you want to tell us?"

"It's about what I think is best for my daughter, Lex. I thought it would be easier to discuss this in person, rather than on the phone."

"Dammit, Jeannie. Would you spit it out?" Amanda's imagination was running rampant, and she feared the worst.

"Fine. Rodney and I talked about this at length, and we both think it would be in Lorrie's best interest if she was in a home where she was loved."

Amanda fought the tears that were threatening to fall. "She's extremely loved here, Jeannie. Or maybe you're conveniently forgetting that."

"No, I'm not." Jeannie moved away from Rodney, so she could stand in front of Amanda. She reached down and lightly touched the toddler's head. "I know you and Lex have been imposed on for these last couple of years, having to take in a baby that wasn't even yours."

"It wasn't an imposition," Lex interrupted. "It was a labor of love." She put her arm around Amanda and pulled her and Lorrie closer to her. "We've never regretted one second of it, Jeannie. She's brought so much into our life."

Jeannie pulled her hand away from Lorrie. "I'm glad you feel that way, Lex. Like I said, Rodney and I deliberated over this for a while now. As much as I love Lorrie, I know you've given her a good home, and that's very important. But it's also important for a child to be with its mother."

"What are you saying?" Amanda began to shake. Her greatest nightmare was coming true.

"I'm saying that, even though I gave birth to her, Lorrie doesn't know me at all. You two are the only parents she's ever known. Rodney and I think our family should start with this little one, here." Jeannie rubbed her abdomen again. "Would you have a problem with adopting Lorrie? I know it was supposed to only be until I got on my feet, but she's obviously very happy here."

Lex wiped at her eyes. "Does this mean you want to give up your rights as her mother?"

"Yes, that's exactly what I mean. Come on, Slim. You don't actually think I'm heartless enough to drag a child away from her family, do you?"

"Damn, Jeannie. You almost gave me a heart attack." Lex stood and moved to embrace her sister-in-law. "We'd be honored to raise Lorrie. She's already so deep into our hearts, I don't know what we'd do without her." She put her mouth next to Jeannie's ear. "Thank you."

Amanda got to her feet. "Are you absolutely sure about this?"

"Completely." Jeannie gestured to her fiancé. "Show them, Roddie."

Rodney reached into his interior jacket pocket and brought out several sheets of paper. He handed the documents to Lex. "These are already signed and notarized. There's also a set in there that you two need to fill out, in order to take legal custody."

"I can't believe this." Amanda looked down into the child's face. "Guess what, honey? You're here for good." She raised her head so that she could lock eyes with her sister. "I don't know what to say."

Jeannie leaned in to kiss Amanda's cheek. "Just say you'll raise her to be half as good a person as you. That's all I ask."

"We'll do our best." With that, Amanda felt her torn heart heal.

THE ONLY LIGHT in the room was from the moon that shone through the bedroom windows. Lex lay on her side, with her head propped on her hand. Amanda mirrored her position with the sleeping child between them. "Look at her, not a care in the world." Lex's gaze tracked upward to meet her lover's. "Can you believe this day? I'm still in shock over what Jeannie did."

"Me, too. I want to file those papers first thing Monday, in case she decides to change her mind." Amanda traced Lorrie's face with her finger. "How could anyone desert such an angel?"

"I think it's like Jeannie said. She knows Lorrie is happy here, and she's very well loved. Why would she want to ruin that?"

Amanda leaned across the baby and kissed Lex. "I know *I'm* very happy here. You've given me everything I could ever want." She ran her hand through her partner's hair, which touched the top of Lex's shoulders. "I love your hair."

"Thanks." Lex took Amanda's hand and brought it to her lips. She kissed the palm, which elicited a moan from Amanda.

"Maybe we should rethink having Lorrie with us tonight."

"I can always put her in her room," Lex offered, although her heart wasn't in it. "She's sleeping so hard, I don't think a train could wake her up."

"No, that's all right. I think I want her to stay, so when I open my eyes in the morning, I'll realize it wasn't a dream." She noticed the sad look on Lex's face. "What's the matter?"

"Hmm?" Lex blinked, and the look was gone. "I guess I was thinking about the doctor's appointment next week. I wish you didn't have to go through that again."

"Are you saying you don't want a baby with me?"

Lex shook her head. "No, of course not. I want that with all my heart. It's hard seeing you put through so many medical tests and procedures. I wish it was the one thing I could give you."

Amanda interlocked their free hands. "I'm glad you can't."

"What?"

"Look at it this way. If you had the right equipment to give me a baby, then we wouldn't be together." Amanda wiggled her eyebrows. "I happen to love your parts."

The teasing tone in Amanda's voice caused Lex to laugh. "Thanks, I think." She squeezed Amanda's hand, and they both settled down in bed. "I happen to be very fond of your parts, too."

"I'm glad. And, when we're alone again, I'll show you how glad I am."

"I can't wait." Lex stretched forward so she was able to place a light kiss on Lorrie's head. "Goodnight, little one." Her eyes glinted with humor. "Oh, and you too, Lorrie."

"I'll have to think of a good way to get you for that one."

"You can try." Lex brought their linked hands to her lips and kissed Amanda's fingers. "Goodnight, sweetheart. I love you." Her eyes closed, and she was asleep almost before finishing her sentence.

"Sleep well, love."

Chapter
Three

PACE. PACE. PACE. Turn. Pace. Pace. Pace. Turn. Pace. Pace.

"Ms. Walters?" A small woman stood inside the open door.

Lex spun around. "Yes?"

"They're ready for you in room two. If you'll follow me, please." The woman, dressed in teal-colored scrubs, led her down the bright and narrow hallway. She paused at a nondescript white door, and knocked. When she received a positive response, she opened the door and waved Lex inside.

Amanda, dressed in a cotton hospital gown, turned her head from where she lay on the table. "Hi, honey."

"Hey, there." Lex went to stand by Amanda's head. "How'd everything go?" She took Amanda's hand in hers, brought it up to her lips, and kissed it.

Over by the sink, a short, gray-haired doctor turned to face them. After writing his notes on Amanda's chart, he smiled at the couple. "Your partner is doing very well, Ms. Walters. As I told her a few moments ago, I don't think we're going to have any trouble at all. We already have your chosen donor's sperm here at our facility. Due to the timing, we should be able to inseminate any day now."

"That soon?" It wasn't that Lex didn't want Amanda to become pregnant, but she wanted to have time to prepare herself. Their trip today was only supposed to be so that the doctor could give Amanda a thorough exam and discuss their options. The way he was speaking, they'd have to stay in town for a few days. "Is there anything special we have to do?"

"No. I've suggested to Amanda that she do a LH surge test twice a day."

The term was something Lex had not heard. "What is that? Our other doctor had her use a thermometer, to check her basal body temperature. Does she need to come to your office for this other test?"

"Monitoring the BBT is less accurate. One of the ways I like to pinpoint the time of ovulation is by identifying the LH surge. It's a hormone that prompts ovulation. It can be detected by testing the urine twice a day, with a home testing kit. If the level of LH is

increased, ovulation should occur within thirty-six hours. All you
have to do is call when you're ready." He shook Lex's free hand.
"Amanda should take it easy for the next few days. Excessive physical
activity can cause inaccurate readings in the test. But, it won't hurt to
do A *little* sightseeing. Try to enjoy yourselves while you're here."

"We will. Thank you, Dr. Hamilton." Lex waited until he left the
room before she helped Amanda sit up. "Let me grab your clothes, and
we'll go have a bite to eat."

Amanda swung her legs over the side of the table. "That sounds
great. Do you think we can take in the Aquarium today? It's on my list
of want-to's, and it shouldn't be too stressful."

"Sure thing, sweetheart, as long as you're the navigator. I always
get turned around when I'm here."

"I CAN'T BELIEVE all the different types of birds and reptiles
they had at the aquarium." They had finished their tour of the Dallas
World Aquarium, and were now sitting in a nearby restaurant.
Amanda waved her French fry in the air to punctuate her point. "I
think my favorite was all the different types of Toucans. Their bills
were so colorful, it looked almost like someone painted them."

Lex took a bite of her steak, chewed, and swallowed. "I know
what you mean. Although, did you see the size of that crocodile? He
was as big as one of our horses."

"No kidding. I could certainly have done without the snakes,
though. They were creepy."

"Yeah. I was always taught that the only good snake is a dead
snake. The monkeys were cool." Lex snitched a fry from Amanda's
plate. "Those with the little white mustaches were cute."

Amanda slapped at Lex's hand. "Hey, watch it." She picked up
another fry and offered it to her partner. "Here, piggy."

"Thanks." Lex smirked. Then she accepted and chewed the
offering. "What do you want to do next?"

"Why don't we head to the hotel? We can always take in a movie
later." Amanda wanted to heed the doctor's orders. "Besides, it's
afternoon, so I can do one of the tests."

Lex blinked. "Uh, sure." She could feel her stomach turn and
hoped that her lunch didn't make a return appearance. The reality of
what they were trying to do hit her hard, and Lex was feeling nervous
about the outcome. She wanted Amanda to be happy, but she couldn't
help but think about the dangers of pregnancy.

"What's the matter? Aren't you ready for this?"

"Of course I am. I guess I'm a little nervous, that's all." Lex placed
her napkin on the table.

Amanda mimicked Lex, and pushed away from the table. "I don't
know what you're so nervous about. It's done every day."

"I know. I'm just worried about you." Lex placed enough cash on the table to cover their meal, and the tip. "Come on. I think I saw an ice cream place close to the hotel."

Following her lover, Amanda couldn't help but frown. This was the first time Lex had mentioned anything negative about her wanting to get pregnant, and she was concerned. The last thing she wanted to do was upset her. She resolved to have a nice, long chat with Lex once they were in their room.

LATER THAT EVENING, Amanda stretched out on the king-size bed in their hotel room and waited patiently for Lex to get out of the shower. She leafed through the television magazine to see what was on the pay-per-view channels. When the door to the bathroom opened, she placed the booklet on the bed beside her. "I found something you might like."

"What?" Lex fluffed her hair dry with a towel. "Why is it that no matter what kind of place you stay at, none of them have ever heard of fabric softener?"

"I think it's so you don't get too comfortable and want to live here." Amanda picked up the journal again. "Which would you rather see? A comedy, action flick, or love story?"

Lex draped the towel around her neck, which matched the one wrapped around her body. "Well." She kneeled on the edge of the bed so that she could lean over her lover. "Since I'm already living the best love story there is, why not something light, like a comedy?"

"You say the sweetest things." Amanda wrapped her arms around Lex's neck and pulled her down for a kiss. Enjoying the contact, she lowered her hands and easily removed Lex's towel.

"I thought you weren't supposed to overdo it?" Lex found her resolve wavering when Amanda's hand slid between their bodies. "Whoa." She rolled over to the side as her towel hit the floor.

Amanda immediately covered Lex's body with her own. "Don't worry," she said, before her mouth began to work its way down her lover's body, "I'll be gentle."

"Isn't that supposed to be my...oh, yeah." Lex closed her eyes.

"Yes?" Amanda grinned and returned to her pleasurable task, which was to see how speechless she could make her lover.

"YOU CALL THAT gentle?" Lex asked, much later. "I think I may have pulled a muscle."

Amanda rubbed her stomach. "Poor baby. You shouldn't have jumped like that."

"Your hands were cold," Lex complained. She rolled over and propped her head on her hand so she could look down onto Amanda's face. "I love you."

"I love you, too." Amanda traced a finger down her lover's face. "Would you like to talk about it?"

"About what?"

"Whatever's bothering you." Amanda watched as several emotions played across Lex's face. "Do you still want to have a baby? You seemed a little off kilter at the doctor's office."

Lex kissed Amanda's finger as it crossed her lips. "Of course I do. I guess I can't help but worry." She sat up and ran a hand through her damp hair. "You mean everything to me, Amanda. I don't know what I'd do if anything happened to you."

Amanda scrambled into a sitting position in front of Lex. "Nothing's going to happen to me. Women get pregnant and have babies every day."

"My mother probably thought that way, too. But she died, having Louis." Lex shifted her gaze to the window so she wouldn't have to see Amanda's face. She was afraid she'd break down otherwise.

"Honey, please look at me." Amanda waited until she had Lex's undivided attention. "I know nothing's foolproof, but we can't go into this thinking that way. Everything's going to be fine. I have to believe that."

Lex swallowed the lump that had grown in her throat. Her rational mind knew what Amanda said was true – childbirth was much easier now than it was during her mother's time. "Okay. But I still reserve the right to worry like crazy." She took Amanda's hands in hers. "And I plan on spoiling you rotten."

"You do, huh? I think that's something we'll have to argue about, when the time comes."

"We'll see." Lex pulled Amanda into her arms. "You won't have a chance."

FOR FOUR DAYS their schedule remained the same. Amanda would test in the mornings before Lex woke, then they'd get up and find something new to do. Since it wasn't often they had such free time together, they spent a lot of it going to see different movies and having leisurely meals. They'd return to the hotel in the afternoons so Amanda could test again, and usually spent the rest of the day either in their room or prowling the hotel and surrounding area.

On this morning, Amanda stepped out of the bathroom with her hands behind her back. She stood in front of Lex, who was on the edge of the bed watching a baseball game. "Lex?"

"Hmm?" Lex rolled her eyes at the television, where the batter had struck out. "What is it?"

Amanda brought out her right hand, which held her ovulation test strip. "There's two lines."

"Okay. Well, maybe you'll have better luck tomorrow."

"No, I don't think so." Amanda placed the strip on the dresser. "We need to make an appointment with the doctor's office for tomorrow afternoon." She watched as Lex connected the dots.

"It was positive?" Lex started to smile as Amanda nodded her head. "Whoo-hoo!" She jumped to her feet and gave her partner a bear hug. "That's great!"

Amanda allowed Lex to spin her around the room. "Easy there. We still don't know if it's going to take or not."

"It will, sweetheart. I can feel it." Lex kissed her soundly. "It's going to work out, wait and see."

Amanda looked into her eyes, which sparkled with happiness. "I'm starting to believe it, too."

THE FOLLOWING AFTERNOON found them at Dr. Hamilton's office. Lex stood by Amanda's head, holding her hand tightly. Although they had been through the same procedure several times, to her it never became any easier. She struggled to keep her hands from shaking, but wasn't successful.

"Honey, you're going to have to ease up a little. That's the hand I write with." Amanda could feel her partner tremble. She was trying to stay relaxed, but worrying about Lex's well-being made it difficult. "Lex, look at me, not the doctor."

Her eyes met Amanda's and Lex nervously swallowed. "I'm sorry. It's—"

"We're done." Dr. Hamilton stood and removed his gloves. "Are you okay, Ms. Walters? You look pale."

Lex nodded but was unable to speak. She hated that Amanda had to go through all of this to have a child of her own. The thought of what the doctor had been doing made her close her eyes. She didn't want to faint like she did the first time. Lex felt Amanda's lips on her hand and she opened her eyes. "Hi."

"Hi, yourself. Are you going to make it?" Amanda noticed that the color was returning to Lex's face, which meant she'd probably miss seeing the floor up close and personal. She remembered how embarrassed Lex had been when that happened.

"Yeah. It's a little warm in here." Lex used her free hand to wipe the perspiration out of her eyes. She turned her attention to the doctor. "So, is that it?"

"It is. Amanda, relax on the table for ten to fifteen minutes, and then you can get dressed." He washed his hands at the sink and then turned to the anxious couple. "Good luck, ladies. Let's hope we won't be seeing each other again, at least until you're ready for baby number two." He winked at them and left the room.

"What did he mean by that?" Lex asked, her stomach doing flip-flops again. "Did the two of you talk about something I don't know about?"

Amanda squeezed Lex's hand. "No, honey. I think it's his way of telling us he hopes we're successful."

"Thank god." Lex pulled up a chair and sat next to her lover. "So, now we wait?"

"Yes. We wait."

Chapter
Four

SHERIFF CHARLIE BRISTOL sat at his desk, thumbing through a stack of paperwork he had managed to ignore for the better part of the week. He was about to get up for a cup of coffee, when the phone on his desk rang. "Yes?"

His secretary, Sarah, was on the line. "Charlie, I have a Lieutenant Eades from Richland, on the line for you. He says it's urgent."

"All right, Sarah. Put him through." Charlie leaned back in his chair. "This is Sheriff Bristol. What can I do for you, Lieutenant?"

"Sheriff, we had several inmates break out of our maximum security facility this morning. We're trying to contact all the neighboring counties to alert them."

Charlie found a notepad on his desk and slid it toward him. "Thanks for calling. How many are there? Do you have names and descriptions?"

"There were three. You should be getting the information sheet by fax any time now." Lieutenant Eades cleared his throat before continuing. "You might also want to notify your deputies these men are armed and dangerous. They broke into a sporting goods store on their way out of town, and have three hunting rifles and two shotguns as well as boxes of ammo."

A knock on Charlie's office door interrupted the call. Sarah stepped in and waved a handful of papers. Charlie motioned her forward. He took the papers from her and quickly glanced at them. "I was just handed the faxed sheets, Lieutenant. Do you have any idea what type of transportation they're using? There's nothing here about that."

"They were last seen in a gray van, but we found that abandoned in Parkdale. We have several officers en route to see if they can get a lead. I'm afraid they may make it into some of your southern rural areas before we pick up their trail."

"All right. I'll gather what men I can, and put them on horseback. It's the easiest way to trek through that part of the county. Thanks for calling." He placed the receiver on its base and rubbed his eyes before speaking to Sarah. "Tell Jeremy to take half a dozen fully-armed men out to Lex's. We're going to have to borrow some horses. I'll call ahead and let her know. Then I'll follow them out."

Sarah nodded. "Will do, Sheriff. Is there anything else you need?"

"No that should be it, at least for now. Thanks." He picked the phone up again and dialed a familiar number. "Hi, Martha. Is Lex around?"

"I believe she's outside with Amanda and Lorrie. Let me run out and see."

Charlie listened to the sound of the phone being set down on the counter. He read the fax while he waited for Lex to come to the phone. This was one conversation he was not anxious to have.

THE MID-AFTERNOON sun warmed Amanda's back as she watched Lorrie play in the sandbox. She rolled her eyes as the toddler tossed handfuls of sand into the air, giggling as it drifted all over herself. She turned her head as Martha sat beside her on the padded glider. "Hi. You look worried. Do you have any idea why Charlie wanted to talk to Lex?"

"No, he didn't give a reason, and that's what concerns me." Martha couldn't help but chuckle at Lorrie's antics, as the child squealed for joy. She continued to throw sand into the air, while more and more of it settled into her dark hair. "It's going to take forever to get her clean. I swear she's exactly like Lexie."

"You should have been out here, earlier. Lex was sitting next to her and Lorrie was trying to bury her with that little plastic shovel." Hearing the back door slam, both women looked up and watched as Lex jogged to the barn. "I wonder what that's all about?"

Martha patted her on the leg. "I'm sure we'll find out soon enough."

Lorrie saw her favorite playmate run past them without a word. "Wex pway?" she asked Amanda.

"No, baby. I'm sorry. Momma Lex has to work." Amanda went to pick up the pouting child. "Let's go take a bath. I'm sure we can talk Mada into helping." Lorrie had begun calling Martha by the name Lex had given her as a child, without any prompting from anyone. Martha was thrilled by the moniker and had gladly taken up the role as the little girl's grandmother.

"Of course I will. What better way to spend the afternoon than to watch this little sprout play in the water?" Martha followed Amanda into the house, although her heart was secretly with the woman in the barn.

LEX WAS SADDLING up the last horse when Roy came in to help. She had called him from the house to have him bring up several men and horses from the stables at the bunkhouse. "Is everybody ready?"

"Sure are. They're armed, like you asked." Roy took the reins of two horses and led them from the barn. "Lester packed some supplies for everyone, just in case. Any idea how long we'll be?"

"Nope. Charlie doesn't even know we're going yet. But since we know the area better than his deputies, I figure he'll take any help we can give." Lex handed Thunder's reins to Chet, who stood nearby. "I'm going up to the house for a minute to get a few things. Anybody need anything?"

The four men shook their heads. They would spend the time checking the horses' gear.

Lex clomped into the house and paused at the downstairs bathroom door. "Hi." She went in and knelt by the tub, next to a damp Amanda. "Who's supposed to be taking the bath?"

"Watch it, or you'll be next." Amanda flinched when Lorrie slapped at the water. "Lorrie, stop that."

Martha stood from where she sat on the closed toilet seat. "I'm going to go check on the laundry." She could tell there was something on Lex's mind, and decided to give the women their privacy.

Amanda saw the concerned look on Lex's face. "It's serious, isn't it?"

"Yeah. Charlie and a few of his deputies are on their way out here. Evidently some prisoners escaped, and they think they may be headed this way. He wants to borrow our horses to check out the southeast properties."

Feeling a trickle of fear, Amanda turned her attention to Lorrie. She ran a washcloth across the child's back. "And? What else aren't you telling me?"

Lex trailed her fingers through the warm water, afraid to look at her lover. "He doesn't know it yet, but me and a few of the guys are going with them."

"What?" Amanda turned and stared at her partner. "Are you out of your mind? What made you even consider doing something like that?"

Lex pulled her hand from the water and dried it on a nearby towel. "None of those deputies, or Charlie for that matter, knows half as much about this area as we do. I can't leave them to wander around on their own." She traced her hand down Amanda's arm in a gentle caress. "Don't worry. A few of the guys are going to stay behind and keep an eye out on the house. You should be perfectly safe."

"I don't give a damn about the house, Lex. What I do care about is you." Amanda pulled Lorrie from the tub and stood. She allowed Lex to wrap a towel around Lorrie. "Why are *you* going?"

"Because I know every inch of this ranch, and more about the neighboring ones than any of them." Lex tickled Lorrie under the chin, causing her to giggle. "On second thought, maybe you and Martha should take Lorrie to see your grandparents, at least until these guys are caught."

Amanda ruffled Lorrie's hair with the soft cloth. "Is Charlie that worried?"

"No, but I am." Lex took the toddler so Amanda could drain the tub. "From what little he said, these guys are bad news. I'd feel a lot better if all of you were someplace safer." She followed Amanda from the room and up the staircase. No words were spoken between the two for several minutes. They trekked to Lorrie's room, where Lex dressed her. "Are you going to say anything?"

"What else is there to say? You've obviously made up your mind, without my input." Amanda took the damp towel to the bathroom, where she hung it over a rod to dry. As she came out, she could hear the sound of several cars driving around to the back of the house. "It sounds like they're here." She blinked the tears from her eyes, determined not to cry.

Lex stood in the middle of the room, holding Lorrie close. She kissed her on the head before handing her to Amanda. "Will you please promise me to go into town?"

Amanda leaned into her lover as Lex pulled them to her. "I promise." She lifted her head. "But only if *you* promise to take your phone, and call me when you can."

"Of course I will, sweetheart." Lex kissed Amanda on the lips. "Walk me down? I need to go into the office for something."

"Sure." Amanda took Lorrie, who reached for Lex. "I don't think she wants you to go."

"Wex, hold me!" Lorrie struggled against Amanda's hold. When Lex brought her close, she snuggled into her shirt and held on.

Lex led them from the room. Once they were in the office, she handed Lorrie to Amanda. "Here, lil' bit. Go to Mommy Amanda." They had added the more familiar names when they returned from Dallas, in order to ease Lorrie into using them. Once Lorrie was safely ensconced in Amanda's arms, she took a key that hung next to a locked door.

Although she'd had Charlie remove the weapons from the house a couple of years before, Lex had recently brought them back. There were too many snakes and wild animals about that necessitated keeping weapons at the house, within easy reach.

Opening the gun closet, Lex selected a thirty-eight caliber revolver, checked to see if it was loaded, and clipped it to her belt. She then grabbed a hunting rifle and two boxes of shells.

"I don't like this." Amanda watched Lex close and lock the door, and then replace the key on the high nail.

"Neither do I." Lex pulled the bolt on the rifle. Satisfied that the magazine was full, she pointed it to the ground away from Amanda and Lorrie. "But I'm not taking any chances." She grabbed her satellite phone from its charger on the desk, slipped it into its holder and placed it on her other hip.

Amanda followed her to the back door and watched Lex place her hat on her head, and drape her duster over one arm. "Be careful."

"Always." Lex kissed her lover, then kissed Lorrie. "Don't stop for anyone on the way into town, no matter what."

"We won't."

"I love you." Lex bit her lip to keep it from trembling. As much as she wanted to help Charlie, a large part of her wanted to stay behind with her family. "We'll stick around until y'all take off."

"Thanks." Amanda pulled Lex to her and kissed her again. "I love you. Please hurry back."

Lex nodded, not trusting her voice anymore. She left the house before she could change her mind.

CHARLIE ARRIVED AS Martha and Amanda pulled away. He waved at the retreating car before turning his attention to the group near the horses. "Lex, what's the meaning of this?"

"We're going with you, Charlie." Lex climbed into the saddle, and her men did the same.

"Oh no you don't. We can manage fine by ourselves." He took the reins of a bay gelding from Jeremy. "Why didn't you stop her?"

Jeremy shrugged before hoisting himself into the saddle. "She had a valid point, Sheriff. I thought I'd leave it up to you."

"And what point was that?" Charlie asked Lex.

Lex brought her horse up next to him. "You're going to need guides. We can help you cover more ground, and show you some of the places those guys might hide."

He hated when she was right. But he'd be damned if he'd say so. "Fine." He studied the gathered group. "It looks like you're all equipped. I assume everyone here knows how to handle their firearms?"

"Don't worry, Charlie. We're all more than capable." Lex pulled her hat down to shade her eyes. "Anything else?"

"Yeah. To make it official, consider yourselves duly deputized." Once everyone was ready to go he shook his head and said under his breath, "I hope I don't regret this."

Lex, who had heard him, leaned over her horse's neck. "You won't. We're not about to take any unnecessary chances. I promise."

Charlie quickly mounted. "I'll hold you to that." He waved to her. "All right. Lead away. I want everyone in pairs, and each of your men with a deputy." He pursed his lips when Lex spun Thunder around, causing the horse to rear. She tipped her hat and winked at him. "Smartass kid."

Chapter
Five

THE KNOCK ON the front door brought Jacob Cauble to the entry. He peered through the peephole and opened the door. "Well. To what do we owe this wonderful surprise?"

Amanda, carrying Lorrie, stepped into the house. Martha followed, hefting Lorrie's bag. They had decided to leave their own bags in the back of the vehicle for the time being. "Hi, Grandpa. I hope you don't mind us invading you for a while."

"Of course not. You ladies are always welcome." He escorted them to the living room and motioned for the three to sit. He noticed Amanda's glum face. "What seems to be the matter?"

Amanda was about to answer him when Anna Leigh breezed into the room. "Mandy, Martha. What a pleasure to see you." She scooped Lorrie out of Amanda's arms and pulled her close, kissing the baby on the cheek. "My goodness. Look how much you've grown in only a week's time." Anna Leigh proceeded to sit on a nearby chair and hold Lorrie on her lap. "Where's Lexington?"

"That's the question of the hour," Amanda grumbled. She crossed her arms over her chest and sank against the sofa cushions.

Jacob raised his eyebrows at his granddaughter's behavior. "What's that supposed to mean? Did you two have a fight?"

Martha decided to step in. "She and some of the hired hands are riding out with Charlie and his deputies to try and find some escaped convicts."

"Surely she realizes how dangerous that could be." Anna Leigh allowed Lorrie to get off her lap.

The toddler raced over to Jacob and raised her arms. "Up." She giggled when he picked her up and raised her over his head.

Amanda brushed her hair out of her face. "Oh, she knows. She has this idea in her head that she's the only one who can help, and nothing I could say would change her mind."

"Honey, for once, I have to agree with her reasoning." Martha patted Amanda's leg. "She's ridden that entire area her whole life. I think she knows every rock and tree."

"That's no reason. She acted like she was almost excited at the prospect of playing posse. Doesn't she realize she has a family to think of?"

Anna Leigh leaned forward in her chair. "Mandy, please. I'm sure that Lexington was thinking of her family. Why else would she go into that sort of situation?"

Amanda gave the question serious consideration. "Honestly? Lately she hasn't been her usual self. It's almost as if she's not happy running the ranch anymore."

"Maybe this is her way of trying something new," Martha added. "She's almost thirty-four years old. And if you remember, ranching wasn't her first choice. It was pretty much thrust upon her."

"If she wanted a different job, she could have said something. Not go traipsing around the woods, looking for men with guns."

Jacob bounced Lorrie on his knee, much to her delight. "Guns? You didn't say anything about them being armed." He tried to keep his voice calm, so he wouldn't frighten the little girl. "That does sound pretty irresponsible."

Martha fiddled with the diaper bag, until Amanda took it away from her. "I think what worries me the most is that Lexie took a couple of guns with her. She's not been comfortable with them for quite a few years." The fearful look on Amanda's face caused her to amend her statement. "I shouldn't have said that. Lexie has always been an excellent shot, and it's not something she's likely to forget."

"That well could be," Jacob admitted. He decided to change the subject. "How long can you stay? I was thinking about cooking up a batch of spaghetti this evening."

Amanda shifted in her seat. "If you don't mind having us, I promised Lex we'd stay away from the ranch until those men are caught. She was worried about us being out there alone."

"We'd love for you to stay. It's been far too quiet since Jeannie and Rodney left last week." Anna Leigh stood. "Mandy, why don't I help you bring in your bags, and we can make up the guest rooms, while Martha and Jacob relax and chat? I'm sure he'll enlist her in the dinner preparations."

Martha handed Jacob a small towel from Lorrie's bag, since the little girl decided his wedding ring was perfect to teethe on. "That sounds wonderful. I'm sure we'll do fine together, won't we, Jacob?"

"Of course, my dear. You're always welcome in my kitchen." Jacob gladly took the towel and wiped the drool from the toddler's chin. "We'll let Mandy and Anna try to contain this one."

"That's going to be a chore in itself," Amanda agreed, as she followed her grandmother out of the room. "I think they got the better end of the deal."

THE ANGRY MAN threw the dirt bike to the ground. "Whose brilliant idea was it to use these damn motorcycles?" He kicked one of the tires and shifted the rifle that was slung across his back.

"How was I supposed to know they didn't have much gas in them, Ed? You liked the idea fine a few hours ago." Gary, the second convict, had already left his empty cycle behind, and his denim shirt and jeans were covered in mud. He was able to jump from where he rode on the back of Ed's bike before it was dropped.

Ed wiped his hands on his jeans, which were in similar shape. "I don't think it was me who said we should go through these woods. We'd have already been several counties away if we'd have stuck to the roads."

The third man drove up on his bike. "What's the holdup, fellas?" He noticed the bike lying in the wet leaves and mud. "That thing get tired of hauling your asses around?"

"No. It ran out of gas, too." Gary, whose greasy red hair was plastered to his head, tucked his hands into his back pockets, careful not to disturb the twin guns draped over his shoulders. "Yours probably won't last much longer, either."

"Tough. I'll ride it until it's dry. You two will have to hoof it." Mack, the leader of the group, flashed the two others a wicked grin. "Just follow my tracks." He spun the bike around, causing it to throw clumps of mud at his comrades. His two guns were in scabbards tied to the motorcycle, which gave him the freedom to race away.

"Asshole!" Ed spat. He wiped his face and started walking. "Maybe we should find the nearest road and take a car."

Gary followed him. "Yeah, like someone's going to stop when they see us. Even if we weren't filthy, we still have numbers stenciled on our shirts." He listened as the sound of the motorcycle got weaker. "I hope he crashes when he runs out of gas."

"Me, too." Ed slipped on some dead leaves. "At least it's not raining."

A LOUD CLAP of thunder caused the horse Charlie was riding to dance sideways. "Whoa, there." He pulled on the reins to get the animal under control. "Lex, do you breed these things to be contrary?"

"Of course not." Lex was in the lead. She had suggested they check along the southern fence, by the highway. It was nearest the convicts' last known location, and the smoothest terrain for them to cross. She reasoned if they could find where the men had entered the woods, it would be easier to track them. Charlie had cursed himself for not thinking of the idea first. Jeremy and one of her men, Jack, followed several lengths behind them. The others were paired off in groups of three, and were all taking positions farther back. "Do you know any particulars about these guys? What exactly are we up against?"

"All I know is that the three of them are career criminals. Robbery, assault, you name it. I believe they were all in the same gang when they were younger." Charlie shifted in the saddle. His rear was already sore, even though they had only been out a few hours.

"City guys, then?" Lex adjusted the collar on her duster as it began to rain.

Charlie buttoned up his coat. "Yeah. Why do you ask?"

"Well, if they're guys who have lived in the city all their lives, being out here in the boonies will unsettle them. That should give us an edge."

He wasn't surprised at her keen understanding of the situation. "You're right. Now, tell me why you're not wearing a uniform? Because you've got more common sense than about half my men."

"It's not like it's something I haven't thought about before. You were always my hero when I was growing up, and following in your footsteps was one of my career choices." Lex wiped the rain from her face. "Unfortunately, my father had other ideas."

"I didn't know." The longer Charlie was around Lex, the less he understood her. "You never said anything."

Lex shrugged. "What good would it have done? My life was already plotted out for me. I made do with what I was given."

"But are you happy?"

She turned in the saddle so that she could give him her undivided attention. "Of course I am. I have a wonderful wife, a beautiful daughter, and the best family I could ask for. That's enough to make anyone happy."

Charlie would not be deterred. "I'm not doubting that for a moment, Lex. But is ranching all that you want out of life?"

"It used to be." Up ahead, she could see where several of the metal fence posts were bent inward, bringing a small section of the fence to the ground. Glad for the interruption, Lex nudged her horse ahead to investigate. "I think we found it."

Charlie brought his horse along side of hers. They both came to a stop a few yards before the intrusion, to keep from ruining the tracks. "We probably wouldn't have, if you hadn't suggested riding this direction. Nice job, Lex."

"Thanks." She swung down from the saddle and let the reins drop to the ground. Well trained, Thunder wouldn't leave. Lex stood near the churned up ground. She turned to Charlie, who had tied up his horse and joined her. "Well, this explains why the fence was so messed up. It looks like they're on motorcycles."

"That's all we need. They'll have a good lead on us." Charlie rubbed the back of his neck, where water dripped from the edge of his Stetson. He used his radio to notify the rest of the searchers, ordering them to take up positions to the east and west of their location.

Lex went to her horse. "True, but at least they'll leave an easy trail to follow. We don't use cycles on the ranch, so theirs will be the only tracks." She waited until he was in the saddle, and nudged Thunder in the direction of the obvious trail.

They rode along in silence for several miles. Charlie had taken the lead, and now pulled up under a dense group of trees. "We might as well take a break. It'll be a decent shelter out of the rain."

The other three followed his advice and they were all soon standing next to the horses, pulling sandwiches from their packs and munching on them. Lex brought out her phone. "If you guys will excuse me for a minute, I'm going to be over there." She pointed to a more secluded spot.

"Tell Amanda hello for me," Charlie teased.

"I will." She leaned against one of the trees and hit a number on speed dial. "Hi."

"Hi, yourself." Amanda had obviously been sitting next to the phone, waiting for her to call. "How's it going?"

"Pretty good. We found their trail, and we're taking a break for dinner." Lex looked around to make certain she had some privacy. "I miss you."

"I miss you, too. Is it raining there like it is here?"

Lex wiped the water out of her eyes. "A little," she fibbed. "Is everyone doing okay there?"

"You're asking about us? We're not the ones out looking for three armed men. We've been watching the news. They keep going on about how dangerous those men are. Why didn't you tell us?"

"Because I didn't know until we got out on the trail. Listen, sweetheart, I'm going to have to go. Everyone is ready to head out." Lex hated knowing she was the cause of the anxious tone in Amanda's voice. "Don't worry. I'm with Charlie and Jeremy. They won't let anything happen to us."

"I hate this. Please be extra careful. Lorrie and I miss you terribly."

"I will." Lex started toward the others. "I love you."

"I love you, too. Be safe."

Lex disconnected the call and placed the phone in the holster. She hoped she could keep her promise.

AMANDA PLACED THE handset down and looked at the concerned faces around her. "They've found tracks."

"That's good, isn't it?" Anna Leigh played with her necklace. "It means they're closer to catching these men."

Amanda sat beside her. "Yes, but it also means they could be riding into danger soon." She tried to steady her hands, which rested in her lap. "I don't know whether to be relieved or scared."

"Charlie's good at what he does. He won't let anything happen to the people who are depending on him." Martha, who sat in a chair opposite of them, did her best to sound calm. "Everything will be fine."

"I wish I had your faith. This whole thing terrifies me. She has no business being out there." Amanda stood and began to pace. "Lex has responsibilities at home. She shouldn't be traipsing around the woods playing cops and robbers."

As she passed, Anna Leigh grabbed Amanda's arm and made her sit. "I think she realizes it's more serious than that. Didn't you two discuss this?"

"Not exactly." Amanda fell against the cushions of the sofa. "She already had her mind made up before she told me about it."

"Are you more upset that she's out there or that she didn't confer with you first?" Anna Leigh asked. She knew how her granddaughter's mind worked.

"We've been partners for nearly four years. I think I deserve to have a say in a decision this important."

Martha understood Amanda well, too. "It's aggravating when she does that, isn't it? But you have to remember, Lexie is an adult. She's pretty good about thinking things all the way through, even when it doesn't seem like it."

"I know. But it doesn't mean I have to agree with her." Amanda stood again. "I think I'll go up and check on Lorrie, to make sure she's sleeping okay."

Anna Leigh reached out and squeezed her hand. "That's a wonderful idea. While you're there, why don't you lie with her for a while? It's going to be a long night and a little rest wouldn't hurt."

"I don't know how much rest I can get until Lex is safely home." Amanda brushed her hands down her blouse, although it was hopelessly wrinkled. "I think I'll take a quick shower and change."

"You do that, dear. We'll come get you the moment we hear something." Anna Leigh watched Amanda leave the room before turning her attention to Martha. "She hasn't changed."

Martha gave her a smile. "Somehow, that makes me feel better."

Chapter
Six

IT HAD BEEN two hours since the last motorcycle had run out of gas, and now all three men were slogging through the dense trees and shrubs. The rain still fell steadily, which made the saturated ground even harder to maneuver across. Gary stopped and sat on a fallen log. "I've got to take a break. My feet are killing me."

"All you've done is complain. I don't know why we didn't leave your sorry ass behind." Ed snapped off a dead tree branch and threw it at his associate. "Get up."

"Why? We're obviously lost, there's no one around for miles, and it's got to be close to midnight. How long are we going to go?"

Mack trudged to the log and kicked Gary. "We're going to keep going until we find some transportation. There's got to be another road around here somewhere."

"It's cold, dark, and I've got blisters on my feet. I'm staying right here." Gary was beginning to rethink his part in the escape.

"Like hell you are." Ed grabbed him by his collar and yanked him to his feet. "We stick together. I don't trust you not to go running to the cops."

Gary wrestled his way out of the angry man's grip. "Let go. I'm not going anywhere." He blocked Ed's attempt at hitting him in the face. "Hey."

"That's enough." Mack got between the two and separated them. He shook his arms to get the worst of the rainwater out of his clothes. Since it was still raining, it didn't do much good. "I hate rain."

"Why don't we make some sort of shelter and wait it out? It's not like we're on a timetable here." Gary gestured to the trees before he sat again. "We're surrounded by material, let's make the most of it."

Ed slapped him on the back of the head. "Dumbass. The longer we stay still, the easier it'll be for them to find us."

"Ouch. We don't even know anyone's out here looking for us. They'd have to be crazy to be out in this mess."

Mack sat beside Gary. "I hate to admit it, but the kid's right. It's the middle of the night, raining like hell, and we've been going all day. I think we need to make camp and get some rest." The area where they stopped was surrounded on three sides by heavy brush. It was about as safe as they'd find.

"I don't like it. The law's not going to give up on us. We need to get as far away from here as we can. Sitting around on our asses is only going to get us caught." Ed kicked the large log the other two sat on. "But I'll be damned if I go running off by myself."

Gary brushed the hair out of his eyes and grinned. "Scared?"

Ed slapped him again. "No, you stupid little shit. I don't trust you to not point out where I went if you got caught."

"Asshole." Gary rubbed his head and glared at Ed. "I still say you're a chicken," he mumbled under his breath.

LEX FOUGHT BACK another yawn. The rocking motion of the horse made her sleepy. The last thing she wanted to do was fall off her horse in front of Charlie and the other two men. She ducked as she rode under a low hanging branch. Thunder stumbled in the mud, causing her to pull up on the reins. "Charlie, hold on. I need to make sure my horse is all right."

"Go ahead. We'll stop here for a while and give all our mounts a rest." He slid from the saddle and loosened the cinch strap. Charlie waved to Jeremy and Jack. "Take a break, fellas."

Satisfied that Thunder was okay, Lex rummaged in her saddlebag for a sandwich. She hadn't eaten when the rest had, and her stomach was reminding her that it was empty and not happy with the situation. While resting against Thunder's neck, she noticed something lying among the trees to the left of them.

Lodged in some thick bushes was a mud-covered motorcycle, perfectly suited for off-road. It didn't appear to be wrecked, but had obviously been dumped recently. Lex placed her empty sandwich bag in her pocket and walked over to kneel beside it. She touched the motor, not surprised to find it cold. "It's been here for a while," she told Charlie, who had stepped up beside her.

"Any idea how long?"

Although she wasn't a tracker, Lex did know enough to make an educated guess. "Probably a couple of hours ago. It looks like at least one of them is on foot."

"Well, so much for our break. I want to gain some more ground on them while it's dark." Charlie brought out his radio and notified the others. After getting verification on where each team was located, he waved to Jeremy and Jack. "You two head a little west of here and we'll keep on this trail."

"Will do, Sheriff. We'll let you know if we see anything." Jeremy set his horse off in an uncomfortable trot with Jack not far behind.

Lex watched them leave and turned to Charlie. "Now what?"

"Let's see if we can pick up their tracks on the other side of these trees."

They remounted and steered the horses through the thicket, oblivious to the continuing rain.

AMANDA STRETCHED OUT on the bed next to the sleeping toddler. She had gotten up to get a glass of water, and now couldn't go back to sleep. It was almost three o'clock in the morning and she hadn't heard from Lex in hours. She didn't know if it was a good or bad thing. When Lorrie stirred, she rubbed her tummy until she settled again. "That's it, sweetie. Everything's going to be okay." She hoped her whispered words were true. A light knock on the open door caused her to look up. "Hi."

"Hello, dear. I thought I heard you, and wanted to see if you needed anything." Anna Leigh sat next to her. She brushed her hand through Amanda's hair in a tender gesture. "You should be trying to rest."

"I can't. I keep thinking of Lex out there in the rain, heading into who knows what. It's scaring me to death."

Anna Leigh felt helpless. Her heart ached at the bleak look in her granddaughter's face. "We have to keep positive thoughts."

About that time Lorrie stirred and opened her eyes. She saw Amanda and reached out to her. "Manny."

"Ssh, baby. It's all right." Amanda picked her up and snuggled Lorrie against her.

Lorrie tangled her hands in Amanda's shirt and whimpered. "Wex?"

Amanda felt like crying, herself. "No, honey. She's not here right now." She looked over Lorrie's head into her grandmother's eyes. "Has there been any word?"

"I'm afraid not. Perhaps they are afraid of disturbing us this late."

As Lorrie settled and went to sleep, Amanda stroked her dark hair. "I hope you're right. This waiting around is killing me." She sent a silent prayer to her lover while she continued to rock the resting child.

CHARLIE STOPPED HIS horse. Lex was so tired she almost allowed Thunder to run into the back of the other animal. She rubbed her face, hoping to wake herself up. "What's up?"

He stepped down from the saddle. "Looks like we've found the last of the bikes." They had run across the second one earlier and continued to follow the last one's trail.

"Good. That means we'll be able to catch up with them faster." Although used to long hours in the saddle, even Lex had a breaking point and she was closing in on it.

"I hope so. My butt is killing me." Charlie gingerly walked to his horse. "It doesn't look like they tried to conceal their tracks too much." He watched as Lex slumped in the saddle. "Let's take a break until sunup. I'd feel a lot better if we're fresher when we find them."

Lex wasn't going to argue with his logic. She knew she wouldn't be any good to anyone the way she was feeling now. Following his lead, she slid gracelessly from the saddle and led Thunder to a clear spot under the trees. She loosened the saddle and tied off the reins on a small branch. As Charlie did the same, Lex took an apple from her pack and cut it in half, giving part of it to her horse.

"You spoil that animal." Charlie gave his horse a piece of his. "But they deserve a treat, considering how long they've been hauling us around, right?"

"Yep." Lex brushed her hands on her jeans before sitting a few steps away. She rested against the tree, glad for the break. Seeing the slump to Charlie's shoulders, she realized he was more exhausted than he let on. "I'll keep watch for a while, so you can get a quick nap."

Charlie almost argued, but the chance to close his eyes for a moment stopped him. "All right. But wake me in an hour and I'll do the same for you." He mirrored her posture and was asleep before she could answer him.

Lex looked on fondly. She would do anything for him, including fighting sleep herself, so he could nap. "Rest well, Charlie."

The hour passed slowly to Lex. She thought about letting him sleep longer but before she could decide, Charlie stretched and yawned.

"I guess my internal alarm clock still works." He stood and walked around. "I'm going to go check in with everyone else. Close your eyes and I'll wake you in a while."

"Sounds good to me." Lex tilted her hat forward so she could rest her head against the tree.

BRIGHT BEAMS OF sunlight covered Amanda's face, causing her to squint as she opened her eyes. She glanced at her watch. It was almost seven in the morning. She turned her head and saw that Lorrie wasn't with her. Alarmed, she jumped from the bed and hurried down the stairs. The sound of Martha's voice led her to the kitchen.

Martha had Lorrie in the high chair that was kept at the house for when the toddler visited. She placed another small spoonful of scrambled eggs on Lorrie's plate and looked up when she heard footsteps in the hall. "Good morning, dear. I hope you don't mind that I brought this angel downstairs. I was afraid she'd wake you."

"No, that's fine." Amanda brushed her hands through her hair before going to the refrigerator and pouring herself a glass of orange juice. "Where's everyone else?"

"I believe they're in the living room watching the news. Why don't you join Lorrie and me for breakfast? There's plenty here on the table."

Amanda kissed the little girl on the head before she sat next to Martha. "I'm not very hungry." She took a sip of the juice and moaned as the cold drink traveled down her parched throat.

"You need to eat. It takes a lot of energy to chase this one around the house. I don't want you passing out on us." Martha picked up a plate and filled it with scrambled eggs, bacon, and toast. She sat it in front of Amanda. "Dig in."

Knowing it was useless to argue, Amanda picked up a fork and began to nibble on the food. She had taken a bite of the toast when a spoonful of eggs hit her in the face.

"Mommy!" Lorrie demanded attention.

Amanda's eyes widened. "Did she say what I thought she did?"

"Sure sounded like it. We were talking about you before you came down. She kept wanting to go upstairs and wake you." Martha used a napkin to wipe the toddler's face. "Cutie, you need to eat that food, not play with it."

Tears of joy welled in Amanda's eyes. "We'd been trying to get her used to calling us that, but this is the first time she's actually used it." She dropped her gaze to her plate. "I wish Lex had been here to hear it."

"Wex?" Lorrie waved her spoon. "Wex!"

"No, honey. Momma Lex isn't here right now." Amanda started to push her own plate away but Martha stopped her.

"Oh, no you don't. There's not much on your plate and I'd like to see it empty before you leave."

Amanda sighed, but did as she was told. "Were you always this stubborn with Lex?"

"You don't know the half of it." Martha cleaned up Lorrie and released her from the high chair. She helped her down and the toddler immediately raced around the table to where Amanda sat.

"Up."

Amanda lifted her into her lap and held her with one hand while she ate with the other. "We're going to have to work on that, Lorrie. How about, up please?"

Lorrie rocked back and forth. "Pease?"

"Yes, please. Do you think you can say that, sweetie?"

"Hmph." Lorrie reached for Amanda's plate and came away with a handful of eggs. She crammed them into her mouth. "Yum."

Martha couldn't help but laugh. "Looks like you'd better get more, so you can share."

When the little girl returned for seconds, Amanda caught her hand. "Lorrie, no. You have to ask nicely. Can you say please?"

Lorrie grunted and reached for the plate again. When her hand was grabbed, she pulled it free. "No!"

"Lorrie." Amanda drew out the word slowly. "Ask please."

The toddler frowned and poked out her lower lip. "Mine." The battle of wills was on.

"Lorrie."

"No."

Martha covered her mouth with her hand to keep from laughing out loud again. She couldn't wait to see how this standoff would play out.

Lorrie reached for the plate again, which Amanda slid out of her reach. "Mommy!"

"Be nice, Lorrie." Amanda was determined to make her point. "What do you say?"

Little hands slapped the table. "Mine!"

Amanda ignored the outburst. She gathered some eggs on her fork and put them in her mouth. After chewing, she placed the fork on the table, away from Lorrie.

"Mommy!" Still being ignored, Lorrie slapped the table again. When she didn't get a response, she pouted.

Not disturbed in the least, Amanda continued to eat.

"Pease."

With a smile on her face, Amanda gathered a small amount of eggs on her fork and fed them to Lorrie. "Good girl."

"Mmm."

Chapter
Seven

AFTER THE BREAK of dawn, Lex and Charlie had begun to walk in front of their horses, because the footprints of the criminals were getting harder to spot. The previous night's rain had washed away much of the trail. They were crossing a clearing when he stopped and pointed at the sky. A plume of dark smoke trailed into the air.

"Do you see that? It looks like it's about half a mile away." Charlie reached for his radio and checked on the others to find their positions. "We're about two miles north of the creek, where it turns away from the eastern fence," he related over the air. "Everyone find a high spot and look for dark smoke. It's less than a mile from our position." Garbled voices answered him. "Okay. Let's set up a perimeter around the area. I want no one closer than two hundred yards, clear?" More jumbled noises came from his radio. "Roger that. Lex and I will be going ahead to scout the area. Again, we'll be coming in from the south."

Lex raised her eyebrows at his last comment. She waited until he placed the radio on his belt. "Should we leave our horses here?"

"Good idea. No sense in giving ourselves away." Charlie walked his horse to the trees they had vacated earlier. He tied the reins to a low branch, took his rifle from the scabbard, and waited for Lex to do the same. "Are you sure you want to come with me? I don't know what we're going to find once we get there."

"I've come this far. Besides, Martha would kill me if I let you go on alone." Lex reached into her saddlebag and brought out a box of shells. She tucked them into a pocket on the duster and hefted her rifle onto her shoulder. It had been hard, but once she'd convinced herself that the weapons were only tools, she'd gotten over her aversion to them. "Well? Are you going to lead, or do I have to?"

He shook his head. "Smartass kid." After filling his own pockets with extra ammunition, he started off toward the smoke.

"WHAT IN THE hell are you doing?" Ed walked over to the fire that Gary had built and began to kick at the smoking branches. He returned from his "trip to the woods" to find Mack missing and Gary tossing green wood onto sputtering flames.

Gary scooted away from the crackling embers. "I was cold and I thought I'd surprise you guys." He waved his hand in front of his face to dispel the heavy smoke. "Why are you putting the fire out? It took me forever to get it lit."

"Because, dumbass, if they're out looking for us, you gave away our position. Where'd Mack go?"

Mack came in from the opposite direction. "Same place you did. Where'd all that smoke come from?"

Ed jerked Gary to his feet. "This idiot thought a fire would be a good idea." He used his grip on Gary's shirt to shake him. "Not such a good idea now, is it?"

"Stop it. I didn't know." Gary struggled to break free.

"Maybe we should leave him here. He's not doing us much good." Mack walked over and slapped Gary across the face. "Were you born this stupid, or do you have to work at it?"

Gary fell to the ground as Ed let him go. He wiped the blood from the side of his mouth and scrambled to his feet. "I'm not stupid. It was my idea to take the motorcycles, wasn't it?"

"Yeah, but you didn't think to check the gas tanks, now did you?" Ed reached for him again, only to be stopped by Mack.

"Forget it. Let's make sure this fire doesn't relight, so we can get moving again." Mack glared at Gary. "You get to bury it in the mud, smart guy."

Grumbling, Gary used a sharp stick to shovel mud onto the smoking mess. "Jerks." He was beginning to think getting captured would be better than staying on the run with the other two. At least he'd be warm.

CHARLIE STOPPED TO peer over a thick mass of brush. He waved his hand to signal for Lex to join him. He kept his voice low. "There they are."

"Now what?"

He held his finger up to his lips and pulled his radio from his belt. After a few quiet sentences, he replaced the radio. "We're going to wait ten minutes, until everyone gets into position. Then we'll—"

"I don't think we have ten minutes." Lex pointed to where the men were. "It looks like they're ready to move on."

"Damn." Charlie pointed to his right and hoisted his rifle onto his shoulder. "I want you to go over there about fifty feet and wait for my signal. If they look like they're going to open fire, get behind that tree."

Lex nodded and followed his instructions. She leaned against the tree and held her rifle in a ready position. Taking a deep breath to steady her nerves, she aimed the gun at the men's camp. *So much for my nerves of steel. More like nerves of silly putty.* She tried to still her shaking hands.

"This is the Sheriff's Department," Charlie yelled. "Step away from your weapons and lie face down on the ground."

The campsite turned to chaos. Each man grabbed his guns and found a safe position behind the log at the campsite. One of them shot in the direction of Charlie's voice.

"Shit!" Lex looked over to where Charlie was hidden behind his own tree. "Are you okay?"

"I'm fine." Charlie jumped as his radio came to life. "Yes, that was a gunshot. No, no one was hit." He wiped the sweat from his face. "Is everyone in position?" At their affirmative answers, he keyed in again. "Good. Hold your fire unless they shoot at you first. I'm going to try and talk them out." He slipped the radio into its holder once again. "Lex? Did you hear that?"

"Yeah." She swallowed hard. "Don't shoot unless they do, right?"

"You got it." He raised his voice again. "Don't make us open fire. We outnumber you."

The only answer he got was another shot, this time closer. He brought the rifle to his shoulder and aimed. Making certain he wouldn't hit anyone, he made a well-placed shot in front of the fallen tree. They answered with several shots.

Lex saw Charlie jump behind the tree. She squeezed off her own round, keeping it low. "Bastards." When they returned her fire, she dropped to the ground and hid behind the tree. "Charlie? Are you all right?"

"Fine, kiddo. Nice shot." He was about to shoot again, when another volley came their way. "Stay down."

"No problem there." Lex propped her gun against her shoulder and wiped her sweaty hands on her jeans. Rustling leaves from her right caused Lex to point her gun in that direction.

Jeremy held up his hands. "Don't shoot, it's only me." He stopped about ten feet from Lex and dropped to his knees. "Jack's with the horses. He told me he didn't think he could point a gun at another person, so I left him where he'd be safe."

More shots came their way. Charlie shot back, but turned in alarm when he heard a grunt of pain to his right. "Lex?" He panicked when he couldn't see her.

Lex crawled over to where Jeremy fell. She saw a circle of blood growing above his hip. Setting her gun on the ground, she wrapped her arms around him and pulled him farther into the trees. Several shots rang over their heads. She tore off the bottom of her shirt and placed it over the wound. "Hang on, bud."

"Dammit, Lex, where are you?" Charlie yelled.

"We're over here. Jeremy's been hit." She grabbed Jeremy's hand

and held it over the wound. "Stay here. We'll get you out of here in a minute." Lex made her way to her rifle, picked it up and squeezed off several shots.

Charlie squatted next to Jeremy. "How bad is it?"

"I think it just grazed me. But it hurts like hell." Jeremy grimaced as he tried to sit up.

"Stay put." Charlie placed his hand on the other man's shoulder. "We'll take care of this." He heard a bullet ricochet off the tree beside Lex. "Dammit, Lex. Watch out!"

She ignored him and made several more shots. Hearing a man scream, she stopped. "Charlie, I think I hit one of them." Her voice shook.

"That's okay, Lex. Hold your fire until I can find out where everyone else is." Charlie bit back a curse when he heard from the others. They were still out of range. One group was circling around behind their position to help move Jeremy out of the line of fire.

Five minutes later Oscar and Roy broke through the trees and dropped next to Charlie and Jeremy. Oscar took one look at his friend on the ground. "Damn, Jer. Why'd you get in the way like that?"

Jeremy chuckled and grabbed his side. "Don't make me laugh, man. It hurts." He allowed the two men to help him to his feet and escort him out of harm's way.

Charlie watched them leave. When he was certain they were safe, he went over to Lex. "How are you doing?"

"Been better." She ducked when another bullet came too close to her head. "These guys are crazy, Charlie. They won't give up."

"It looks that way. The worst part is, they've got a pretty defensible spot. The cover is too thick on three sides, so there's no way we can get to them from there."

She reloaded her rifle. "How long are we going to do this?"

"As long as it takes." He squeezed her shoulder. "We should be getting some backup anytime, now."

"Good." Lex gripped her gun tighter to keep her hands from shaking. "I'm not ashamed to admit this scares the hell out of me."

Charlie gave her a tiny smile. "Me, too. I've never had to use my gun like this before, and I've been Sheriff for almost thirty years."

Lex felt better after his confession. She was about to say something else, when she realized it had gotten quiet. "I wonder if they've run out of ammo?"

"I don't know." He raised his head high enough to see over the bushes. There wasn't any movement from the criminal's camp.

Suddenly, a voice rang out. "I want to give myself up." One of the men stood, holding his hands above his head. He started out in the open, walking slowly.

"Dammit, Gary, get back here," one of the other men yelled.

"No! I've had enough, Ed." Gary continued to walk forward.

Ed stood also, pointing his rifle at the other man's back. "I said, get back here!"

Gary ignored him. When a shot rang out, he crumpled to the ground. A spot of blood grew on his back as he lay still.

"Teach you to run out on us." Ed ducked behind the fallen tree they used as cover.

Lex started breathing hard. "Did you see that, Charlie? He shot his own man."

"Yeah." Charlie was relieved when several of their party joined them. "You guys fan out the best you can."

Daniel, one of his newer deputies, came up to him. "Oscar and Jack are taking Jeremy to the main road. There's an ambulance on the way to meet them."

"Good, thanks." The return of gunfire from the convicts stopped their conversation. "Stay down."

With adrenaline racing through her body, Lex no longer felt nervous. She continued to take careful aim before pulling the trigger on the rifle, but returned the felons' fire bullet for bullet. Another scream caused her to pause, but only for a moment. She didn't know if it was her shot, or one from another deputy that hit. Remembering Jeremy's pain-filled face, she decided she didn't care. "Bastards."

"Hold your fire," Charlie commanded his group. He waited but no more shots came from the escapees.

Lex held her rifle against her chest. "Should we go check on them?"

"Not yet. I don't want to risk anyone."

Wayne, another one of Charlie's men, came up and squatted next to the sheriff. "I think I can get closer to them and see what's up."

"Okay, but don't take any chances." Charlie used his radio to communicate with the others. "Wayne's moving in. Cover him." After receiving the acknowledgements, he nodded to Wayne. The deputy took off, using trees and brush to conceal his whereabouts.

Lex held her rifle at the ready and blinked the sweat from her eyes. She watched as Wayne moved closer and closer. He stood and waved. "They're both down." More men followed. They handcuffed the criminals and dragged them out of their hiding place.

Charlie stepped out of the trees and went to kneel next to the man who had been shot in the back. He looked up as Lex joined him. "He's dead."

"Damn." Lex looked down at the man, who appeared years younger than herself. "Why would they shoot one of their own guys?"

"I don't know. We may never find out. The other two aren't in very good shape." He stood and put an arm around her shoulders. "How are you doing?"

She shook her head at the senselessness of it all. "Tired." Watching the deputies take the injured men out of the area, she sighed. "Are you going to need any help with them?"

"I think we can handle it from here. Why don't you take your guys to the house? We'll do the cleanup."

"Sounds good." Lex gave him a weary smile. "I've got a date in town anyway."

Charlie pushed her in the direction of where they left their horses. "Give Amanda and Lorrie a kiss from me. And tell Martha I'll call her when I can."

Lex turned and waved. "You got it, Charlie."

Chapter
Eight

ANNA LEIGH AND Martha stood in the doorway to the living room. Seeing Amanda and Lorrie asleep on the sofa, they decided not to intrude. "Poor thing. Mandy looks completely exhausted." Anna Leigh could feel a chill in the air, so she tiptoed into the room and covered the two with a quilt.

Martha waited until she was out of the room and they were in the kitchen. "I'm glad they're finally taking a nap. They were both getting a little cranky."

"I hope Mandy isn't coming down with anything. I can't remember the last time she took a nap in the middle of the day." Anna Leigh walked over to the counter and raised the coffee pot. When Martha nodded, she took out two mugs, filled them and brought them to the table. "I wish we'd hear from Lexington. That would do her a world of good."

"Thank you." Martha took a sip. "I put a call in to the dispatcher at the sheriff's department. Carla's a sweet girl and she promised she'd let me know as soon as she heard anything."

A knock on the front door brought Anna Leigh out of her chair. Martha followed her and stood by the staircase. As the door opened, Martha covered her mouth with one hand and gasped. "Lexie?" She rushed over and enveloped the exhausted woman in a hug. "Oh, baby. Look at you."

Lex was covered in dry mud. Her hat was still damp from the earlier rain and her face was drawn and shadowed. "Sorry for the mess, but I came straight here." She forgot who had taken her horse to the barn for her and barely remembered the drive into town. "Charlie said to tell you he'd call when he got a chance."

"That's fine, honey." Martha could feel the clammy skin underneath the moist clothes. "You need to get out of these wet things."

Lex acted as if she hadn't heard her. "Where's Amanda?"

Martha took her by the arm and led her to the living room. "She's napping, but I think she'd rather see you." She exchanged glances with Anna Leigh and left Lex alone.

Kneeling next to the sleeping woman, Lex watched her for a moment. Unable to help herself, she reached out with a trembling hand and brushed the hair away from Amanda's face. "Sweetheart?"

At the sound of her lover's voice, Amanda's eyes popped open. She sat up quickly, waking Lorrie. "Are you really here?"

Lorrie began to cry, until she noticed who was beside them. "Wex!" Her arms reached out and she latched onto Lex's neck, knocking the hat off her head.

"Whoa!" Lex tumbled backward as she was greeted similarly by Amanda.

Amanda ran her hands all over Lex's body. "I can't believe you're finally here." She moved until she sat across her partner's hips. It was then she noticed bloodstains on Lex's shirt. "Oh, my god. What—"

"It's not mine." Lex caught Amanda's hands and held them. "Jeremy got nicked, but he's okay." She grinned as Lorrie patted her face.

The child giggled as Lex caught one of her hands in her mouth. She pulled it back and placed it on Lex's lips, chortling as she was captured again.

Now that she was looking, Amanda could tell how worn out Lex was by the dark circles under her eyes. "I think we need to get you upstairs and into a nice, hot bath."

"Bath!" Lorrie squealed and hopped up and down on Lex's chest. "Me likes bath."

Lex closed her eyes and enjoyed the love of her family. There would be time later to think about what she'd gone through.

AMANDA RAISED HER head from Lex's shoulder. They had both gone to bed after Lex's quick shower, and she was surprised to see hints of the morning sun coming through the window. Once again, Lorrie was missing from the room. Her grandmother had obviously taken her downstairs for breakfast. The little girl refused to let Lex out of her sight the day before, so they had brought her to bed with them while they took their "nap", which had turned into fifteen hours of sleep. She looked down into Lex's face. "What happened to you out there, love?" The dark circles were still evident under her eyes and there were lines between her eyebrows and around her mouth as she frowned in her sleep. Lex had cried out several times during the night, and only Amanda's comforting words settled her. Amanda was about to lay her head down, when her bladder made itself known. Grumbling, she hurried to the adjoining bathroom.

The movement of the bed awakened Lex, and she looked around the room in confusion. It took her a moment to realize where she was. She didn't remember anything after her shower and was surprised to see that she was wearing a pair of Jacob's pajamas. Her body ached all over from sleeping in one position for so long. Seeing the sunshine streaming through the blinds, she rubbed her eyes. A heavy weariness weighed on her shoulders as she remembered the events from the previous two days.

Amanda left the bathroom to find her partner sitting up on the bed with her arms wrapped around her legs. "Good morning, sleepyhead."

Lex raised her head. "Who are you calling sleepyhead? I see you're still wearing your jammies." When Amanda sat beside her, Lex leaned into her body. The soothing fingers that were massaging her scalp caused her to moan in appreciation. "I'll give you twenty years to stop doing that."

"Only twenty? I was thinking more along the lines of seventy or so."

"Mommy!" Lorrie raced into the room and tried to climb onto Amanda's lap.

Amanda saw movement in the doorway. "Hi, Gramma."

"Good morning, you two. Someone got up around eight last night for dinner and you were sleeping so well that we kept her with us for the night." Anna Leigh joined them and sat on the edge of the bed. "How are you feeling, Lexington?"

"Not too bad. Although I don't know why I'm tired, after all that sleep." Lex brushed her fingers through Lorrie's hair. "Wait a minute. Did she call you mommy?" she asked Amanda. "When did that start?"

Lorrie tapped Amanda on the chest. "Mommy, pway."

"Sure, honey, in a little while." Amanda turned to Lex. "She called me that yesterday morning and hasn't stopped. I have a feeling I'll be hearing it a lot."

Lex took the little girl from Amanda and hugged her. "She's a good mommy, isn't she, lil' bit?"

"Yep."

Anna Leigh laughed. "That sounds familiar. I wonder where it came from?"

"I'm pleading the fifth." Lex ducked behind Lorrie, much to the child's delight. She felt her hair grasped in two small fists when Lorrie turned around. "Ouch!"

Amanda untangled Lorrie's fingers from Lex's head. "Lorrie, be nice to Momma Lex."

Lorrie put her hands on Lex's cheeks and gave her a kiss. "Momma, good."

Lex felt tears trickle down her face. She had never heard a sweeter sound. "Momma loves you, Lorrie."

LEX WATCHED QUIETLY as Lorrie sat on the floor with Jacob, playing with a wooden toy train he had built for her. They pushed it back and forth, and she would clap in delight when he made puffing sounds along with the action. At Amanda's urging, they had decided to spend another day at the Cauble's home. A large part of her was glad, because she didn't feel like doing anything more than watching their daughter play.

Out of the corner of her eye, Amanda took a surreptitious glance at her partner. Lex had barely spoken all day. Her listlessness was unusual and Amanda was concerned. She squeezed the hand she was holding. "Can I get you anything?"

"No, I'm good, thanks." Lex turned her head when Martha and Charlie walked into the room. "Hey, there."

Martha sat on the edge of the sofa and placed her hand on Lex's shoulder. "How are you feeling? We were on our way to the ranch and thought we'd drop by."

Lex leaned into the touch. "I'm fine. A little tired, but okay."

"Can I talk to you in the kitchen, Lex?" Charlie ignored the pointed look from Amanda. "I need to fill you in on a few things."

"Sure." Lex released Amanda's hand and followed him from the room.

Charlie put his hands in his pants pockets. He looked everywhere in the kitchen except at Lex, until she cleared her throat. "There's no easy way to tell you this."

"Tell me what?"

"Maybe you should sit down."

Lex crossed her arms over her chest, but didn't leave the spot where she stood. "Tell me."

Suddenly, the pattern on the tile floor was fascinating to Charlie. "That man you shot, Mack Wilkins?"

"That was his name?" Lex felt bad that she never asked.

"Yeah." Charlie rubbed the back of his neck. "I'm sorry to be the one to break this to you, Lex. But he died last night on the operating table."

Lex paled and slid down the wall to the floor. "No. I couldn't have."

"It's not your fault, honey. He lost too much blood on the way to the hospital." Charlie stepped forward and reached out to her.

"No!" Lex encircled her torso with her arms. "No." She choked back a sob.

Amanda had heard Lex cry out and she rushed into the kitchen. "What's going on?" She saw Lex huddled against the wall. "Charlie?"

"He was fine when I left. I couldn't have killed him." Lex closed her eyes and leaned forward.

Surrounding her grief-stricken lover with her arms, Amanda gave Charlie an accusing look. "What did you say to her?"

Lex raised her head. "I killed him, Amanda. I didn't mean to, but I did."

"I know you didn't, baby." Amanda had no idea what she was talking about. Feeling he was responsible for her lover's anguish, she glared at Charlie.

"Yesterday, when we caught up to the escapees, they began to shoot at us," he explained. "Did she not tell you any of this?"

"We haven't talked about it. What happened?"

"We had to return their fire, and one of Lex's rounds hit the leader of the group. We traded shots back and forth for a while, and he lost a lot of blood during that time. Once it was resolved, we took them into custody and brought them to the hospital. He was too weak and never made it out of the operating room." Charlie twisted his hat in his hands. "I didn't want her to hear about it on the news."

"Thank you." She pulled Lex closer. "I'm sorry I yelled at you. I know it was as hard for you to tell her as it was for her to hear."

He touched Amanda's arm. "Let me know if I can do anything for her." Saddened by Lex's distress, Charlie left the room.

"Come on, love. Let's get you off this floor." Amanda helped Lex to her feet.

"I don't want to go back there."

Amanda rubbed her hand across Lex's back. "You don't have to. We'll go home and try not to think about it."

"No, I'm not going."

"What do you mean?"

Lex shook her head. "I can't go to the ranch. I killed him there."

In the doorway, Martha had heard what Lex said. "Bull. That man was shooting at you." She moved into the room and stood in front of Lex. "Don't you dare feel bad about defending yourself and Charlie. He told me how brave you were."

"I didn't—"

"You most certainly did. Had you not been with Charlie, I could have lost him. Please don't let some lowlife scum ruin your life, or make you run away from the only home you've ever known."

Lex bit her lip and thought about what Martha said. Coming to a decision, she straightened her posture. She knew when she was deputized that she might have to use her firearms. It was the criminal's own actions that killed him, not her. "I won't." She brought Martha close to her and kissed her cheek. "Thanks."

Martha blushed. "Don't thank me. I only told the truth." She nodded to Amanda and left the room.

"She's something else, isn't she?"

Lex gathered Amanda into her arms. "That she is."

Amanda rested her cheek against Lex's shirt. "Are you going to be okay?"

"Yeah. It's going to take me a while to accept the fact I had a hand in a man's death, but it was in self defense. Can we go home in the morning?"

"We could leave now, if you want." Although the last thing Amanda wanted to do was leave the warm cocoon of love enveloping her.

"Nah, tomorrow's soon enough. Lorrie can spend more time with her great-grandparents this way.

"Sounds good to me." Amanda closed her eyes and inhaled her lover's scent. "I could stay like this forever.

Chapter
Nine

AMANDA'S EYES OPENED and she squinted to get her bearings. The room was dark and the digital reading on the alarm clock next to the bed showed it was only five o'clock in the morning. She wasn't sure what had caused her to awake, until she felt an unusual queasiness. It was the third day in a row she had been disturbed in this manner, but she chalked it up to her frazzled nerves. Even after they returned to the ranch, Amanda couldn't help but think about the escaped convicts and all she and Lex could have missed if things had turned out differently.

"Why are you awake?" Lex rolled over and faced Amanda. "Is everything okay?"

"I'm thinking about how lucky I am." Amanda palmed Lex's cheek. "We could have lost all of this."

Lex covered Amanda's hand with her own. "But we didn't. Besides, I made you a promise that I would come home. And you know I don't break my promises."

"I know. I was so scared."

"To tell you the truth, so was I. When we finally caught up to those guys, I wasn't too sure if I could even raise my gun." Lex brought Amanda's hand from her face and kissed the palm. "The last thing I wanted to do was let Charlie down. He was depending on me to cover his back. Once things got going, I only did what I had to do to keep us both safe."

Amanda moved so she could snuggle against her lover. "And you have no idea how thankful I am for that."

"I think I do. I was glad you were in town with your grandparents. I wasn't as scared for me as I was you. Now things can get back to normal." Lex tucked the bedding around Amanda. "Get some rest, sweetheart."

Her eyes already sliding closed, Amanda yawned. "Love you."

Lex kissed the top of her head. "I love you, too."

SEVERAL DAYS LATER, Lex trotted down the stairs en route to

joining Amanda and Lorrie for breakfast. A firm knock on the front door caused her to change direction. She opened the door and then took a step back. A man and woman faced her. Lex directed her glare at him. "What are you doing here?"

"What? You're not glad to see me? It's been a few years, little sister." Hubert Walters had his arm around a petite blonde woman. "Aren't you going to ask us in?"

Getting over her surprise, Lex couldn't contain her curiosity. "Okay, fine. But there better not be any funny business or I'll throw you out." She moved to allow them to enter. "Let's go into the den."

Hubert led the silent woman with him into the room and took a seat on the sofa. "The place looks good."

Unsettled by his demeanor, Lex followed them and sat on the loveseat. "Thanks. I didn't even know you were out of jail. What brings you here?"

"I thought I'd show Janine where I grew up." He put his arm across the back of the couch and his fingers grazed the top of the woman's shoulders. "Oh, yeah. Janine, this is my sister, Lex." With a proud look on his face, Hubert pulled her close. "Sis, this is my wife, Janine."

Wife? Lex blinked. *Sis? He's never called me that.* "It's nice to meet you, Janine." Lex continued to stare at her brother. She was relieved when Amanda came into the room carrying Lorrie.

"Momma!" Lorrie struggled in Amanda's arms until she was set down. As soon as her feet hit the floor, she raced to Lex and climbed into her lap. Standing up, she wrapped her arms around Lex's neck and gave her a sloppy kiss on the cheek.

Hubert's eyes widened and his jaw dropped. "Momma? You have a kid? How did that happen?"

"Didn't dad ever go over the birds and bees with you?"

Amanda joined Lex and Lorrie on the loveseat. She gave a friendly smile to the woman who sat next to Hubert. "Hi, I'm Amanda, Lex's partner. This is our daughter, Lorrie."

"It's nice to meet you, Amanda. I'm Janine."

"Hubert's wife," Lex added.

"Oh?" Amanda quickly covered her surprise. "How long have you two known each other?"

Janine leaned into Hubert's embrace. "A little over a year. I was Hubert's anger-management counselor. Once he was paroled he started sending me flowers, asking for a date. After several months I finally gave in and we've been together ever since."

"How long have you been out, Hube? I didn't think you'd be coming home to Somerville so soon." Lex bounced Lorrie on her knee to keep her occupied.

Hubert squeezed Janine's arm. He turned and looked at her with adoration. "Janie's been my rock. Thanks to her, I got out early, about eight months ago. I'm only on parole for a year, then I'm free and clear. We've decided to settle down here since that's where my family is."

"Family?" Lex stopped moving, much to Lorrie's dismay.

The little girl patted Lex's leg. "More." When she was ignored, Lorrie patted it harder. "More." She raised her eyes to Lex's face and frowned. "Momma?" Trying another tactic, she kicked her legs. "Pease?"

"I'm sorry, lil' bit." Lex resumed the action.

"Yeah. You, our grandfather. And it looks like I've got a niece now."

Amanda stood. "Would you like some coffee?" She needed a few minutes to get her equilibrium back. "There's a fresh pot in the kitchen."

Janine also got to her feet. "That would nice, thank you. Let me give you a hand so these two can get reacquainted."

"Um, sure." Amanda left the room with Janine on her heels. Once they were in the kitchen she pulled out a tray and placed four mugs on it. "Do you take anything in your coffee?"

"No, black is fine." Janine touched Amanda's arm. "I know this must be a shock to you, us showing up like we have. Hubert told me all about the animosity between him and his sister. He's let go of his anger and forgiven her."

Amanda spun around. "He's forgiven her? Did your husband happen to mention why he was locked up?"

"Of course. He was quite remorseful about the whole misunderstanding."

"What?" Amanda shook her head as if trying to clear it. "Just what exactly did he tell you?"

Janine poured the coffee into the mugs, not seeing the incredulous look on Amanda's face. "Oh, he admitted that what happened to the two of you was wrong and he was terribly upset by it. As a matter of fact, he feels like it was his fault. If he hadn't mentioned to those men how upset he was with his sister, they would have never run your truck off the road."

"I hate to break this to you, Janine, but Hubert didn't mention something to those men. He paid them to hurt us. He even admitted that to us right before he was arrested. I can't even begin to tell you all the horrible things he's put Lex through."

"Well, that's your opinion of course. I go by what he's told me. Hubert has always been honest with me and I trust him."

Amanda picked up the tray and started to leave the kitchen. "A word of warning to you, Janine. This is a wonderful family you've married into, but Hubert's never been a part of it. Watch your back. When you least expect it, he'll turn on you."

In the living room, Lorrie tired of using Lex as a horse and curled up in her arms. She had one hand tangled in Lex's shirt and her eyes closed. To keep from disturbing her Lex kept her voice low. "I don't know what your game is, Hubert. The last time I saw you, I remember you threatening to kill me. Don't you think for one minute I've forgotten what you did to us."

He leaned forward in his seat. "I'm not sure what you're saying. Can't you be happy for me?"

"The only thing that would make me happy is to never see your face again. You're a sorry excuse for a human being and nothing you do or say is going to change that fact."

Janine heard the last of the conversation as she came into the room. "Excuse me? What gives you the right to pass judgment on him? From what I've been told, you're as much to blame as anyone."

After Amanda placed the tray on the coffee table, Lex handed Lorrie to her and stood. "I think you two should leave."

"That's a good idea." Janine got her purse. "You were right, Hubert. She is an unreasonable and hateful person." She took his arm. "Let's go. You shouldn't have to be subjected to her nasty temper."

He waited until his wife's back was to the others and grinned. "Thanks, baby. I told you it wouldn't do any good to come out here." To Lex, he mouthed, "Bitch." Then, out loud, he said, "Bye, sis. I had hoped to have a better relationship with you."

"Go to hell, Hubert." Lex got to her feet and held her fists at her side, wanting more than anything to knock the self-satisfied look off his face. "Get out."

Amanda put her hand on Lex's chest to keep her from going after her brother. "Honey, it's okay."

"We'll be leaving now." Janine led her husband from the house, muttering her fears of what his volatile sister might do to him.

Lex waited until the door was closed. "That went well." She exhaled heavily and dropped down to sit on the loveseat again. "I'm sorry, Amanda. I don't know what's wrong with me."

"You have nothing to apologize for. I talked to Janine in the kitchen and apparently she is completely deluded as to who he is. Hubert has obviously lied to her about everything."

"She's an idiot." Lex rubbed her face with her hands. "I wonder how long it's going to be before she meets the real Hubert. There's no way he can keep up the charade for long."

Amanda sat next to her with Lorrie still sleeping in her arms. "They say love is blind." She nudged Lex with her shoulder. "It's obviously stupid, too."

"Yeah." Leaning her head back and closing her eyes, Lex suddenly felt very weary. "I don't know what he's up to."

Amanda placed her head on Lex's hand in a show of support. "I don't either, but maybe he'll be too busy with his new wife and leave us alone."

"I hope so, but I'm not counting on it."

Neither was Amanda. She had a feeling they hadn't seen the last of him and the thought scared her.

HEAVY RAIN SETTLED into the area again the following day. Lex decided to use the time to work in the barns. She was reorganizing the tack room when Jack appeared at the door. "Can I talk to you for a minute, boss?"

Lex took off her hat and wiped her brow. She propped herself up against the rack where the saddles were kept. "What's up?"

"I've been doing a lot of thinking." He mirrored her posture on the opposite wall.

"What about? Is there something the matter?"

Unable to meet her eyes, he ducked his head. "I owe you an apology."

"For?"

"Being a gutless coward." Sticking his hands in his front pockets, he looked everywhere but at her. "I've come to give you my notice."

Lex moved to stand in front of him and waited until she had his attention. "Hell, Jack. I don't think you're gutless at all. If it had been anyone else but Charlie, I wouldn't have gone in the first place."

He raised his hopeful eyes to hers. "Yeah?" Jack was only in his early-twenties, and looked up to his boss. "Were you scared, too?"

"Shitless."

"How did you get over it?"

She clasped his shoulder. "I didn't. But I wasn't about to let anything happen to Charlie or any of you. And I didn't want those assholes near our place." Lex escorted him from the room. "Do you honestly want to quit? I'd miss you."

"No, I guess not. But I didn't think you'd want a coward working for you."

They stood at the main door and watched the rain come down. "You're not a coward. I'd trust you to watch my back, any day."

"You would?"

"Yep." She noticed he wasn't wet. "How did you get here? It's pouring rain and you look dry."

He scuffed his toe in the dirt. "Roy dropped me off. He was heading into town for a few supplies." Jack frowned at the rain. "I guess I'm stuck here until it lets up some."

"Nah." Lex adjusted her hat and grabbed her coat, which was lying on a bale of hay. "I'll give you a ride."

"Thanks." Feeling relieved, Jack followed Lex out into the rain.

Chapter
Ten

MARTHA WAS UP to her elbows in dishwater when the front doorbell rang. She was the only one in the house. Amanda had taken Lorrie in to town for her regular checkup with her pediatrician. With a heavy sigh, Martha wiped her hands on a dishtowel as she hurried to answer the door. Upon opening it she came face-to-face with a man in his mid-twenties. His hair was rusty brown and his hazel eyes were set in a tanned face.

He took his straw western hat off and held it in his shaking hands. "Ma'am? May I speak with Rawson Walters?"

"I'm afraid not, young man. He passed away a few years ago. Is there something I can do for you?"

Lowering his eyesight to the hat he was holding, the stranger shook his head. "I guess not, ma'am." He raised his head and noticed the wedding band she wore. "Are you Mrs. Walters?"

Unable to help herself, Martha chuckled. "Lordy, no. I only take care of the place." She held out her hand. "I'm Martha Bristol."

"Pleased to meet you, Mrs. Bristol." He shook her hand. "My name's Cleve Winters."

"Mr. Winters. Were you here to see Mr. Walters about a job? I know we can usually use an extra hand."

Cleve began to fiddle with the brim of his hat. "Not exactly. I was hoping to meet with him and talk."

Feeling he was no threat, Martha stepped aside. "It's nasty out here. Why don't you come in and I'll get you a cup of coffee? We can discuss this more in the kitchen."

"ANOTHER CUP OF coffee, Lex?" Lester, the bunkhouse cook, waved the pot in the air. "It's still raining pretty good. I'd hate to see that old Jeep of yours end up in a ditch somewhere."

Lex choked down the rest of her cup. It was a lot stronger than she was used to, but a welcome offering to warn her after being out in the damp air. She grinned at the men seated around the scarred old table. "Nah. Since I've already whipped these guys in poker, I might as well head on up to the house."

No fair. We should get a chance to win our pennies back," Roy complained good naturedly. "I'm out almost a dollar as it is."

"Is it my fault you can't bluff?" Lex stood and jiggled the change in her pockets. "At least you're not the one rattling when you walk."

Chet, another one of the hands, tossed a penny at Roy, hitting him in the chest. "here. Don't say I never gave you nothing."

Roy picked up the offering and studied it. "Gee, thanks. Now I get that new truck I was thinking about." He flipped it in the air. "Since you have all my others, do you want this one too, boss?"

"That's okay. Save it for next time, then I'll take it off your hands." Lex ducked as the penny went sailing over her head. "You're going to have to do better than that."

Before Lex could make it to the door, the telephone near the stove rang. Lester limped over and answered it. "Lex? It's for you."

She walked to where he stood and took the handset. "Thanks."

"Lexie, you need to get up to the house." Worry colored Martha's tone.

"What's up?"

"I don't want to get into it over the phone, but you've got a visitor."

Lex propped herself against the wall and studied the fingernails on one hand. She frowned when she saw dried mud underneath them. "Who is it? Not Hubert again?"

"No. It's a fellow you should talk to. Now quit playing twenty questions and get your rear to the house."

Lex's cocked her head at the no-nonsense tone in Martha's voice. Whatever it was, she was upset. "Yes, ma'am." Lex hung up the phone. She moved to the door and took her coat from its peg, shrugging into it. "Gotta go, guys. I'll be back some other time to take your money."

Roy made a shooing motion with his hands. "Go on. I'll try to find something constructive for this lot to do." He waited until the door was closed and turned to Lester. "Is Martha on the warpath?"

The old cook shrugged. "Didn't sound like it. At least not until the boss was giving her a hard time." He hitched up his pants. "Since it's still raining, it's a good day to move all the furniture and clean the floors. Come on, boys. I'm going to put y'all to work." He was answered by a roomful of groans.

STANDING ON THE back porch of the ranch house, Lex took her hat off and shook the rain water from it. "I'm starting to feel like a damned fish." She stomped her feet to clear some of the mud off, then wiped them on a thick mat outside the door. Satisfied they were clean enough, she stepped into the house and hung her hat and duster on the hooks by the door. "Martha?"

"Stop your yelling, Lexie." Martha came out of the kitchen and swatted her with a towel. "I know you like to spend all your time there, but I didn't raise you in a barn."

Properly chastised, Lex took the towel from Martha and wiped the water from her own face. "Sorry about that."

Martha took the towel away from her and dabbed at Lex's hair. "You're soaked."

"Couldn't help it. It's coming down in buckets out there." Lex ducked out of the way. "Stop that."

"Maybe you should go upstairs and get into some dry clothes."

"It's not that bad. I'll dry."

Martha slapped at Lex's arm. "You'll catch cold is what you'll do. Go change and I'll have your guest wait for you in the den."

Knowing she was beat, Lex kissed Martha's cheek. "Yes, ma'am." She hurried up the stairs, leaving small bits of mud as she went.

"I'm going to kill that girl one of these days." Martha could always count on Lex keeping her mop bucket in use. She went to keep Cleve company until Lex returned.

Less than five minutes later Lex returned to the first floor of the house. She walked into the living room where Martha was talking with a man who sat next to the fireplace. "Hello."

He jumped to his feet. "Ms. Walters. Thanks for seeing me."

"No problem." Lex held out her hand, pleased with his strong grip. "Call me Lex."

"Okay, Lex. My name's Cleve Winters."

Lex motioned for him to sit. She took the chair opposite him. "What can I do for you, Mr. Winters?"

"Cleve, please." He propped one foot on his opposite knee and began to jiggle it nervously. "I wasn't expecting to see you."

"Who exactly were you expecting?"

Realizing his foot was moving, Cleve stopped. "I actually came here looking for Mr. Walters."

"Why? Did he offer you a job or something?" Out of the corner of her eye, Lex saw Martha twisting her ever-present dishtowel. "Martha?"

"I think I'll get you two some coffee." Martha stood and left the room, unable to meet Lex's gaze.

Lex got to her feet also. "All right, Cleve. I'm not in the mood for games. What the hell's going on here?"

His foot started wiggling again. "I'm sorry, ma'am. I didn't mean to upset Mrs. Bristol. I only came here to—"

"To what?" Lex was on the verge of jerking him out of the chair and shaking him. "Spit it out. Why were you looking for my dad? What was he to you?"

Cleve studied the stitched pattern on the top of his boot. "My father."

"Excuse me?" Lex was sure she didn't hear him correctly.

"I said...he was my father."

Lex felt like she had been kicked in the stomach. She fell into her chair. "I don't believe this."

He rose from the chair. "Look, Ms. Walters. I didn't come here to cause any problems. I wanted to meet my father."

"What makes you think my father, Rawson Walters, was yours, too?" Lex ran her hands through her hair, which was still damp from the rain.

"Because my mother told me so."

"How do you know she was telling the truth?"

Cleve's face reddened. He grabbed her by the shirt and pulled her from the chair. "Are you calling my mother a liar?"

"Get your damn hands off me." Lex clutched his wrists in an effort to break free.

"What's going on in here?" Martha came into the room and almost dropped the tray she was holding. "Lexie, stop it!"

Lex pushed Cleve away from her and brushed the front of her shirt. "I didn't do anything. This jackass attacked me."

Embarrassed by his actions, Cleve backed away from Lex and stuck his hands in his front pockets. "I'm sorry, Mrs. Bristol." He glared at Lex. "Just don't talk about my mother like that."

"Like what? All I did was ask a simple question." Lex took the tray from Martha and set it on a nearby table. "Thanks."

"You insinuated my mother was a liar." He clinched his fists at his sides. "I don't appreciate that."

Lex adjusted her shirt. It was still wrinkled where he grabbed it. "Well, I don't like when someone manhandles me either. So I guess we're even."

Martha was tempted to spank her. "Behave."

"Fine." Lex sat again. "Okay, Cleve. Why don't you tell me why your mother thinks we have the same father?"

He reached into his back pocket and pulled out his wallet. Digging through it he finally found what he was looking for. Cleve handed Lex a small photograph. "See for yourself."

She took the wallet-sized print and studied it. The grainy print was of a man astride a horse. Lex squinted to make out the face. "Okay. So you have an old picture of a guy. What's this supposed to prove?"

"Mom says it's the only shot she has of my father. And she told me his name was Rawson Walters and he lived in Texas."

Lex looked at it again. The man in the photo did favor her father. "This could be anyone. How do I know you're not trying to get a piece of this ranch? Maybe you read the obituary and waited awhile before showing up."

Cleve took a step toward her. "You're full of shit, lady." He looked at Martha. "Excuse me. I didn't mean to say that in front of you."

"I've heard worse." Martha stood nearby, not trusting either of them to control themselves. "Why don't you show her what you showed me?"

"Oh, yeah." Cleve reached into his other back pocket and pulled out a ratty folded envelope. He handed it to Lex, who accepted it gingerly. "Go ahead. Read the note inside."

Lex removed a rumpled piece of paper and unfolded it. She read it silently, then looked up. "Where did you get this?"

He appeared smug. "My mother's name is Marcy. That's who it was written to. Do you recognize the signature?"

Although the scrawled name was nearly illegible, Lex knew exactly whose it was. "Yes, dammit." The letter, although short, was written to someone named Marcy. In it, the author explained that although he cared about her, he was going to Texas to make amends with his family. He mentioned how his wife at home was pregnant with their third child and he was determined to be a better husband and father.

"He didn't even know Mom was pregnant with me when he left." Cleve took the letter from Lex. "She never heard from him again."

Lex lowered her head. She closed her eyes to ward off the headache that began to make itself known. "I don't need this right now."

WHEN AMANDA RETURNED with Lorrie from the appointment, she was surprised to find that Lex was nowhere to be found. The house was quiet. Normally her partner would be anxiously waiting, wanting to know every detail of the doctor's visit. Lorrie began to fuss so Amanda placed her in the high chair in the kitchen in order to feed her an overdue snack.

The back door closed and Amanda looked up hopefully. When Martha came into the room, Amanda's hopes fell. "Hi Martha."

"Hello, there. How was the check up?" Martha went to the refrigerator and took out a gallon of milk. She shook the container before pouring a small amount into Lorrie's favorite sippy cup. "I swear, this little girl is a miniature of Lexie. She loved the 'moo juice', too."

"Moo juice?"

Martha put the milk away while Amanda set a couple of graham crackers on the tray in front of the impatient toddler. "That's what Lexie called it when she was little. It used to drive her daddy crazy. I personally think that's the reason she did it."

"I wouldn't be surprised." Amanda took a place at the table next to Lorrie. "Honey, slow down. The cookies aren't going anywhere."

"Yet another trait of her momma's. That girl would barely slow down to eat. When she did, she ate so fast I thought she'd choke. As soon as she was done, Lexie would race from the table and be off again."

Amanda found the revelation quite humorous. "She still does it. I can only get her to take her time in bed." Her face flushed suddenly when she realized how the comment sounded. "I mean eating." The innocent explanation embarrassed her more. "Oh, hell."

"Don't worry, honey. I knew exactly what you meant." Martha patted Amanda on the shoulder before joining her at the table. "But you sure are cute when you blush."

Waving her hand in front of her face in an effort to cool off, Amanda cleared her throat. "Let's see, what were we talking about? Yeah. Where's Lex?"

Still amused, Martha accepted the subject change. "She took a fellow up to the bunkhouse."

"Doesn't she usually call Roy to come get them? Why the special trip?" A gooey hand slapped Amanda's arm. "Lorrie, no." She took a paper napkin from the holder in the middle of the table and wiped herself clean.

"More!" Lorrie crumbled what was left of her last cracker and added a few drops of milk from her cup. "Mommy, more."

Amanda winced at the mess. "Lorrie, that's gross."

The little girl laughed and slapped at the sodden pile. Her laughter soon turned to tears when Amanda used another napkin to clean it up. "No." She swatted her mother's hand. "Mine!"

"Lorrie, stop." Amanda flinched when an errant glob landed in her hair. "That's it. No more cookies for you." She ignored the indignant wail that came from the child.

Martha covered her mouth with her hand to prevent a laugh from escaping. When Amanda glared at her, she shook her head and pantomimed zipping her mouth shut.

"I suppose Lex did that, too?"

"Did?" Martha stood and began removing items from the fridge to start dinner. "You know as well as I do that she still loves to make a mess. It takes me half the day to clean the mud from the house when it rains."

Lorrie settled down and watched Martha as she began chopping vegetables for stew. She noticed that Martha was close to the open box of graham crackers. "Mada, cookie?"

"Oh no, little one. Your mommy would never forgive me."

"Pease?"

The sweet entreaty melted Martha's heart. She turned to Amanda. "Shouldn't good manners be rewarded?"

Amanda raised her hands in defeat. "Go ahead. Dinner's several hours away." She didn't know who was happier about the decision,

Lorrie or Martha. Both beamed.

"She's hard to say no to." Ruffling the child's hair, Martha returned to preparing the stew.

"That's because she has you wrapped around her little finger, Mada. Now, since you've appeased the tiny terror, do you want to get back to why Lex felt the need to take a new hire up the road?"

Martha heated the previously browned stew meat in a skillet before adding it to the pot. "I'm not sure how much to tell. Maybe it would be best if Lexie told you herself."

"Told her what?" Lex asked as she came into the room. Her hair was damp and she was in her stocking feet. She dropped into a chair and stretched out her legs.

"Amanda was curious why you took Cleve up to the bunkhouse."

Lex turned to her partner. "She told you about him?"

"No. Martha mentioned you had taken a man up. Don't you normally have Roy do that?"

"Oh."

Lorrie, no longer occupied with her food, heard Lex's voice and immediately started slapping her tray. "Momma, momma."

"Have you been having fun, lil' bit?" Lex got up and walked around the table. She couldn't help but laugh at the mess that was her daughter.

Lorrie's hair, filled with clumps of soggy crackers, stood in several directions. She also had more squished between her fingers and bits in her eyelashes. "Momma!" Lorrie waved her hands in Lex's direction, causing particles of cookie to fly everywhere.

"Watch out there." Lex took a dishtowel and wiped the toddler's hands. Once they were clean, Lex picked Lorrie up and held her close. "How's my girl?" Her question was aimed more at Amanda. "Were you good at the doctor?"

"She was an angel, although I think when she pulled his stethoscope out of his ears he was a little rattled."

Lex kissed Lorrie's forehead. "That's my girl."

"So, Lex. About the new guy?"

"His name is Cleve Winters. He showed up here this afternoon and I thought I'd give him a chance."

Confused, Amanda frowned. "I thought this was the time of year you let a few men go. There's not that much to do with winter coming on."

Lex went to her chair. She accepted the mug of coffee that Martha placed in front of her. "Thanks."

"You're welcome." Martha returned to her preparations, trying to be as unobtrusive as possible.

Realizing she had stalled as long as she possibly could, Lex bounced Lorrie on her knee. "Cleve actually came by to see dad." Her voice softened, so much that Amanda had to strain to hear it. "He claims that he's dad's son."

"What proof did he have? Was he trying to get a piece of the ranch?"

"That's pretty much what I said, too. This guy had a picture of dad and a letter he had written Cleve's mother. It explained why he was leaving her to go to his family. From the way it read, I think he wrote it right after he found out my mother was pregnant with Louis. He never knew about Cleve."

"Do you think he's telling the truth?"

Lex played with her coffee cup. "Dad wrote the letter. I'd know his handwriting and signature anywhere. And the timing's about right. He spent almost as much time in Oklahoma as he did here, then." She raised her mug to her lips and snorted derisively. "His excuse was always rodeoing or buying stock. I can't believe he did something like that to mom."

Amanda squeezed Lex's forearm in a show of compassion. "Maybe he got lonely up there."

"Don't try to make excuses for the man. We both know he was pretty much a bastard." Tiny hands touched her cheeks.

"Momma, pway?"

Lex pushed down the anger she always felt when she thought about her father. The child in her lap was much more important. She nibbled at the little fingers before standing. "Come on, kiddo. Let's go upstairs and see what we can get into." Bending slightly, she kissed Amanda. She grinned when Lorrie mimicked her. "We'll see how things go with him. I couldn't turn him away."

"I know, honey. You two go on. I think I'll help Martha down here for a while." Amanda watched as Lex took Lorrie from the room. Satisfied they were gone, she got up and walked to the counter. Picking up a knife, she took over the vegetable slicing chores from Martha. "What do you think about all this?"

Martha wiped her hands on a dishtowel. "To tell you the truth, I wasn't too surprised. Although I didn't start working here until Mrs. Walters was well along in her pregnancy, I could see that something besides the ranch was on his mind."

"This whole thing doesn't seem quite right. I remember him speaking of his wife with only the utmost love. Why would he feel the need to mess around on her?"

"That's something we'll never know, Amanda. But I think part of his grief after she passed was because he felt guilty for messin' around. He sure wasn't the devoted family man he'd claimed to be." Martha dumped the vegetables Amanda had chopped into the stew pot. "Having another woman in Oklahoma explains why he made so many trips away when he had two young children at home."

Amanda shook her head. The more she thought about it, the more she was able to believe Cleve Winters' claims. "You're right. It makes me wonder what would have happened if he knew he had another son."

"Me too. Let's hope this doesn't blow up in Lexie's face."

Chapter
Eleven

THE EXCITABLE HORSE danced sideways before the man atop could bring her under control. Unsettled, he jerked hard on the reins. "Whoa!"

"Dammit, Cleve. Are you trying to ruin her mouth?" Lex ducked between the slats in the corral and went over to grasp the bridle. "Where in the hell did you learn to ride a horse?"

Exasperated, he slapped his hands on his thighs. "I've been riding on a horse probably as long as you have. It's not my fault this nag is out of control. At least my horse has some sense. Thank god I'm going into town tomorrow to pick her up where I've stabled her."

"Get down."

"What?"

Lex grabbed his arm and jerked Cleve from the saddle. "Get your ass off the horse."

He barely had time to get his legs underneath himself before he hit the ground. "Hey, watch it!"

Ignoring Cleve's sputtering, Lex swung up into the saddle and held the reins loosely. "Watch and learn, boy."

"Bitch." But Cleve couldn't help but marvel at how the filly reacted in Lex's hands. He moved over to the edge of the corral and watched as she rode the animal around the arena.

Although Roy felt almost sorry for the new hire, he was secretly glad it was his boss who took over the horse's training. "She may be abrupt at times, but Lex *does* know her way around a horse." He'd heard from several of the hands about Cleve's attitude. For the life of him, Roy didn't understand why Lex allowed the man to stay on. It wasn't as if they were short-handed and needed the additional help.

Cleve acted as if he hadn't heard him. "Has she always been so high and mighty?"

Roy shook his head. "I don't know what bug bit you in the ass, but you'd better watch your mouth. She hired you on the spot and she can fire you just as fast."

The other man let out a derisive snort. "That ain't happenin', bud. She doesn't want the trouble I'd cause."

"Is that a threat?" Lex had ridden up to the two men and overheard Cleve's comment.

He tipped his hat and stuffed his hands in his rear pockets. "Nope. Only stating a fact." Trying to save face, he turned and sauntered to the bunkhouse without another word.

"That's a major asshole, boss."

Lex swung down from the horse and stood behind Roy. "You can say that again." She waited until she was sure Cleve was out of earshot. "He been giving you much grief?"

"Nah. I've heard some grumbling from a couple of the other guys, but I think I can straighten him out." Roy turned and leaned against the top beam of the corral. "If you don't mind me asking, why *did* you hire him? Was it his sparkling personality?"

"Yeah, right." Lex tied the reins loosely to the nearest post. "I guess you can say it's a favor to my old man."

"I see. He offered the guy a job or something?"

Lex sat on the top rung. "Not exactly." She looked around to make certain they were alone. "This goes no further, okay?"

"Sure."

"When I was little, my father would go up to Oklahoma on cattle buying trips." She glanced down at her knees and scratched at a clump of mud. "That wasn't all he was doing. He had a girlfriend up there, too. Cleve's a result of that."

Not wanting to upset Lex, Roy tried to keep his eyes on a distant point. "So that's what he meant, by causing trouble. Do you think he'll make a claim to the ranch?"

"I doubt it. Other than the chip on his shoulder regarding me, he seems like a decent enough guy. Martha liked him okay."

"All right. But give me the word and he's out of here. You don't need his crap."

Lex patted him on the back before hopping down from the fence. "Thanks, my friend. I may take you up on that."

IT WAS NEARING midnight before Lex returned to the house. She stepped quietly into Lorrie's room and looked down into the crib at the sleeping child. Sometime during the night, Lorrie had kicked off her covers. With a small shake of her head, Lex tucked her in once again. She bent over and kissed Lorrie on top of the head before leaving the room.

She stood at the doorway to the master bedroom. In the glow of the banked fire, the sight before her brought a smile to Lex's face. Amanda was curled around Lex's pillow in the middle of the bed. Like Lorrie, she had kicked off the blanket and sheet. Walking as silently as she could, Lex went into the bathroom to take a shower.

Lex stepped out of the steamy room, toweling her hair dry. A second towel was draped around her hips. She was almost to the dresser when she heard a shifting on the bed.

"Lex? What time is it?" Amanda sat up and blinked blearily at her. She turned and glanced at the clock on the nightstand. "What have you been doing? It's almost one o'clock in the morning."

"Sorry, I didn't mean to wake you." Lex crawled into bed and moaned in relief. "Damn, that feels good." She stretched her legs over the clean sheets and snuggled deeper into the bed.

Amanda cuddled next to her and draped her arm across Lex's stomach. She kissed her lover's cheek. "I'm glad you're here. I missed you today."

Lex turned her head and met Amanda's lips with her own. "Is everything okay?"

"Yeah, I guess so. I'm being a baby."

Lex rolled over so she was facing her. "Sweetheart, you're never a baby." She gripped Amanda's hand and pulled it close. "Did something happen today?"

"No. Well, Lorrie did pull a bag of flour out of the pantry and proceed to powder the entire kitchen. I was helping Martha bake cookies and our backs were only turned for a second." Amanda couldn't keep the amused look from her face. "She looked like a little ghost. Of course, so did I before I could get the bag away from her."

Unable to control herself, Lex laughed. "I would have paid good money to see that one."

"Yeah. Needless to say, we took a bath together. Martha wouldn't let me help clean the kitchen, either. She did bust up over it though."

"I can see that she's going to be in her terrible two's until we're old and gray." Lex released Amanda's hand and brushed her fingers through her partner's hair. "Makes my day seem tame by comparison."

"Hmm?" Amanda closed her eyes as Lex's nails gently scratched her scalp. "Anything exciting?"

"Nope. Well, other than almost strangling Cleve."

Amanda opened her eyes. "Why?"

Embarrassed, Lex concentrated on the head massage she was giving Amanda. "He's an ass. The idiot can't handle a horse worth a damn."

"What'd he do?"

"He nearly tore the new filly's mouth by jerking the reins everywhere." Lex stopped the scratching and sat up. She was getting angry all over again. "I wanted nothing better than to knock that damned smirk off his face."

Amanda rose also. "You didn't."

"No, but I wanted to. He's bringing his own horse out tomorrow. I can't wait to see what kind of glue factory reject he rides."

Amanda rubbed Lex's arm in an attempt to calm her down.

"Maybe he's not used to training horses. It does take a different ⸻ of knowledge than riding."

"But if that's the case, he should have said something. I swear that jackass has a chip on his shoulder the size of Texas." The light touch had the desired effect, as Lex exhaled heavily and leaned against the headboard. "No matter what I say, he either argues or ignores me completely. I don't know what to do."

"Would you like me to try talking to him? Maybe I can find out what skills he has. He might not know how to talk to you, since you're related."

Lex sighed heavily. She knew Amanda was right, but it still rankled her. "I guess it wouldn't hurt. I'll take all the help I can get."

Turning to snuggle into Lex's side, Amanda wrapped her arms around her lover's waist. "Now that all of that is settled, tell me what you were doing until after midnight tonight."

"I was so pissed after arguing with Cleve that I decided to organize the hay barn. I didn't want to come into the house in the mood I was in."

"That bad, huh?"

"Yeah. Y'all didn't need to put up with me." Lex hugged Amanda to her tightly. "But maybe if I came in and did this, it wouldn't have mattered." She kissed the top of her head then went for her lips when Amanda's face tilted toward her. They spent a few leisurely minutes enjoying the contact. When Amanda's hands threaded through Lex's hair, Lex rolled her onto her back and kissed her in earnest.

"You're not too tired, are you?" Amanda asked when she took a breath.

Lex kissed her on the nose. "Sweetheart, I'm *never* too tired for this." She proceeded to prove her point, much to Amanda's delight.

AMANDA NERVOUSLY SPUN the coffee cup on the table. She was waiting for Cleve to arrive at the main house, so they could talk. Lex had taken Lorrie for a "ride" and Martha was spending the day with Charlie, which left her alone in the house. The silence in the large home unnerved her. When a knock came at the back door, she jumped in response.

Cleve opened the door and stuck his head in. "Hello?"

"I'm in here," Amanda called. She stood as he came into the room. "Hi. Would you like a cup of coffee?"

He shrugged and pulled out a chair. Twisting it around, he sat and propped his arms over the back. "So, what do you want? Roy told me to come here."

Amanda grabbed a mug from the cabinet and filled it. She brought it to the table and set it in front of Cleve. "Do you take anything in it?"

"Nah. Milk and sugar are for wimps." He wrapped his hands around the mug. "Well?"

After sitting, Amanda met his hostile gaze with her calm one. "I wanted to see how things are going for you. Are the guys treating you okay?"

He pushed his hat back on his head. "They're fine. Why do you care?"

"Because you're family."

"Yeah, right. That's why she banished me to the bunk house." He sipped the coffee. "I'd hate to see how she treats someone she doesn't like."

Amanda took a deep breath and released it slowly. "You haven't given Lex a chance to get to know you."

"It's her own damn fault. Every time I open my mouth, she cuts me off at the knees."

"Maybe it's not what you say, but how you say it. I know that sometimes things can be taken out of context and misunderstandings happen."

He got to his feet. "Look, lady. I know you think she walks on water, but the truth is, my *sister* is a stuck up, smart-ass, know-it-all. Every queer I've ever known is the same way."

"I think that's enough." Amanda stood also. "Your attitude is why Lex has trouble with you."

"I don't have an attitude, she does." He slammed the chair to the floor. "I don't need you telling me how great she is."

Amanda's heart pounded at his violent response. She moved to keep the table between them. "I think you should leave."

With his fists clutched at his sides, Cleve stalked her. "You're as high-handed as she is." He pushed her chair out of his way so that he was standing inches away. "You don't look like a dyke. Maybe you need a guy to show you what you're missing."

It was then Amanda could smell the alcohol on his breath. "You've been drinking."

"So what?" He pulled a flask from his hip pocket. "Want a nip?"

"I don't think so." Amanda backed up as he moved closer. Her progress was stopped when she butted up against the stove.

Cleve caught up with her and grabbed her shoulders. "Come on, babe. Loosen up."

"Hey, sweetheart. Lorrie wanted to see her Mada, so I thought we could—" Lex walked into the kitchen in time to see Cleve kiss Amanda roughly. "You sonofabitch!" She rushed over and spun him around. Pulling her fist back, Lex put everything she had into a solid left hook.

With a pained grunt, Cleve's body slammed into the counter. He spit blood onto the floor, lowered his head and rushed Lex. They fell into the table, flipping it over. "I've had about all I can stand of you, dyke bitch!" His flailing hands landed several good blows.

"Stop it," Amanda screamed. She pulled at Cleve ineffectually. When he stood and started kicking Lex, Amanda grabbed the nearest thing she could find and whacked him on the head. The coffee pot shattered, dropping him like a stone. Not caring about the damage she may have done to him, Amanda pulled Cleve's body off her lover's. "Lex, are you all right?" She dropped to her knees beside her.

Dazed, Lex rolled over onto her back. She open and closed her eyes several times, trying to clear her vision. Feeling something sticky, she wiped her face with one hand and was surprised to see blood. "Whoa."

"Oh, honey." Amanda helped her sit up. She kept her arm around Lex's shoulders for support. "Maybe I should call Charlie."

"No." Finally able to focus her eyes, Lex noticed the broken glass around them and the unconscious form nearby. "What happened?"

"I couldn't...he was..." Amanda waved one hand around. "I thought he was going to seriously hurt you." She brushed Lex's bloodied face with her fingertips. "Are you sure you don't want me to call Martha's house? Charlie could be here in a second."

Lex pinned Amanda's hand to her face. "I don't think so. But we should see if Cleve is okay."

"But he attacked you."

"I hit him first. Hell, he could probably sue us both. Go ahead and check him out."

"You were protecting me. There's no way that can be construed as anything but self-defense." Amanda got to her feet and knelt next to Cleve's prone body. She saw blood on the back of his head and shakily checked his neck for a pulse. "He's—"

Cleve groaned. He raised one hand to touch his head. "Fuck." With Amanda's help, he was able to stand. He glowered at her as he held his hand over the sluggishly bleeding injury. "What the hell did you hit me with?"

"The coffee pot." Lex gingerly stood and put her arm around her partner. "Serves you right."

They all turned when they heard the back door close.

"Lexie, I hate to bother you, but—" Martha stopped in the doorway and covered her mouth with her hand. The first thing she noticed was the upturned table and glass scattered all over the floor. Her eyesight moved from that to the three people in the kitchen. "What's going on?"

Lex accepted the hand towel that Amanda gave her and wiped at her face. "Only a little misunderstanding, nothing serious." Her words would have been more effective if she hadn't been bleeding from several places on her face.

"Good lord." Martha started toward them, but was pushed aside by Cleve as he wordlessly left the house. She ignored him and hurried over to check Lex's damaged features. "I swear, it's always something with you, isn't it?"

"He had it coming." Lex swatted away Martha's hands. "Stop that."

Martha took her by the arm and began to drag her from the room. "Let's go. The first aid kit is in the bathroom across the hall." She gestured to Amanda with her free hand. "Come on, honey. I want to take a look at your bloody knees. You two kids like to keep me on my toes, don't you?"

"We don't—" Lex tried to stop, but ended up allowing Martha to pull her along.

"Hush. At least I know where Lorrie gets it. She is always into something or another. I'm glad she wanted to stay with Charlie." Martha pushed Lex down to sit on the edge of the tub. "Now behave, or I'll have to get rough with you." She brought out a package of gauze pads and set to work.

Chapter
Twelve

"TRUST ME, BABE. He's going to love you." Hubert studied his reflection in the mirror as he adjusted his tie. Prison had actually been good for him. Once bloated from his over-consumption of alcohol, the time he spent locked away gave him a chance to dry out. With nothing better to do, Hubert spent a lot of his time exercising, which brought him down to what he referred to as his "fighting weight". He grinned rakishly at his image.

Janine looked around the tiny room with disdain. When her husband explained to her that he had a house in Somerville, she had no idea how small it would be. Her old apartment in Huntsville was larger and much nicer. She knew she would have her work cut out for her if she was to convince him to find something more suitable. She checked her perfectly painted fingernails. "If you say so." Personally, she wasn't so sure. He rarely spoke of his family and had even less to say about the people he knew in the town. "How long will this take?"

"Why? Do you have an important hair appointment?" He was getting tired of her whining. All she had done since they arrived was complain. The town was too small, the restaurants were too rustic, the people too nosey. She also admitted to him that she was more than a little frightened by his sister. Hubert wasn't about to tell his wife about his family dynamics, or the reason behind Lex's animosity. "Are you about ready to go?" He shrugged into his suit jacket, which was now too large for his frame. "Let's get this show on the road."

"I've been waiting on you, Hubie dear." Janine quickly checked her lipstick and followed her husband out of the room.

Once inside the car, she wrinkled her nose. They had returned their rental the day before, and Hubert found the used brown Corolla for a cheap price. He told her that in order to pay for his legal fees, he had been forced to sell his BMW convertible. "How long will we be forced to drive around in this old junker?"

"Like I told you before, as soon as I get my business going again, we'll get something more suitable. Have some patience."

Perturbed by his condescending tone, she crossed her arms over her chest. "So far, all I've heard are a lot of vague promises. What happened to the big plans you told me about?"

Stopping at a red light, Hubert turned to face his wife. "Believe me, babe. Once I get my old clients back, we'll be well on our way. I also plan on getting what's owed to me."

"And how do you plan to do that?"

"Trust me." He drove through the intersection, a grim look on his face.

CHARLIE NOTICED THE glum figure sitting alone on the bench near Lorrie's sandbox. Lex had her elbows propped on her knees and her chin rested on her open palms. He sat next to her. "You sure seem to be thinking hard."

She raised her head. "Nah." The small cuts on her face were healing, but the black eye she had received courtesy of her half-brother hadn't faded. Cleve had made himself scarce for two days after the incident in the kitchen. Martha had wanted Charlie to arrest the man, but Lex refused to press charges, preferring to handle the matter herself. "What brings you out here? I thought you and Martha were going out to dinner tonight."

"We are. But I saw you out here and wanted to see if you were okay."

Unable to meet his eyes, Lex suddenly found the sandbox fascinating. "Yeah."

She didn't know how to broach the subject that weighed heavily on her mind. The ranch was prosperous, her relationship with Amanda was more than she could have ever hoped for, and they now had a beautiful little girl. She should have been the happiest person in the world. But something deep inside was off-kilter and she didn't know how to fix it.

"If you want to talk about it, I'm here." Charlie's voice was low. He mimicked her posture, settling against the wooden slats.

She stretched her legs out and crossed them at the ankles. "Did you always want to be a lawman?"

The question caught him off guard, but he did his best to conceal his surprise. "No. It's something I had an aptitude for, I guess."

"What was your first choice?"

"Uh, well, when I was in high school, I was involved in all the usual sports. Baseball, track, basketball. But what I enjoyed was football. I got a scholarship, played on the varsity team all through college, and was all prepared to enter the professional draft."

Lex turned her head to look at him. "What happened?"

He pointed to his left leg. "Last game of the college season, I tore up my knee. Back then there wasn't much they could do. Sure, it was good enough to do everyday things, but my football-playing days were definitely behind me. My uncle was with the sheriff's

department at the time, and he talked me into taking the exam."
Charlie raised his hands out to his sides. "And here I am."

"Huh."

"Why the sudden interest?"

She fiddled with her watch. "Just wondering."

Charlie tapped Lex on the leg to get her undivided attention. "No,
I think it's more than that. You've been acting out of sorts for awhile.
What's going on with you?"

"I'm not sure." She got to her feet and put her hands in her front
pockets. "I feel, I don't know, restless or something." She began to
pace back and forth. "I don't know what's wrong with me. I'm bored
and I don't give a damn anymore."

"Have you talked to Amanda about this?"

She shook her head. "I can't. She's got so much going on right
now. The last thing she needs to hear is me whining about something
I'm not sure of. The custody issue for Lorrie shook her up. Add to that
her trying to get pregnant, and then that whole mess with the
escapees, she's had more than enough stress." Lex kicked at the dirt.
"I'll get over it."

"It sounds a bit more serious than that, kiddo." Charlie stood and
put his arm around her shoulders. "Don't let this thing fester inside
you. Let your family help." He led her toward the main house. "And
for God's sake, talk to Amanda. She's pretty darned sharp."

Lex leaned into him as they walked. "Yeah, I know. Makes me
wonder why she hooked up with me in the first place." She couldn't
help but laugh when he hip-checked her for that comment.

WHEN THEY PULLED up to the diner, Janine rolled her eyes and
sighed heavily. "Don't tell me we're eating at this dump."

Hubert ignored her comment and got out of the car. He walked
around to the passenger side and opened the door. He took a firm grip
on her arm and pulled her from the vehicle. "Let's go."

"Stop it, you're hurting me." Janine slapped his hand away. She
straightened her skirt and fussed with her hair. She was beginning to
think marrying him was a mistake. The man she was with now bore
little resemblance to the kind and soft-spoken inmate she thought she
fell in love with. It seemed the instant they arrived in his home town
Hubert had changed. And she wasn't happy with the result. "I'm not
some bubble-headed bimbo, Hubert. Don't treat me like one."

"Then quit whining. I'm getting tired of it." He opened the door
and waited for her to step through, before he followed.

Janine looked around as she moved into the diner. Half a dozen
worn out booths lined the wall on the right, while a long counter with
barstools stood on the opposite side. It was crowded, and the sound of
dishes clattering and the murmuring of voices made her ears ache. A

harried blonde waitress pushed by them without as much as a word, carrying a food-laden tray high over her head. "My god, I've moved to fucking Mayberry."

"Shut up." Hubert put his hand against her back and none too gently pushed Janine toward the rear of the room. "I think I see him in that last booth. Come on. I can't wait to see the look on his face."

The man he was so anxious to see was engrossed in the newspaper and never noticed the couple's approach. The sound of Hubert's hand slapping the table caused him to drop his paper and look up. "What the—" His jaw dropped in surprise. "Oh, my god. Hubert?"

"In the flesh." Without waiting for an invitation, Hubert guided his wife to sit in the opposite seat and slid in next to her. "Been a while."

"That's putting it mildly." The older man folded his paper. "How long have you been out?"

Hubert took the newspaper away from him and threw it on the floor. "Long enough. What's the matter, aren't you glad to see me?"

"Not particularly. Have you come back to cause trouble?" Once a poker buddy and Hubert's former lawyer, Kirk Trumbull now had no use for his ex-friend. He had almost been disbarred over Hubert's past antics and didn't want any part of his schemes.

"Depends on what you call trouble." Hubert held his hand up and snapped his fingers at the passing waitress. "Hey, babe. We need some coffee over here."

She stopped at the booth and glared at him. "Well, look what the cat dragged in. Hubert Walters. They let you out so soon?" She made no move to answer his demand.

"Francine. Nice to see you, too." He gestured to the woman sitting next to him. "This is my wife, Janine. Try to show a little respect."

"You, of all people, asking for respect. That's a laugh." Francine eyeballed the other woman. "My sympathies, hon." She touched a finger to her brow in a mock salute and went about her business.

Hubert considered throwing the salt shaker at her. "Stupid broad." He stood and turned to his wife. "Why don't you go wait in the car? I'll be out in a minute."

"Fine with me." Janine scooted out of the booth and walked out of the noisy restaurant. She was more than a little peeved at Hubert's demeanor and planned on taking him to task when he stepped outside. "We're going to have a nice long talk soon, my dear husband. I won't tolerate being treated like this."

Kirk waited until she left. "So, are you going to fill me in on why you're here?"

"Some things have come up, and I'm going to need your help." Hubert leaned across the table to keep from being overheard.

AMANDA WAS ON her knees, scrubbing at a dark stain on the kitchen wall. She heard the back door open and waited until she heard footsteps before getting to her feet. "Lex? Is that you?"

"Yep." Lex stopped inside the doorway. "What's that?"

"*Your* daughter decided it would be fun to finger paint on the walls with her chocolate pudding."

Lex struggled to keep from laughing. "Oh, so suddenly she's *my* daughter? Why is that?"

"Because," Amanda handed her the sponge, "no child of mine would be that, um, creative. I've been chasing after her all day and now it's your turn to clean up after her."

"Oh." Lex tossed the item into a nearby bucket. She put her hands on Amanda's hips and pulled her close. "That sounds fair." She kissed her on the lips for a long moment. "How about this – I'll finish up down here, while you go upstairs and soak in a hot bubble bath. Then, I'll come upstairs and give you a nice, long massage."

Amanda locked her hands behind her lover's neck and returned the kiss with one of her own. "You're my hero." She tucked her head beneath Lex's chin. "I don't know why I'm so exhausted today. I joined Lorrie for her afternoon nap, so I shouldn't be dragging like this."

"Sweetheart, taking care of Lorrie is a full time job and then some." Lex squeezed Amanda to her. "Go on, I'll be up in a minute." She nuzzled the top of Amanda's head before releasing her. Watching the tired woman trudge from the room, Lex waited until she was completely gone before turning her attention to the messy wall.

It took longer than she thought it would. Lex finally gave up and decided that the kitchen would need a new coat of paint. After putting the cleaning supplies away, she made her way upstairs. A quick peek into Lorrie's room assured Lex that the child was down for the night. She did her usual job of tucking the little girl in before placing a kiss on the tiny dark head and leaving the room.

The sight that greeted her as she walked into the master bedroom caused Lex to stop dead in her tracks. Amanda was on her stomach, stretched out across the bed. Completely nude. And sound asleep. Lex paused to enjoy the view, before shaking her head, closing the door and going into the bathroom to clean up.

After her shower, Lex returned with a bottle of baby oil. She got up on the bed next to her slumbering partner and poured a small amount of the oil into her hand. She waited until her body heat warmed the oil before rubbing it across Amanda's back.

"Oh, God, that feels so good." Amanda's eyes opened slightly. "Marry me."

Lex chuckled. "I think I already did that. Do you want to go through it again?"

Amanda moaned as Lex found a sore spot. "As much as I enjoyed it, I'd have to say no. My grandmother nearly drove me nuts."

"Martha, too." Lex straddled Amanda's hips and used her thumbs to work along her spine. "Next time, we elope."

"Works for me. Oh, yeah, right there." Amanda winced. "Ungh."

"Too hard?"

"Never." Amanda quieted as the massage continued. Before long, she was out again.

Lex heard the soft snores and finished up. She returned to the bathroom to put away the oil and wash her hands. That completed, she moved Amanda under the covers. "Sleep well, love." It wasn't long before she joined her in sleep.

Chapter
Thirteen

"BUT HOW LONG will you be gone?" Lex stood in the kitchen, her back against the counter and her arms crossed over her chest. "Are you sure you don't want me to go with you?"

Martha put the last pot away in the cabinet. The question was one of many that she had fielded from Lex. "No, honey. You've got too much going on here. But I do appreciate the thought." Earlier that day, Martha received a phone call from her uncle in Raleigh, North Carolina. Her Aunt Nattie, who was in her late eighties, had fallen and broken her hip. While she was in the hospital, she had a severe heart attack and wasn't expected to live much longer. "Uncle Ronald thinks it will be soon. I need to be there for him."

"Of course you do. I only wish you'd let us be there for you. This damn ranch isn't as important as you are."

"There are too many folks that depend on you. You can't go running off and babysitting me. I'll be fine." Martha took off her apron and loosely folded it. She headed for the laundry room with Lex right in behind her.

"Roy can handle it."

Martha tossed the apron into the empty clothes hamper. "Yes, I know he can." She left the wash room and started for the back door. "But that's not the point. Now let's not have any more of that kind of talk. I need to go pack. Why don't you keep me company and then I'll give you the chocolate cake I finished up this morning."

Lex followed her like a dutiful puppy, wanting to spend as much time as possible with Martha before she left. They walked along the path between the two houses until they got to Martha's. "You don't have to bribe me with cake, you know. I enjoy getting to visit with you." Lex waited until Martha entered, then closed the door behind them.

The living area was uncluttered and tidy, and the bedroom was the same. "Grab my bag from the closet, will you?" Martha began to take clothing items from the dresser.

Lex took an empty suitcase from the back of the closet and placed it on the bed. "Would you like for me to drive you to the airport?" Not knowing what else to do, she stood next to the dresser and watched.

"No, but I wouldn't mind a ride into town. Charlie is going to quit work early this afternoon and take me." Martha added a few more items to the case before going into the bathroom to gather her toiletries. She came out and noticed the glum look on Lex's face. "What?"

"I hate the thought of you going alone." Lex pushed off from the dresser and moved to stand next to Martha. "Promise me you'll call if you need anything? I can be there in no time at all."

Martha patted Lex's side. "I promise. And I want you to promise *me* that you'll stay out of trouble while I'm gone."

"You have nothing to worry about. I'll be good."

"That's what I'm afraid of." Martha kissed Lex on the cheek and returned to her packing.

MARTHA HAD BEEN gone two days when Amanda decided to take Lorrie into town to spend part of the day at Mother's Day Out, where Lorrie could interact with other children her age. She'd then head to the office, and afterwards they would visit her grandparents. The morning started out with a heavy thunderstorm, which hadn't let up. She was gathering up Lorrie's things when Lex came upstairs. Rain dripped from her clothes and Amanda thought she looked like a drowned rat. "Don't you have a raincoat?"

"Yeah, but I forgot it." Lex moved through Lorrie's room and into her bathroom, where she took a towel from the cabinet. She came out, attempting to dry her hair. "It's nasty out there. Are you sure you want to drive in?"

"Momma!" Lorrie heard Lex's voice and raced across the room. She attached herself to one leg. Feeling the clammy wet jeans, she slapped the material. "Uck! Momma, you wet."

"That's what happens when you play in the rain," Amanda scolded. "You need to go change."

Lex picked the little girl up, careful to not hold her against her wet clothes. "In a minute. How are you doing, lil' bit?"

"Pway ussl?"

"What?" Lex looked over to Amanda.

"She's got a new wooden puzzle. Charlie brought it this morning." Amanda finished packing and placed the small backpack near the door. She waited until Lex put Lorrie down before using the towel around Lex's neck to wipe her lover's face. "We'll be back this evening. Go change and you can come out to play."

"Yes, mommy." Lex stole a quick kiss before leaving the room.

Amanda dropped her gaze to Lorrie. "Your momma's a brat."

"Yep." Lorrie raced to where her toys were kept and sat at the tiny table. She took the pieces from the wooden puzzle block and placed them on the table surface. The puzzle consisted of a flat, rectangular piece of wood, with six separate cutouts, shaped and colored like farm pieces. Each individual piece had a tiny raised knob, to make it easier to grasp. One at a time, Lorrie took the pieces and placed them where they belonged. When she finished, she clapped her hands. "Done!"

"Wonderful, Lorrie." Amanda squatted next to the table. She took the pieces out again and mixed them up on the table. "Now try."

Lorrie clapped again. "Yay!" She picked up a piece, studied it and put it in its proper place. "Good?"

Amanda nodded. "Very good." She felt, rather than saw, Lex come into the room. Turning her head, she was relieved to see her changed, right down to her dry boots. "You're a good girl, too."

"Gee, thanks." Lex took a position on the other side of the table. She sat cross-legged on the floor and picked up a puzzle piece. "I swear, Charlie's going to spoil this kid."

"That's what I said. He told me that she was his first grandchild and it was his job to spoil her." Amanda handed Lorrie another piece. "Where does this one go?"

The little girl slapped the part in place. "Dere."

They sat quietly for a few minutes and watched Lorrie play. She never seemed to tire of the puzzle and continually put the parts in and took them out. Sometimes she would hand Lex or Amanda a piece and expect them to place it correctly. The sound of the heavy rain hitting the roof finally abated and Amanda stood to look out the window. "The rain's finally stopped. Guess we'd better get going, while we can."

"Yeah." Lex got to her feet. "I'll walk you down." She grabbed Lorrie's bag.

Once they were all downstairs, Lex helped Lorrie with her coat. The child squirmed and it took several minutes to get it put on and zipped. "Kiddo, I swear you're part worm." She finished and helped Amanda with her coat as well. "Enjoy lunch with your grandparents, sweetheart. Give them my best."

"We will." Amanda led the way to her "mom mobile", as Lex called it. The silver Xterra was her concession to a safer ride and it easily handled all the rough roads between the house and the highway. Her Mustang sat in the garage Lex had built for it and now was only driven during the comfortable spring months. She waited patiently while Lex buckled Lorrie into her car seat behind the passenger seat. "All done?"

Lex kissed Lorrie before closing the door. "Safe and secure." She moved around to the driver's side and wrapped her arms around Amanda. "Be careful."

"You know it." Giving her partner a kiss, Amanda climbed behind the wheel. "Try to stay dry, if you can. I don't want to have to tell

Martha you caught cold."

"Yes, ma'am." Lex patted the side of the vehicle and watched it until the tail lights faded from view.

THE FALLING RAIN matched Lex's mood. It had been hard not to join Amanda and Lorrie on their trip. Her mature side understood that if she had gone, Lorrie would have spent more time playing with her and not Amanda's family. Still, staying behind alone hurt. She stood at the corral near the house, ignoring the light rain that soaked into her clothes. So engrossed in her thoughts, she never heard anyone come up behind her until a hand touched her arm. Startled, Lex spun around.

Charlie's frowning visage greeted her. "Martha will throw a fit if you get sick from being out here without a coat."

"What she doesn't know won't hurt me." She checked her watch. "It's only nine. What are you doing home?"

"To tell you the truth, I didn't feel like being there. I'll go in after lunch." Charlie took off his hat and shook the excess water from it. "Come on to the house and keep me company. Martha left a pie or two and I don't want her to return home and find any leftovers."

Lex sighed. "Might as well. I can't get much done until the damned rain lets up." She followed him over to the cottage he shared with Martha. He hung his coat on one of the hooks by the door and they both placed their damp hats next to it.

While Charlie made the coffee, Lex took out plates, removed the apple pie from the refrigerator, dished up two slices and placed them in the microwave to heat. "How hot do you want yours?"

"Warm enough to eat, but not so much that I have to wait for it to cool." He brought two steaming mugs to the table and sat as Lex put the plates down. They each took a couple of bites before speaking. "Why don't you tell me what you were doing out in the rain?"

"Thinking, mostly."

"About what?"

She took a sip of coffee. "Different things. Hey, what all is involved in joining the department?"

"Department?"

"Yeah. You know, where you go to work everyday?"

His attention was quickly buried in his cup. "Well, the usual. Background check, medical assessment, written and physical tests. If those all are passed, then a sixteen week course at the academy. Why?"

Unable to look into Charlie's eyes, Lex used her fork and scooted what was left of her pie around the plate. "It's something I've been thinking about."

"For how long?"

"About a year or so, I guess."

Charlie leaned back in his chair. "I know it's not something that happens around here a lot, but I got the impression you weren't comfortable when we went out after those guys."

She raised her head. "It wasn't so much that, as I was afraid of doing something wrong. Maybe with the right training, I would feel more comfortable with it."

"You could be right. Hell, Lex. I've always said you'd be better at the job than a lot of the men we already have. But it should be something you're sure of." He moved forward and placed his elbows on the table. "Have you talked to Amanda about this?"

"No, not yet. I wanted to see what you thought, first. No sense in getting into it with her, until I got your opinion." Lex ran her hand through her hair. "I'm tired of working this ranch. There's no challenge in it anymore and it practically runs itself. Do you think I'm out of my mind?"

He placed his hand on her forearm. "No, I don't. We all need to do what's best for ourselves. But we also have to take into account the people around us. That's one of the reasons I've been thinking about retiring."

"What?"

"I'm not getting any younger and I've finally got the life and family I've always wanted." He stood and cleared the dishes from the table. "I'd like to spend some quality time with Martha before we're too old to enjoy it."

Lex helped Charlie clean the kitchen. "Seems like we both have some serious thinking to do. I'd sure like to know what Amanda and Martha think about it, though."

"The only way we're going to find out is to talk to them." He took his coffee cup and went into the living room, knowing that Lex would follow. "Although I'm betting that Martha will accept my retiring a whole lot better than Amanda will take your thoughts about a career change."

"That's the part that worries me."

"MOMMY!"

Amanda peeked in the rearview mirror. Lorrie was in her car seat and her hand was crammed in the small snack bag on her lap. "What is it?"

"Pway?" Lorrie took several Cheerios out of the bag and shoved them into her mouth. "Mrumph."

"Yes, honey. You're going to go play with your friends at school." Amanda returned to watching the road. A couple of months ago, her grandmother had suggested they enroll Lorrie in the "Mother's Day Out" program at her church. It was only one day for a few hours a week and the little girl thrived on the social interaction with others her age. Amanda jumped slightly when a piece of Lorrie's snack hit her in the head. "Lorrie, behave." Another bit went flying over the seat. "Lorrie."

"Pway!"

Amanda brushed one hand through her hair, dislodging several more pieces. "Do you want to go home?"

"No."

"Then stop throwing your snack."

Nonplussed, Lorrie grabbed another handful and sprinkled them in the floorboard beneath her. She looked up at Amanda with an innocent grin.

"Well, you didn't throw them." Amanda turned off the highway and onto a sedate city street. Softly so Lorrie wouldn't hear her, she murmured, "You look like Lex when you smile like that."

When she noticed where they were, Lorrie began to brush the tidbits of food from her lap. "Yay! Me pway now."

Amanda parked the vehicle and walked around to get the excited child from her seat. "You have to promise to be a good girl. Mommy's going to do some shopping, then we'll go see Gramma and Grandpa Jake."

"Otay." Lorrie put her arms around Amanda's neck and gave her a sloppy kiss on the cheek. "Me good." She started trying to hop while in her mommy's arms. "Pway."

"Yes, honey." Amanda took her into the building, cringing when she heard the laughter and screaming of a roomful of toddlers. "You couldn't pay me enough to do that."

AT CHARLIE'S URGING, Lex returned to the ranch house instead of going out to the barn to mess with the horses. She wandered around downstairs for a while before finally settling in her office. The paperwork for the ranch was almost a week behind, so she decided to take the quiet time and get caught up. Lex had only been at it for an hour when she heard a vehicle pull into the driveway. She was on her way to see who it was when there was a knock on the front door. Opening it, she was surprised to see Cleve again so soon. "What do you want?"

"Roy sent me." He stayed about five feet away. "The rain knocked out the phone at the bunkhouse and he wanted you to know that several of the horses from the east pasture are missing."

"Damn. Guess I'll be playing in the rain too, then. Anyone checking the north range? They could have headed there." Lex held the door open further. "Do you want to come in?" She didn't want him inside the house, but she felt she should at least make the offer.

Cleve took another step back. "No. I said what I came to say. Roy and a few of the guys are going to check the fences on the east side, not the north. He wanted you to know."

"Fine. I'll do it myself."

He shrugged. "Whatever." With once last glance, Cleve turned and left the porch as quickly as he came. The old work truck roared to life and skidded out of sight.

"Asshole." Lex slammed the door. "Might as well get a move on." She checked her watch. "Amanda will be picking Lorrie up from her play date about now. Since they were going to have lunch with her folks, they won't be home for hours." She hurried down the hall and took her hat and coat from the hooks by the back door. "I should easily beat them back to the house."

"GRAMMA!" LORRIE RAN through the front door of the Cauble's house and tangled her hands into one leg of Anna Leigh's slacks.

Bending to scoop the happy tot into her arms, Anna Leigh hugged her close. "Hello, my darling. Have you been a good girl?"

"Yep."

"Not." Amanda followed, with Lorrie's bag over her shoulder. "She got put in time-out at school for playing tug-of-war with another girl's doll. Not to mention the inside of my car looks like a cereal box threw up."

Jacob relieved her of the backpack and put his free arm around Amanda's waist. "It sounds less messy than when you were her age and decided ketchup made a nice shampoo."

Groaning, Amanda allowed herself to be led into the living room. "I can't believe you still hold that one against me."

"You'll have to admit, you were quite a frightful sight, dear. I hope you get to enjoy this little one's early years as much as we did yours." Anna Leigh patted Lorrie's bottom. "Although I don't see how this beautiful girl could be anything but angelic."

"Dad has already cursed me with the old, 'I hope you have kids like yourself,' speech. Believe me, after the 'angel' you're holding got through finger painting the kitchen with chocolate pudding, nothing will surprise me." Amanda stopped and shook her head. "She's growing so fast. While she played with her friends, I picked up a few new outfits for her." She flopped tiredly onto the sofa. "I can't believe I'm so tired."

Jacob sat next to her as his wife took Lorrie to the corner of the room where they kept her toys. "Are you not getting enough rest? I know taking care of Lorrie can wear a person down."

"Actually, I've been getting more than my share. We've been taking naps together. I think she sleeps better if I'm with her." Amanda laughed as she saw her grandmother sit in the floor with the toddler and pull out the wooden building blocks. "Watch out, she likes to stack them high and then swat them across the room."

Anna Leigh turned to Amanda. "You used to do the same thing. Oh, by the way Mandy, your father called earlier. He's bringing Lois over for lunch."

"That's great. I was hoping to get a chance to see them while we were in town today." Amanda stretched her legs out in front of her. "I feel like I could take a nap right here."

Her grandfather patted her on the leg. "You could always go up and take a quick nap. I'll come up and get you when they arrive."

Yawning, Amanda shook her head. "No. I'll be fine. I guess it's the weather." She rested her head against the pillows. "Or maybe some sort of bug. I've been a little queasy lately."

"Then you definitely should go lie down." Jacob stood and pulled her up with one hand. "Come on. I'll get you some tea."

"Okay, you win." Amanda looked at her grandmother, who waved then continued to play with Lorrie.

Chapter
Fourteen

HUBERT STOOD AT the door, hesitant in knocking. It had taken him some covert research to find the address. He didn't want to look bad in front of Janine by admitting he didn't know where he was going. Taking a deep breath, he rapped his knuckles on the wooden door.

A woman, close to his own age, answered the door and peered at him. Her light brown eyes held a question, but no concern. "Is there something I can do for you?"

"Yeah." Hubert straightened his tie. "I'm here to see Travis Edwards. Is this the right house?"

She cocked her head. He looked vaguely familiar, although she had never seen him before. "What's this in reference to?" Before she could question him any more, a tall, elderly gentleman came up behind her.

"Who is it, Ellie?" Travis looked around her and recognized the man she had been speaking to. "Hubert?"

Hubert plastered what he thought was a sincere smile on his face. "Hello, grandfather. It's been awhile."

"Yes, it has." Travis almost didn't recognize his grandson. The man standing before him was thinner and looked much healthier than he remembered. It was then he noticed the woman beside Hubert. He was curious as to the reason for the visit. "Come in out of the rain and I'll make a fresh pot of coffee."

Ellie stood to the side as the couple moved into the house. "I'll take care of the coffee, grandpa. Why don't you go get comfortable?"

"Thank you, dear." Travis gave her shoulder a friendly squeeze before leading his unexpected guests to the living room. He waited until they were seated and Ellie was out of earshot. "I had no idea you had been released from prison. What brings you to see me?"

"I wanted to touch base with my family again. No harm in that, is there?"

Travis fought to keep the surprise from his face. "No, I suppose not." He turned his attention to the woman sitting next to his wayward grandson. "I'm sorry, I don't believe we've met."

"This is my wife, Janine." Hubert put his arm possessively around her waist. "Babe, this is my grandfather, Travis Edwards."

Janine was charmed as Travis stood and shook her hand. "It's a pleasure to meet you, Mr. Edwards. Hubert has spoken highly of you." He actually hadn't spoke more than a couple of sentences about any of his family, but Janine didn't want to hurt the older man's feelings.

"Um, thank you." Travis returned to his chair. He wasn't sure what Hubert was up to, but he certainly wasn't going to turn his back on him. He was saved from making a comment when Ellie returned to the room, carrying a tray with four cups of coffee.

She held the tray out in front of each person until there was only her own mug left. "Would anyone like cream or sugar?" At everyone's negative response, she put the tray on a side table and took a chair near Travis.

"Who are you?" Hubert had never been known for his ability to lead a polite conversation. "Did I hear you call him grandpa?"

Travis cut in. "That's right. Ellie is your Uncle William's daughter. She's staying here with me."

"I didn't know there even was an Uncle William. Who the hell is he? Oof." Hubert jerked as Janine elbowed him in the ribs. "What?"

Janine gave Ellie a friendly look. "You'll have to forgive my husband. He's been under a lot of pressure since we got here." She was beginning to see Hubert for what he truly was. So far, everyone they had come in contact with didn't want anything to do with him. His stories of a close-knit family and good friends were starting to look more like fairy tales.

"Don't worry. I'm very well aware of how Hubert is." Travis placed his coffee cup on the table in front of him. "So tell us, son. What is your real reason for coming here?"

The tone in his grandfather's voice set Hubert off. He leaned forward and glared at him. "I've told you before, old man, I'm not your son." To cover his outburst, he cleared his throat. "I mean, can't a guy want to see his own grandfather? Neither one of us is getting any younger, and I—"

"You wanted to see what you could get from me." Travis stood. "I think you should leave."

Getting to his feet, Hubert pointed at Travis. "You've never liked me, you old coot. It's always been my damned sister."

Janine took her husband's arm in a firm grip. "I think you've said enough, Hubert. Let's leave these nice people alone." She forcefully pulled him toward the door. "I'm sorry we disturbed you, Mr. Edwards."

"You're more than welcome anytime, Janine." Travis wasn't surprised when Ellie stood between him and her cousin. He put his hands on her shoulders as the other two left.

"That was different." Ellie closed and locked the door. She turned and rested one arm around Travis' hips. "Are you all right?"

He nodded. "But I won't be unhappy if I never see that boy again. I'd bet everything I have that he's up to no good."

A LIGHT TOUCH on her forehead woke Amanda from a deep sleep. She slowly opened her eyes. "Dad?"

"Hello, sweetheart." Michael Cauble sat on the bed next to her. "Are you feeling okay?"

She pushed herself up into a sitting position. "I don't know. I think I may have a touch of the flu. I haven't been quite myself for the last week or so."

"I'm sorry to hear that. Lois and I brought Chinese. Will you be able to eat it?" He stood so she could swing her legs from the bed. "Or would you rather stay up here and get some more rest?"

Amanda ran her fingers through her hair to give it some semblance of order. "No, I'll be okay." She got to her feet and embraced him. "It's good to see you."

"Same here, kiddo." He stepped away and studied her for a moment. "Maybe you should go see a doctor, if you've been feeling bad for that long."

"I think you're right." She followed him down the stairs. "I'll call next week."

They were met in the kitchen by the rest of the family. Lois sat at the table holding Lorrie, who squirmed away from her when Amanda came into the room.

"Mommy, I do good." Lorrie proceeded to climb Amanda as if she were a jungle gym.

Amanda hefted her up and settled Lorrie onto her hip. "What did you do, sweetie?"

Lorrie pointed to the counter, where there were cookies cooling on a rack. "I cookded."

"You did? That's wonderful." Amanda looked at Jacob. "I'm assuming you assisted her in this culinary surprise?"

"A little," he admitted. "But she sprinkled the chocolate chips in the batter all by herself."

Amanda then noticed a smudge of chocolate behind her daughter's ear. "I can see that." She sat next to Lois and took a paper napkin from the holder on the table. She tried to clean the mess from Lorrie's head, but seemed to be fighting a losing battle. The little girl kept moving from side to side, trying to pull the napkin from her hand.

"No." Lorrie stretched toward Lois. "Help!"

Laughing, Lois took the child into her arms, which allowed Amanda the opportunity to get her clean. "You're a handful."

"She certainly is." Michael sat next to his wife. They had been married almost two years and he couldn't remember ever being happier. "She reminds me of Mandy at that age."

"Gampi?" Lorrie reached out for Michael. No one knew where she came up with the names she used, but they good-naturedly took them in stride.

He chuckled and lifted the little girl over Lois' head. "Come here."

While everyone else took turns entertaining Lorrie, Jacob and Anna Leigh put the containers of Chinese food and plates on the table. Michael placed Lorrie in her high chair, while his mother dished up some rice and vegetables on a small plate for her.

After they filled their plates, Amanda took a few bites of her food. Frowning, she got up and opened the refrigerator. She took a jar from one of the shelves, closed the door and went to her seat. She fished several green olives from the container and began to munch on them happily. The silence in the room caught her attention. "What?"

Jacob watched as more of the olives disappeared from her plate. "It's nothing, Mandy. But when did you develop a fondness for those?"

She chewed hastily and swallowed. "I don't know. It seemed like something that would taste good." Amanda checked the jar, which was now over half empty. "Weird, huh?"

"Not necessarily." Anna Leigh exchanged knowing looks with Lois. They had been talking of this very subject while Amanda napped. To her, all the signs were there. She was curious to see if her granddaughter had any inkling of what could be causing her "symptoms". She pushed her plate away and stood. "Dearest, could I see you for a moment in the living room?" The last thing she wanted to do was to embarrass Amanda, or say something in front of everyone, without cause.

"Uh, sure." Amanda speared another couple of olives and popped them in her mouth. She got up and followed her grandmother into the other room. "Is everything okay?"

Anna Leigh studied her closely. Yes, she did appear tired, but there was something else about Amanda that made her certain of her thoughts. She took Amanda's hand and led her to the sofa. "Let's sit for a moment. I have a few questions for you and I didn't want to get into them in the kitchen."

"Okay." Amanda appeared confused, but did as her grandmother asked. "Go ahead."

"How long have you been feeling under the weather?"

Amanda shrugged. "I don't know. A week or two, I guess."

"You've been tired? Moody? Feeling nauseous?" Anna Leigh gently questioned her. "And, I hate to ask a delicate question, but have you been running to the bathroom more than usual?"

"Yes. That's why I think it's the flu or at least a bladder infection.

But I haven't been running any fever. Do you think I should go to the doctor? I'd hate for Lex or Lorrie to catch whatever this is."

Anna Leigh couldn't keep a gentle smile from appearing. "If I'm right, I don't think you're contagious."

"But what—" Amanda's eyes widened. "But—" A slow smile began to stretch across her face. "Oh, my God. Do you think it's possible?"

"I think it's more than possible. You two have been trying for so long. Why haven't you tested before now?"

Amanda raised a shaky hand to her mouth. "There's been so much going on lately, it had completely slipped my mind. I've been so tired and Lorrie's been more rambunctious than usual. The days have blurred together." She jumped to her feet. "I've got to call Lex."

"Hold on." Anna Leigh hung on to her hand. "Let's run to the drugstore and pick up a test kit first. There's no sense in getting Lexington all excited until we know something for certain."

Bouncing in place, Amanda swung their hands. "Let's hurry. I can't wait."

Chapter
Fifteen

THE RAIN HAD let up and Lex used the opportunity to saddle up the new filly and take her out. She rode across the northern part of her property, following the fence line to make sure no trees had fallen and taken it down. She hadn't come across any tracks that would indicate the direction the missing horses took, but Lex knew that it would only take a small break in the fence to give them an escape route.

A loud rumble of thunder caused the young horse to prance sideways. Lex tightened her grip on the reins and used her knees to bring the animal under control. Once they were headed in the right direction again, she checked her watch. "Damn. It's almost three o'clock. I can't believe I've been out here that long." She grimaced when a few drops of water hit her cheek. "Great. It would start to rain while we're at the back end of the place. Maybe it won't get too heavy." As the words left her mouth, the sky opened up and Lex found herself caught in a deluge. The horse reared, and it took all of Lex's considerable talents and strength to keep from falling to the ground. "Whoa!"

A crack of lightning caused the filly to scream and race off through the wooded area. Lex hung on as the rain stung against her face. She pulled hard against the reins, to no avail. The terrified horse slipped through the mud and leaves with no apparent concern for its own safety. "Dammit, horse. I said whoa!" Lex stretched in the saddle and used the strength in her arms and shoulders to finally bring the animal under control. They stopped under a canopy of leaves as the rain fell around them.

Lex used one gloved hand to rub the heaving filly's neck in an attempt to calm her. She thought about dismounting but was afraid it would be harder to control the horse from the ground. Her own heart was pounding from the frenetic race through the trees. "That was more excitement than I cared to have today, girl." Lex continued to speak to the creature in a soothing voice. "I think we're going to have to come up with a better name for you than 'horse' or 'girl'. Got any preferences?" When no answer was forthcoming, Lex laughed and patted the animal's neck. An evil thought crossed her mind. "Since you've got enough sense not to want my jackass half-brother near you, I think I'll call you Mine. That'll piss him off."

Once the newly named Mine had calmed somewhat, Lex guided her through the trees. Since they were both already drenched, she didn't see any reason why they shouldn't finish checking the fence line. It wouldn't be long before they would be heading down the opposite fence on the way to the stables and Lex didn't feel like sitting alone in the house until Amanda and Lorrie returned from town.

They had traveled quietly for over half an hour when the thunderstorm worsened. Thunder rumbled ominously while lightning raced through the dark clouds. The rain continued to fall heavily and it was getting harder for Lex to see very far ahead. When a large, obviously dead tree shuddered and fell beside them, Mine took off, causing the reins to slip through Lex's rain slicked gloves. Lex's curses were swallowed up by the storm as she ducked forward and pawed frantically at the wildly whipping leather strips. Her left boot slid from the stirrup and she struggled to stay on the horse.

She had gotten her hands on one of the reins when the ground fell out from underneath them. The horse pitched over to the right and fell hard into the churned mud. Lex was tossed with her as they dropped into a newly formed sinkhole.

AMANDA AND HER grandmother returned from the drug store before anyone knew they were gone. The co-conspirators tiptoed up the stairs and were neatly hidden away in the guest room while those downstairs were none the wiser. Amanda took the home pregnancy test from the plastic bag and stared at the bathroom door. "I guess now's as good a time as any, huh?"

"It's going to be fine, dearest." Anna Leigh opened the door for her.

"Thanks." After she closed the door behind herself, Amanda struggled to tear the outer wrapping from the box. She didn't know why she was so nervous. She had been through the routine before and was now an expert at reading the small indicators. Her hands shook as the plastic finally came free and she was able to take the test stick out.

For her part, Anna Leigh sat on the edge of the bed with her hands folded neatly in her lap. Her outside demeanor appeared calm, but inside she was as anxious as when she had waited to find out she was pregnant with her son, Michael. She knew of Amanda's previously failed attempts and hoped more than anything that this time would be lucky for her. Bits of her granddaughter's childhood played through her head. Anna Leigh remembered how excited they were when Amanda came to stay with them during the summer months. Having been confined to a playroom when at her own home, the little girl was quite boisterous when she was allowed to run freely.

Climbing trees, walking across the top of the picket fence and swinging from anything she could reach brought Amanda to the emergency room more than once every year. Her penchant for finding trouble followed her into adulthood, Anna Leigh realized fondly, as she thought about how Lex came into their lives. She was nudged from her reminiscing by the opening of the bathroom door.

Tears streaked down Amanda's face as she stepped into the room. Her lower lip quivered when her eyes met Anna Leigh's.

"Oh, baby." Anna Leigh held out her arms. "It's going to be okay." She rubbed her granddaughter's back and rocked her gently. "Don't worry, dearest. You can try again."

Amanda pulled away until she was able to see her grandmother's face. "It's positive," she choked out. "I'm going to have a baby." Her tears continued to flow as her face creased into a smile. "Lex is going to go nuts."

Kissing her on the head, Anna Leigh chuckled. "Of that, I have no doubt. Your father will be ecstatic."

"I know." Amanda shook her head. "No, wait. Can we keep this between the two of us, for now? I want to tell Lex before anyone else knows."

"Of course. That's how it should be." They both stood and embraced again. "I would love to be a fly on the wall when you tell her, though." Anna Leigh kept her arm around Amanda's waist. "Now, the fun part will be trying to keep this a secret. Your joy is written all over your face."

"I feel incredible. I want to dance around the room and yell." A loud clap of thunder caused them both to jump. "Thank goodness we got home from the store when we did. I'd hate to be out in that mess."

Anna Leigh released her and walked over to peer out the window. "It appears you may be stranded here for a while. I can't even see the cars through all the rain."

Joining her at the window, Amanda looked outside as well. "I hope Lex has the sense to stay inside." She closed the curtains and went to the bed and sat. "I think I'll call her and let her know we'll be here until the weather clears."

"Good idea." Anna Leigh looked at her watch. "It's getting late. I know you want to run home and tell her your good news, but maybe it would be wise to stay the night and get a fresh start in the morning."

Nodding, Amanda dialed the phone. She returned her grandmother's wave as Anna Leigh left the room. While she patiently waited for Lex to answer the phone, Amanda rubbed her stomach. She couldn't believe that a tiny life had begun. It was almost overwhelming. When the answering machine at the ranch picked up, she sighed. "Lex, it's me." She bit her lip to keep from blurting out her news. "Um, since it's raining so hard, Gramma asked me to spend the night. So Lorrie and I will be home in the morning, okay? I love you."

She hung up the phone. "I hope you're not out playing in the rain, again." She looked down at her belly. "Your momma is determined to make me old and gray before my time, little one."

THE POUNDING OF the rainwater and the thrashing of the horse shook Lex awake. She didn't know how long she had been out, since the heavy clouds effectively covered the sky and made telling time impossible. She blinked several times and took stock of her situation. Both she and the horse were covered with mud and they were a good six feet from the top of the ground. She had ended up wedged against the wall of the hole, while Mine's hooves sunk into the quagmire on the bottom.

The sinkhole had sucked them down without warning and didn't appear to be releasing them any time soon. Mine was on her side, trapping both of Lex's legs beneath her. Lex's right shoulder was stuck deep into the thick mass of sodden earth. The more the frightened horse struggled, the deeper Lex was buried. "Easy, girl." Lex tried to pull herself free, but a sharp pain from the right side of her body caused her to stop. With her free hand, she rubbed Mine's flank. "It's going to be okay. Ssssh."

Tiring, the horse settled and dropped her head. Ever so often she would attempt to get some traction with her feet, which only trapped her further. Eventually, the soothing voice finally calmed her and her breathing settled.

Lex closed her eyes when the horse stilled. She continued to stroke the creature's side; whether for its benefit or her own, she wasn't sure. The rain tapered off and gave way to the coolness of the evening.

Some time later, Lex opened her eyes again. The night breeze chilled her bare face, but she was thankful that Mine's body heat protected her from the worst of it. Somewhat more alert, Lex tried to figure out how she fared, physically. The pounding headache reminded her that she had hit her head as she fell. She was buried in the mud, and the pain from the right side of her body was excruciating. Whether from the weight of the horse or from injury, she was numb from her hips to her feet. That part worried her more than anything. She wanted to call for help, but her cell phone was attached to her belt, above her right hip which was crammed deeply in the mud. Lex didn't even know if it was still working. "Well, Mine," she rasped, "we're screwed."

ANOTHER SUITCASE HIT the bed. Janine took a handful of clothes and stuffed them inside, not worrying about wrinkling them. She had heard enough excuses from her husband and was more determined than ever to end things with him.

Hubert stood nearby. He hadn't stopped whining since they arrived home and she delivered her ultimatum. "Come on, Janine. This was all a big misunderstanding. There's no reason to act like this." He ducked as his alarm clock sailed through the air, barely missing his head. "Dammit, woman. Stop this bullshit right now."

"Excuse me?" She paused in her frenetic packing and placed her hands on her hips. "Did you yell at me?"

He stomped over to where she stood and grabbed her arm. "You're fucking right, I did. You're my damned wife. Now act like it."

Janine's face reddened and her voice dropped. "Let go of me."

"Not until you come to your senses." He shook her arm for good measure. "You need to learn who the boss is around here."

Without warning, Janine slammed her free hand into his nose. It caused an audible crack and blood began to pour from Hubert's face. "I believe I settled that."

Hubert released her and screamed. "You broke my fucking nose!" He quickly brought both hands to his face.

"That's not all I'll do to you if you ever grab me again." Janine turned and resumed her packing. She was hard-pressed not to laugh at the way her husband was dancing around the room, cursing.

"I'll kick your ass, bitch." He blindly reached for her, but howled again as the heel of Janine's foot met his shin. "Dammit!"

She looked around the room to see if she had missed anything. "If this wasn't such a dump, you'd be the one leaving. But I think you deserve to stay in this rat hole." Gathering up the two suitcases, Janine carried them to the door. "You'll be hearing from my lawyer, Hubert. Be prepared to pay," she paused and grinned at his bloody countenance, "through the nose." With a final flip of her hair, she left the room.

He limped to the front door and watched as she drove off. "Hey, wait. That's my damned car!" Wiping his bloody hands on the front of his shirt, Hubert turned and went into his house, grumbling under his breath. "She fucking took my car. That bitch is going to be sorry she ever met me."

JACOB CARRIED LORRIE upstairs. She had fallen asleep in the middle of the living room floor with plastic animals still held in her hands. She snuggled closer to him and clutched his shirt. Already wrapped around her finger, Jacob felt his heart melt even more. He placed Lorrie into the crib and changed her into her pajamas. After kissing her on the forehead, he turned to see Amanda standing in the door. "You could have stayed downstairs. She wasn't a problem."

"I knew you could handle her. Dad and Lois left, so Gramma and I decided we might as well come upstairs and go to bed, too." She walked over and peered into the crib. "She's so peaceful when she's sleeping."

"That, she is." He put his arm around Amanda. "You look like you're feeling better."

Amanda leaned against him. "I am, thanks. Guess that nap today did the trick."

"Uh-huh." Jacob tried to keep a serious look on his face. "Well, you should try and get as much rest as you can, while you have a chance. Babies can take a lot out of you."

"True." Amanda gasped when she realized what he had said. "What do you mean?"

Jacob squeezed her close. "Kiddo, I'm not completely clueless." He used his spare hand to gently pat her tummy. "I pretty much figured it out, even before you and your grandmother took off today."

She closed her eyes and released a heavy breath. "Damn." Opening her eyes, she looked up at him. "Does anyone else know?"

"Nope. Why the secrecy?"

"I want to tell Lex before anyone else finds out." She moved over to the bed and sat. "I wish she'd call."

He took off his glasses and cleaned them with a cloth he kept in his pants pocket. "Knowing Lex, she's probably out playing with her horses."

"I wouldn't be surprised. But I still miss her. I can't wait to tell her, Grandpa. It's taking all I have not to rush out to the ranch right now."

"I know. But morning will be here before you know it. Rest well, sweetheart." He kissed the top of her head and left the room.

Amanda watched the door close and fell on the bed. "Dammit, Lex. Where are you?"

AFTER LEAVING A message on the machine, Roy hung up the phone. He turned to the men who sat at the table. "She's not answering." He made a point of looking at Cleve. "You were supposed to go up to the house and tell Lex about the missing horses. What did she say?"

"Nothing." Cleve rocked in his chair until the front two legs were off the ground. "That little SUV was gone, though." Knowing full-well that Amanda wasn't home when he was there, he decided to lie to Roy in order to cause Lex trouble. He was embarrassed at the way Lex talked to him, and figured she left to look for the horses after their conversation. "Maybe she went into town."

Roy took a seat at the table. "That's possible. I didn't want her to worry about the horses." He glared at Cleve. "They wouldn't have gotten as far as they did, if you would have latched the gate right. I'm glad we were able to round them up quickly."

Cleve shrugged. "Whatever." He allowed the chair to land flat against the floor. "I'm going out for a smoke."

"Check the water in the stables while you're out there," Roy yelled after him. After the door slammed, he shook his head. "I don't know what crawled up his ass and died, but I'd love to be the one that buries it." The other men in the room laughed. None of them liked the newcomer and many were looking for an excuse to knock the chip from his shoulder. Roy knew it was only a matter of time before someone did.

Chapter
Sixteen

THE MORNING SUN hit her face and awoke Lex. She squinted and brought her hand up to shield her eyes. Now, in the light of day, she could see what kind of situation she had fallen into. Their muddy prison wasn't as large, or as deep, as Lex had previously thought.

Her movement startled Mine, who began to struggle. Due to the drying mud, the filly was finally able to kick her legs free. Her hooves fought for purchase on the slick surface as she rocked back and forth.

Lex cried out as the animal's weight pressed against her. She tried to calm Mine, but the horse began to flail wildly. "Whoa, girl." Her voice failed as the panicked creature's flank shoved her deeper into the mud.

The ten-minute struggle paid off as Mine was finally able to stand. Lex's right foot dropped limply from the stirrup as the horse stepped away. She gasped from the excruciating pain and wrapped her left arm across her body in an attempt to ward off the worst of the agony. Mine shook herself, scattering bits of mud everywhere. She stretched her neck out and sniffed at Lex.

Opening her eyes, Lex turned her head enough to see Mine standing above her. The horse didn't seem injured. "Maybe I should have named you Lucky instead." She looked down at her body, which was still partially buried in the muck. "Looks like you're on your own. I'm not getting out of here any time soon." Lex closed her eyes at the hopelessness of her situation. No one knew where she was and she realized that Amanda would be frantic by now.

AMANDA WALKED INTO the house, with Lorrie following behind. "Lex?" She checked the upstairs and was concerned when she noticed the bed was still made up as she had left it the day before. Lex always turned the pillows in the opposite direction than she did, so it was always easy to tell who had made the bed.

"Momma?" Lorrie looked under the bed. She wanted to look for Lex, too. "Where's Momma?"

"I don't know, sweetie." Amanda reached for Lorrie's hand and led her downstairs. They went into the office, where the light blinked on the answering machine. Amanda sat in the leather chair and listened to the messages. The first one was from her, so she deleted it. The second, from Roy, later the same day. "That's weird."

Lorrie climbed into her lap. Since her mother wasn't paying attention, she was able to reach out and pick up the pen that had been left behind. The large calendar that sat flat on the desk looked like the perfect place for her artwork. She began to scribble away until Amanda realized what she was doing and captured her hand.

"Lorrie, no." Amanda reached into one of the drawers and pulled out a notepad. "Here, use this."

Satisfied, Lorrie happily scrawled on the notepad.

Amanda picked up the phone and hit the speed dial for the bunk house. "Lester, this is Amanda. Is Lex up there?" At his negative answer, she took a shaky breath. "Can I talk to Roy?" She waited several minutes before the foreman picked up the line.

He sounded slightly out of breath. "Amanda? What can I do for you?"

"I'm sorry to bother you, but have you seen Lex today? We got home, and it doesn't look like she's been here."

"No, I haven't. We thought she went into town with you. Give me a minute and I'll be right there."

"Okay." More concerned than ever, Amanda hit another button on the speed dial. "Hello, this is Amanda Walters. Is Charlie available?"

After a few moments, the sheriff's voice came on the line. "Good morning. To what do I owe this pleasure?"

Trying to stay calm so as not to alarm the child on her lap, Amanda cleared her throat before speaking. "I hate to disturb you at work, Charlie. But have you heard from Lex, lately?"

"No, not since yesterday, around lunch time. Why?"

"She wasn't here when I got home this morning and the bed hadn't been slept in. I was hoping she had said something to you about where she was going."

There was silence on the other end of the line for a long minute. "I'm on my way out there and we'll get this all straightened out. Hang tight." He disconnected the call without another word.

Amanda hung up the phone. The more she found out, the less she actually knew. Even though her heart pounded in her chest, she knew she had to act as normal as possible. She looked down at the paper Lorrie was working on. "That's pretty, honey. What are you drawing?"

Lorrie looked up. "Cow," she said matter-of-factly, as if Amanda should have known. She resumed her art work.

"I see." Amanda stood, bringing Lorrie up with her. "Let's go into the kitchen, and I'll get your crayons. Would you like that?"

"Yep." Lorrie slithered out of her grasp and took off for the kitchen.

It wasn't long before Roy knocked on the back door and came into the house. He went into the kitchen and saw Amanda at the table with Lorrie. "Hi." He took off his hat and squatted next to the little girl, who gave him a friendly smile. "Hello, Lorrie."

"Hi." She pointed at the paper she had been working on. "See? Cow."

Roy gave the drawing the careful consideration it deserved. "And a fine cow it is, youngster." He glanced across the table. "No one's seen her, Amanda. I checked the barn, and one of the horses is missing, along with Lex's saddle."

Amanda felt her stomach drop. "Do you know how long?"

"No." He stood and brushed his hands down the legs of his jeans in a nervous manner. "When was the last time you heard from her?"

"Yesterday morning, before Lorrie and I left. I tried calling late yesterday afternoon, but she didn't pick up the phone."

"Damn." He belatedly remembered they weren't alone. "Sorry about that. I shouldn't talk like that around her."

A slight smile touched Amanda's face. "Don't worry, she's heard it before." She got to her feet and stepped around the little girl's chair and lowered her voice. "What are we going to do?"

"I'm going to get the guys together and go hunting for her. If you don't mind, could you stay here and coordinate things by radio? I'd get Lester to do it, but," he gestured toward Lorrie, "I know you'll have to stay here with her."

Hating to concede the fact, Amanda nodded. "Okay. But please keep in touch."

"You bet." He ruffled Lorrie's hair. "I'll see you later."

Lorrie never looked up. She was used to tuning out the adults when she was busy. "Bye."

Amanda was about to sit next to her daughter, when she got a sudden thought. "I'll try her cell." She grabbed the kitchen phone and dialed the number by memory.

THE MUTED STRAINS of "Bolero" woke Lex from the light doze she had fallen into. It took her a moment to realize where the sound was coming from. Since she had assumed that her phone was damaged in the fall, she thought she was dreaming. Using her teeth, she removed the stiffened glove from her left hand. She slipped her hand inside her coat and stretched as far as she could, choking back a cry as the pain radiated from her right shoulder and lanced down her side. Her fingertips grazed the top of the phone but glided off. The harder she tried, the more she shoved her right side into the ground, bringing new waves of agony. Between the stress, the pain and the heat from wearing the heavy coat, rivulets of sweat beaded up along Lex's brow and into her eyes. She paused in her attempts, spent from the effort.

Thunder began to roll across the skies again. Mine, who up to that time had been content to stand by Lex, jerked her head and skittered sideways. Her reins swung close enough to Lex for her to get her hand tangled in one. "Whoa. Easy there." She wrapped the leather strap around her wrist several times. Knowing it was only a matter of time before the horse bolted, Lex hoped that she'd be able to hold on long enough to be pulled from the drying mud.

A sharp blast of lightning struck nearby, causing Mine to jump. Lex felt the reins tighten and her last conscious thought was of how much the sudden movement was going to hurt. The jolt not only pulled her free, but brought renewed misery to her already screaming body. She slipped quickly into unconsciousness as she was dragged up out of the pit.

The light, drizzling rain on her face brought Lex back. She found herself flat on her back with her left arm hanging uncomfortably from the reins, several yards from the hole she had spent the night in. Her legs still felt useless. Frightened by the thought, Lex struggled to wriggle her feet. It took longer than she had hoped, but she was finally able to move her left foot from side to side. The slightest movement of her right leg was painfully impossible and Lex worried at the condition.

More rumbling from the sky caused the horse to begin walking. Lex winced but didn't want to lose her connection to her only transportation. "Hold up, there. Whoa." She tugged at the reins. "Dammit, horse. Stop!" Her serious tone brought Mine to a halt. "Good girl." Now her only concern was to find a way to remount and get home.

"JACKASS MOTHERFUCKER. DRAGGING my ass out in the rain, for no good reason." Cleve continued to mutter to himself as he rode along. He had not been happy when Roy made him saddle up. "Stupid bitch is probably already at the house, laughing because I'm out here." He was one of the three men assigned to the north end of the property and the only one who knew that it was likely where Lex had ended up.

A wet blast of air dropped rain down the back of his jacket. "Shit." He wanted nothing more than to return to the bunkhouse and get dry. "Even that old coot's coffee would taste good about now." Cleve was about to turn around when he saw a movement through the trees. Curious, he kicked his horse's sides and went to investigate.

As he ducked under a low lying branch, Cleve could make out the form of a horse not far away. When he got closer, he noticed the struggling figure beside it. "Well, son of a bitch." He spurred his horse on.

Lex struggled to turn her head to look in the direction of the hoofbeats. The movement caused sharp pains to shoot into her head. "Thank god." Her relief was short-lived when she realized who was riding up. "Damn."

"Look at what I found." Cleve stayed in his saddle and made no move to get down to help Lex. "Having trouble?"

"You could say that." Lex was in a sitting position on the ground and had her left arm draped through the stirrup. "Could you give me a hand?" It galled her to ask him for help, but at this point, she'd make a deal with the devil himself to get out of her predicament.

He propped himself against the saddle horn and looked down on her. "I don't know. What's in it for me?"

Lex felt her temper snap. "Less than a total ass-kicking when I finally get on my feet, that's what. You still work for me."

"Now, now. That's no way to talk. Maybe I'm tired of working for you. Hell, I was making better money, for less hassle, when I did the rodeo." He jerked on the reins and began to turn his horse around. "Find your own way home, bitch." Cleve kicked his horse's flanks and disappeared off into the trees.

"Hey! Get back here, you son of a bitch!" Lex dropped her head to rest on her good arm. "Dammit." More determined than ever, she slowly pulled herself up until she was able to lean against Mine's side. Unable to place any weight on her right leg, she stood shakily on her left, trying to catch her breath. "I'm going to kill him when I catch up to him. To hell with who he is." With the last of her strength, Lex grabbed the saddle horn and drew herself up onto the horse.

Cleve rode for almost a mile before he came upon Chet. The other man waved him down, so he had no choice but to stop. "Hey."

"You're riding pretty hard. Did you find anything?" Chet pulled his horse next to Cleve's and looked him in the eye. "Why are you in such a hurry?"

"I wanted to let you know that it was clear back there. I couldn't find any tracks." That much was true. He never bothered to look for tracks.

Chet wasn't convinced. "Fine. You go on to the bunkhouse and I'll take over from here." He wanted to check the area over himself. Roy had contacted him earlier and let him know that they had come up empty in their searches.

"Sure. Whatever." Cleve went about his business. He was confident that Chet was too stupid to find Lex, so he wasn't very worried. "I'm out of here."

"Good riddance," Chet mumbled under his breath. He waited until Cleve was out of sight before riding off in the direction he had seen him coming from. "Let's see what you were running from, asshole."

AMANDA PACED BACK and forth in the office while Charlie did his best to calm her down. "What the hell is going on out there? I haven't heard from anyone in hours."

"Getting all upset isn't going to help matters any." He peeked out into the den, where Lorrie was enthralled by a man and an animated blue dog interacting on the television screen. Satisfied that the little girl was occupied, he turned to Amanda. "Roy has everyone out there looking, so the best thing we can do is stay calm and let them do their jobs." He would rather have been out searching also, but Charlie knew that his time would be better spent keeping Amanda company.

She dropped into the office chair and sighed. "I know. It's the waiting that's killing me." The phone rang, and she grabbed it immediately. "Hello?"

"Hello, honey. How's everything going?" Martha tried to sound upbeat, but her voice was too tired to pull it off.

"Hi, Martha." Amanda exchanged looks with Charlie. "Um, yeah. We're doing fine, here." She closed her eyes and hoped that she wouldn't be struck down by lightning for her lie. "How's your aunt?"

"She's finally at peace, God rest her soul. Her funeral service is set for tomorrow, and I'm on a flight to come home later that afternoon." Martha paused for a moment. "Is everything all right?"

Amanda blinked away tears. "Um, hold on." She held the phone out to Charlie, who took it immediately.

"Hello, sweetheart. How's Nattie?"

"Charlie? What are you doing home this time of the day? There's something going on, isn't there?"

He rubbed the back of his neck nervously. "Work was dull, so I came home for lunch. You know how I hate to eat out all the time."

"Okay, now I know something's wrong." Martha's tone became hard. "Blast it, Charlie. Don't give me that load of crap. What is it?"

"Now don't get upset. It's Lex. She's out somewhere on a horse and we're trying to find her." He leaned against the desk and put one arm around Amanda to give her support. "For all we know, the horse could have come up lame and she's having to walk it to the house. But we've got men out looking, just in case."

"That settles it. I'm taking the next plane out of here."

Charlie sat up. "No, there's no sense in you doing that. What about your aunt?"

"She passed peacefully in her sleep. Funerals are for the living, not the dead. My uncle will understand." Her tone brooked no argument. "I'll call you with my flight number. Will you be able to have someone pick me up at the airport, or should I take a cab?"

He sighed and shook his head. Charlie knew that he would never win against her when she had her mind set on something. "I'll get Jeremy to do it. Have a safe flight."

"I will. Give Amanda my love."

The dial tone in his ear was not unexpected. Charlie was well aware of how single-minded his wife could be. He hung up the handset. "She's on her way."

"But—"

"I know. But there's no arguing with her when she gets her mind set on something." He picked up one of the extra radios. "Let's join Lorrie. I know how you love that guy who sings to his dog."

Amanda rolled her eyes, but allowed herself to be led from the office. "Yippee."

CHET HAD BEEN following the tracks Cleve left for close to thirty minutes. He didn't trust the man, and wanted to see for himself that the area had been properly checked. He pulled his horse to a stop when he heard cursing on the other side of a thicket. "Hello?"

Lex rose from where she was bent over the saddle horn. "Hey!" Every movement brought renewed pain to her head and back.

Following the voice, Chet steered his horse through the heavy brush. He saw a mud-covered apparition a few yards away. "Lex? Is that you?"

"Yeah," she groaned. Her voice cracked on the word. "Damn, I'm glad to see you."

"That goes both ways, boss." He jumped from the saddle and approached her horse on foot. "If you don't mind me saying, you look like hell." He placed one hand lightly on her leg.

"Then I look a lot better than I feel."

Chet gently took the reins from her hand. "Can you make it to the house, or do you want me to go get some help?"

"Let's go. I want out of this damned rain." She held her right arm against her body and her right leg was hanging limply against Mine. "I think you're going to have to drive, though."

"Not a problem." He tied a length of rope to her horse's bridle, so it would be easier to lead. "Let me know if you need to stop for a break. I'm going to get on the radio and let them know we're on our way."

She leaned forward again until her forehead touched Mine's neck. "Thanks."

THE CRACKLE OF the radio caused Amanda to jump from the sofa and hurry into the office. "Hello?"

"This is Chet. We're on our way in."

"Thank god." Amanda's shaky hand pressed the button on the microphone. "Is she okay?"

"Covered in mud and tired, but she looks all right."

Amanda closed her eyes as tears trailed down her cheeks. The relief was almost too much and she wasn't even aware when Charlie took the mike from her and guided her to a chair.

"We'll be waiting, Chet. Thanks for letting us know." He replaced the mike and wrapped Amanda in his arms. "Let's go put some coffee on. They'll need something to knock the chill off when they get here."

It was over two hours before they heard the sounds of horses and men behind the house. Amanda raced to the back door and opened it wide. She watched as Roy and Chet assisted Lex down from her ride. The way her lover dropped into their arms scared Amanda.

One of the other men, Jack, jogged up the steps to meet her. "Roy thinks it would be better if we took her straight to the hospital. He's sent one of the guys for the truck."

"No. We'll use mine." Amanda went and took her keys from the kitchen counter. "Here. The back seat folds down. I'll get some blankets." She turned and bumped into Charlie. "We need to—"

"Go get Lorrie ready. I'll drive you both in my car. Those lights should be good for something, right?"

She nodded. "Thanks."

BRIGHT LIGHTS ASSAILED her senses and the first thing Lex was aware of was that her left hand was held in a vise-like grip. She blinked her eyes to get used to the glare and realized she was stretched out in a hospital bed. Her neck was immobilized by a plastic collar and her right arm was strapped tightly across her body. She could also feel her right leg in a heavy brace. The hand holding hers squeezed a little tighter.

"Lex?" Amanda leaned over since Lex wasn't able to turn her head. "Hey, honey." She put on her best smile, although it took some effort. "We were so worried about you."

"Sor—" Her dry throat stole the words from her mouth. Lex was extremely grateful when Amanda placed a straw in her mouth for water. She took several sips and closed her eyes in relief. "Thanks." The light touch of fingers across her brow gave Lex the will to open her eyes again. "How long have I been here?"

"A couple of hours. Do you remember what happened?"

"Yeah. I took the new filly out to look for the missing horses and we fell into a sinkhole." Lex pulled her hand away from Amanda's and touched the casing around her neck. "What's wrong with me?"

Amanda brought her hand away from the brace. "That's only a precaution." She touched the strapping that held down Lex's arm. "You have a concussion, a dislocated shoulder and you sprained your back and your knee. Since you had some bruising on your back and neck, they wanted to keep you in the brace for a day or so."

"That's all?"

"Isn't that enough?" Hours of worrying finally came to a head, causing Amanda's temper to ignite. "Why didn't you tell anyone where you were going? Do you have any idea what it was like, to come home and realize you were missing? My God, Lex. You could have died out there and we would have never known it." She released Lex's hand and spun away, putting one hand on her hip and the other over her mouth.

"Sweetheart, please." Lex reached for her. "Come here."

Amanda shook her head. "I can't. I need —" She raced out of the room and ran directly into Martha, who had came straight from the airport.

"Hold on there." Martha put her hand against Amanda's back. "What's the matter?"

"She's awake. I need to get some air. Excuse me." Amanda stepped around the confused woman and hurried down the hall.

Martha considered chasing after her, but the pull of checking on Lex was too much. She went into the room and walked over to the bed. "Looks like you did it up good this time."

"Hi." Lex leaned into the cool touch of Martha's hand on her cheek. "Where's Amanda?"

"She went racing out of here like her tail-end was on fire. Said she needed air, whatever that was supposed to mean." Martha tapped Lex's left forearm. "Is this one okay?"

"Yeah. Why?" Lex yelped when that same arm was swatted. "What'd you do that for?"

Martha crossed her arms over her chest and glared downward. "For scaring us all to death, that's why. That poor little gal's a wreck. You know better than to head off somewhere without telling anyone. What are you using for brains? Rocks?" She tapped Lex on the forehead. "I swear, if you weren't laid up, I'd whup your butt."

She was right. But Lex would be damned before she let Martha know that. "I was planning on being home long before Amanda got home. It was an accident and it could have happened to anyone."

"You foolish kid. Don't you know that every time you think something like that you are bound to get into trouble?" Now that she knew Lex would be okay, Martha felt as if a huge weight had been lifted from her shoulders. She swatted Lex's arm again.

"Ow!"

"Stop your whining."

It finally dawned on Lex that Martha was no longer in North Carolina. "How's your aunt?"

"She passed peacefully in her sleep, thank the good Lord. Her services are tomorrow."

"I'm sorry, Martha."

"That's all right, honey. She had a long and happy life. I'm glad she's no longer in pain." She brushed the hair away from Lex's eyes. "Is there anything I can get for you?"

Lex nodded, or at least she tried to. "Could you go check on Amanda for me? I'm worried about her."

Martha patted her arm. "You bet. She's probably gone to call her grandparents to see about Lorrie. I'll be back in a flash."

She was partially right. Martha found Amanda in the waiting area, holding her daughter and talking to Anna Leigh and Jacob. The first one to notice her was Lorrie, who immediately held out her arms and kicked her legs. "Mada!"

Everyone turned to see her come into the waiting room. Amanda released Lorrie, and the child raced over to Martha. "Mada, up."

"You sure know what you want, don't you, little one?" Martha took Lorrie into her arms. "Are you all right, Amanda?"

Amanda felt ashamed of her earlier behavior. "No. I feel like a complete ass. Lex is lying in a hospital bed and I went off on her. I can't believe that."

"Well, she does have a tendency to bring that out in a person." Martha kissed Lorrie's cheek. "Have you been a good girl?"

"Yep."

With a soft chuckle, Amanda ruffled the little girl's hair. "Her definition of good is a little off base, I think." She hugged her grandparents. "Thank you for coming. I'm going to go and apologize."

"Don't let her off the hook," Martha warned. "She might think it gives her permission to do something this boneheaded again." She took Lorrie over to the play area, with Jacob and Anna Leigh following.

Taking a deep, cleansing breath, Amanda opened the door to Lex's room and stepped inside. She was happy to see that they had turned down the lighting until only a soft glow was cast across her lover's features.

Lex heard the door close. "Who's there?"

"Someone who owes you an apology," Amanda said, her voice almost at a whisper. She was relieved to see Lex hold out her hand to her and quickly crossed the room to accept it. "I'm so sorry, honey."

"You have nothing to apologize for." Lex pulled her hand close and kissed her knuckles. "It was all my fault. I'm sorry I put you through that."

Amanda placed her head on Lex's chest. "I was so scared." She finally released the tears she had been holding at bay.

Lex held Amanda as best she could, whispering words of comfort. "Everything's going to be fine, baby."

Sniffling a few times, Amanda raised her head and smiled. "I know." She took Lex's hand and placed it on her own belly. "Speaking of which, say hello."

"Hello?" Lex thought about where her hand was. "No, really?"

"Yes."

Her grin was almost painfully wide. "Hot, damn! We're

pregnant!" Lex wanted to jump out of the bed and swing Amanda around the room. Instead, she settled for pulling her down for a kiss.

Chapter
Seventeen

AS HE STEPPED through the door to the bunkhouse, Roy could hear the men talking among themselves. He ignored them for the moment and went over to the coffee maker and filled a mug. Before he took the first sip, he felt someone standing right behind him. "Hello, Lester."

"Is that all you've got to say? We've been waiting all day for some news and you come traipsing in here like you don't have a care in the world. I figured you'd be up at the hospital." The old cook moved in closer. "How's she doing? Chet told me she was hurting something awful."

"She's got some bruises and sprains, but nothing broken. I swear, that woman has more lives than a cat."

Chet came into the house and hung up his coat. He saw Roy with Lester and waved at the two of them. "Got the horses all taken care of, Roy. Is there anything else you need me to do?"

"Nope. Thanks for your help." Roy turned to Lester. "He's a good man."

Lester nodded. "Yup. One of the better ones, that's for sure." He heard Cleve's voice. "That one, now, is pure trouble. I don't know why he's still around."

"Hey, bud. You finished licking boots?" Cleve laughed as Chet's face reddened. "I bet ol' Lex keeps you busy, huh?"

"Shut your mouth." Chet sat at the table across from the obnoxious man. "That reminds me." He leaned forward and raised his voice so the men around him could hear. "It's interesting that Lex was in the exact area where you checked, but didn't see anything."

Cleve shrugged. "Not my fault."

Ben, one of the older ranch hands, got up from where he had been sitting. "What are you saying, Chet?"

"After Cleve came riding hard from the north range, I followed his tracks and ran right into Lex." Chet stood also. "Funny, how that was."

Cleve got up and kicked his chair away from the table. "You're full of shit." He started toward to the door. "Besides, she got out of it all right. No big deal." He went outside for a smoke.

Several of the men, including Ben and Chet, followed him. "I think that son of a bitch needs to be taught a few things," Ben muttered. He nodded to Roy, who raised his coffee cup in salute.

"If I were twenty years younger, I'd join those boys," Lester commented. "What are you going to do about it?"

"Not a damned thing." Roy grinned over his cup and took another sip.

Chet was the first one through the door. He cleared his throat, causing Cleve to turn around.

Cleve took a drag from his cigarette and turned when he heard footsteps behind him. "What the fuck do you guys want?"

"You know, we don't much like you." Chet knocked the cigarette from Cleve's lips.

"Hey! What the hell did you do that for?" Cleve turned his head. He realized he was surrounded by four men. "Uh, guys. What are — ugh." He bent over when Chet punched him in the stomach.

Ben grabbed one arm and Jack the other. "Lex isn't only our boss," Ben explained, "she's a damned good friend, too." They stood Cleve upright so Chet could hit him again.

Raising his right fist, Chet slammed it into the side of Cleve's face. "We're tired of your damned attitude, asshole." He punched him again, this time in the nose, causing a crunching sound and blood to spray everywhere. Another blow to Cleve's cheek opened up a wide cut.

"Stop," Cleve wheezed.

"I don't think so." Chet slugged him in the gut several more times. He stopped and rubbed his reddened knuckles.

Jack released his hold, which caused Cleve to drop to his knees. "Had enough, you prick?"

"Fuck you." Cleve spat blood at his feet.

"You're an idiot, boy." Ben held Cleve up by his shirt. "I think it's time you moved on." He shoved him into the wall of the bunk house. "Get your stuff and get out of here."

The battered man knelt in the dirt with his arms wrapped around his middle. "I'm glad I left that bitch behind. She's as pathetic as the rest of you." He never saw Ben's boot coming toward his face. Cleve was unconscious before he toppled forward into the dirt.

"THIS SUCKS!" LEX reached her fingers into the cervical collar in an attempt to loosen the constrictive piece. "Why won't they take this damned thing off me? There's nothing wrong with my neck."

Amanda pulled her hand away. "Stop it. You're going to pull out your IV if you keep that up." She was on the verge of asking for a tranquilizer. Not for her partner, but for herself. Lex had been fidgeting for over an hour and it was about to drive Amanda insane.

The door opened and a nurse stepped into the room. "I'm sorry to do this, but visiting hours are almost over." She held a needle and waved it in the air. "And it's time for someone's sedative."

"I don't need it."

"Oh, I think you do." The nurse gave a sympathetic look to Amanda as she inserted the needle into the intravenous drip. "You have about five more minutes, and then you'll have to leave, dear."

Amanda waited until the nurse closed the door behind her. She leaned over the bed until she was close to Lex's face. "Guess that's my cue." Placing a soft kiss on her lover's lips, she pulled away and brushed the hair from Lex's eyes. "Hopefully we can take you home in the next day or two. Are you going to be all right here by yourself?"

"Sure." Lex felt a lethargic wave wash over her. "Probably sleep all night, anyway." Her eyes closed. "Love you."

"I love you, too." Amanda kissed her forehead. "Rest well, honey." She slowly backed out of the room and was startled when she almost ran into her grandmother.

Anna Leigh caught Amanda around the shoulders so they wouldn't collide. "Careful. How's Lexington?"

"She's doing pretty well. The doctor is optimistic that she can go home tomorrow or the next day if her tests come back all right."

"Wonderful." Anna Leigh put her arm around Amanda's waist. "Come home with me. Jacob took Lorrie there earlier and I've been able to talk Martha and Charlie into staying the night."

"I guess I'll have to since they won't let me stay here." Amanda followed her down the hallway. "Let me leave the number at the nurses' station in case they need me."

They had walked through the outside doors when they met Michael and Lois. He was wearing a plain white tee shirt with his dress slacks, which was unusual for him. "How's Lex? I called the ranch to see how you were feeling and Roy told me what happened."

Amanda ran into her father's arms and leaned against his chest. "I'm so glad you're here." She turned her head to smile at Lois. "Thanks for coming."

"We came as soon as we heard." Lois rubbed her back in a comforting motion. She had grown quite fond of Amanda over the past couple of years and thought of her as a daughter. "How is she?"

Anna Leigh kissed Lois on the cheek in greeting. "She's resting. I was about to take Mandy home with me. Why don't you two join us?"

Michael squeezed his daughter before releasing her. "That sounds like a great idea. We'll peek in on Lex, and then come over."

"Thanks, Dad." Amanda released him and gave Lois a brief hug, which was gently returned.

"Let's go, dearest. We can visit more when we get home." Anna Leigh took Amanda by the hand and directed her to the car.

Once they were inside and buckled up, Amanda let her head drop against the seat. She closed her eyes and released a heavy breath. "My God, it's been a hell of a day."

"It certainly has. How are you faring?" Anna Leigh drove the car out of the hospital lot and headed toward her home.

"I'm a little queasy and I have the worst headache," Amanda admitted. "It took a lot of self-control to keep from climbing into that bed with Lex." She stifled a sob as the day's horrors caught up with her. Bending at the waist, Amanda covered her face with her hands and began to cry.

Keeping her eyes on the road and one hand on the steering wheel, Anna Leigh put her other hand on Amanda's back. "That's it, honey. Let it all out." She slowed the car down and brought them into a nearby parking lot. Unbuckling her seat belt, she quickly took her granddaughter into her arms and held her close. "Sshh. Everything's going to be fine." Anna Leigh ran her fingers through Amanda's hair in an attempt to calm her.

Amanda didn't know how long they sat there, but she was finally able to sit up. She accepted several tissues from Anna Leigh and gently blew her nose. "Thanks. I don't know where that all came from."

"We all have to give in and have a good cry now and then. It cleanses the soul." She used her fingertips to wipe the tears from Amanda's face. "At least that's what I've always been told. Personally, I think it's the only way to stay sane."

"I think you're right. Although I don't know how sane I am."

Anna Leigh laughed. "I'm afraid that's the Cauble coming out in you, my dear. We've never been known for our sanity." She kissed Amanda's cheek. "Are you up to going home?"

"Now, I am. Thanks, Gramma." Amanda sniffled and sat up straighter. "Let's go see what kind of trouble my daughter has gotten into."

WHEN SHE HEARD the front door open, Lorrie dropped the crayon she had been using, climbed down from her seat at the kitchen table and raced into the entryway. Before her mother could even walk completely into the house, she attached herself to Amanda's leg. "Mommy! Me 'n Gamps clorled."

"He did? What did you and Gamps color?" Amanda picked Lorrie up and hugged her. "I missed you, honey. Have you been a good girl?"

Jacob came out of the kitchen. "She's been a little angel. We played with her building blocks, watched a video, and have been drawing and coloring for about half an hour. You'd have been proud of her."

"I always am." Amanda carried her over and kissed her

grandfather's cheek. "It sounds like you two have had a busy evening."

"We have." He followed Amanda and Anna Leigh into the living room. Amanda and Lorrie sat on the sofa, while Anna Leigh and Jacob took their favorite place on the loveseat. "How's our big girl doing?" He refrained from calling Lex by name, to keep from upsetting Lorrie.

Amanda nuzzled Lorrie's soft hair and then kissed her head. "She's in quite a bit of pain, but already wants to leave. The nurse sedated her before I left." She looked around and realized who was missing. "Where's Martha and Charlie?"

"They've gone to pick up dinner. Lorrie had hers already, but the rest of us are getting deli sandwiches."

"That sounds good." Amanda shook her head at Lorrie's antics when the little girl slid off her lap and started dancing in front of her. "What are you doing?"

Lorrie wiggled her rear end. "Me bubbet."

"Bubbet?"

Jacob laughed. "I think that it's my fault. We watched a video with dancing puppets. So now she wants to be one."

"Ah." Amanda nodded and clapped as Lorrie danced. "That's wonderful, sweetie." Unable to control the yawn that escaped, she leaned against the back of the sofa.

Anna Leigh stood and picked up Lorrie. "I think it's about someone's bath time. Would you like to go play in the tub for a while?"

"Yep." Lorrie gladly wrapped her arms around her grandmother's neck. She looked around the room. "Where's momma?" Lex was her favorite bath buddy.

Amanda felt tears sting her eyes. "Momma's got an owie and she's at the hospital."

"Hopil?"

"That's right, darling girl. Your Momma's at the hospital, but she misses you very much." Anna Leigh turned her head when Michael and Lois stepped into the room. "Hello, you two."

Lorrie struggled to get out of her grandmother's arms. "Gampi!" She held out her hands to Michael, who immediately took her.

"How's my sweet girl?" He kissed her cheek. "I swear, I think you've grown overnight."

"Good." Lorrie leaned to get her kiss from Lois, as well. "Mimi, tub?"

Lois gave Anna Leigh a questioning glance. "I'm assuming it's bath time?"

"Yep." Lorrie wriggled to a tune in her head while she was in Michael's arms. "Tub!"

He handed her off to Anna Leigh. "I think I'll let you handle that bit of fun, Mom."

"Yay!" Lorrie clapped her hands. "Gramma, me go!"

"The princess has spoken," Anna Leigh announced. "Lois, would you care to join us?"

"I'd be delighted." Lois took Amanda's hand and squeezed it. "How are you holding up?"

Amanda wiped a tear from her face and tried to smile. "I'm doing all right, thanks." She gestured to the doorway, where her grandmother held Lorrie. "You'd better go. Lorrie gets impatient when it's time for her bath."

Nodding, Lois squeezed her hand before releasing it. "If you need anything, let me know."

"I will." After they left the room, Amanda exhaled heavily. "That child's energy is exhausting."

Michael sat next to her and put his arm around her shoulders. "Don't take this the wrong way, but you look completely worn out. Why don't you go on to bed and we'll tuck Lorrie in?"

"You're right, I'm beat. But she usually sleeps with me."

"Let your grandmother and me take her," Jacob offered. "I can move the crib into our room."

The thought was tempting, but Amanda didn't want to be alone for the night. "No, that's fine. I'd like her with me, if that's okay with you."

Jacob understood. He knew that without Lex, Amanda could feel lost. He felt the same way about Anna Leigh. "Of course. At least let us get her ready for bed, so after you eat, you can join her."

"All right." She leaned into her father's embrace. "I'm glad this day is almost over. I've had about all I can stand." She knew the next few days would be trying and hoped she'd get through them without losing her mind.

THE ROOM WAS dark and quiet. Although it was after visiting hours, Travis had charmed one of the evening nurses into allowing him access. He moved hesitantly to the bed and looked down at his granddaughter's face. The nurse had explained her injuries, but it was still a shock when he saw her for himself. Lex's eyes were closed, but he could still make out the faint lines in her face that showed her discomfort. Travis brushed the hair away from her eyes and was surprised when they opened.

"Gran'pa?" Lex squinted at his shadowy figure. "What time izzit?"

"I'm sorry, Lexie. I didn't mean to wake you." He continued to stroke her hair. Her eyes were glassy from the medication she was on. "It's pretty late. I wanted to see how you were doing." He silently cursed himself for not being home when Amanda called to tell him of Lex's accident. He and Ellie had traveled to Austin to settle some old business of his and he couldn't get to the hospital quick enough after finding the unsettling message on his answering machine.

"S'okay. M'glad you're here." She blinked several times in an attempt to clear her vision. "Didja see 'Manda?"

He couldn't help but smile at her speech. Every word sounded like a great effort. "No, honey. It's well past visiting hours and she's probably home in bed by now."

A goofy look covered Lex's face. "I mish her. Hey, we're gonna have a baby, ya know."

Travis' eyes widened. "You are?"

"Yep. Well, 'Manda is. I'm jus' gonna help." Her eyes closed, although Lex struggled to stay awake. "She's such a good mom." One lid partially opened, but only for a moment. "I love her."

Travis bit his lip to keep from laughing at her. "I know you do. She loves you too, you know."

"Uh huh." Lex opened her mouth again, but only a soft snore came out.

He chuckled and shook his head. "Rest well, Lexie." After placing a kiss on her forehead, Travis left the room.

Chapter
Eighteen

UPON WAKING, CLEVE tried to take a mental inventory of his aching body. First and foremost, the pain was close to unbearable. There wasn't a muscle or body part that wasn't in agony. He slowly rolled onto his back from the fetal position he had fallen asleep in. He stared at the ceiling, which was the roof of the hay barn.

The previous day, after he regained consciousness, he left the yard of the bunk house and pulled himself up into his truck. Unable to drive very far, Cleve ended up parking behind the barn and crawling behind a tall stack of hay, only to pass out again.

It was all her fault. He was certain of that. The more he thought about his situation, the more Cleve hated his half-sister. She had everything he always coveted—a home, the respect of her peers and a woman to share her life. He closed his eyes and smiled. Amanda. Her gentle smile, her soft hair and the way she carried herself, were what attracted him to her. He considered the last time he saw Amanda. Those once-friendly eyes blazed with anger and she never looked more beautiful. He believed that if he could spend more time alone with her, he could get her to forget all about his controlling sibling. Cleve knew in his heart he could have her with very little effort on his part. She was beautiful and he fancied himself as quite the ladies' man. It would be a piece of cake.

With a pained grunt, he sat up. Once again, he cursed Lex. She probably paid the men in her employ to knock him around. It would be just like her. Maybe Amanda mentioned an interest in him, which made his sister so jealous that she wanted Cleve out of the picture. Yes, that was probably it.

He cautiously prodded his side. It didn't feel like anything was broken, only bruised. His nose was a different matter entirely. It was bent to one side and impossible to breathe through.

"Damn bitch. I hope she hurts like hell." He thought about the look on her face right before he rode away. The pain and the anger she showed brought another smile to his face. It would have made him happier if Lex had never been found. Maybe then he could have taken his rightful place as head of the ranch and in Amanda's bed. Cleve was determined to make her his, and not even his sister's interference would stop him.

LEX BLINKED HEAVILY at the bright light above. It had been a rude awakening, being hauled to radiology so early in the morning. She was hoping they'd get the answers they wanted so she could get out of the cervical collar. At the sound of footsteps she tried to see who approached, but her head was immobilized.

"Well, hello there." The x-ray technician leaned over Lex to make eye contact. "There are a few questions I have to ask, then we'll get right to it."

"Ugh." Lex cleared her throat and tried again. "Like what?"

The woman waved a clipboard. "The usual things we ask everyone before giving them an x-ray. If possible, of course."

"Okay." Lex swallowed several times.

"Good." The tech patted Lex lightly on the arm. She checked her questionnaire and shook her head. "Some of these questions are silly, but bear with me."

Lex closed her eyes. "Go ahead."

"All righty. Your name?"

"Lexington Walters."

The woman made a notation. "Good. Date of birth?" After Lex answered several more of the questions, she turned the page. "Only a few more and we're through. "Are you pregnant?"

"No!"

"Now, now. Don't get upset. Like I said, these are all routine. Are you taking birth control?"

Lex sighed. "Of course not."

"Oh? Are you trying to become pregnant?"

"Not me, but—"

"All right. Fine." The tech checked off several more boxes on her paper. "I assume you use condoms?"

To Lex, the questions kept getting more ridiculous. "No. We don't use anything."

"Well, you know it's not a good idea to have unprotected sex. Even if you're careful, you can have an unplanned pregnancy. Not to mention all the sexually transmitted diseases."

That comment caused Lex to laugh, then moan. "We're safe. Don't make me laugh, it hurts."

"Honey, it's not a laughing matter."

"Lady, I'm gay. My wife is good, but she's not that good." Lex closed her eyes as the ache in her head became a constant pounding. "Can we get this over with?"

"Um, sure." Her horizons suddenly expanded, the technician quieted and got to work.

RELIEVED TO HAVE finally gotten rid of the cervical collar, Lex scratched determinedly at her throat. The constant itching drove her nuts. She could already feel the places where her skin was raw and there didn't seem to be any relief coming in the near future. She shifted slightly in the bed and bit back a moan. Even though she wanted to leave the hospital, her body had other ideas. Shooting pains down her back made Lex consider hitting the call button for another dose of pain killing medication. The only drawback to being on the medication was not being coherent and she was looking forward to visiting hours.

The door opened and Amanda came in, carrying a large bouquet in one hand and a piece of paper in the other. "Hi honey." She walked over to the bed, put the flowers on the adjustable table and gave Lex a kiss. "How are you feeling this morning?"

"A lot better. Do you think you can talk to the doctor and maybe get me out of here today?"

Amanda ran her fingers through Lex's hair. She was relieved to see the confining head gear missing. "We'll see." She held up the paper she was holding. "Lorrie colored this for you." It was a picture from a coloring book, with a cow eating grass. Scribbles of different shades of crayon were scratched across the page.

"It's great." Lex closed her eyes at the gentle head massage. "I want to go home." She caught Amanda's hand and held it close to her chest. "I missed you last night." At least she did whenever the pain would wake her and she lay in the darkness waiting for relief. That quiet time, when no one stirred in the halls and it took what seemed like forever before the nurse arrived to assist her, was the loneliest part of the night.

"I missed you, too. Lorrie keeps asking where her Momma is. Do you feel up to a visit?"

Lex's heart swelled at the thought of seeing their daughter. Knowing that she was missed made her aches fade and she found herself looking forward to seeing Lorrie. "I'd like that. Do you think it would scare her, seeing me laid up like this?"

"I don't think so. As long as I explain it to her, she should be fine. She's pretty sharp." Amanda brushed her thumb across Lex's cheek. "You're hurting, I can tell."

"Some," Lex admitted. "But I don't want to stay hopped up on drugs all the time. I'd rather be able to talk to you."

Amanda smiled at that. "I'd rather not see you in pain. But, I can appreciate where you're coming from." She gestured toward the vase of flowers. "Lorrie helped me pick these out. She liked the ivy, but it was too big to carry."

"I love them and the picture." Lex brought Amanda's hand to her lips and kissed the knuckles. "I love you."

"I love you, too. Were you able to get any sleep at all?"

"A little."

"Yeah, I didn't, either. Lorrie kept singing the new song Gramma taught her in the tub last night. I thought she'd never settle down."

Lex grinned. "What song was that?"

"Eeebee 'pider."

"What?"

Amanda held out both hands, twisting them so that her pinky fingers were pointed in opposite directions. She touched the tips of her thumbs together. "Well, at least that's what Lorrie called it. Itsy, bitsy, spider." She moved her hands up and down, so that her pinky fingers waved in opposite positions.

Rolling her eyes, Lex mentally pictured the little girl's antics. "She got into it, huh?"

"Oh, yeah. I may have to do some serious harm to my grandmother for that one. Old MacDonald is bad enough."

"As I can see from the artwork you brought, she still has that thing for cows, doesn't she?" Lex remembered Lorrie's excitement every time she saw one of the animals.

"Uh-huh. And now, she's also going on about dogs. One of the kids at the church brought pictures of his new puppy and I think she's a little jealous."

Lex considered that. As a child, she was never allowed to have a dog. The times she would ask, her father would refuse. He claimed it would upset the cattle, but Lex thought it had more to do with his fear of the animals. He had mentioned one time that when he was a child, he had been bitten by a neighbor's terrier. She mentally shook off the thought. "What do you think? Should we get her one?"

"I don't know. I thought I'd mention it to you, so that you'd know." Amanda propped one hip against the bed. "It might give her something to concentrate on, besides the baby."

"Maybe so." Lex touched Amanda's stomach. "How are you feeling?"

Covering Lex's hand with her own, Amanda sighed. "A little nauseous. But it's a lot easier to tolerate now that I know what's causing it." A rueful smile touched her face. "Although I'd gladly give up the constant trips to the bathroom. And, speaking of which, I'll be right back." She rolled her eyes and went into the adjoining washroom.

As the outside door opened, Lex looked up to see Charlie and Martha walk in. "Hi."

"Hey there, kiddo." He lightly squeezed Lex's good leg. "Aren't you about through lazing around?"

Lex laughed then grimaced. "Ow. Don't make me laugh, Charlie. Hey, why aren't you at work?"

"Like he could stay away from here." Martha straightened the bedcovers. "You're looking a mite better than yesterday."

"Thanks. I'm doing all right." Lex grabbed her hand. "Stop fussing."

Amanda came out of the bathroom. "Who's fussing?"

"Martha." Lex soaked up the love from her family. She looked up into Martha's eyes. "I'm fine."

"Damned kid." Martha sniffled. "Don't you dare scare me like that again, you hear? I'm getting my gray hair fast enough without you helping."

Lex clasped her hand tighter. "I'm sorry. I'll try to do better." She looked over at her lover. "Have you given them the news?"

Charlie turned his gaze back and forth between Lex and Amanda. "What news? Are you getting released?"

"Nope. Better." Lex grinned at Amanda. "You haven't told them?"

Amanda shook her head. "No, I wanted to wait until we were together." She stood on the other side of Lex and placed her hand on her shoulder. "I'm pregnant."

Martha raised her hands and clapped them together. "I knew it!" She turned to her husband. "See? I told you."

"You sure did." His smile almost covered his whole face. "Congratulations, you two. That's wonderful news."

"Wait a minute. What do you mean, you knew it?" Amanda asked Martha. "How did you know?"

"Please, honey. Even I knew that you had all the classic symptoms. Surely you had some inkling." Martha hurried around the bed and hugged Amanda. "You're so cute."

Amanda returned the embrace and pulled away slightly. "There has been so much going on lately, that I didn't realize how long it was since we had seen the doctor. I had to have Gramma tell me."

Lex turned to look at her. "Your grandmother figured it out?" She started laughing. "I would have loved to have heard that conversation."

"Hush." Amanda crossed her arms over her chest, then chuckled herself. "It was pretty funny. I can't believe, after wanting this baby so badly, that I didn't realize what was going on in my own body."

"Don't you worry about it." Martha shook her finger at Lex. "And don't you be giving her a hard time. Just because you're stuck in that bed, it doesn't mean I can't take my spoon to your behind."

Holding up her good hand, Lex surrendered. "I'll behave, I promise." She turned her eyes to Charlie. "Are you going to stand there, or are you going to help me?"

"Oh, no. Don't get me involved in this." He backed away from the bed. "I'm afraid you're outnumbered this time."

"Gee, thanks." Lex tried, but was unable to keep the grin from her face. She was too excited about Amanda's pregnancy to care.

THE BANDAGE COVERED his nose and close to half of his face. Hubert grimaced at his reflection and straightened his tie. He had one more idea to make some quick money. Picking up his jacket from the bed, he left the house. Hubert looked in the driveway and cursed. Losing the car upset him more than the loss of his wife. He took off down the sidewalk, still grumbling under his breath.

It took him almost half an hour to reach the diner. When he stepped inside, he noticed his old friend sitting in a corner booth. Ted Hotchiss only lowered his newspaper when he realized someone had sat in the booth across from him.

"Hubert? I heard you were in town. What on earth happened to your face?" Ted laid his paper on the seat next to him. He wasn't too surprised to see Hubert. Once he heard he had returned from prison, Ted figured it was only a matter of time before Hubert looked him up.

"Long story." Hubert waved to the waitress, who took her time coming over to the table. "Hey, babe. Get me a coffee."

Francine wrinkled her nose and shrugged. "All right." She checked the table. "Would you like anything else, Ted?"

"No, I'm fine. Thanks."

With another disdainful look at Hubert, she turned and left.

Hubert stretched against the back of the booth. "So, how are you doing, bud?"

"Not bad. Business has been pretty good."

"Uh-huh." Hubert leaned forward. "Listen, I'm in a bind. Someone closed up my old office while I was gone and now the damn place is a sewing shop." He took the coffee Francine placed on the table and brought the cup to his lips. Blowing on the hot liquid, he took a cautious sip. "Since your business is so good, what do you say to having a partner?"

Ted felt a sudden chill at those words. The last thing he needed was trouble and he knew the man across the table from him was chock full of it. He had been trying to distance himself from Hubert since he'd been in jail, for that very reason. "I don't think I have enough clients to justify that, Hubert. Wouldn't it be better for you to reopen somewhere else?"

Slamming his coffee mug onto the table, Hubert cursed as some of the drink spilled onto his hand. "Dammit!" He sucked on the skin between his thumb and index finger in an attempt to squelch the pain. "Are you saying you're not going to help me? After all I've done for you?"

"Give me a break." Ted had heard enough from his former friend. "You never do anything for anyone else, unless it suits you. Now if you'll excuse me," he picked up his paper and opened it, "I've got things to do."

Hubert glared at him. He waited several minutes for Ted to say something, but all he got was a rustling of the paper the other man held in front of himself. "You've got to be kidding me." He grabbed the paper and yanked it down. "Hey, dammit. I'm talking to you."

Ted shook out the paper and resumed his previous position. "Goodbye, Hubert."

"Goddammit!" Hubert slapped his hands on the table and stood. "This is bullshit. You haven't seen the last of me, asshole!"

Watching him leave, Ted shook his head. "That's what I'm afraid of."

LEX'S GRIMACE TURNED into a smile when Anna Leigh stepped into her room, balancing Lorrie on one hip. The little girl squealed and held out her hands.

"Momma!" Lorrie wriggled in her grandmother's grasp. She continued to struggle until Anna Leigh brought her next to the bed.

"Hold on there, lil' bit." Lex raised her good arm and caught Lorrie's hand. "Put her here next to me."

Anna Leigh continued to hold the squirming child. "Are you certain that's a good idea, Lexington? She's quite rambunctious today."

"Please." Lex bit back a groan as Lorrie joined her on the bed. She was glad Amanda had left the room a few moments earlier, otherwise she might not have gotten away with having Lorrie with her. "How's my girl? Have you been good for Gramma?"

"Yep." Seeming to sense her mother's pain, Lorrie lightly touched Lex's injured shoulder. "Momma's owie hurt?"

Lex nodded. "A little." She kissed the tiny hand that touched her lips. "But it's feeling a lot better since you're here."

"I brought—" Amanda came into the room, holding a paper bag. Her words died on her lips while she watched Lex with their daughter. She stood next to her grandmother and kept her voice low so as not to disturb them. "Thanks for bringing Lorrie in, Gramma. Lex has been dying to see her."

Anna Leigh leaned closer to her. "It was my pleasure. I did try to explain to her that Lexington wasn't feeling well and she had to be easy on her. And from the looks of it, I believe she understood."

Lorrie lay against Lex's side and propped her head on her uninjured shoulder. She closed her eyes and snuggled as close as she could. In no time at all, she was asleep.

Lex put her arm around Lorrie to keep her from falling. Once she realized the child had fallen asleep, she looked up and noticed Amanda in the room. "Oh, hi."

"Hi, yourself." Amanda put the paper bag on the small table beside the bed. "I brought you something to eat."

"Please tell me it's barbequed ribs."

Amanda shook her head. "I'm afraid not. But I did think about it.

I didn't know how you would have handled eating them." She took a wrapped package from the bag. "You'll have to settle for a barbeque brisket sandwich, instead." She used the controls to raise the top of the bed, until Lex was upright. Lorrie never stirred. Amanda unwrapped the top portion of the sandwich and handed it to her lover.

After the first bite, Lex rolled her eyes in ecstasy. "Mmm. That's fantastic." It didn't take her long to finish her lunch and she wadded up the paper the best she could. She exchanged it for a paper napkin from Amanda and wiped her mouth and chin. "Thank you."

"You're very welcome." Amanda tossed the trash into a nearby receptacle. "Has the doctor been by?"

"No, not yet. I'm hoping that means I'm getting out of here today."

Anna Leigh placed her hand on Lex's uninjured leg. "Please don't rush things, Lexington. I know you are tired of being here, but you need to follow the doctor's orders."

"Don't worry, she will." Amanda pinched several strands of Lex's hair and tugged. "Isn't that right?"

"Yes, ma'am."

Bending over to kiss her lover's lips, Amanda whispered, "Good." She straightened up and looked down into Lorrie's peaceful face. "She's been going nuts without you."

Lex stroked the sleeping child's hair. "I've missed her, too. You never realize how much you love and care for someone until you almost lose them."

"Yeah." Amanda brushed her knuckles across Lex's cheek. "Let's keep that from happening, okay?"

"You bet. I plan on being around to see her kids graduate from college." Lex put her hand behind Amanda's head and pulled her forward. "Come here, beautiful." Their lips touched and neither of them noticed when Anna Leigh slipped quietly from the room.

Chapter
Nineteen

IT HAD BEEN a long week. Lex had spent the majority of it relegated to the lower floor of the house. When she was very lucky, she was allowed to spend time sitting on the front porch. She had conveniently "lost" the sling for her arm not long after returning from the hospital. The sturdy brace she wore on her injured leg made it hard for her to walk. Refusing to use the wheelchair Amanda rented for her, she instead relied heavily on a cane.

Martha came outside and placed her hands on her hips. She stared at Lex, who used her good foot to push the porch swing back and forth. "Are you still pouting?"

"I'm not pouting."

"You could have fooled me." Martha wiped her hands on her ever-present dishtowel and sat next to the sullen woman. "She did it for your own good, you know."

"Hmph." Lex didn't care for the reason behind Amanda's betrayal. At least that's what it felt like. She had hoped, of all people, her partner would understand. But no, Amanda had sided with Martha. She assumed Amanda would remember how it felt, to be stuck at the house all the time with nothing to do. Surely she would have realized Lex's feelings on the matter. Lex lowered her gaze to her feet, which were only covered with heavy socks. "She hid my damned boots."

Failing in her attempt to stifle her laughter, Martha patted Lex on the leg. "That's what you get for trying to go riding, Lexie. You know you're supposed to be taking it easy."

"I feel like a bum." Lex fussed with the sturdy brace that covered her right leg, from mid-thigh to her ankle. "I'm tired of lazing around. There are things I need to be doing."

"Like what? Roy and the others have everything under control. And how do you plan to do these things? You can barely walk." Martha understood where she was coming from, but refused to allow Lex to injure herself further by over-stressing her knee.

Straightening in the swing, Lex crossed her arms over her chest. It was the same argument she had heard from Amanda. It's wasn't like she wanted to go out riding or anything. Only a short trip to the barn to see the horses. Surely that wasn't too strenuous. But both Amanda and Martha took turns not letting her out of their sight. If it hadn't been for getting to spend time with Lorrie, Lex would have mutinied sooner. "I'm using the cane, aren't I? Besides, it's not that far to the barn."

"Ahem."

Lex turned to see Amanda leaning against the door jam. "Um, hi."

"Don't hi, me." Amanda's arms were also folded across her chest, and she wore a perturbed look on her face. "Has she been giving you a hard time, Martha?"

Not wanting to get into the middle of another disagreement between the two women, Martha stood. "Actually, I believe now would be a good time to bake that cake. And I'll see if Lorrie is up from her nap." She went in the house.

Amanda didn't move. Although she thought Lex looked adorable when she didn't get her way, she knew it wasn't the right time to admit it. She continued to stare at her lover, unwilling to break eye contact. "Well?"

"What?"

"Are you still mad about your boots?"

Lex turned away and found the grass in the front yard fascinating. She didn't like being treated like a child and couldn't understand why a short walk to the barn was such a big deal. "No."

"Liar." Amanda pushed off from the door and joined Lex on the swing. "I suppose we have been a little rough on you. Will you ever forgive us?"

"I guess."

Amanda snuggled against Lex. "How about," she unfastened a button on Lex's shirt and sneaked her hand inside, "tonight, after dinner," her nails lightly scratched Lex's belly, "Lorrie and I go down to the barn with you?" She noticed her partner's eyes closed. "Lex?"

"Mmm?" Lex inhaled and trapped Amanda's hand. No longer upset, she forgot what she had been mad about to begin with. She turned her head and easily found Amanda's lips with her own. The barn could wait. It was turning out to be a nice afternoon. Very nice, indeed.

CLEVE TURNED HIS head first one way, then the other. No matter how he looked at his reflection, his flattened nose mocked him. The purple bruises beneath his eyes were still dark and the jagged tear across one cheek would leave a nasty scar. He blamed Lex for his appearance. The men who beat him worked for her and he believed they were only doing her bidding. There could be no other explanation for their behavior. He was a great guy. No one would do him harm, unless they were paid to do so. He touched the scab on his face. The bitch would pay.

He moved away from the mirror and gathered his personal belongings. Cleve tucked his wallet into his back pocket. The ragged leather bifold had been a gift from his mother and he carried her picture inside. He couldn't wait for her to meet Amanda. Maybe when he took over the ranch, Marcy would come live with them. "That's right. Mom will be so proud of me. She's always wanted a daughter." Cleve took his keys from the dresser and picked up the duffle bag he used for his clothes.

After checking out of the run down motel, Cleve decided he needed to find a place to board his horse, at least temporarily. He didn't want Lex to do anything to it out of spite. Once he was in control of the ranch, he'd bring his horse to the main barn, so it would be nearby.

Cleve stopped for a newspaper and took it into the diner. Not seeing any empty tables, he found a stool at the counter.

A smiling redhead stopped in front of him. "What can I get you to drink, hon?"

"Coffee, black." He opened the paper and started reading the classified ads. He had to give the woman credit. She never looked twice at his puffy face. When a white ceramic mug was placed in front of him, Cleve raised his eyes. "Thanks."

"You're welcome." Francine wiped the counter next to him. "Can I get you something to eat?"

He folded his paper over and pushed it out of the way. "What do you suggest?"

Francine leaned over and gave him a nice view of her considerable assets. "A nicer place." She winked and straightened. "But, if you're determined to eat here, the pot roast hasn't killed anyone. Yet."

"Sounds good." Cleve waited until she left before he returned to reading the ads. Maybe he'd wait until the waitress got off work, and see if she'd show him around town. He could use a good distraction.

AFTER TEN MINUTES of non-stop chattering, the silence in the kitchen came as a surprise to Amanda. She placed her fork next to her plate and touched Lex's hand to get her attention. "I think someone has finally lost the battle."

Lex turned to see what she was talking about. A smile crossed her face at the sight. "Poor kid. Looks like she's out for the count."

Sound asleep, Lorrie's head was bent at an almost impossible angle. Her chin rested on her chest, and she still held her spoon with one hand. Mashed potatoes covered both cheeks. What appeared to be bits of meatloaf clung to her chin.

"She enjoys her food, that's for sure." Amanda stood and pried the utensil from the sleeping child's hand. She never saw Lex leave the table, but was thankful for the damp towel that was handed to her. Between the two of them it took no time at all to get Lorrie clean. Amanda tucked her against her chest. "I'll take her upstairs."

"While you're doing that, I'll get things put away down here." Lex brushed her palm over Lorrie's hair and kissed her head.

Putting Lorrie to bed was more of a chore than Amanda expected. Lorrie had partially awakened while Amanda put her pajamas on her and started to fuss. With the promise of having a book read to her, the little girl cooperated and was asleep in no time.

A noise across the hall got Amanda's attention. She took one last look at her daughter's sleeping face before going into the master bedroom. The bathroom door opened, and Lex hobbled out. She was wearing a tee shirt and boxers, and the long knee brace she'd been forced to wear home from the hospital was missing. "What are you doing?"

"Getting ready for bed." Heavily favoring her leg, she plopped onto the bed.

"Sometimes I wonder how many children I'm raising. What am I going to do with you?" Amanda didn't expect an answer. She went about her own nightly rituals and soon joined Lex. Her partner reclined on the bed, leafing through a child development magazine. "Anything interesting?"

Lex lowered the periodical. "It warns that toddlers tend to be argumentative." She placed it on her nightstand. A standoff between Amanda and Lorrie earlier in the day came to mind. "I think whoever wrote the article knew our daughter."

"No kidding." Amanda waited until Lex was stretched out comfortably again. She edged closer and ran her hand softly across her lover's knee. "It's looking better."

"Yep." Although still tender, her knee was able to bear more weight. Lex was confident that she could begin wearing a smaller brace, and was glad to be free of the cumbersome stabilizer for the evening.

Amanda snuggled against Lex's side. "I didn't expect you to be here."

"Where was I supposed to be?"

"After our talk this afternoon on the porch, I thought that you'd go to the barn after dinner." Amanda traced her finger across Lex's stomach. "Not that I'm complaining or anything. You seemed so antsy today."

"I guess I was." Lex ran her fingers through Amanda's hair.

Lifting her head slightly, Amanda turned to face her. "Why didn't you?"

"Because I promised Lorrie she could go with me. But since she fell asleep at dinner, I changed my mind."

"You could have still gone. She would have never known." Caught up in the light in Lex's eyes, Amanda almost forgot what they were talking about.

A small grin appeared on her face when she saw the far off look in Amanda's face. "She might not have, but I would. I'm not going to break my promises to her, if I can help it."

"You're a good mom, Lex. She's a lucky little girl."

Lex pulled Amanda's face to her for a kiss. "I think I'm the lucky one. Many times over." She started to tug on Amanda's shirt. "You're over-dressed again." She easily divested Amanda of her top, the years of practice making it almost second nature. With a half roll of her body, Lex playfully pinned her lover to the bed. "Let's see if I can finish what we started on the swing today."

Amanda worked her hands beneath Lex's shorts to pull her closer to her. She lifted her chin as soft lips claimed her throat. The exhaustion she felt from the long day slowly receded as Lex lovingly worshipped her body.

HUBERT HATED SHOPPING. He would rather order things off the Internet. But some things, like groceries, were a necessity. It still rankled him. He wondered if Somerville would ever join the twenty-first century and have grocery deliveries. Still grumbling to himself, he wandered the aisles, pushing a cart that seemed to have a mind of its own. Turning a corner, he slammed into another cart. "Why don't you pay attention to where you're going, asshole?"

"Hubert?" Ellie leaned on her cart with an amused smile on her face. "Looks like someone finally got tired of your mouth."

"Fuck you."

A firm hand grasped his shoulder. "You should watch your language, young man."

Hubert spun around. His grandfather held a bag of coffee beans in one hand. "Leave me the hell alone, old man." A sudden thought flickered through his mind. "Actually, I was thinking about you, grandfather."

"Oh?" Travis didn't like the sound of that. "What are you up to, now?"

"It's nothing like that. I feel bad for how we left things the other day." Hearing a snicker from his cousin, Hubert glared at her. "It's true."

Ellie had her elbow propped on the handle of the cart, and placed her chin in her open palm. "This ought to be good."

Biting his tongue to hold a sharp retort, Hubert tried to smile. "Janine explained to me how things might have sounded. I apologize if I was out of line."

"Oh?" Travis didn't believe him for a moment, but was curious as to how Hubert's little ploy would pan out. "Where is your lovely wife?"

"That stupid bi— I mean, she went to Huntsville. To visit," he added quickly.

"She do that to you face?" Ellie questioned, innocently.

His face reddened. "Yes! No, it was an accident."

Travis had heard enough. He was tired of Hubert's games. "What is it that you want, son?"

"I'm not your—" Hubert caught himself. "Actually, I wanted to talk to you about a business deal."

"Oh?" Travis held up his hand to forestall Ellie's objections. "Ellie, would you mind getting the fresh vegetables? I'll be along shortly."

She sighed, but took the coffee from him and placed it in the basket. "Sure." Glaring at Hubert, she added, "I'll be back in a few minutes."

Once she left, Travis put his hands in his front pockets to appear less threatening. "Go on, tell me what you have to say."

"It's like this. While I was away, the lease expired on my office. Those jackasses didn't give me a chance to do anything about it, and when I got home, all my shit, I mean, furniture and stuff, was gone. I wanted to ask if you'd loan me the money to get started again. I could make you a silent partner."

"You can't be serious."

He didn't know why his grandfather looked at him that way. Hubert thought it sounded like a perfect solution, and he wouldn't have to pay him back. "Of course I am. It's a good opportunity for someone your age. You'd have a steady income. I know how hard it is for you elderly guys. You don't think she'll take care of you in your old age, do you? Elsie is sponging off you. God knows at her age she'll never find a guy to take care of her."

"Her name is Ellie. And for the record, I'm not about to give you one red cent." Travis stepped closer to Hubert. "You leave her, and your sister, out of your petty schemes. If I hear one word about you bothering anyone in my family, I'll have the law on you so fast it will make your head spin."

"For what?"

Travis smiled, but it wasn't friendly. "For whatever you're up to. Trust me. I have enough friends to help put you back in prison, where you belong."

Rattled, Hubert swallowed nervously and straightened his jacket. "Fine. But don't come crying to me when that broad bleeds you dry." He brushed by Travis and hurried to the next aisle.

Ellie returned in time to see Hubert's retreat. "Is everything all right?"

"Yes." Travis put his arm around his granddaughter. "I don't think we'll have to worry about Hubert anymore."

"I sure hope not. He's even more of a jerk than Lex says." Although she still had her problems with Lex, Ellie could tell that Hubert was nothing like her. "Do you think he was adopted?" She sincerely wished she'd never see him again, but didn't think she'd be that lucky.

Chapter
Twenty

AMANDA WOKE TO a light breath on her exposed stomach. She was charmed by the look on her wife's face. "Good morning. How long have you been up?"

"A while." Lex kissed her tummy. "I've been visiting with Junior."

"Oh? And what does Junior say?"

Lex grinned and kissed the same spot again. "She told me that you're an awesome mommy, and she can't wait to meet you."

Amanda grabbed Lex's face and pulled. "Get up here, you nut." She kissed her, purring when the contact was deepened. "Now that's how to say good morning."

"Yep." Lex rolled over onto her side and brought Amanda with her. "Have I told you lately how much I love you?"

Amanda kissed her again. "You may have mentioned it a time or two dozen last night." She ran her hands under Lex's shirt and up her back. "And showed me, too. But I'll never get tired of hearing it."

"Good. Because I don't ever plan on stopping." Wandering hands caused her to squirm. "You keep doing that, I'll show you all over again."

"And that would be a bad thing?"

"Mommy!" A loud voice called from across the hall. "Momma!"

Lex chuckled at their daughter's timing. She forced herself away from Amanda and went next door to fetch their demanding offspring. Without the brace for her leg, she limped heavily. But she loved being the one who helped their child in the mornings. "Hold your horses, Lorrie."

In a few minutes, Amanda heard the pounding of tiny feet. She barely had time to prepare herself before Lorrie climbed on the bed and launched herself at her. "Good morning, sweetie."

"Mommy, I pottied."

"You did?" Amanda looked at Lex, who nodded and joined them on the bed.

"Yep," Lorrie answered. "Big girl."

Amanda tickled her. "That's wonderful. You are getting to be a big girl."

Lex braced herself on her left arm and put her chin on her hand. "No accidents, either. I think someone is ready for her big girl panties." They had bought her underwear in several designs. Lorrie's favorites were decorated with cartoon princesses. She knew that once she was able to go to the "big girl potty" she'd get to wear them all the time, not just during the day.

Lorrie clapped her hands. "Yay! Big girl panties." She bounced on the bed. "Now?"

"Yep." Lex started to get up, then remembered something. "How do we ask, Lorrie?"

She batted her gray eyes at Lex. "Pease? Big girl panties?"

"Good girl." Lex scooped her up and carried her off to her room to change into her new underwear. A new obstacle faced, and conquered.

AFTER BREAKFAST, AMANDA caught Lex in the bedroom, placing a smaller brace on her injured knee. "Isn't it a little soon for that?"

"Nope. The doctor told me I could put as much weight on it as was comfortable. It's not going to get better if I don't walk on it. I've had similar problems before, and it worked out okay."

"If you say so." Amanda handed Lex her cane. "Stick with this for a while, please? I don't think I could carry you very far."

Lex stood and embraced her. "I don't know. After lugging Lorrie around so much you've developed quite a set of muscles there."

Amanda felt hands grab her butt. "That's not where my muscles are, Slim."

"Feels pretty muscular to me." Lex kissed her on the nose and started for the door. "Let's relieve Martha of the kiddo, and head over to the barn. I promised her."

"And that's all she's talked about this morning, other than her new underwear." Amanda linked her arm with Lex's spare one and walked down the stairs with her. "You've created another horse fanatic."

Lex was quite pleased with herself. "Yep. That's my girl."

They found Lorrie "helping" Martha with a pie. The little girl had a small amount of dough and was beating it with a miniature rolling pin. She had a few smudges of flour on her face and arms, but was otherwise neat.

She looked up as they came into the kitchen. "I cookded," she related proudly.

"I bet you did." Lex limped to the table and sat next to her. "What are you making?"

"Pie," Lorrie answered, as if it were obvious. She put the rolling pin on the table and began to slap at the dough. "Gots to go flat," she explained. "Make yum."

Lex gave her full attention to the little cook. She dutifully ate the small bite Lorrie offered of the dough. "You're right, lil' bit. That is yummy."

Amanda stood next to Martha while they both watched Lorrie give Lex a cooking lesson. She marveled at her partner's patience. She seemed perfectly content to sit and listen to their daughter chatter about the pie dough, even though Amanda knew she was itching to get out of the house and to the barn. She had no doubts that their next child would receive the same caring attention, and was looking forward to seeing how their lives would unfold.

"Done!" Lorrie turned to Martha. "Mada? We cookded?"

Martha gathered the dough and placed it in a three and a half inch tart pan. She ladled on a spoonful of apple mixture, and covered it with the dough she had put aside for the occasion. When she was through, she showed the finished product to Lorrie. "How's that?"

Lorrie clapped. "Good!" Her eyes never left the "pie" as Martha placed it in the oven.

"Did you ever do that with Lex?" Amanda asked, quietly. "You're so good with Lorrie."

"Thank you, but it's a labor of love." Martha handed Lex a damp dishtowel to clean the flour and dough from Lorrie's face and hands. "I wish I could have done the same with Lexie, but her father wouldn't hear of it. He said she didn't have time for such nonsense." She scrubbed the counter. "It was a pure shame, too. She was forever sneaking into the kitchen. I know she wanted to learn more than how to feed horses, poor thing."

"You still did a wonderful job. I can see a lot of you in Lex. She was lucky you were here for her." Amanda saw Lex help Lorrie from the table. "It looks like you'll be getting the kitchen to yourself again."

"Mommy, go!" Lorrie wrapped her arms around Amanda's legs. "See ossie's."

Lex started to use the dishtowel to wipe the table. Martha took it away from her and swatted her on the rear. "Hey."

"I'll finish this, honey. You have more important things to take care of." She shooed them out of the kitchen. After they left, Martha leaned against the counter and wiped her forehead with her hand. "Now maybe I can get some things done."

Lorrie raced ahead, while Lex and Amanda took a more leisurely pace to the barn. Lex limped slightly, and tried to only use her cane for balance. Her knee ached, but it wasn't anything she couldn't handle. She'd had numerous injuries growing up on the ranch, and refused to let any of them take her down for long. Lorrie stretched as far as she could to reach the handle on the barn door but could only touch it with her fingers. "Take it easy, kiddo. We'll be there soon enough."

Amanda picked Lorrie up as Lex opened the door. They had a rule. Because there were so many things she could hurt herself with, she wasn't allowed to have free rein in the barn. "Now remember, Lorrie, let's use our inside voice, so we don't scare the horses," she reminded her.

"Yep." Lorrie's favorite was Amanda's paint pony, Stormy. She rubbed the animal's nose gently. "Good ossie."

Lex stopped at the new filly's stall. She did a cursory check and could see that someone had taken very good care of her. "How are you doing, girl?" She patted the horse's neck. "You look none the worse for wear. Wish I could say the same."

"She's the horse you were on when you got hurt?" Amanda asked, bringing Lorrie with her to stand by Lex. "New, isn't she?"

"Yep." Lex scratched behind the filly's ears, much to the horse's delight. "Even as new as she is, she did me proud out there."

Amanda rubbed under the animal's jaw. "Does she have a name?"

"Mine."

"Huh?"

Lex grinned at her. "I call her Mine."

"Okaaay." Amanda drew the word out. "Isn't that a silly name for a horse?"

"Nope. I bet Lorrie would agree with me." Lex patted Mine's neck again. "Lorrie, do you like this horse?"

The little girl grinned, looking like a miniature of her momma. "Yep. Mine!"

"See? Perfect name." Lex couldn't keep the satisfied look off her face. "Lorrie, do you want to help me feed the horses?"

"Yep!" Lorrie squirmed until Amanda put her down. She happily followed Lex into the feed room while Amanda continued to pet Mine.

"You poor thing. I have a feeling you've gotten a new owner." She laughed as Mine bumped her in the chest with her nose. "Don't blame me, I only raise them."

LATER THAT AFTERNOON, Amanda and Lorrie were in the kitchen putting together a puzzle, while Lex went over the ranch's books. The front door slammed. Seated at her desk in the office, Lex was about to go investigate when Cleve strode into the room. "What do you want?" She noticed the cut and fading bruises on his face. "What the hell happened to you?"

"I came for my check." He pointed at his broken nose. "Don't act like you don't know about this. Those assholes at the bunkhouse worked me over. I bet you got a good laugh out of it."

"You want your check? Fine." Lex took her checkbook from the top drawer and quickly filled it out. She tore off the top page and thrust it at him. "Take it." She put her pen down and pushed away from the desk. "When did this happen?"

"The day they took you to the hospital." He lurched forward and placed his hands on the desk. "I hope you paid them well, because I plan on suing your ass for it."

Lex leaned in her chair. "I do pay them well, because they do a good job. Unlike you. And for the record, I had nothing to do with it." She smirked. "Although it only helped your looks."

"Bitch!" He raked his hand over the table top and scattered the contents to the floor. "I should have done more to you out there than leave. Maybe worked you over."

Amanda stood in the doorway. She had heard the commotion and came to see what was going on. "Lex, what is he talking about?"

It wasn't the way Lex wanted to tell Amanda. They had yet to discuss her ordeal. "Can we talk about this later?"

"No, I'd like to hear it, now."

He spun and gave Amanda a cocky grin. "I'm the one who found her. Out there." He took a step closer. "You should have seen her. Hanging by one hand to that worthless horse, begging for help. I should have got off my ride and knocked her around some more. She couldn't even stand up. It was great."

Amanda's eyes sparkled with hatred. "And you left her there like that?" She turned her gaze to Lex. "Why didn't you tell me?"

"We haven't talked about it. It's kind of embarrassing." Lex started to get to her feet, but Amanda's upraised hand forestalled her.

"Lex, could you give Cleve and me a minute?"

The patter of small feet caused them all to look behind Amanda. Lorrie peeked around her mother's legs to see what was happening. "Mommy? Who dat?"

"No one, baby." Amanda clasped the top of Lorrie's head against her in a protective gesture.

"Mommy mad?" Leave it to a child to see to the heart of things. Lorrie nervously stuck a thumb in her mouth and stared at Cleve. "Who you?"

Cleve took another step toward Amanda and Lorrie. "Can't you shut that brat up?"

Amanda backed up, taking Lorrie with her. She didn't like the look in his eyes, and she could smell the alcohol on his breath. "Don't come any closer."

Lex cleared her throat. In a deceptively soft voice, she spoke to her wife. "Sweetheart, would you mind taking Lorrie into the kitchen? I don't think she needs to be around our guest."

"All right." Amanda didn't want to leave Lex, but knew her top priority was their daughter's safety. "Holler if you need anything." She picked up Lorrie and slowly backed out of the room.

Lex waited until they were gone. She stood, picked up her cane and shoved the end of it into Cleve's chest. "I've had about all I can stand of you, you little pissant. I've put up with a lot of your bullshit, because I thought I owed you something. But your free ride is over." She punctuated her words with a poke of the cane. "If... you... ever... yell at my daughter again, I'll kick your ass all over the place."

"Is that a threat?" He glared at her. "Because if it is—"

She dropped the cane on the desk and grabbed him by the front of his coat. Her voice dropped so low he could almost feel it in his bones. "Oh no, asshole. That wasn't a threat. It was a promise." Lex released him and stepped away. "Now get out before I call the sheriff and have you thrown in jail for trespassing."

He couldn't resist a final dig. "You know, I bet that girlfriend of yours is a sweet piece of ass. All she needs is a good man to show her what she's missing." The look in her eyes froze him. Cleve crumbled up the check and tucked it in his coat pocket. "You can have her. I don't need this shit." Deciding that a retreat was better than facing his half-sister, he straightened his coat and left.

When she heard the front door slam, Lex fell against the desk and sat on the edge. Her hands shook, and it took all her self-control not to follow Cleve and tear him apart. Soft footsteps approaching calmed her instantly.

Amanda, holding Lorrie, walked in and took her place next to her lover. "Are you all right? Charlie's on his way."

Lex leaned into her and closed her eyes. "I'm fine. Mad as hell, though." She smiled slightly when she felt tiny hands on her head. Raising her face, she kissed Lorrie's fingers when they touched her lips. "Hey there, lil' bit."

"Love Momma." Lorrie stretched and put her arms around Lex's neck, causing her to take her.

"I love you too, Lorrie. You're such a sweet girl."

Lorrie nodded. "Me good." She gave Lex a slobbery kiss on the lips.

All of Lex's anger faded into nothing. This was what mattered, not some idiot who thought the world owed him. No, she'd let life handle Cleve. She was content to bask in the love of her family.

Chapter
Twenty-one

FREEDOM. LEX REVELED in it. A month after her accident, things were finally returning to normal for her. Her shoulder hadn't given her any trouble for well over a week. She still wore a brace on her right knee, but that was more for Amanda's benefit than her own. She was glad to be on her own again. It was nice, spending extra time with her partner and their daughter, but she couldn't stop the happiness that bounced inside of her as she walked into the old feed store.

A hearty voice hailed her from the back of the store. Three old men sat in one corner. "Hey there, young 'un. Haven't seen you around." Claude picked the old coffee can off the floor beside him and spit into it. "We heard you had a little trouble awhile back."

His brother, Ted, grabbed another chair for Lex. "You're looking pretty good, considering we heard you was half dead."

"Where did you hear something like that?" Lex took the offered seat. "Thanks."

Ted took off his sweat-stained Stetson and scratched his head. "You know how things are around here. Get a hangnail and suddenly folks got you at death's door."

"Ain't that the damned truth." Jesse noticed the brace on her leg. "Heard tell it was more than a hangnail, though."

Lex stretched her right leg out slowly. Her knee did bother her a little, but she decided to keep that information to herself. Amanda worried enough as it was. "Yeah, I messed my knee and shoulder up a little, but nothing too serious. What exactly did y'all hear?"

"Roy came in the same week it happened, and he talked to Tom at the front counter. Tom told us that you were practically crushed under a horse, and spent days out in the weather."

Good grief. Now she understood how little stories got so quickly out of hand. Tom was a worse gossip than the ladies at the Auxiliary Hall. She'd have to warn Roy about him. "Actually, we stumbled into a sinkhole. I spent the night out there, but it certainly wasn't as horrible as you heard." She released a heavy sigh. "Damned Tom."

Claude slapped her on the back. "Glad to see you in one piece, girl." He gave her a sly look. "Oh, and congratulations, by the way."

"For?"

"That new young 'un that's on the way. We heard that gal of yours is having a baby." Claude winked at her. "Keep it up and you're going to have to build a bigger house."

Lex couldn't help but laugh. "Thanks. We're pretty excited about it." Nothing surprised her about these old men. She had grown up around them, and although she never told them about her lifestyle, they didn't blink an eye about her and Amanda. She wished the people her own age were as accepting. "You guys are better than the Somerville Times-Dispatch. Who needs to read the paper as long as you're around?"

They were interrupted when a young man came up to Lex. "I've got all that stuff loaded for you, Lex. Dad says he put it on your bill."

"Thanks, Bobby." As much as she enjoyed the men's company, she also wanted to get the supplies to Roy. She rose from her chair. "Guess that's my cue to leave, guys. Try to stay out of trouble."

Jesse swatted her leg with his hat. "We're not the ones who are always getting into things, kid. Keep yourself in one piece."

She tipped her hat. "Easier said than done, friend. But I'll do my best." With a quick wave, Lex left the comfort of the feed store. She decided on one more stop before going to the ranch.

THE SQUALLING BOY was beginning to get on his nerves. Michael was gratified he was almost finished with this particular portrait. The child, nearly two years old, was spoiled and demanding. He wore a cute Dalmatian puppy costume, which was completely out of character with his temperament. The worst thing was how the mother acted. She whined and begged the child to behave.

"Snookums, be a good widdle boy for mommy-kins. Daddy-waddy wants your picture for his office. You're such a handsome boy." She rubbed her hand over the child's head, causing the cotton hood, complete with cloth ears, to slide. "That's right. Mommy will give you a new toy if you'll sit still for the nice man." She batted her eyes at Michael. "Have you ever seen such a beautiful child?"

Michael summoned his old boardroom demeanor to maintain a professional air, despite having to fight the urge to gag. He thought the boy would be better served by wearing some sort of mask, but kept his opinion to himself. "He is something, all right." He took several more shots, hoping that his lens would stay intact from the view. "All done." The boy grabbed a plastic pumpkin and began to chew on it. As far as Michael was concerned, the prop would be tossed in the trash the moment his client left.

"Mr. Cauble, thank you for working with us on such short notice. My little Andrew is so precious, we wanted a nice picture to commemorate Halloween this year."

Michael handed her his card. He had gotten all of her information down before the shoot. It was a lesson learned a long time ago. Anytime a child was involved in the photograph, filling out the paperwork before getting started made things much easier. "I'll give you a call when the proofs are ready, Mrs. Davis." He did his best to ignore the child racing around the room, barking like a dog.

"Thank you. Come along, precious. It's time for din-din." Mrs. Davis reached for the door. Her son growled and barked and ran into the woman who held the door open for them.

Lex looked down at the child. He had his hands wrapped around her leg and continued to bark. "Have I come at a bad time?"

Mrs. Davis took in Lex's appearance. Her jeans, cowboy boots and a blue and white flannel shirt were well-worn, and the black western hat sat low over her eyes. Everything about her screamed cowhand and Mrs. Davis wanted no part of her. "We were leaving. Let's go, darling." She took her son by the arm and pulled him from the office.

"I thought there was a leash law inside the city limits." Lex removed her hat. "Didn't know you were into pet shots."

"Ha, ha. Very funny." Michael took an antibacterial wipe and proceeded to clean his hands. "Not that I'm not happy to see you, but what brings you into town today?"

She took a seat and stretched her legs out in front of her. "Had a few errands to run and thought I'd drop by and see if you were free for lunch."

"I'd love to. Give me a second to clean up." Michael went into the adjacent bathroom and washed his hands thoroughly. He didn't think he'd ever get the feel of Andrew's slobber from his skin.

The walk to the restaurant was pleasant for both of them. Lex related Lorrie's latest antics. Her daughter had recently discovered the joys of climbing. Unfortunately, her favorite place was the kitchen. The drawers were perfect for pulling out and making a ladder and Lorrie caused Martha to lose her composure when she caught her sitting on the counter.

"I imagine poor Martha almost had a heart attack." Michael held the door open for Lex, ignoring the wry look his action brought. "Where was Amanda during all of this?"

Lex nodded to the hostess, who led them to a table near the window. She took off her hat and placed it in an empty chair. "She was, um, helping me in the hay barn." They didn't get much hay stacked, but both of them returned, hours later, covered with straw.

Michael loved the blush that had worked its way across Lex's face. "I bet I don't want to know what kind of help you're talking about, do I?"

"Ahem." Lex opened her menu. "I think I'll have the chicken fried steak. What about you?"

The rest of the meal was spent sharing stories. Lex filled Michael in on how Amanda's pregnancy was progressing. "I'm not even allowed to mention food before noon. God help me if she smells breakfast on my breath." She took a sip of her iced tea. "Hell, the other day, I had been in the kitchen while Martha cooked. I guess some of the smell clung to my clothes. When I went upstairs, Amanda made me shower and change."

He commiserated, having been through it twice himself. "At least she's talking to you. Elizabeth was so mad at me when she found out she was pregnant with Jeannie, she relegated me to the guest room for nine months. That was a blessing in disguise."

"Yeah." Lex remembered all too well what a monster her mother-in-law was. She used her fork to stack individual kernels of corn around her mashed potatoes. "I wish there was something more I could do for Amanda. I hate seeing her so miserable."

Michael placed his hand on her arm. "She's going to be fine. The morning sickness will leave as quickly as it came, trust me. Now, to change the subject a little, Lorrie's birthday is coming up. Do you have any plans?"

"Nothing definite yet. Although Amanda and I have talked about having a party and inviting all her friends from the daycare."

"That sounds like a lot of work. Why would you want to subject yourselves to that?"

Lex continued to play with her food. The mashed potatoes were now mountains and had a gravy river going through them. "I want Lorrie to have all the opportunities that I didn't. I was so isolated at the ranch and never had a chance to make friends my own age." She looked him in the eyes. "I'll be damned if I let that happen to her. I'll sell the ranch and move into town, if that's what it takes."

The vehemence in her tone surprised Michael. He knew Lex was dedicated to her family, but to hear her discount the one thing that defined her, shocked him to his core. To think of Lex not living on the ranch was incomprehensible. "I don't think you'll have to go to that extreme, Lex. You and Amanda are doing everything possible to give Lorrie everything she needs. And I think living on the ranch is a big part of that."

"Why? Wouldn't she be better off in town, so she could make friends easier?"

"Not necessarily." He wiped his mouth on his napkin. "There are so many ways kids can get into trouble these days."

"Are you talking about drugs?"

He waved her off. "No. Well, that too. But I meant inactivity. They have their video games, movies and generally hundreds of things that cause them to plant their butts on the couch. Kids get bored so easily. Living out on the ranch is a great deterrent to being lazy."

Lex couldn't agree more. She couldn't think of a time, as a kid, that she was ever bored. There was always something to do. "I never thought about it that way." She took out her wallet and placed some cash on the table. "Thanks."

"Anytime. Now," he stood and stretched, "tell me what I can get my granddaughter for her birthday." He followed Lex out of the restaurant, while they discussed the appropriate gifts for a certain three-year old.

"GRAMMA, PLEASE. DO you honestly think we can get her to wear that?" Amanda vetoed the cute yellow dress. She had spent the entire morning shopping with her grandmother while Lorrie was at the daycare. "Every time I try to put her in a dress, she strips it off within five minutes and races around the house in her underwear."

Anna Leigh put the frock on the rack. "That's a shame. She'd look so adorable in ruffles. Although, I shouldn't be too surprised. You were like that at her age." She smiled at the woman who had been assisting them. They had found out, quite accidentally, that she had gone to school with Lex. Her insight into Lex's early years made their shopping experience much more interesting.

The saleswoman held up a pair of denim overalls. "What about this? If she's anything like Lex, I think something along these lines would be more her style."

Amanda wasn't paying attention to the selection, but focused on what the clerk said. "What do you mean by that?"

"Don't get me wrong. I think the world of Lex. But she is a little, shall we say, rough and tumble? She was the biggest tomboy in school. She was never in anything but boots and jeans. And those god-awful tee shirts. She'd always hide under that ugly cowboy hat, too. I'd hazard to guess that her attitude influences your daughter."

"Excuse me?" Amanda brushed off Anna Leigh's hand, which touched her arm in an attempt to calm her. "There's not a damned thing wrong with how Lex dresses." She tossed the clothes she held on a nearby chair. "Let's go, Gramma. There are better places than this to shop."

Anna Leigh cocked an eyebrow at the surprised clerk. "I would advise you to learn a little tact in the future, young woman. Your next customer might not be so forgiving." She hurried to catch up with Amanda, who paced outside the door to the shop.

"I can't believe the nerve of that woman! I ought to go in there and—" Amanda threw her hands up in the air. "Maybe a good whack in the mouth would teach her."

"Dearest, violence never solved anything." Anna Leigh led the furious woman to their car.

"Maybe not, but it would sure make me feel a hell of a lot better." Tossing her purse on the floorboards, Amanda got in on the passenger side and slammed the door. "Obnoxious bitch."

Using a touch more decorum, Anna Leigh slid behind the wheel and started the car. She wasn't used to hearing Amanda use that kind of language, and, for a moment, she was startled into speechlessness. She wasn't sure how to handle her volatile granddaughter.

As the silence lengthened, Amanda realized how she must have sounded. She felt ashamed of her actions, if only because it embarrassed Anna Leigh. "I'm sorry." She cut her eyes over to her grandmother. "I don't know why I went off like that."

Anna Leigh relaxed. She patted Amanda's leg. "I do. It's called hormones. I'm afraid it's only going to get worse, the further along you are."

Great. It was the last thing Amanda wanted to hear. Her short temper had always gotten her into trouble and she certainly didn't need any help in that area. She leaned her head against the seat and closed her eyes. "Poor Lex."

"She'll survive," Anna Leigh assured her. "But I'll make up the guest room, just in case." Her joke had the desired effect as Amanda burst out in laughter. She expected her granddaughter's pregnancy was going to be quite enlightening, for all involved.

Chapter
Twenty-two

IT WAS AFTER dinner the next evening before Lex and Amanda had a chance to talk about Lorrie's birthday. Through mutual agreement, they decided to have a family get-together for her instead of a party with a bunch of children. There would be plenty of opportunities in the ensuing years to forsake their sanity in such a matter.

That accomplished, they were upstairs in her room while Lex attempted to assemble their daughter's first gift. The toddler bed was small, low to the ground and the headboard was a heavy duty plastic, covered with cartoon characters. Since it was to be a surprise, Martha had volunteered to keep Lorrie at her house for the night.

Lex tightened another bolt. "I can't believe she's going to be three already. It doesn't seem possible." The wrench slipped, and she banged her knuckles on the floor. "Ow! Dammit!" She glared at Amanda, who stood nearby with her hand over her mouth to keep from laughing out loud. "Gee, thanks." Lex sucked on the injured joint. "Tell me again why we're doing this?"

"Because you promised she could have her own bed when she turned three. Be thankful she wanted the 'princess' bed, instead of the one that came in about a hundred pieces. You'd probably still be putting it together when she graduates from high school."

"Please, don't mention high school. It's going to be hard enough to let her go to kindergarten." Lex checked the instruction page again. "How the hell do they expect anyone to understand this gibberish? And how many different sizes of damned nuts and bolts does a kid's bed have to have?"

Amanda knelt beside her and turned the paper. "I think it would be easier to read if you had it going the right direction." She handed it to her partner.

"Smart ass." Lex picked up the wrench. She was tempted to throw it across the room, but looked closely at the bolt instead. "Would you mind handing me the box of sockets? I think I'm using the wrong size."

"Sure." Amanda used her foot to scoot the container. "Is there anything, besides handing you tools, you'd like me to do?"

Lex gave her the instruction sheet. "I think I'm on step eight, but I'm not sure. Maybe you can make sense out of this damned thing."

"I'll try." She read the first few steps before checking Lex's progress. "Is that piece upside down?"

"What?" Lex took the paper and looked at it. "Dammit." She'd have to disassemble half her work in order to fix her mistake. She exhaled heavily and started to take it apart.

Two hours and several more scraped knuckles later, the bed stood proudly in place. Beside it was a child-sized dresser, compliments of Jacob, where Lorrie could pick out her own clothes. Her closet was already equipped with short rods, an easy reach for someone of her stature.

Lex put the final tool away. "Next time, if something says, 'some assembly required', shoot me if I even think about buying it."

"Oh, I don't know. You did a great job, honey." Amanda placed her arm around Lex's waist. "I'm looking forward to seeing you put together her first bicycle." She was unable to hold her laughter when her lover groaned. "Maybe a swing set?"

"Uh, no. If we do that, you'll have to get me one of those pretty white jackets that tie in the back. There's no way in hell I'm going through this again." Lex flinched as a sharp elbow jabbed her in the ribs. "At least until next year."

Amanda patted her on the stomach. "Good girl. I knew you'd see it my way." She kissed Lex's jaw. "It's nice and quiet and we have the house to ourselves for the night. Know what I'd like to do?" She punctuated her question by nibbling on her lover's throat.

"Mmm?" Lex tilted her head back and closed her eyes. "I know what I'd like to do." She started walking backward while insistent hands unbuttoned her shirt. "Guess you have the same idea."

"Uh-huh." Amanda steered her across the hall and into the master bedroom. She slid the shirt off Lex's shoulders and quickly relieved her of her bra. Before they reached the bed, she found herself losing her top. Lex's hands covered her exposed breasts and she leaned into the contact.

Lex covered Amanda's lips with her own as they divested each other of their clothes. When the back of her knees hit the bed, she toppled over, bringing Amanda down on top of her. Blanketed by warm skin, Lex moaned. "You feel so good."

"So do you." Taking her time, Amanda kissed her way down her lover's throat, stopping in various places to leave soft bites behind. "I love you." She took a tender spot of flesh into her mouth and sucked gently.

"I love you, too." With pleasure chasing all thoughts from her mind, Lex relaxed and enjoyed Amanda's touch.

TWO DAYS LATER, brightly colored wrapping paper was strewn across the den floor. New toys, momentarily abandoned, surrounded their owner, who was stretched out in the midst of the paper. Lorrie lay on her stomach, sound asleep, still clutching a small baby doll that was already missing its clothes.

Amanda and Lex were snuggled together on the sofa. Once everyone left it had turned into a quiet evening. The birthday party had been a complete success, even if their guests had bent the "one present per couple" rule. Amanda's grandparents each brought a gift, which caused Lex to complain they cheated. When her grandfather and cousin showed up similarly laden, she shook her head and grumbled under her breath that she should have known better. Michael and Lois did the same.

Amanda thought it was all rather funny, especially since she and her partner did the same thing. They got Lorrie her new bed, and, so that she'd have something to "unwrap", Lex had searched the Internet for over a month until she found the perfect rocking horse. The Radio Flyer plastic spring horse came complete with colored rope mane and tail and a leather saddle. Lex made certain the wide base was safe and only had slight difficulty putting it together the previous week. It took all her considerable control not to give it to Lorrie the minute it was finished. Instead, Amanda coerced her into hiding it in the storage room until the day of the party.

Not too far away from the "ossie", was Michael's gift. The sturdy double easel was made of durable plastic. One side was a chalkboard, while the other held a large blank pad of paper. His daughter almost threatened his life when she saw the paint set he bought to go with it, until he volunteered to supervise Lorrie's artistic endeavors. By the end of the evening, both were well-covered in watercolors.

Lois gave Lorrie a painter's smock that had her name embroidered on the front. She admitted it had taken her the better part of a month to complete the project, but everyone was duly impressed with her attention to detail.

Although Jacob had already given a gift of a handmade dresser, he didn't want to show up empty handed. The matching rocking chair was Lorrie's size and she spent over fifteen minutes showing everyone how fast it "rockded".

The baby doll Anna Leigh brought was an instant hit. Lorrie wasted no time in undressing the life-like doll. She was even more thrilled by the extra clothes the doll had, and allowed her grandmother to help her dress the baby. It wasn't long before Lorrie quickly had the doll undressed again.

Travis had to enlist Lex's help in bringing in his gift. The kitchen play set now took up an entire corner of the den. Lorrie had wanted to place it in the real kitchen, but Martha vetoed that suggestion quickly. Ellie contributed a set of play dishes, and spent the better part of an hour having "dinner" with the new little chef.

Martha and Charlie were more subdued in their selection, but their gift was well received by the birthday girl. The set of rhyming books had Lorrie climbing up in everyone's lap, each person getting to read her a story.

Before she and Charlie left, Martha had dimmed the lights, with a promise to return later and help with the cleanup. Lex waved her off. Now, looking around the room, she was having second thoughts. "This place looks like a tornado tore through here."

"True." Amanda snuggled closer and rested her head against Lex's shoulder. "Once we get the birthday girl to bed, it won't take us any time at all to get it cleared away."

Lex tightened her hold on Amanda. "If I knew it would still be here in the morning, I'd say leave it. But knowing Martha, she'd get here bright and early and take care of everything. It's bad enough I can't get her to stop picking up after me."

"Well, honey, you are a full-time job." Amanda gestured to the sleeping child. "And she's growing up to be just like you."

"You say that like it's a bad thing."

"Nah. But it does keep both Martha and me busy." Amanda squirmed when Lex unbuttoned her blouse and edged her hand beneath her bra. "Your fingers are cold." She jerked slightly. "Ow."

Lex quickly removed her hand. "What's the matter? Did I hurt you?"

Amanda caught Lex's hand and held it close to her body. "It's nothing serious. I'm a little tender there."

"Oh." At first she was hesitant to go any further. The last thing Lex wanted to do was cause Amanda any discomfort, but when Amanda placed her hand inside her shirt, Lex carefully placed her fingers near the top of her bra. "How's this?"

"Not good enough." Once she was certain Lorrie was still sleeping soundly, Amanda removed her shirt completely and took off her bra. She held her lover's hands and used them to cup her breasts, enjoying the touch. "That's much better." She was about to suggest something even more enjoyable when it hit. "Damn." Amanda slipped the shirt on, but left it unbuttoned. This constant rushing to the bathroom was already getting on her nerves, and it was only the beginning.

"Did I—"

Amanda quickly stood. "Sorry. I've got to," she tipped her head to the door. "Be back in a minute."

Lex watched her leave. "That's definitely a mood killer." She got up also and decided she might as well get Lorrie ready for bed. She knelt next to the dozing child and scooped her up into her arms. The little girl was so sound asleep she stayed completely limp. It was very easy for Lex to carry her out of the den and up the stairs to her room.

Lorrie was already undressed and tucked into bed when Amanda came into her bedroom. Lex was nowhere to be found. Amanda came in and kissed Lorrie goodnight and went in search of her missing mate. She found her where she had left her – in the den. The discarded wrapping paper and empty boxes had been wadded up and piled in trash bags. Lex was wiping down the tabletops with a dishtowel when Amanda came into the room. "Someone's been busy."

Lex raised her head at the sound of Amanda's voice. "Yep." She took in her wife's attire. Amanda had taken the time to get ready for bed and the shimmering navy blue satin nightgown hugged her curves in all the right places. "You look beautiful."

"Thank you." Brushing her hand across the material, Amanda gave Lex a sexy smile. "I'm hoping not to be wearing it for very long." She turned and left, knowing she'd be followed.

"Good guess." Lex crossed the room after her. She decided her "mood" hadn't been killed in the least. In fact, things were progressing quite nicely. She turned out the light in the den and hurried after Amanda.

STEAM ESCAPED FROM the bathroom as Lex stepped out. Her wet hair was slicked back and dripped on the towel that hung around her neck. She was barefoot, and her jeans adhered to her damp skin. She was completely unaware of her appreciative audience, until a wolf whistle caught her attention.

Amanda was in bed, lying on her side so she could watch her partner get ready for the day. She crooked a finger in Lex's direction. "Come here." They had the morning to themselves, since Martha had taken Lorrie into town to visit Charlie at work. He loved showing his granddaughter off to the rest of the department and they all appreciated a chance to spoil the precocious little girl.

Never one to turn down an invitation, Lex walked over to the bed and sat. She leaned over to get a kiss, when Amanda's hand blocked her. "What?"

The nausea came without warning. "No. The smell. I can't—" Amanda quickly climbed out of the bed and raced for the bathroom.

Concerned, Lex followed. The sight of her wife kneeling in front of the toilet and retching was like a cold slap in the face. Uncertain what to do, she dampened a washcloth and moved Amanda's hair away from her face. "I'm sorry, sweetheart." She placed the cloth across the back of Amanda's neck, doing her best to keep from joining her.

After what seemed like hours to Amanda, she was able to scoot away from her new morning spot. She propped herself up against the wall listlessly while Lex fussed over her. "Honey, please. I'm okay." She took the damp cloth from Lex's hands. "Honestly."

"I'm so sorry. What made you feel bad? I'll fix it, whatever it is." Lex backed away, afraid of causing another bout of sickness. She didn't even realize she was standing in the bathroom topless.

Amanda closed her eyes. It was going to be a very long pregnancy if Lex panicked every time she got nauseous. "It's nothing you did. The weirdest things can trigger it."

"Is it my soap, or my shampoo? I can change," Lex continued to babble. She felt a chill and crossed her arms over her body. "I know that sometimes I come in from the barn and I have to shower. Between the usual horse smell and then when I clean out the stalls, I—" she stopped when she saw Amanda cover her mouth and pale. "Oh. Um, sorry."

"Why don't you finish getting dressed? I'll be out in a few minutes."

Lex nodded almost frantically. "Sure." She backed out of the bathroom. "Holler if you need anything. I'll be right outside the door."

After she left, Amanda took a deep breath and released it slowly. The sick feeling had subsided for the moment, but she was leery of moving too quickly. She slowly got to her feet and washed her face in the sink. Eyeing herself in the mirror, Amanda noticed the redness in her eyes, and her pale skin. "I thought you were supposed to be beautiful when you're pregnant. Not look like death warmed over."

"You are beautiful, love." Lex stood at the door, afraid her presence would set Amanda off again. "And you get more beautiful every day."

"I certainly don't feel like it." Amanda was pleased to see her partner now wearing a denim shirt. A cold front had moved through during the night, and she didn't want her to become chilled and catch cold. She took several steps toward Lex until she was close enough to touch her and held out her hands. "Come here."

Lex worried that being near her would make Amanda ill again. "Are you sure?" At her lover's nod, she moved forward and pulled Amanda into her arms.

There was no better feeling in the world. Amanda took a cautious breath, hoping against hope that whatever caused her to be sick in the first place was gone. Another, deeper breath brought no ill effects, for which she was eternally grateful. She buried her nose against Lex's throat, inhaling deeply. "Perfect."

"Thank god." Lex helped her to the bedroom. After Amanda crawled into bed, she started to step away when a hand grabbed her shirt.

"Come snuggle for a while?" Amanda patted the spot beside her. "And lose the clothes."

"Yes, ma'am." Lex broke a speed record for getting undressed, and quickly slipped beneath the covers. She'd call Roy later to have someone else take care of the horses. She had much more important things to do. Snuggling being on the top of the list.

Chapter
Twenty-Three

HALLOWEEN. LEX ALWAYS hated this time of year. The streets of Somerville were overly crowded with people gathering decorations for a holiday she thought frivolous. Pumpkins were used at almost every turn by shop owners, and Lex thought it was ridiculous that Amanda ask her to pick up some. "One of these days, I'm going to tell her no." Lex realized the folly of her thoughts. "Right. Tell Amanda 'no'. That's not going to happen."

She was on her way to Sunflower Realty. They had mutually decided that it would be all right for Amanda to go to work part time. Amanda was getting restless at the house and so was Lorrie. Martha was the one who suggested they let Lorrie go to daycare half a day, which would allow Amanda to go to the office. It worked out well for all concerned, except Lex. She missed her playmates.

She adjusted the bags she held in her hands and struggled to get inside the office without dumping her bounty. Several women called out to Lex when she came in. Wanda held the manager's door open for her. "I'm glad you're here. She's been asking us every few minutes if any of us had heard from you." Wanda leaned in to whisper conspiratorially, "She's been driving us all nuts."

"Sorry about that. I had to scrounge everywhere for these damned pumpkins." Lex stepped into the office. The woman who sat behind the desk was concentrating on an open binder and talking on the phone.

Amanda raised her head after she heard the rustling of bags. "There you are. What took you so long? Did you get them? How many did you get? How big are they?"

"Hold your horses. One question at a time." Lex placed the bags in the middle of the desk. "Your pumpkins, ma'am." She stood by in amusement while Amanda took them out of the sacks and sorted them.

"These are great. Did you find a big one to carve?"

"Huh?" Lex thought the one on the far left was more than adequate. It was six inches in diameter. "What about that one?"

The pumpkin was a nice shape and a perfect shade of orange.

Amanda hefted it in one hand. "It's perfect for Lorrie to take to school. They're going to decorate their own jack-o-lanterns."

"You've got to be kidding me. A roomful of three-year-olds carrying around carving tools? Have they lost their mind?"

Amanda placed the pumpkin on the desk. Sometimes Lex could be so literal. "I don't think their insurance could handle that, honey. No, they use markers and draw on them. It's still messy, but much safer."

Lex dropped into one of the visitor's chairs. "That's a relief." She stretched her legs out and crossed them at the ankles. Her hands were loosely clasped together on her stomach. "Speaking of Halloween, has Lorrie made up her mind what she wants to dress up as?"

"We've narrowed it down to three things: a princess, a ballerina, or a cow."

"A ballerina? Where did that come from?"

Why wasn't she surprised? It didn't seem to faze her partner that their daughter was considering dressing up like a farm animal. Amanda wondered what a young Lex would have wanted to go as. "It's not my fault your daughter has a cow fetish."

"Hey, wait a minute. Now she's my daughter? And it's not a fetish. More like a..." Lex had to think about it. "A deep appreciation. Yeah." She looked extremely pleased with herself.

"Appreciation? Lex, her first word was 'moo'. And you're the one who got her so enamored of our bovine friends."

Lex studied her boots. She did have a point. But it was so much fun to tweak Amanda. It couldn't hurt to goad her a little more, could it? "Do you think we could find her a costume with little ears and maybe a tail?"

"Oh, no. My daughter isn't going out dressed like Elsie the Cow." She couldn't believe this. Had Lex completely lost her mind? "What else? Udders?"

"Now she's yours? Make up your mind, sweetheart." Lex appeared to think. "Hmm. You know, little udders would be cute. She could carry a milk bucket instead of a trick-or-treat bag."

Amanda had heard enough. "I don't think so." She walked around the desk and sat on Lex's lap, facing her. "Are you trying to say you want Lorrie to go out looking like a farm animal?"

Lex pursed her lips to keep from laughing in Amanda's face. "She won't have hooves, but some shiny black shoes and black mittens would work."

Amanda playfully grabbed her shirt front and tugged her close. "There's no way in hell that'll ever happen. Our little girl will be dressed in something more traditional. I think she'd look cute as a ballerina or a princess. And you'll be the one to help her pick it out."

A slow smile formed on Lex's face. "Moo." She burst into laughter when Amanda released her grip and goosed her instead. "Wait, wait."

Her lover hit a ticklish spot below her ribs and Lex jerked in response. She had to grab Amanda around the waist to keep her from falling.

"Oops." Amanda decided Lex needed to be rewarded, so she gave her a quick peck on the lips.

"Is that the best you can do?"

It sounded like a challenge. And Amanda never backed down from one of those. She raised her arms and locked her hands together behind Lex's neck. Her lips touched Lex's again, this time prolonging the contact.

"Amanda, I've got those... oh." Wanda stood at the door, her face flushed with embarrassment. "Don't you two ever get enough?"

Lex broke the kiss and turned to Wanda. "Jealous?"

"Heck, yeah. Dirk's idea of romance is to only watch one football game on Sunday so we can eat dinner together." She rested against the edge of Amanda's desk. "And that's the dinner that I cook." She quirked an eyebrow at her boss. "Would you like to rent her out?"

Amanda reluctantly scooted off her lover's lap. "How much are you offering?"

"Hey!" Lex sat taller in her chair. "Don't I have some say in this?"

"Nope." Amanda decided that paybacks were sweet. Lex should have never teased her about Lorrie's Halloween outfit.

"Uh-uh." Wanda handed a file to Amanda. "Maybe we should make it an even trade. Dirk's housebroken. Does she snore?"

Lex couldn't believe what she was hearing. They were bartering back and forth about her. "Now wait a damned minute—"

Both Wanda and Amanda burst into laughter. Amanda was the first to recover. "Don't worry. I would never give you up."

"That's more like it." Lex resumed her earlier position with her legs stretched out in front of her.

"I don't blame you. It takes a while to get them trained." Wanda lightly popped Lex on the head. "Don't forget to bring Lorrie over on Halloween. Dirk's looking forward to seeing her all decked out. We've decided to let Ally go as a witch. She fell in love with the makeup we saw at the store." Allison was their daughter, who was only a few days older than Lorrie and in her class at day care. The two girls got along well. Sometimes too well. They were constantly getting each other into trouble. Actually, Lorrie instigated and Ally followed. Wanda feared for the day the two started school.

Amanda dropped the file onto her desk. "Don't worry, we'll be there." She waited until Wanda closed the door behind her before she leaned against her desk and crossed her arms over her chest. "Now, where were we?"

Lex patted her lap. "Here?"

"No, before that. I believe we were deciding between a princess and a ballerina."

Neither choice appealed to Lex. "How about after we pick her up at school, we take her shopping? We can decide then." Maybe if she went with them they wouldn't get too carried away. She dreaded all the frills and such that either costume would entail.

"All right." Amanda pointed her finger at Lex. "But no whining." Before Lex opened her mouth, she added, "and no animals, either."

Lex personally thought Lorrie would look cute as a little heifer, or puppy. Her big expressive eyes would be perfect. She'd have to see what she could talk their child into. "Whatever you say, sweetheart."

THE DISCOUNT STORE had not been ready for Lex and Lorrie shopping together. Amanda seriously considered killing her partner after Lex tried to get Lorrie to pick out a ninja costume. It was hard to say no when both of them looked at her with the same hang dog expression. "For the last time, no. Lorrie, you don't even know what a ninja is." She got extremely nervous when Lex squatted and whispered something into the child's ear. "Lex—"

Lex hung up the black costume and took another down from a hook. "Okay, then how about this?"

A brightly colored vest, fluffy shirt, brown pants and...a sword? "Oh, no way. We're not giving her a weapon."

"But it's plastic." Lex showed the outfit to Lorrie. "What do you think, lil' bit?"

Lorrie eyed the costume dubiously. She zeroed in on the attached saber. "Yay!"

Amanda closed her eyes and raised her face upward. "Give me strength." She glared at Lex, who did her best to appear innocent. "No."

"But—"

"No." Before Lex could utter another word, Amanda put one hand on her hip and held her hand up. "Forget it. I know you're only doing this to get me for this morning." She recognized the embarrassed look on Lex's face that meant she knew she was caught. "Go to the front of the store and sit in the coffee shop. We'll come and get you when we're through."

"But—"

"Go." Amanda hated to be the bad guy, but she was tired of shopping. Her feet hurt, her back ached and she had developed the headache from hell. Banning Lex was the only way she'd ever get done. "All right, Lorrie. Let's look around and see what we can find."

HALLOWEEN EVENING HAD arrived and Lex was anxious to see her daughter's costume. Amanda refused to let her know what it was, and even Lorrie had been able to keep it a secret. So here she was, sitting in the living room and waiting impatiently for them to come downstairs. They had quite a few houses lined up. Both of their families, the women from Sunflower Realty and many of the people they knew from the historical society and women's auxiliary had extended invitations. Lex was afraid they wouldn't get home until midnight if they went to every house.

Amanda stood in the doorway. "Close your eyes."

"What?"

"Close your eyes. Lorrie wants to make an entrance. On second thought, cover them up." Amanda mimed putting her hands over her eyes. "Come on, hurry up."

"Good grief." Even though she thought it was unnecessary, Lex did as she was told. She heard heavy footsteps come in and stop right in front of her. It was hard to keep from peeking. Lex could hear Amanda speaking to Lorrie quietly, although she couldn't make out her words. She heard Lorrie giggle, which made her even more curious. "Well?"

"Almost," Amanda promised.

More giggles and what sounded like a small foot stomp. "Now?"

"Otay. Momma, look."

Lex removed her hands. She couldn't believe her eyes. Their daughter stood proudly next to Amanda, who looked extremely smug. "Whoa. And who are you supposed to be?"

Lorrie slapped her own legs in frustration. "You, Momma."

It didn't take a genius to figure out Lorrie's "costume". She wore new jeans, black cowboy boots, a matching belt, and a light blue shirt. On top of her head sat a crisp, new, black cowboy hat and to set the outfit off, a lightweight brown duster. Lex lost her voice for a long moment. She was in total shock. "You look great, kiddo. Where did the coat come from? I know they don't make them that small."

"Martha whipped it up. It's more for show than protection from the cold, but she couldn't resist." Amanda plopped down on Lex's lap and put one arm around her neck. "Cute, isn't she?"

"And then some. Come here, lil' bit." Lex grunted when Lorrie climbed onto Amanda. "I guess I'm furniture now."

Lorrie took off her hat and put it on her momma's head. "Yep. We go pway?"

Lex placed the hat on her daughter's head. At least now she understood why Amanda was so adamant she wear new jeans and her pale blue shirt. "This was a great surprise, sweetheart." She noticed her wife wasn't wearing anything special. "Where's your costume?"

"I'm wearing it."

"And what are you supposed to be? A mom?" Lex tugged at the soft cotton leggings, topped off by one of her old sweatshirts.

"Nope. A pregnant mom." No matter how many times she said it, the word still felt surreal to her. She gave her thanks every day for the gift and couldn't wait to bring their new child into the world. Amanda jumped when she felt a pinch to her bottom. "Watch it."

"Actually, that's one of my favorite pastimes, watching it." Lex ran her hand over Amanda's rear and squeezed it. "And I'd love to show you how much, but I think we promised a certain little girl she could go harass the town for goodies."

Lorrie bounced on Amanda's lap. "Yay! We go now." She slid off and stood in the middle of the living room floor. When they didn't move, she tried again. "Go." Her lower lip stuck out when her moms ignored her and started kissing each other, instead. "Go, pease?" She considered stomping her new boots on the floor, but knew it wouldn't do any good. "Mommy? Momma?"

Amanda turned and looked at mini-Lex. "All right, honey. We'll go." She stood and helped Lex off the couch. She brushed her fingertip across her partner's lips. "And we'll finish this conversation later."

"I'm looking forward to it." Lex followed them out of the room, wondering how long a three-year-old hopped up on candy would stay awake. Longer than her, she imagined. It was going to be a long night.

Chapter
Twenty-four

THINGS WERE GOING smoothly. Amanda was relieved that her morning sickness had disappeared. Now in her fourth month, she was feeling much better. Lex also settled down into a routine. On the weekend she would take Lorrie for the morning and the two of them would spend several hours together. It gave Amanda much-needed quiet time. They would be gone until lunch, then Lorrie would take a nap with Amanda while Lex spent the rest of the day with the hired hands.

Amanda closed the bookkeeping program on the computer screen. When their friend Janna moved to Wisconsin to take care of her mother, Amanda took over the books for the ranch. Thanks to the program the accountant had made for them, it was a quick and easy job. It only took her an hour a day, then she was free to surf the Web.

One quick click and she was on the Internet. Amanda opened the folder she had her favorite pages saved in. Another click and she was on her most-visited site. "This is so cool." The page covered the stages of pregnancy and how the fetus developed.

She read for well over an hour. When she found a page that was particularly fascinating, she decided to print it and share with Lex. She wasn't the only one interested in the topic. Sometimes late at night, Amanda would wake, only to find Lex downstairs on the computer.

The printer spit out three pages and stopped. It was out of paper, so Amanda opened the desk drawer to get more. On top of the package was a thick envelope addressed to Charlie from a law enforcement academy in Houston. "What is this doing here?" She was torn between satisfying her curiosity and leaving the packet alone.

Amanda used unbelievable restraint and bypassed the envelope for the printer paper. She finished printing her pages and closed the session. But the bottom desk drawer haunted her. There was no reason Lex should have something of Charlie's in her office. "Maybe it got mixed in with her mail and she forgot to give it to him." She opened the drawer and stared at the envelope. Her traitorous hands took the packet out of the drawer and placed it on top of the desk. One end was sliced open neatly. Someone had obviously already seen inside. Was it Lex, or Charlie?

Her curiosity got the better of her. Amanda slipped the contents out carefully. The top sheet was a form letter addressed to Charlie at the Sheriff's Department. Amanda's confusion grew when she read the letter. It thanked him for his inquiry, and told of the next testing date for the Academy. "What the hell?" She continued to read then scanned the following pages. There was an application, a long form to fill out for a background check and a map to the testing facility in Houston. "This isn't for Charlie. He must have gotten it for Lex."

The thought of Lex wanting to do something so life altering, without discussing it with her, hurt Amanda's feelings. She had no idea Lex wanted to do such a thing. She had never mentioned it. "Why would she keep something like this from me?"

"What's up?" Lex stood in the doorway with Lorrie sitting on her shoulders.

"Hi, Mommy. We rode 'ossie's.'" Lorrie bounced as she talked. "We go fast."

Amanda gathered the papers and placed them in the envelope. "You did?"

"Yep." Lorrie swatted Lex on the top of her head. "Down, pease."

They had been working hard on her manners. She caught on quickly, although there were still times she stubbornly refused. Amanda called them her "momma" moments. Lex didn't find it as amusing.

Lex carefully lifted Lorrie over her head and stood her on the floor. "There you go." She sat on the edge of the desk. "What do you have there?"

"That's what I'd like to know." Amanda turned the packet around so Lex could see it more clearly. "I was looking for printer paper and accidentally ran across this." While Lex picked it up, Amanda helped Lorrie up into her lap. She automatically put a piece of paper and a pencil on the desk. Lorrie began to draw, unaware of the drama unfolding.

"I'd forgotten all about this." Lex tossed the envelope in the box reserved for incoming mail.

Amanda's hurt expression conveyed more than words. She took the papers and placed them in the desk drawer. "When were you going to tell me about it? After you filled it out and mailed it in?"

"No, of course not. It was something I talked about with Charlie months ago. He gave it to me right after I got out of the hospital and I put it away. I wasn't hiding it from you." Lex walked around the desk and knelt next to Amanda's chair. She put her hand on her lover's leg. "I would never consider something like that without talking to you." She felt a wave of relief pour over her when Amanda took her hand in her own. "Before you got pregnant, I guess I was going through some sort of mid-life crisis or something. I honestly thought I couldn't be happy ranching anymore."

Amanda remembered all too well how Lex acted then. She only went through the motions of her daily life and nothing seemed to interest her. Amanda chalked it up to being overworked. The thought of Lex going through that all alone tore at her heart. "Why didn't you talk to me? I would have done anything in the world to help."

Lex lowered her gaze and concentrated on their linked hands. "There wasn't anything you could have done, sweetheart. For the longest time, I had no idea what was wrong. Then when I did know, I was at a loss as to what to do." She raised her head. "And leaving the ranch wasn't an option."

"Why not?"

"I know how much you love it here. I could never take you from all this. I even thought for a while that Lorrie would be better off living in town." Her heart skipped a beat when Amanda took her hand away.

"That would be a mistake. This ranch is her home." Amanda skimmed her fingers through Lex's hair. "And ours. Don't get me wrong. I'll follow you wherever you want to go. But don't think for a minute we're not happy living here."

The touch was soothing and Lex began to relax. Her eyes closed. "I realize that now."

"Good." Amanda pulled on her hair hard enough to get her attention. "Don't you ever suffer through anything like that alone, got me?"

Lex opened her eyes and was relieved to see understanding and love looking at her. "Yes, ma'am."

Amanda stood, bringing Lorrie up with her. "It's time for lunch, isn't it?"

"Yep." Lorrie dropped her pencil on the desk. She slid out of Amanda's arms and took off for the kitchen.

Neither of them remembered moving, but soon Lex and Amanda were in each other's arms. Their lips met and they spent a quiet moment reconnecting. They would talk about the packet later.

LATER THAT SAME evening, the house was quiet and Lorrie was tucked into bed, sound asleep. Amanda and Lex were snuggled together in bed. Amanda sat against the headboard, with her partner stretched across the bed and her head pillowed in her lap. They hadn't said much to each other, both lost in their own thoughts.

Amanda trailed her fingers through Lex's hair. "What made you think about joining the sheriff's department? Is it what you always wanted to do?"

"I don't know. I guess when we were out there, looking for those

escaped prisoners. It seemed like something different from ranching."
Lex closed her eyes and enjoyed the gentle touch. "I was so burned
out. This is all I've ever done and it started getting to me." She stayed
silent for so long, Amanda thought she had fallen asleep. "You know,
Charlie has been around here for as long as I can remember. He's
always been someone I looked up to. When Dad was off at some
rodeo, he'd always come out and take me for rides in his squad car. I'd
even get to run the siren, if we were here on the ranch." The memory
was one of the few happy ones she had growing up. She hadn't exactly
been unhappy on the ranch. But because of the added responsibility of
having to handle things when her father was away, she grew up more
quickly than other kids her age. Lex had no idea how miserable her
existence was until she pulled a complete stranger out of a flooded
creek, a few years earlier. "Charlie was more of a father to me than my
own. I've always looked up to him."

"Do you think you'd be happy as a deputy?" Amanda was fearful
of the answer. She realized ranching was a hard life. But the thought
of Lex purposely doing something so dangerous terrified her. Seeing
her unhappy was worse. "I think if it's something you want to do, you
should."

Lex raised her head. "You do?"

It was one of the hardest things she'd ever said. "Yes." Amanda
swallowed her fear. "I want you to be happy, honey. And if working
with Charlie will do that, I'm all for it."

"Thank you." Lex put her head down but kept her eyes on
Amanda. "But I decided it wasn't for me."

"Why?"

She wasn't certain she could find the right words, but Lex felt
Amanda deserved to know. "When I fell into that sinkhole, a lot of
things went through my mind. My family, my friends, the ranch. But
the most important thing I couldn't stop thinking of was you. And if
something happened to me, how it would affect you." She used her
thumb to brush away a tear that fell from Amanda's eye. "You and
Lorrie mean everything to me. I can't knowingly do something that
would put my life in jeopardy and leave you behind." She sat up and
rested on one hand so they were eye to eye. "We're a family." Lex put
her other hand on Amanda's stomach. "And growing. I promise I'll be
here until we're both old and gray."

Amanda couldn't say anything. She pulled Lex to her and began
to cry. She knew in her heart that everything would be all right. Lex
promised, and she never went back on her word.

THE HORSE MOVED along at an easy gait, its head bobbing with
each step. A gentle breeze blew across Lex's neck, drying the
perspiration that gathered around her tied-back hair. To her, the quiet

surrounding them was relaxing, and she could make out several different birds by their song.

"Momma, what's dat?" Lorrie, seated in front of her, pointed to the left.

At least it had been quiet. Lex stopped Mine and squinted in the same direction to see what her daughter was talking about. A sudden movement caught her eye. "That's a rabbit."

Lorrie twisted around and stared at her mother. "Ribbit?"

"No, rabbit. Raa-bit."

"Rabbit. Can it pway?"

Lex had to think about the best way to answer her question. "No, lil' bit. It's a wild animal and we can't play with those. He might hurt you."

"Why?"

Lex had to admit it was a good question. She remembered when she asked her father a question and he would brush her off with, "because I said so". She vowed if she ever had children, she would give them the best answer possible. But sometimes, especially lately, Lorrie tended to question everything. The answers were becoming harder to come by. "Uh, well." Lex lowered her voice, so as not to startle the rabbit. "Wild animals aren't used to us, and when they get scared, they only want to get away. Even if they don't mean to they will scratch and bite to be left alone. If we try to catch them we could hurt them. You wouldn't want to hurt it, would you?"

Lorrie scrunched up her face while she thought. "No." She waved as the rabbit disappeared into the brush. "Bye, rabbit. Momma?"

"Hmm?"

"Is puppies wild?"

Lex couldn't help but chuckle. "Not all of them. Why?"

"Derek has puppies. His mommy says no pway. Why?" Derek was a friend of hers from daycare. He constantly bragged about the litter and he had even brought pictures to show everyone. Although it had been over a month ago, Lorrie hadn't stopped talking about it.

Oh, boy. Lex wished Amanda was with them. She knew what the next question would be. "They're probably too little to play with. Do you remember the baby horse you saw?" Earlier in the week, one of the mares on the ranch gave birth, and Lorrie had wanted to play with the foal. She had gotten upset when Lex told her it was too young to play.

"Yep."

"Puppies are like that, too. You have to wait until they're old enough before you can play with them."

"Otay." Lorrie was quiet for the next five minutes, until something else came to her. "Momma?"

Lex sighed. "Yes?"

"When can puppies pway?"

There it was. Lex knew that no matter how she answered, the next question could get her into trouble. "You have to wait until their eyes are open and they can get around real well."

"Oh. Otay." She was appeased, for the moment anyway. They had ridden along for another minute or so when something else popped into her head. "Momma?"

Lex was beginning to wish they had found something else to do, other than riding. "Yes?"

"Can I gets a puppy?"

Great. Now what should she say? Lex could only hope Amanda wouldn't kill her for the answer. "I don't know, Lorrie. We'll have to see what your mommy says about it."

"Otay." Lorrie bounced in the saddle. "Momma?"

Her patience was wearing thin, but Lex tried to keep it out of her voice. "Yes?"

"We go fast?" Lorrie had obviously become bored. "Mine wanna goes fast." She rocked forward. "Pease?"

How could she resist such a plea? Lex tightened her hold on Lorrie and urged the horse into a canter. "Hang on, kiddo." They headed to the house, while Lex silently prayed that Amanda was in a good mood.

"DON'T YOU DARE lay this on me now!"

Even though she was in the kitchen, Martha cringed as she heard Amanda's voice rise in the den. "I'm sure glad it's not me in there." She started to hum in order to drown out the argument.

In the living room, Jeannie was getting dizzy watching her sister pace back and forth. "I don't see why it's such a big deal. I thought you'd be glad."

Amanda glared at her. "Right. I've been busting my ass, trying to get everything organized for your wedding, and then you dump this on me?"

"But Mandy, I don't want to be as big as a house on my wedding day. Surely you of all people can understand that." Jeannie had decided to wait until after her baby was born to get married, much to her sister's displeasure.

"What's that supposed to mean?" Amanda put her hands on her hips. "Are you saying I'm fat?" She was extremely self-conscious of her appearance. Even though she only had a slight "baby pooch", she could already tell that her clothes were fitting differently. She spent too much time in the mornings trying to find pants that weren't too tight. Her clueless partner was no help. Lex had rubbed her stomach and mentioned how cute she was, which caused Amanda to burst into tears and lock herself in the bathroom for over an hour.

Jeannie rolled her eyes. "Of course not." She touched her own stomach. "I'm the one who looks like she's going to have twins."

"Mommy!" Lorrie raced into the room and stopped suddenly when she saw Jeannie on the sofa.

Lex followed, her boots thudding as she chased after her daughter. "Lorrie, wait. You can't—" She practically skidded to a stop. "Hi, Jeannie."

"Hey there yourself, Slim." Jeannie watched the little girl, who hid behind Lex's legs. "She doesn't like me, does she?"

Amanda held out her arms and Lorrie jumped into them. "How's my girl?" She kissed Lorrie's head. "It's only because she doesn't know you very well." Amanda sat on the other end of the couch and Lorrie cuddled closer. When Lex sat on the arm of the sofa, Amanda leaned against her. "Did you two have a good ride?"

"Uh, yeah. About that," Lex ran her fingers through Lorrie's hair. "I think I may have gotten in a little over my head."

No longer upset at her daughter's snub, Jeannie found Lex's words humorous. "What else is new?"

Amanda ignored her sister. "Lorrie, did you and momma have fun?"

"Yep." Lorrie cut her eyes at Jeannie and stuck her thumb in her mouth. The woman scared her. When Jeannie scooted closer, she tucked her face into Amanda's shoulder.

The child's gesture hurt Jeannie's feelings more than she cared to admit. She purposely softened her voice. "Hi there, cutie. Do you remember me?"

Lorrie burrowed deeper and her voice was muffled. "Yep."

"I'm not that scary, am I?" Jeannie lightly touched Lorrie's back. "After all, I am your mo—I mean, aunt." Now more than ever, she regretted her absence in the child's life. It also made her realize how smart she was, allowing Amanda and Lex to adopt Lorrie. She was obviously very well loved.

Lex could see the sadness cross Jeannie's face. "Any word on Rodney's job search?"

"Actually, he was offered a chance to join another doctor's practice. Now all we'll have to do is find a place to live."

"Which doctor?"

"Dr. Anderson. He told Roddy his other partner decided to move to Houston."

Lorrie decided the strange lady meant no harm. She turned and curiously stared at her. "Hi."

Jeannie's face glowed. "Hi, sweetie."

Now that Lorrie had relaxed, Amanda wanted to hear more from Lex. "You were trying to say something, earlier?"

"It's not that important. We can talk about it later." Lex hoped Lorrie had forgotten about their previous conversation. Unfortunately, the child had a one-track mind.

"Mommy?"

Amanda looked into Lorrie's eyes. "What is it, honey?"

"Can I gets a puppy?"

Lex lowered her head. She knew what was coming next. The tone in Amanda's voice promised Lex a slow and painful death.

"Lex, did you and Lorrie talk about a puppy today?"

"Not exactly. Well, sort of." Lex lifted her face and couldn't decipher her partner's tone. "I mean, we were riding along, and she saw a rabbit. And then—" Her mouth was covered by Amanda's hand.

"Mommy, we sawed a rabbit." Lorrie saw what Amanda did to Lex and thought it was fun. "Can I help?"

Amanda quickly jerked her hand away and wiped it on Lex's shirt. She should have remembered how Lex would lick her palm to get it off her mouth. "Gross."

Lex smirked. "I thought you liked it when I—" She cut her sentence off when Amanda waggled a finger at her.

"Very funny. Now, explain to me why Lorrie wants a puppy."

"You remember, she's been asking for a while. Ever since she saw those pictures at daycare." She tried to explain the scenario to Jeannie, who appeared confused. "A friend of hers at the church daycare has new puppies, and he brought pictures to show everyone. Now, all we hear about is how much Lorrie would like one, too."

Lorrie followed the conversation. "Yay! Puppy!"

"Not yet. Why don't you ride your pony for a while?" Amanda allowed her to get down. Lorrie went to her rocking horse and climbed aboard. Now that the little girl had been sidetracked, she went to Lex. "You were saying?"

Lex rubbed the back of her neck. "Um, well. Like I said, she saw the rabbit and wanted to play with it. I explained how she should leave wild animals alone, and then she changed directions and asked if puppies were wild, too."

Jeannie cracked up. "I would have loved to hear your answer to that one."

"Hey, I did all right." Lex felt a finger tapping her leg. "Oh, right. I told her puppies weren't wild, but couldn't play until they were old enough. Then the little interrogator asked if she could have a puppy. I told her we'd have to ask you, first."

"Gee, thanks." Amanda glanced at Lorrie, who was still riding in a private adventure. "What do you think?"

"I don't know. I was going to ask you."

Amanda shook her head. "You're worse than she is." She turned to Jeannie. "I finally have the two of them housebroken. What's your opinion?"

"Don't drag me into this."

"How about," Lex lowered her voice, "we get her a young dog, not a puppy? She'd still have a dog to play with, but it wouldn't be as hard to train."

It sounded good to Amanda. "Okay. But we leave her at home with Martha while we're looking. I don't need to have both of you giving me that pouty face."

"I don't know what you're talking about." Lex gave her the exact look.

Amanda did her best to ignore Lex. It was going to be a long week.

"LORRIE, COME BACK here," Lex grumbled, chasing into the kitchen after her wet and naked daughter. A small, excited terrier yipped happily at her heels. Its white, smooth coat was liberally covered with black spots and its head was black, with brown eyebrows and cheeks. The high-strung dog loved chasing games, especially ones as impromptu as this.

Less than a week after they decided to find a pet for their daughter, a woman at the realty office approached Amanda. Peggy Kincaid was recently divorced and she was moving into a one-bedroom apartment. She had raised her rat terrier, Freckles, from a pup. The idea of cooping the frisky animal into such a tiny space wasn't fair and she would rather give Freckles to a good home than subject her to apartment life. As she was only three years old, the sweet dog immediately hit it off with Lorrie. They became friends and were now inseparable.

Martha spun to one side, almost dumping the bowl of liquid gelatin she carried. "Lexie, watch out." She raised the bowl higher to keep from dumping it on the giggling child.

"Mada, catch me," Lorrie squealed, grabbing Martha's apron.

Lex dropped to her knees and wrapped a fluffy towel around Lorrie. "Gotcha."

"Nooo!" Lorrie jerked, the movement enough to loosen Martha's tenuous grip on the bowl.

The cold mixture hit Lex perfectly on the head, falling down the collar of her shirt. "Dammit." She held Lorrie away from her body to keep her from getting any of the green mess on her.

Lorrie took the opportunity to twist out of the towel. She laughed maniacally and took off. Freckles barked and dutifully followed.

Laughter could be heard in the living room, where Lorrie had obviously headed. Martha placed the empty bowl on the counter and helped Lex to her feet. "You should keep the bathroom door locked when you bathe her."

"I know." Lex used the towel to wipe her face. "It gets so damned steamy in there, though. I always feel like I need a bath after hers."

"That's certainly true this time." Martha used a dishcloth to dab at the green streaks of liquid dripping from Lex's hair. "I guess we won't be needing extra Jello tonight, after all. Why don't you go on upstairs and —"

"Martha, have you seen —" Amanda paused in the doorway, holding one hand over her mouth. She willed herself not to laugh. "Uh, Lex? Ronnie caught Lorrie. He and Lois took her to her room to get dressed."

Lex tossed the towel on the floor to clean up the mess. "Thanks." She leaned against the counter and took off one of her formerly white socks, which was now a lovely lime color. "Let me get this cleaned up so I can a shower."

"I'll take care of it," Martha offered. "Put those clothes in to soak so they don't stain."

"Yes, ma'am." Lex was tempted to remove her shirt altogether, but having a houseful of guests quickly vetoed that idea. She edged around Amanda. "Go ahead, laugh."

Amanda uncovered her mouth and burst into giggles. She followed her partner up the stairs. "I'll help you, honey." She ran a finger across Lex's throat for a taste. "Mmm. Refreshing."

"Smartass."

Halfway up the stairs, they were almost run down by Lorrie and Freckles. "Mommy, catch me," Lorrie shrieked.

"Don't even think about it, kiddo." Lex held out her hands. "You know better than to play on the stairs."

Lorrie stopped short and frowned at Lex. "Momma, you ucky."

Ronnie, who was home from college for the holidays, exchanged grins with Lois. He'd been around Lex long enough to know when to keep his mouth shut.

Lex mirrored Lorrie's posture, both hands on hips. The others were hard-pressed to control their mirth. "You had a hand in it, remember?"

"Mada did it," Lorrie added for good measure. "Uck."

"Lorrie —"

Amanda decided to cut in before Lex got too mad. "Lorrie, go downstairs and apologize to Mada for playing in the kitchen."

"Mommy, you go too?" Lorrie gave Amanda her most adorable grin and captured her hand. "Pease?"

"Well, I was going to help your momma."

Lex started up the stairs again. She moved past Ronnie and Lois. "Nah. You guys go on. I'll be down in a little while."

Twenty minutes later, Lex was clean and almost to the living room when Jeannie caught up with her. "Hey, Slim. Got a few minutes?"

The sounds of a football game could be heard from the television in the living room, and Lex sighed. She hoped to catch at least part of the first game. "Sure. What's up?"

"I was going to try and walk off these stupid false labor pains."

The harmless contractions had been making Jeannie uncomfortable for the past week. She held out her hand. "Would you like to join me?"

"Only for the walking," Lex teased. She gripped Jeannie's hand and followed her through the back door. "It's a little cool. Are you sure you don't need a jacket?"

Jeannie rubbed her belly with her free hand. "Are you kidding? I'm carrying my own personal furnace. But if you can't handle a little cool air—"

"Hrumph." Lex tugged Jeannie outside. "It's not that cold." She allowed her sister-in-law to control the pace as they followed the sidewalk toward the barns. The breeze ruffled her still-damp hair. "How are you feeling? Other than the obvious?"

"Fantastic. This pregnancy is so much different. I was sick for most of Lorrie's." She stopped for a moment and gasped.

"Are you all right?"

Jeannie squeezed Lex's hand before straightening up. "That was a strong one." She couldn't help but smile at the look of concern she received. "I'm fine."

Lex wasn't convinced, but decided to stay close, just in case. "If you say so." She was surprised when Jeannie wrapped her arm around hers and tucked her head against her shoulder.

"Actually, I'm scared." Jeannie's voice was so low it was hard to hear. "It seems like things are going too well, you know? I keep waiting for something bad to happen."

"You can't think like that. Everything's going to be fine." Lex shivered as another blast of air gave her a chill. She opened the barn door. "Come on."

Jeannie found a bale of hay and sat while Lex checked the horses. "Lex?"

"Yeah?"

"What if I'm not a good mother?"

Lex rose quickly from where she had been filling one of the water troughs and whacked her head on a board. "Ow." She rubbed the back of her skull and stepped to where Jeannie was perched. "You're going to be a great mom."

"How do you know? You're raising my firstborn, and she doesn't even like me." Tears began to leak from Jeannie's eyes. "What if—"

"Shh." Lex sat beside Jeannie and pulled her into her arms. "You didn't have much of a choice, sweetheart. And for the record, Lorrie loves you. She just didn't know you very well, at first. But y'all get along great, now."

After blowing her nose, Jeannie exhaled and sat up. "Thanks. You're pretty good with emotional, pregnant women, Slim."

"Lots of practice."

Jeannie laughed and picked up Lex's hand. "Rodney and I have talked about it, and we'd like to name you and Amanda as the baby's godparents. And," her voice softened, "we'd also like for you to raise him, should anything happen." When Lex stayed silent, she was afraid she'd said too much. "I mean, you know as well as I do, that life doesn't go smoothly. And I realize your family is growing already, but—"

"Of course we would. And we hope you'd do the same for us. It only seems right for you to take care of Lorrie if we can't." Lex kissed the side of Jeannie's head. "But nothing's going to happen. In another week or so, you're going to bring a healthy son into the world."

"Thanks." Jeannie hugged Lex and started to stand. She felt a strong pain and covered her abdomen with both hands. "Oh!"

Lex's eyes widened when she noticed the wetness on Jeannie's dress. "Is that...?"

"Yeah." Jeannie doubled over. "I don't think he's going to wait. My water broke."

AMANDA KNOCKED SOFTLY on the wooden door. She glanced at her daughter, who stood dutifully by her side. "Is that too heavy?"

"Nope." Lorrie adjusted the stuffed cow in her arms. The black and white toy was so large it hung past her knees, but it was what she picked out at the store as a gift.

The door opened and Rodney appeared. "Well, hello there." He winked to Amanda before squatting in front of Lorrie. "That's some toy you have there."

"Izza moo cow." Lorrie raised it and held it close to his face.

"I see." Rodney stood and beckoned them inside. He closed the door and pointed toward the living room. "You've got great timing. Teddy finished his lunch a few minutes ago."

Lorrie walked next to Amanda, but stayed close to her leg. She saw Jeannie in a large, cushy chair, holding a squirming bundle. Her curiosity got the best of her and she moved to stand close by Jeannie. She pointed at the blanket, which squeaked and moved. "What's dat?"

"This is your bro...cousin, Teddy." Jeannie gave Amanda an apologetic look at the near slip. She moved the blanket so Lorrie could get a better look. "See? He's a baby."

"Bee bee?" Lorrie's brow wrinkled as she considered what Jeannie had told her. She turned to Amanda for confirmation. "Mommy?"

"That's right. A baby. Remember? We went shopping for him?" Amanda sat on the arm of the chair. "He's adorable, sis." She happily accepted him from Jeannie. "Rodney, I think he takes more after you."

"So Jeannie tells me." He sat on the floor close to Lorrie, who immediately sat in his lap. "Do you like the baby?"

She waved the stuffed animal. "Gots moo cow for bee bee." Lorrie was completely comfortable with Rodney, who had always treated her well. "Gots cookies?"

"Lorrie!" Amanda cringed at her daughter's lack of manners. "We'll get cookies at Gramma's."

Lorrie stood and tossed the toy on the floor. "No! Wants cookies."

Amanda handed Teddy to Jeannie. "Lorrie, I told you we'd have cookies later. Now apologize for your behavior."

"No." Lorrie's lower lip jutted out and her eyes narrowed. "Wants cookies."

Amanda bent over enough to get on her daughter's level. "Lorraine Marie Walters," she pointed to the sofa, "Go sit in time out."

Lorrie glared at her for a moment before stomping to the couch and climbing on the far end. She crossed her arms and pouted, but didn't say another word.

Jeannie stifled a chuckle. "She looks like Slim when she does that."

"I know." Amanda straightened and placed her hands on the small of her back. "You should see when they both get into trouble at the same time. I think the terrible twos extend into the threes, and are contagious."

Rodney stood and dusted off his jeans. "Hold on, Amanda." He pushed a cushioned rocker close to her. "This was Jeannie's favorite while she carried Teddy."

"Thanks." Amanda lowered herself into the chair and sighed in relief. "That's much better." She noticed Lorrie looking contrite. "Lorrie, are you going to behave now?"

Lorrie nodded.

"All right." Amanda held out her hands. "Come here, sweetie."

With tears in her eyes, Lorrie scrambled off the sofa and hurried into her mother's arms. "Me sowwy."

Amanda held her close and rocked. "I love you, Lorrie."

Jeannie looked on with a pang of sadness. Although she had given birth to Lorrie, she knew that now, without a doubt, Amanda was her mother.

Chapter
Twenty-five

IT WAS ONLY ten days until Christmas and Lex was ready for the holiday to be over. She usually loved this time of the year, but between Amanda's pregnancy and Lorrie's exuberance, it was more than she was used to. Her partner alternated between giddy happiness and spur-of-the-moment crying jags, keeping Lex continually on edge. And Lorrie was, well, a typical three-year-old. At least that's what Martha assured her. Lex wasn't so certain.

The festive, piped-in music was beginning to grate on Amanda's nerves. She had agreed to go Christmas shopping with Lex, but she didn't take into account that everyone else in the county would be doing the same thing. If one more person shoved her, she was sure Lex would start breaking kneecaps as she had threatened to do earlier. She tightened her grip on Lex's arm and followed her into what she hoped was the final store.

Lex found an empty chair near the women's cologne counter. "If we don't find it here, I'm going to cut out a picture of it and put it in a card." She stopped and waited for Amanda to sit, which she did. "I'm sorry it's taking so long, sweetheart." The perfume hadn't been her first choice for Martha's present, but after she had heard her go on and on about it after seeing the commercial, Lex knew it had been a thinly veiled hint. So, here they were. "I'll be right back."

"Take your time." Amanda sank into the soft leather chair and closed her eyes. Her feet were killing her, and her back complained with every step. She was ready for the baby to arrive. And she was jealous of Jeannie, who was home with her son and planned to have her wedding on Valentine's Day. Amanda thought the whole idea of a big ceremony was silly when they had a newborn to care for. If it were her, she would have gone to City Hall and been done with it.

The exhausted saleswoman checked her watch again. Muriel patted her dyed, platinum-blonde hair, knowing it was no longer in the neat bun she had started with that morning. She didn't think she'd last the two hours until closing time. When she noticed the casually dressed woman peering at the different fragrances, she pasted a smile on her face. She hated browsers. This one looked even poorer than the rest. Her denim shirt was old and worn and her jeans were faded. Even her battered leather jacket looked as if it had seen better days. "Is there something I can help you with?"

Lex raised her eyes. "Uh, yeah. What sizes does that," she tapped the glass over a dainty bottle, "come in?"

"I'm sure I can find you something more affordable. We've got a shelf of suitably priced colognes over by the ladies' shoes." Muriel pointed in that direction. "The fragrances in this cabinet are imported."

"So?" Lex couldn't understand what the woman's problem was. "Don't you want to make a sale? This is exactly what I've been looking for."

Muriel looked down her nose at the stubborn woman. She leaned across the counter and lowered her voice. "Listen to me. If you start to cause a problem, I'll call security."

"What?"

"You heard me. Go to the discount store. It's more in your price range."

Lex checked her clothes. They were pressed and didn't have any holes. She looked at the soles of her boots. No, they were clean. She didn't know why this woman was so hostile, but she was determined to find out. "Lady, I'm not in the mood for your games. Give me the damned perfume." She reached into her inner coat pocket for her wallet.

All Muriel could see was the woman's hand disappearing inside her coat. She panicked, fearing she was about to be robbed. Her hand groped beneath the counter until she felt the alarm button. She pushed it and hoped she'd live long enough to see security take this woman down.

Amanda heard hurried footsteps rush by her, and she opened her eyes in time to see two large men head toward the perfume counter. "Now what?" She struggled to get out of the chair to see what was going on.

Lex saw a commotion out of the corner of her eye and turned her head right before she was tackled and knocked down. "What the—"

"Shut up." The larger of the two guards pinned her to the floor, face down, and wrestled Lex's hands behind her. "Don't try anything stupid." He handcuffed her and flipped her over onto her back. While straddling her hips, he carefully searched her pockets. "Where's your weapon?"

Amanda wanted to yank the security guard off her lover. "What do you think you're doing? Lex, what's going on?"

"How the hell should I know? This big ape attacked me for no reason." Lex rocked her shoulders in an attempt to get more comfortable. His hand brushed her breast. "Hey, watch it!"

The man climbed off her and lifted Lex to her feet by her coat.

"Don't move. The police should be here any minute." He pushed her face against the counter and started to frisk her. His partner stood by and watched the scene silently.

Amanda had seen enough. "Would you please stop? She hasn't done anything wrong."

"She was trying to rob me!" Muriel pointed a shaky finger at Lex. "I saw her reach for a gun."

"That's ridiculous. We came in to buy a present." Amanda bristled when Lex raised her head and the guard slammed her down again. "Stop! You're hurting her!"

The second guard pulled out a notebook. He glanced at the saleswoman's nametag. "Muriel, if you'll give me your statement, we can get the perp out of your hair."

At that moment, two uniformed deputies arrived. Both had their hands on their holstered guns, but relaxed when they noticed Amanda. The first one couldn't believe what he was seeing. "Amanda?"

She almost cried in relief. "Jeremy, thank god. Would you please tell this jackass they've made a mistake, and to let Lex go?"

Jeremy waved off the other deputy and grabbed the big security guard's arm. "Stand down, buddy. Uncuff her."

"I can't do that. She threatened to rob one of our employees." He hitched up his pants. "We've got to process her."

Lex cautiously raised her head. Her cheek ached, and she had a feeling it was going to bruise. "I did not. She was giving me a hard time about buying some damn perfume. I was taking my wallet out to show her my credit card, when this guy body-slammed me."

Everyone turned to Muriel. "She was being difficult." She brushed her shaky hand against her hair in an attempt to calm herself. "I mean, look at her. There's no way someone who looks like her can afford a bottle of our finest fragrance." She looked haughtily at Jeremy. "I want to press charges."

"You've got to be kidding me." Jeremy glared at the guard until he relented and removed the handcuffs from Lex.

Lex stepped away from the counter and rubbed her wrists in an attempt to restore circulation. "Can we go home?" The whole incident had unnerved her. She began to feel calmer when Amanda stepped into her embrace.

Jeremy patted Lex on the back. "I think that can be arranged. Go on, I'll handle this." He waited until she and Amanda were out of earshot, then gestured for the guards to leave. The dirty looks he received from the men didn't faze Jeremy at all. "Lady, you're damned lucky it was me that showed up. Because if it had been my boss, you'd be in deep trouble."

She drew herself up and glared at him. "Why? What's so special about that hooligan?"

"She's my boss's daughter. And she has more money than you'll see in a year." He enjoyed her shocked look. "Now, which one of these was she looking at?" Jeremy knew it wouldn't make up for the embarrassing day Lex had suffered, but it would be fun to tweak this snotty saleswoman. "While you're at it, get your manager over here. I think he needs to be filled in on how you treat customers."

Once outside, it didn't take long for Lex and Amanda to reach the truck. Amanda led her partner to the passenger side. "I'll drive." She brushed her fingers over Lex's cheek, which was still red from her mistreatment. "Are you all right?"

"Yeah." Lex closed her eyes at the gentle touch. "Do we have to tell anyone about this?"

"We'll keep it between us, love. Let me call my grandparent's and see if they'll watch Lorrie for the night. I think we need a little alone time." Amanda waited until Lex got into the truck before she went to the other side and climbed in. Some world-class pampering would be needed tonight. And she would be more than happy to be on the giving end for a change.

FIVE DAYS UNTIL Christmas. The last place Lex wanted to be was in a doctor's waiting room, but here she sat across from another couple. The obstetrician's office was close to the Somerville hospital, and the doctor had been recommended by their primary physician, Dr. Anderson. They liked Dr. Vaughn very much, and she always explained everything to them well. Still, Lex felt uncomfortable around strange pregnant women. Some were with husbands, while others came in alone. She bounced her leg anxiously.

"Would you please calm down?" Amanda put her hand on Lex's thigh. "You'd think you're the one who has to expose herself to the doctor."

"I can't help it. You know how these places get to me."

Amanda sighed. "Maybe I should have come alone."

"No!" Lex blushed when everyone in the room stared at her after her outburst. "Sorry." She leaned closer to Amanda and lowered her voice. "I promised you I'd share as much of this as humanly possible and I meant it. I want to be here." She laced their fingers together and privately vowed to keep her nervousness to herself. Amanda had enough going on without having to worry about her.

"Thank you." Amanda squeezed Lex's hand. While Lex was jittery, Amanda was actually looking forward to the visit. Although she had already had one ultrasound earlier in her term, they were hoping today to be able to find out the baby's sex.

The woman across from them noticed their linked hands. "Is this your first?"

"Yes."

"No."

Amanda shook her head at Lex. "It's my first pregnancy, but our second child."

"I see." The woman looked at Lex. "Did you —"

Lex's eyes almost bugged out of her head. "Me? Hell no!" The thought of going through what Amanda was freaked her out. She jumped slightly when her lover lightly slapped her leg. "Sorry."

"We adopted our daughter." Amanda didn't feel the need to go into all the details.

The lady nodded knowingly. "And this one? Artificial insemination?"

Lex was relieved when a door opened and a nurse announced Amanda's name. She stood and helped her lover to her feet. The conversation made her twitchy. She hated speaking about their personal life to strangers. A voice inside of her wanted to tell the woman to mind her own damned business, but she figured it would only get her into more trouble.

Amanda linked her arm with Lex's and looked at the other couple. "Artificial insemination? This baby seems real enough to me. Come on, Slim." She led Lex to the door.

Lex smirked and strutted after her. Before going through the door, she turned and gave the woman a wink. The look of surprise she received made the whole trip worthwhile.

The nurse escorted them to an exam room and handed Amanda a cotton gown. "I'm sure you're used to this by now, Ms. Walters. I'll be back in a couple of minutes to take your vitals." She closed the door behind her, leaving Lex and Amanda alone in the chilly room.

"This is one of the parts I wouldn't mind sharing." Amanda handed the gown to Lex so she could undress. "I don't know why they have to make these places so blasted cold." She hurriedly covered up and wrapped her arms around herself.

"Here." Lex helped her onto the table and draped her coat around Amanda's shoulders. "This should help, at least for a few minutes."

Amanda pulled the leather jacket closed in front of her. It was nice and warm, and she could faintly detect Lex's cologne. "Thanks. Have I told you lately that I love you?"

"Yep. But I still love to hear it." She put her arms around Amanda. She turned around when the door opened and the nurse stepped inside. "Do you have to keep it so cold in here?"

The nurse set her chart on the nearby counter. "Of course we do. It keeps us from having to refrigerate our stethoscopes." She placed a digital thermometer into Amanda's ear. It beeped and she checked the reading before writing it on the chart. "I hate to do this to you, but you're going to have to remove the jacket, so I can check your blood pressure."

Lex removed the coat and watched while the nurse completed her preliminary exam. As soon as the woman was finished, Lex replaced the jacket on Amanda.

Dr. Sandra Vaughn came into the room. She was of average height and her light brown hair framed her delicate features. She gave Lex and Amanda a friendly smile and took the proffered chart from her nurse. "Good morning. Amanda, it looks like your blood pressure is a few points too high, so let's try to keep an eye on that. But I see no cause for alarm as of yet." She placed the chart on the counter and washed her hands at the sink before donning a pair of gloves. "Why don't we get the uncomfortable part of the exam out of the way, then we can move on to the fun stuff."

Lex stood by Amanda's head and concentrated on her partner's face. Amanda handled the exams much better than she did, which was a private source of embarrassment. But, she figured passing out would be worse. So, she held Amanda's hand and listened carefully while the doctor related her findings.

"Everything is looking great." Dr. Vaughn scooted her stool away and stood. She removed the gloves and washed her hands again. "All right." She snapped on a fresh pair of gloves. "Let's have some fun. Terri, bring the ultrasound machine over. And grab the gel from the freezer." At the couple's nervous looks, she laughed. "Only kidding."

Terri took the gel from the warmer and handed it to the doctor. Dr. Vaughn smeared a liberal amount over Amanda's bare belly then ran the transducer across the area. She pointed out several things to them on the screen while manipulating the device. "Quite an active one you've got there."

"Tell me about it," Amanda sighed. Being awakened in the middle of the night by the baby's movements was already getting old.

Dr. Vaughn chuckled. "Looks like she's an exhibitionist, too."

Amanda perked up at the pronoun. "She?"

"Most definitely." Sandra gestured to a certain area on the screen. "She's very cooperative. And a little bigger than I expected." She saw the concerned look on Lex's face. "Not too surprising, considering how big you are." She caught herself. "Oops. Sorry about that. Sometimes I forget."

Lex shrugged good naturedly. "That's okay. I think of her as mine, too." She accepted a towel from the nurse and used it to clean the gel from Amanda's skin. "So, Junior looks all right?"

"Junior?"

Amanda pulled the gown down and swatted Lex on the arm. "Silly joke. Lex has been teasing me about naming the baby Junior, even if it was a girl." She cut her eyes at her partner. "But now that we know for sure, that's a definite no, right?"

"Yes, ma'am." Lex helped Amanda sit upright. "Is there anything special we should be doing right now? It seems like every book I've read says something different."

The doctor finished washing her hands again and dried them. "No, I think you're doing fine." She directed her next comments to Amanda. "Rest with your feet up when you can." She shook both their hands. "I'll see you next month."

"Thank you, Dr. Vaughn." Amanda waited until the doctor and nurse were both out of the room before she turned on Lex. "I can't believe you called the baby Junior."

"I didn't mean to." Lex's face changed from chagrined to elated. "We're going to have another daughter. Isn't that cool?"

Amanda's faced mirrored hers. "It is. I was hoping for a girl."

"So was I." Lex helped Amanda get dressed. "Want to go celebrate?" It didn't matter to her what the baby's sex was as long as both of them were healthy. She was more excited to hear that Amanda and the baby were both doing well. But, the announcement still made her want to run outside and shout it to the world. She couldn't wait to tell everyone.

THE FIRE HAD burned down to embers, and the once boisterous house was now silent, except for an occasional exclamation from Lorrie. She sat on the den floor, close to the twinkling Christmas tree, surrounded by toys, empty boxes, and discarded wrapping paper.

Lex breathed a sigh of relief. Christmas evening had gone better than she had hoped. Everyone in their family seemed to have enjoyed themselves. But she was more than happy to have the house quiet once again. She was stretched out along the leather sofa, with Amanda propped against her, dozing. Her hands cradled Amanda's stomach, and she found herself stroking the surface from time to time.

"Momma, look." Lorrie bounced the blocky toy farmer around with one hand. It had come with one of her favorite gifts – a plastic barn with several animals and people.

"That's great, lil' bit. Is that you?"

Lorrie looked at her as if she were an idiot. "No." She waved the piece at Lex. "It's Momma."

It felt funny being chastised by a three-year-old. Even though she was pleased with the gifts she had been given, Lex's favorite part of the evening was any time Lorrie opened a package. She'd always hug the item to her as if it were the most important thing in the world. After it had been suitably loved, she would run over to whoever gave it to her and give them a big hug and a kiss. Lex couldn't understand why Lorrie wasn't exhausted after all the excitement. She felt the body propped against her chuckle. "I thought you were asleep."

"I was, until I heard you and Lorrie talking. She set you straight, didn't she?"

"Yep." Lex kissed Amanda's ear. "Is it close to her bedtime? I believe I promised you a massage."

Amanda stretched. "Oooh. I like the sound of that." She noticed the paper still cluttering the floor. "Lorrie, it's time to clean things up and go to bed."

"Don't want to." Lorrie looked around and grabbed a piece of wrapping paper and put it on her head.

"Mommy's right, kiddo." Lex waited until Amanda scooted away before dropping to her knees on the floor. "I'll help."

Lorrie stood, the wrapping paper still on her head. It was covered with cartoon cows, wearing Santa hats. She dodged out of Lex's reach and took off around the room at a gallop. "Moo!"

"Lorrie!" Lex dove for her again and missed.

"Moo!" Lorrie giggled as she evaded her momma. "Moo!"

Amanda aimed an unreadable look at Lex.

"What?"

"You had to wrap her farm in that paper, didn't you?"

Lex gathered up several piles and stuffed them in a nearby trash bag. "I kind of thought she'd want to be the rancher."

"No, not your daughter. She wants to be the cow."

"Moo!" Lorrie hopped around Lex, who finally gave up and sat in the middle of the floor.

Chapter
Twenty-six

THE THUMP OF small feet running, punctuated by sharp, staccato barks, made Amanda rub her temples with her fingertips and close her eyes. It had been going on all morning and she felt like she was slowly losing her mind. She wished Lex was home. But her partner had been "volunteered" by Martha to help set up chairs and tables for the Ladies' Auxiliary New Year's Eve dance. So, Amanda found herself alone for the day, with only Lorrie and her best friend to keep her company. A high pitched bark in the next room startled her. "Lorrie, what are you two doing?"

Clattering nails on the hardwood floor announced the arrival of her daughter's four-footed partner in crime. One quick, yet effortless leap and the excited dog sat beside her. The terrier cocked her head and looked at Amanda.

"I swear, Freckles, you look like you understand everything I say." Amanda stroked the animal's soft head. Her daughter stomped into the room, dragging an old tee shirt of Lex's. "Lorrie, why do you have Momma's shirt?"

Lorrie waved the dark blue cloth. "Fleckles is cold. She wants dis."

Amanda prayed to whatever deity would listen to grant her strength. Lorrie's "terrible two's" had been a cakewalk compared to how her three's were starting. "I don't think your momma would be happy to come home and see Freckles dressed in her favorite tee shirt. Please go upstairs and put it away."

"No." Lorrie tossed the shirt onto the floor and crossed her arms, in an uncanny imitation of Lex. "Fleckles wants it."

"Excuse me?" Amanda was all for her daughter asserting her independence, but she was becoming tired of Lorrie's favorite word. "Lorrie, I'm not asking you again. Please put the shirt back where you got it."

"No." Lorrie stomped her foot for good measure.

Freckles watched the goings on with great interest. She wagged her stubby tail at Amanda, expecting the treat her playmate's mommy always had close at hand.

It was almost amusing how much Lorrie favored Lex when she was being stubborn. But no matter how cute she was, her attitude couldn't be tolerated. Amanda stood and held out her hand. "Please give me the shirt, Lorrie."

"N—" Lorrie could see that her mommy meant business. She exhaled heavily and gave her the garment. She knew what came next. Her parents had learned of the "time out" chair from the daycare teachers and quickly instituted it at home, much to the child's disappointment. Lorrie stuck out her lower lip and walked slowly to a small chair near the office door. She flopped hard onto the wooden seat and pouted.

"Thank you." Amanda took the kitchen timer that resided on the bookshelves and set it for one minute. Lorrie would be allowed up once it went off. She folded the shirt and placed it on the coffee table. A sharp bark caused her to turn. "Yes, Freckles?"

The terrier lay on the ground with her rear high in the air. She wriggled her butt and barked again.

Amanda took a dog treat out of the container that was on a lower bookshelf. "I think Lex is spoiling you." She gave the bone-shaped treat to Freckles, who snapped it up and raced into the office to eat it. "You're welcome." The timer dinged and she waited until Lorrie got up and came to her. Amanda kneeled and gave her daughter a hug.

"Love you, Mommy." Lorrie tucked her head into Amanda's neck and sniffled. "I sowwy."

"I love you too, sweetie. Would you like to help me put Momma's shirt where it belongs?"

Lorrie nodded. She dutifully took it from the table and held it close to her chest. "Fleckles, you help." She led the way, the frisky dog by her side.

LEX STRETCHED UPWARD as far as she could reach. She was perched precariously on a rickety chair fighting for balance. With a final swing of the hammer, she had the banner draped across the wall. A sudden grasp on her calf caused her to almost fall.

"Lexington, are you sure that's straight? It seems a touch crooked to me." Mrs. Pendleton tugged on the jeans once more. Her bluish white hair was cropped close to her head and the glasses she peered through were so thick, it was a wonder she could see anything at all. "I don't think it's centered very well."

"No, ma'am, it's centered and straight. I measured before I hung it." Lex fought the strong urge to kick her leg free from the old woman's grasp. Martha was going to owe her big time for what she'd gone through all morning. It seemed as if every woman in Somerville over seventy was crammed into the Knights of Columbus Hall, decorating it for the big New Year's Eve dance. The old women had run her ragged. She started to step off the chair, but Mrs. Pendleton's hold on her leg caused her foot to slip. Lex tumbled off the chair, her fall only broken by the frantic grip she took on the banner. She fell against the wall but landed on her feet. "Damn."

Mrs. Pendleton slapped her arm. "Mind your language, young lady." She craned her neck and glared at the drooping sign. "Well, it's certainly crooked now." She tsked and toddled away.

"Ornery old bat." Lex raised the hammer as if she were going to throw it. Her arm was grabbed and held tight.

Martha pulled Lex's arm down. "Lexie, what am I going to do with you? That's no way to talk about Gladys. She was only trying to help." She eyeballed Lex's handiwork. "Run to the kitchen and fetch the ladder. I don't know why you were climbing on that old chair, anyhow."

"It's not my fault. That old biddy —"

"Hush." Martha took the tool away from her. "Go on. If you'll hurry up and get this hung, I think there are a couple of ladies who want to take you to lunch."

"Oh, no. Not the Holstein, I mean, Goldstein sisters. They've been giving me grief since I got here." Lex backed away from Martha. "I'd rather starve, thank you very much."

Martha held the tool by the head and waggled it at Lex. "Be nice. They're only trying to be helpful. This is the one big thing they get to do all year long. Behave yourself."

Lex took another step away. It was a good time for a retreat. "You say the ladder is in the kitchen?" She didn't wait for a response. "Got to run, bye." She turned and jogged away.

"Brat." Martha flipped the hammer in the air and caught it before laying it on the chair. "I'll get her for that one."

The kitchen was bustling with activity. Women maneuvered around each other while they cleaned and got things ready for the refreshments that would be arriving the next morning. Lex saw the ladder near the pantry, but a woman was already using it. She moved closer, hoping to be able to borrow it once she was finished.

Mrs. Pendleton brushed by Lex, causing her to bump into the ladder. The woman who had been standing on the top rung began to fall and Lex instinctively caught her. She cradled her in her arms and looked into her face. The young woman was in her early twenties, and her auburn hair fanned across her face.

"I'm sorry about that. Are you okay?" Lex realized she was still holding the redhead and immediately set her down.

"Oh, I'm more than okay." The woman brushed her hair out of her face. Her dark brown eyes sparkled. "Thanks for saving me. I'm Ashley."

"Nice to meet you, my name's Lex. I'm sorry about bumping into you like that. How did you get roped into helping around here?"

Ashley wrapped her fingers around Lex's arm. "Why don't we go somewhere quieter to talk? It's like a madhouse in here."

"I'm sorry, I can't. I've got to get the sign in the main room hung. I came in here for the ladder." Lex wriggled out of her grasp and took a step away. She wasn't comfortable with the look Ashley was giving her. "Do you need it anymore?"

Ashley's face took on a predatory gleam. "No, I'm done. How about I help you? I'm sure it would be easier with two of us."

Lex grabbed the ladder and kept it between them. "No, I can handle it." She backed through the kitchen door. "Thanks." She quickly dragged the ladder across the room, intent on finishing so she could get out of there.

A happy yell echoed in the Hall. "Momma!" Lorrie raced to where Lex was setting up the ladder and attached herself to Lex's leg. "We gots foods."

"Hey there, lil' bit." Lex bent and hoisted Lorrie into her arms. The reprieve was a welcome one.

Amanda followed at a more sedate pace. She stood next to her partner and rubbed her on the upper arm. "Martha told us you were about finished. And, as our daughter so eloquently put it, we brought a picnic lunch. I thought it would be fun to sit in the gazebo in the square."

"Sounds great." Lex kissed Lorrie's cheek and set her down. "Give me a second, and I'll be done."

THE DECEMBER AFTERNOON was unseasonably warm, which allowed the trio an opportunity to enjoy an outdoor lunch. Amanda and Lex were sitting on an old blanket, both propped up against the inside wall of the gazebo, enjoying the relative privacy it afforded them. They snuggled while Lorrie galloped around the grass that surrounded the structure, riding an invisible horse.

Amanda was sitting between Lex's legs and her head was pillowed on her chest. "You're quiet. What's up?" The hand that had been lightly rubbing her belly stilled.

"Huh?"

"Is everything all right?" Amanda covered Lex's hand with her own, stroking the long fingers.

Lex exhaled heavily and resumed her rubbing. "Nothing's wrong. I was just thinking."

"About what?"

"Are you sure you want to go to the dance?"

Amanda turned her head slightly to look at her partner. "Why? Don't you?"

"Well yeah. I guess so. It's that this year you're, you know." Lex patted Amanda's stomach, which seemed to grow larger every day.

"I'm pregnant, not an invalid. What's the matter, are you ashamed of being seen with me?" Amanda felt tears sting her eyes. She hated how easily she cried these days. "It's because I'm fat, isn't it?"

"No!" Lex kissed Amanda's head and pulled her closer. "You're not fat at all, sweetheart. I think you get more beautiful every day. I didn't want you to get worn out tomorrow night, that's all."

Although she enjoyed how attentive Lex had been lately, Amanda was tired of her over-protective streak that had grown to epic proportions. "I know and I appreciate it. But we've already planned on staying at my grandparent's house after the dance, and Jeannie and Rodney are excited about watching Lorrie for the evening. If I start to get tired, I promise I'll tell you, and we'll leave."

"Okay." It was a battle she'd never win, so Lex caved. She was looking forward to the dance and they hadn't missed a year since they were together.

They sat quietly for a while, exchanging kisses while keeping an eye on their daughter. Lex was about to doze off when Amanda gasped. "What is it? Are you okay?"

Amanda sat perfectly still. There. She felt it again. "I think I felt the baby move."

Lex placed both hands on her belly. Since she had read every book on pregnancy she could get her hands on, Lex knew it was too soon for her to feel the baby's movements from the outside. But it didn't keep her from getting excited. "What did it feel like?"

The excitement in her lover's voice brought a smile to Amanda's face. "It was kind of a flutter, I guess. Wait." She paused for a moment and her smile widened. "That's such a weird feeling."

Lex felt like jumping up and hollering. The miracle they were a part of continually amazed her. She raised the bottom of Amanda's top and covered her stomach with her fingers and kissed her ear. "I can't wait to meet Junior. I bet she's going to be beautiful, like you." Her hands were playfully slapped.

"Hush. I've told you if we have a girl, you're not naming her Junior."

"Why not? I think Amanda Junior has a nice ring to it." Lex couldn't help but tease her wife. "We could call her Junie for short."

Amanda chuckled. "No way. How about naming her after you?"

"Not a chance. I don't want our daughter going through life having to fight every time someone teases her."

"You know, I've always wondered how you got your name. Do you know?" Amanda loved Lex's name. It suited her.

Lex thought about the question. Her name had been the source of many fights while she was growing up. Kids could be mean, and she never wanted to subject her children to such a fate. "I asked Dad about it when I was around ten. I got sent home from school for fighting and after he busted my ass, he finally got around to asking why I did it."

"What happened?"

"Stupid kid stuff. Some of the guys in my class started hassling me. I got tired of it and threw a few punches. I don't think Dad would have gotten so upset, but I got my butt kicked. He hated losers." She rested her forehead on Amanda's shoulder. "I asked him why he named me something so stupid. He said it was where he was when he found out my mother was pregnant with me, and he liked the way it sounded. They thought I was going to be a boy and when I was born, he was too damned stubborn to change it." Lex shrugged. "I guess I should be thankful he wasn't in Hoop and Holler, Texas, at the time."

"You're kidding me, right?"

"Nope. It's in Bell County." Lex released a heavy sigh.

Amanda's well-developed protective streak made her want to hold Lex in her arms and never let her go. "I'm sorry. I should have never brought it up."

Lex pushed the thoughts away. "That's okay. Promise me we won't name her Dallas."

"Oh, I don't know. Dallas Walters has a distinctive ring to it." Chills went down Amanda's arms when she felt Lex nibble on her neck. "Don't start something you can't finish." But she tilted her head to one side to give her lover better access.

"Believe me," Lex whispered in her ear, "I have every intention of finishing." She slid her hands higher until they were gently cupping Amanda's breasts.

Amanda squirmed when she felt Lex's thumbs barely brush across her overly sensitive skin. "Please."

"Hmm?" Lex kissed her way across Amanda's neck and took her earlobe into her mouth. She knew it drove her lover wild.

"We've got to stop." Amanda's right hand rose and tangled in Lex's hair, pulling her closer. "Oh, god." She felt like she was going to combust on the spot. With what little strength she had she struggled to her feet. "Take me home. Now."

Lex's face was flushed. She stood and took Amanda's hand in hers. "Let's see if Martha will watch Lorrie. I plan on keeping you busy for the rest of the afternoon." She headed for the Knights of Columbus Hall on shaky legs. Amanda would be lucky if she let her out of bed at all.

LEX WAS STRETCHED out on the bed, when another dress landed on top of her legs, adding to the growing pile. They had enjoyed a fun afternoon, at least until Amanda realized she had nothing to wear to the dance the following day. Now Lex was stuck watching as the clothes flew out of the closet. She lifted a dress from the stack. "What about this red one?"

Amanda stuck her head out of the closet and glared at her

partner. "Are you kidding me? I look like a tomato in that one." She ducked inside. "I'm too fat for anything," she wailed.

No matter what she said, Lex knew she'd get into trouble. She slipped from the bed and quickly put her clothes on. "Sweetheart?"

"What?" Another outfit sailed across the room.

Lex decided to take her life into her own hands. She peeked around the door and was shocked at the disaster their closet had become. Almost every piece of Amanda's clothes was now decorating the floor and her lover stood in the middle, clad only in a bra and slip. "It's still fairly early. Why don't we go into town and buy you something new?"

"Like what? A tent?" Amanda tossed another hanger onto the floor. She stared at her body and burst into tears. "I'm huge!" She crumpled into Lex's arms and began to sob. "I don't know how you can stand to look at me. I'm as big as a house."

"You're beautiful." Lex brushed at her face with the end of her open shirt. She cringed when Amanda took the cloth and wiped her nose. Her more immediate concern however, was her wife. "Baby, look at me."

"No." Amanda tucked her face into Lex's chest.

"Please?"

She knew she was being unreasonable, but Amanda couldn't help it. Her tears continued to dampen Lex's skin. The embrace she found herself in finally calmed her. She sniffled a few times and moved away slightly. "I got you all wet."

"That's not necessarily a bad thing." Lex kissed her forehead. "I know that while the baby is growing, you're uncomfortable with how your body is changing."

"I'm fat."

Lex's smile was sincere. "No, you're pregnant. A beautiful, sexy, pregnant woman. And I understand that you want to wear your regular clothes. But sweetheart, maybe those clothes are uncomfortable for Junior." She ran her hands down Amanda's sides and rested them on her hips. "Let's spoil you and go buy some new clothes."

Amanda tried to keep her petulant look in place, but the love that shined from Lex's eyes made it extremely hard. "Then everyone will see how big I am."

"No, they'll see how beautiful you are." Lex framed Amanda's face with her hands. "You don't know how wonderful it is, to see our baby growing within you every day. It only makes you more stunning. You take my breath away, Amanda." She kissed her, trying to convey with action what she couldn't find in words.

The words soothed Amanda's wounded psyche and she melted into Lex's embrace. When they finally parted, she knew that the time of regular clothes was over, at least for another four months or so.

"Thank you." She kissed Lex on the chin and left. One of her older dresses would do while they shopped for new outfits.

AMANDA STOOD BESIDE Lex on the front porch of her sister's house. The thought of leaving Lorrie with them disturbed her more than she was willing to let on. She knew they were more than capable of taking care of her, but she still worried. "Are you sure about this? She's quite a handful."

Jeannie seemed to have recuperated well from Teddy's birth. In fact, she had never looked more radiant. Now Jeannie was standing behind her husband, holding her sleeping son. "Mandy, please. Go and have fun."

"We'll be fine." Rodney hitched Lorrie higher on his hip. His new best friend had her arm wound tightly around his neck. "I wouldn't have suggested it if I didn't think so." He turned his head and touched noses with Lorrie. "We're going to have a great time, aren't we?"

"Yep." Lorrie brushed her hand along his cheek and giggled at the feel of his stubble. "Yuck."

When her eyes met Jeannie's, Amanda smiled. They'd both matured over the last couple of months, and the shared joys of motherhood had brought them closer together. "You're absolutely positive?"

Jeannie covered Teddy's head with her hand and kept her voice low. "Of course we are. Now go on."

Lex put her arm around Amanda. "Come on, sweetheart." Truth be told, she was feeling separation pangs as well, but did her best not to show it. "Call us if you need anything?"

"We will. It's only for the night. Enjoy it while you can." Jeannie stepped beside her husband. "You won't get many more opportunities for a while."

Amanda lightly yanked on Lorrie's hair. "Be good for your Uncle Roddy and Aunt Jeannie. Your Momma and I will be back to get you in the morning." They were going to stay with her grandparents after the dance, so they wouldn't be on the roads after midnight.

"Tay." Lorrie leaned toward Amanda and gave her a sloppy kiss. "Love Mommy." She did the same for Lex. "Love Momma." She then rested her head against Rodney's shoulder. "Love Woddie."

Lex cleared her throat and felt Amanda's hand in hers. "Yeah. You be good, lil' bit. We'll see you later." She turned and led her wife away, before one or both of them broke down.

AMANDA TUGGED SELF-CONSCIOUSLY at the edges of the jacket draped around her. She was afraid to remove the coat she borrowed from Lex. The new dress she wore wasn't uncomfortable. In fact, it was the opposite. The black crinkle chiffon dress was stylishly cut and it complemented her figure. It was sleeveless, with a scoop neck and had a band of glittering oval rhinestones in a line above her waist. But the fact that it was a maternity dress, no matter how nice it looked, made her feel matronly instead of sexy.

Lex had gone crazy at the maternity boutique. For someone who didn't like to shop, she certainly had a great time dressing her partner. Now Amanda had enough of a wardrobe to last her several months. Dresses, jeans, sweaters, tops and even new undergarments filled her closet. She put her foot down when Lex wanted to buy her a new coat. She'd rather wear Lex's old leather jacket. She started to panic when Lex tried to remove it from her shoulders. "Wait."

"It's okay." Lex gently eased it from her, but left the black lace shawl. She hung the coat next to her own then placed her arm around Amanda's waist. "You look great." In fact, the dress complemented her growing belly quite well. Because Amanda was petite to begin with, it hadn't taken long for her to start showing.

Martha took that moment to show up. "Don't you two look spiffy. Amanda, is that a new dress?"

No matter how hard Amanda prayed, the earth didn't open and swallow her. She was certain people had heard Martha's exclamation on the other side of the crowded room. Embarrassed by the attention, she shrank against Lex. "Yes, we got it yesterday afternoon."

"Goodness." Martha took Amanda by the arm and pulled her away from Lex. "Step over here where I can get a good look at you." She made Amanda turn around. "You look positively radiant, sweetie."

For the first time since she noticed her stomach growing, Amanda felt her self- esteem peek out from its hiding place. She knew that while Martha loved her dearly, she would never say anything she didn't mean. "Do you think so?"

"Most definitely." Martha slapped Lex on the arm. "Haven't you told her how lovely she looks? Shame on you."

"Hey." Lex looked offended. "Of course I have."

Amanda stepped in front of her. "Lex has been extremely supportive. It's been my own stupid insecurity that's been the problem. But thanks. I needed to hear it from someone other than my obviously biased wife."

"I'm not biased. I've got good taste." Lex put her hands on Amanda's shoulders. "Do you want me to get you something from the kitchen?"

"Not at the moment. You know what happens when I drink anything. I'm not ready to start that cycle of fun."

Martha took Amanda by the hand. "Why don't you two sit with us at our table? It's not far from the refreshments. Or the ladies' room." Her last words were whispered to Amanda. She knew of the frequent bathroom breaks Amanda took at home, but she didn't want to embarrass her.

"Thank you. That would be great." Amanda allowed herself to be led through the crowd, with Lex close behind.

Wanda, who noticed them when they arrived, stopped them. "Amanda! You look fantastic." She turned to her husband. "Isn't she beautiful?" He opened his mouth to speak, but she cut him off. "What a gorgeous dress. Where on earth did you find it? I mean, you always dress so nice, but I can never find anything that fancy around here." She chattered on, not giving Amanda a chance to answer. "Did you go shopping in Austin? I bet you found it at some fancy boutique, didn't you?" She elbowed Dirk. "Well? Isn't she lovely?"

He wore his usual suffering look. It was rare that he got a word in whenever his wife got started talking. "Yes, dear." He shook Lex's hand. "It's good to see you both. You do look beautiful, Amanda. Now if you'll excuse us, I'm going to try and find a muzzle." He escorted Wanda away, ignoring her squawks of complaint.

"I'm not through visiting, Dirk. Let go of my arm." Her voice could be heard all over the room, even with the noise of the crowd.

Lex waited until they were out of sight. "She's something, isn't she?"

"You can say that again." Amanda tucked her arm around Lex's. Martha had gone ahead of them and they could see her standing by a table close to the kitchen. Charlie was there, sitting next to another couple. "I'm not quite ready to sit down. Would you like to dance instead?"

"That's the best offer I've had all day." Lex led Amanda to an unoccupied spot on the dance floor and pulled her close. She loved how they fit together. Amanda's head was at the perfect height so she could nestle her face in her hair.

Amanda rested her cheek against her lover's chest and closed her eyes. The sounds of the crowd slowly receded until all she was aware of was the sound of Lex's heartbeat. They swayed slowly to the music and Amanda couldn't think of anything more perfect.

They had been on the floor for three songs when Amanda's bladder demanded to be acknowledged. "Honey? Can we take a break?"

"Sure." Lex followed her off the dance floor. Before they got to the table, she paused. "Are you ready for that drink now?"

"That would be great. Thanks." Amanda draped her shawl over an empty chair and continued on to the restroom.

Lex was ladling them each a cup of punch when someone touched her back. She turned, her hands full, to see Ashley in front of her. "Hi." The red dress she wore shimmered in the lights. It was short-sleeved, cut well above her knees and skin tight.

"I'm glad you made it tonight. I was hoping to talk you into a dance or two." Ashley stood leaning slightly forward, to accentuate the way her breasts almost fell out of her low cut dress. "We didn't get much of a chance to talk yesterday." She ran her red painted fingernail down Lex's arm.

Amanda stepped out of the ladies' room and noticed Lex wasn't at their table. She scanned the room and spied her at the concession table. She felt her blood pressure rise when she saw a strange woman with her hands on her partner. It didn't take long for Amanda to weave her way through the crowd. She was almost upon them when Lex noticed her.

"Hi, sweetheart." Lex felt somewhat guilty for talking to Ashley, but she didn't know exactly why. "I was about to bring you some punch."

Amanda cut around Ashley and put her arm possessively through Lex's. "I don't believe we've met."

Lex cringed as Amanda's fingers dug into her arm. She didn't have to see her face to know she was pissed. "Uh, yeah. Amanda, this is Ashley. She was helping with the decorating yesterday. Ashley, this is Amanda, my —"

"Wife," Amanda finished for her. She gave Ashley a barely perceptible nod. "If you'll excuse us, we have friends waiting." She practically dragged Lex from the refreshment area. "Who the hell does she think she is? That bitch was hanging all over you." She continued to grumble as they reached the table. It was vacant for the moment, as the other couples were on the dance floor.

"Amanda, hold on." Lex held out a chair for her lover and waited for her to sit. "I think she was only being friendly."

"Too friendly, if you ask me." Amanda sat and kicked off her shoes beneath the table. "Damned grabby whore."

It was time to diffuse the situation. She covered Amanda's hands with hers and looked into her eyes. "You're the only one for me, sweetheart. I met her yesterday in the kitchen, surrounded by a roomful of old ladies. We said maybe half a dozen words to each other. Let's forget her." She kissed Amanda, deepening the contact.

They separated and Amanda opened her eyes dreamily. "Forget who?" She put one hand behind Lex's neck and pulled her close again.

"I swear I can't leave you two alone for a minute." Martha sat next to Amanda. She enjoyed the way the two women reddened at her words.

"Can you blame me?" But Lex moved away from her lover. A little. She placed her arm around the back of Amanda's chair and stretched her legs under the table. When Charlie sat next to Martha and wiped the perspiration off his forehead with a handkerchief, she couldn't help but tease him. "What's the matter? Is Martha wearing you out?"

He put the damp cloth in his jacket pocket. "Isn't she always?"

"Don't blame me if you're tired." Martha took a sip of her punch and wiped the residue from her mouth with a paper napkin. "It's not my fault you stayed up so late last night."

"Are you sure about that?" Lex never saw the wadded paper sail toward her. She picked it up from the table after it bounced off her chest. "Shame on you, Martha. You should let the poor man rest sometime." She tossed the napkin at Martha, who batted it away.

Amanda popped Lex on the arm. "Behave."

"She started it." But Lex relented. She'd find another way to torment Martha, later. "Nice suit, Charlie. I guess you're off tonight?"

He did look dapper in the navy suit. The pale blue shirt and red tie went together well. He adjusted the tie. "Uh-huh. I've decided to cut back on my hours, since Jeremy practically runs the department anyway. I'd rather spend more time with my lovely wife."

"I don't blame you at all." Lex rested her hand on Amanda's shoulder. "I'm thinking of cutting back some, myself."

Amanda turned her head. "What do you mean?" This was the first she'd heard about Lex's plans. It rankled her when Lex would do something without even talking to her. They usually shared everything. "What's going on with you?"

"I'm tired of spending all day, every day, with the guys or the horses." Lex never noticed when Charlie stood and took Martha away from the table. "Is it so wrong to want to be with my family more? I thought you'd like it."

"Of course I do. But you can't suddenly drop what you've spent your whole life working for." Amanda scooted closer to her and put her hand on Lex's thigh. "I can't let you do that."

"Let me?" Lex grew angry. "Shouldn't I have a say in how I spend my life? I don't want my kids to grow up thinking that the damned ranch is more important to me than they are."

"Lex, please. I'm trying to understand, not tell you what to do."

The plaintive tone in Amanda's voice touched a cord in Lex's heart. Her anger faded away, leaving a weary resignation behind. "I know and I'm sorry. It's something I have to work out in my head, not take out on you." She stood. "I'll be back in a minute. I need some air."

Amanda watched her leave. She wanted to find out if Martha had any idea what was going on with Lex. Before she could get up to find her, someone sat beside her.

"She's quite a catch." Ashley gestured toward the outside door, which Lex had disappeared through. "Don't you love how safe it feels in her arms? She's so strong. God, I could stay there forever."

"I beg your pardon? Are you talking about Lex?" It took a lot of effort, but Amanda controlled the urge to dump her punch over the woman's head.

Ashley laughed. "Oh, honey. Don't misunderstand me. I don't think I'm woman enough to keep up with tall, dark and sexy. But I wouldn't mind giving her a whirl." She leaned closer. "You can tell me. Is she the dominating type in the bedroom? I get all hot and bothered thinking about her." She licked her lips. "I bet she's a wild one."

Amanda was able to silence the little voice in her head that stopped her earlier. A glance at her near-empty glass kept her from tossing it into Ashley's face. Instead, she picked up Lex's full cup and carefully poured it over the smirking woman's perfectly coiffed head.

"You bitch!" Ashley jumped to her feet and held out her shaking hands. Mascara ran down her face and punch dripped off her nose. "Well, I never!"

"And you never will." Amanda got right in her face. "If I find out you so much as think about Lex again, I'll kick your skanky ass."

Lex saw the commotion across the room and jogged through the heavy throng to reach the two women. "What's going on here?"

"Your girlfriend is a freakin' lunatic!" Ashley shoved by them both and stomped away. Catcalls and laughter followed her out into the night.

"Amanda?" Lex took the empty cup from her lover's hand. "Hey, it's almost midnight. Let's go watch the fireworks." She'd wait until Amanda calmed down before she asked about the altercation again. Red punch wouldn't look good on her gray shirt, and she noticed several more glasses on the table.

Amanda was still fuming. "Hateful cow. I should have decked her."

"Um, sweetheart? Do you want me to hunt her down for you?" Her partner had always had a temper, but the hormone-induced emotions were beginning to scare Lex. She'd have to check with Martha and see if there was something she should do besides hide for the next few months. For now, a diversionary action was called for. She held out her hand. "Come on. We've never missed the fireworks. We'll worry about her later."

Amanda took her hand and squeezed. Lex was cute when she was flustered and it always had a way of calming her. "Never mind. She's not worth the trouble. Besides, I think we've seen the last of her." She followed Lex out of the building and across the lot to the gazebo. There were much more important things to think about. Like when they could sneak away from the dance and ring in the New Year in a much more private way.

Chapter
Twenty-Seven

THE BRIDAL STORE felt unreasonably warm to Amanda. She wished Jeannie would decide on a wedding dress so they could leave. Amanda was grumpy, hot, and miserable and she wanted to go home. She could feel the beginnings of a headache and wanted more than anything to be able to sit somewhere and prop up her swollen feet. "Jeannie, that's the fourth dress you've picked out. We still have to drive to Somerville, you know." The sudden trip to Austin had not been on Amanda's agenda for the day and she would have much rather stayed at home with Lex and Lorrie.

Jeannie gave her a dirty look, but kept browsing through a rack of expensive lace gowns. She would stop ever so often, take one from the rack, hold it up to herself, and replace it. This went on for another ten minutes, until she heard her sister sigh heavily. "Now what?"

"How can you have so much energy? It's only been about six weeks since you had Teddy." Amanda found a bench and slowly lowered herself onto it. Her back thanked her. She couldn't wait to get home so she could talk Lex into another massage. Her lover was very adept at making all her aches go away. If she closed her eyes, she could almost feel Lex's hands working their magic on her. "Aren't you tired?"

"Truthfully, I've never felt better." Jeannie carried another dress to where Amanda sat. "I'm sore from the incision, of course. But, it's so great to be able to enjoy the whole experience this time." She held the white lace and pearl-beaded creation up to her. "What do you think?"

Amanda gave the choice careful consideration before answering. It was a beautiful dress, but far too formal for a small, intimate wedding. "It's nice. But, isn't it a little much?"

"I don't think so." Jeannie held the gown against one leg, which she lifted slightly. "It would look great on me, and the way it's cut it would hide my 'baby belly'."

"Jeannie, it's white. It's also extremely formal. You're not planning on having the ceremony at a cathedral. I don't think it's suitable for our grandparent's backyard."

Her sister glared at her. "I look good in white."

"Maybe, but I think it would be more appropriate for you to look for something in a cream or neutral color."

"You're jealous." Jeannie placed the dress on the nearest rack.

The unladylike snort slipped from Amanda by accident. "What gave you that crazy idea?"

Jeannie did her best to ignore Amanda's attitude. Her sister could be such a snot, sometimes. She had been snippy all day. "Well, I am marrying a doctor. Not that there's anything wrong with Slim, but Rodney is a professional."

"He'd have to be, to put up with you." Amanda fought the temptation to kick off her shoes. From Jeannie's tone, they weren't leaving anytime soon.

"Smartass."

"You started it."

Jeannie stuck her tongue out, which caused them both to laugh. She took another dress from the rack and brought it over for Amanda's inspection. "This one's nice."

Amanda fingered the tag that hung from one sleeve. "It'd better be. You could make a month's house payment for this."

"So? I want this to be special."

"It will be. But Dad said he was going to pay for your dress. You can't honestly expect him to spend that much money."

With a roll of her eyes, Jeannie draped the dress over the rack. "He helped pay for yours, didn't he? I don't see what the big deal is."

"No, Lex and I paid for everything. He offered, but we knew he was trying to use all his money on his new business."

"You think you're so superior to me, don't you?" Jeannie put her hands on her hips and glared at her sister. "If our father thinks it'll cost too much, he can always ask our grandparents for help. Or tell me no."

The throbbing of her temples signaled to Amanda an impending headache. It was the third one this week. "Fine. You're going to do whatever you want to anyway. Leave me out of it." She stood. "Pick out a dress so we can go. I'm too tired to argue with you anymore."

Jeannie's entire demeanor changed. "Are you all right?"

"I will be once we're done. Can we please stop arguing and get this over with?"

"Of course." Jeannie remembered too well how uncomfortable shopping could be when pregnant. "You know, I think you had the right idea at your ceremony. Something tasteful and less formal would be the way to go."

Amanda was grateful for her sister's return to sanity. "Thank you. I think you'll be a lot more comfortable, since it's going to be an outdoor ceremony."

"That little tidbit had slipped my mind." Jeannie picked up her bags. "Let's go. I owe you lunch." They left the trendy boutique in search of a good meal and more sensible clothing choices.

THE HOUSE WAS quiet, except for the movie that flickered on the large television screen. The animated musical about a mermaid was Lorrie's favorite, at least for the moment. Lex and Amanda sat next to each other and their daughter was stretched across both their laps.

Amanda brushed her fingers through Lorrie's hair. The dark strands were fine, and she carefully detangled the unruly locks. The motion relaxed Lorrie and soothed Amanda. Her shopping trip with Jeannie the previous day had worn her out more than she cared to admit. She leaned into Lex's shoulder and closed her eyes. It wouldn't take much for her to doze off.

With the hand that rested on Amanda's far shoulder, Lex scratched the back of her lover's neck. "Are you feeling okay?"

"A little tired I guess."

"Is there anything I can do? Maybe another massage tonight?" Lex enjoyed the almost nightly ritual. She never tired of touching Amanda's body, whether making love or making her feel better.

"I'd like that."

The end credits for the movie rolled across the screen. Lorrie twisted until she was on her back and patted Amanda's stomach. "Mommy?"

"Hmm?"

Lorrie raised Amanda's shirt. "You growing."

"That's right." The comment didn't upset Amanda. She knew how curious their daughter was. She shifted when cold little hands ran across her sensitive skin.

"Why?"

When Amanda first started to show, Lex and Amanda sat Lorrie down and explained to her what was happening. She seemed to understand, but now Lex wasn't too sure. She was curious what was on Lorrie's mind. "Remember what we talked about? Your mommy has a baby growing in her tummy." She tickled Lorrie's belly and caused the child to giggle.

"No, Momma." Lorrie squirmed and slapped at Lex's hand. She settled down soon after. "Why a baby?"

Amanda gestured to Lex, wanting to see how she handled the question. "Yes, Momma. Tell us."

"Um, okay." Lex scooped Lorrie up. "We loved you so much, that we wanted to give you a little sister to play with."

"Like Christopher's? His mommy gots baby."

Lex kissed her head. "Yep. Just like Christopher's mommy."

Lorrie considered the answer. "Did Christopher's daddy give you the baby?" She couldn't understand why her Momma and Mommy started laughing. It sounded perfectly logical to her.

Amanda got her laughter under control first. "No, honey. Christopher's daddy loves his mommy and that's why he gave her a baby."

"Otay." Lorrie was quiet for over a minute before she thumped Lex on the chest. "Momma, you loves Mommy?"

"Yep."

The facts, as she knew them, all fell into place for Lorrie. "Momma, you gave Mommy the baby?"

"Um, well." Lex looked to Amanda for help. How much knowledge should you give a three-year-old, anyway? "Mommy?"

"Gee, thanks." Amanda subconsciously rubbed her stomach. "It's hard to explain, sweetie. We went to the doctor and he helped us get a baby."

"Otay." Lorrie slipped off her momma's lap. Freckles, who had been sleeping in her nearby dog bed, jumped up and raced over to her. "Can we gets a puppy, not a baby?"

Amanda buried her face in Lex's neck to keep from laughing out loud. Sometimes their daughter's one track mind surprised even her.

"No, lil' bit. I'm afraid that's not how it works." Lex struggled to keep a straight face.

"But Fleckles wants a puppy." Lorrie wrapped her arms around the happy dog's neck. Freckles proceeded to lick her cheek.

"I'm sorry, kiddo. But mommies can't have puppies."

The petulant look which crossed Lorrie's face was a carbon copy of Lex's when she didn't get her way. She frowned and started to stomp from the room, grumbling to herself. It would have been a lot more fun to have another puppy.

IT WAS HARD to tell who enjoyed going to bed more that evening. After the promised massage, Amanda was stretched out on the bed, dozing. Lex had her head propped on Amanda's thighs, reading aloud.

"Compared with last week, feeder steers and heifers weak. Slaughter cows and slaughter bulls steady. Stock cows and pairs weak. Trading and demand moderate." Lex thumbed through the computer generated pages. "Supply included fifteen percent feeders, fifteen percent stock cows and pairs. Of the feeders, sixty percent were steers and forty percent heifers with fifteen percent weighing over six hundred pounds."

Amanda sighed. "What on earth is that?"

"The producers livestock auction report."

"Uh-huh. And why are you reading this out loud?"

Lex raised her head. "I saw in one of the baby books that it was good to read to the baby." She placed her ear against Amanda's belly. "You want to be well educated, right, Junior?" Amanda's stomach gurgled in answer. "I think she agrees with me."

Amanda lightly slapped her on the head. "Couldn't you find something a little more, I don't know, relevant?"

"What's more relevant than the stock report? I haven't been to the auctions in a few months, so it's important to know what's going on." Lex suddenly got very quiet and still.

"What is it?"

"I'm not sure." Lex splayed her hand next to her head, lightly rubbing. "Junior? Are you listening?" She started humming a tune while she continued to stroke Amanda's distended stomach.

"Lex?"

There it was again. Now Lex was sure. "She kicked me." She sat up and put both hands where her head had been. "Come on, Junior." Another small motion caused a huge smile to cover Lex's face. "Yes!" She leaned closer. "You like when I talk to you, don't you?" It wasn't much, but she could feel a slight movement beneath her hands. "I guess that means you want me to tell you a story."

It was a toss up as to who was happier. Amanda caressed her partner's hair while Lex chattered.

"I can't wait to show you everything. Of course, the first one you'll see is your beautiful mommy. Then, we'll introduce you to your sister. I bet when you're older, the two of you will cause all sorts of trouble." Lex was almost giddy at feeling their daughter move. She kissed Amanda's belly. "I think she likes it when I talk to her."

"Maybe she's kicking to see if you'll be quiet."

Lex stuck her tongue out at her wife. "Don't listen to her, Junior. Mommy is grumpy. We know you like the sound of my voice." The baby kicked again and she raised triumphant eyes toward Amanda. "See?"

Amanda groaned. "I'm doomed." But she played with Lex's hair and had a fond smile on her face. "You're cute."

"I don't know about that, but I'm extremely happy." Lex kissed her stomach and scooted up to lay next to Amanda. She propped her head on her hand so she could look down into Amanda's eyes. "Every time I think it's impossible to fall in love with you any more, another day comes and proves me wrong." She bent and touched her lips to Amanda's.

Chapter
Twenty-Eight

AMANDA TYPED A few more words on the computer and stretched. She knew it would take awhile for the report to print, so she stood and decided it was time for another cup of decaffeinated tea. She stopped drinking coffee when she found out she was pregnant, and one of the women in the office had suggested tea. It had taken some getting used to. She had always been a coffee drinker, and the only way she liked tea was if it was poured over ice. But it was better than going completely without. Amanda made her way to the office kitchen where Wanda greeted her.

"Hi there, boss. I figured you'd be gone by now. It's been pretty slow." Wanda made herself a cup of coffee and dumped several packets of sugar and creamer into it.

Amanda's mouth watered at the strong fragrance. "I'm finishing up some paperwork before I pick up Lorrie at daycare." She dunked a tea bag into her mug of water. She wanted to dump the cup over Wanda's head when the other woman took a sip of coffee and groaned in pleasure. "Do you have to tease me like that?"

"Hmm?"

"I'd kill for a cup of coffee about now." Amanda swirled a teaspoon of sugar into her tea. "I hate hot tea."

Wanda could sympathize with her. When she had been pregnant with her daughter, Allison, she cheated on her dietary restrictions more than once. "What about decaf?"

"I've tried. But all it does is give me indigestion." Amanda took a sip of the brew and frowned. "Yuck." She poured the contents down the sink and rinsed out the mug. "Maybe I'll stick with milk and juice. This stuff is too nasty."

"How about a caffeine-free coke? Those aren't bad."

Amanda grabbed a bottle of water out of the refrigerator and opened it. She took a healthy swig before she leaned against the counter. "That's true. But I know I need to drink something healthier. I never realized how much I'd miss my daily infusion."

"You're a better woman than I am. I constantly cheated on my diet. Of course, Dirk would tell the doctor on me. If we had a doghouse, he would have spent most of my pregnancy in it." She sat at the small table and waited until Amanda joined her. "Has Lex driven you crazy, yet? I think it's in the handbook somewhere that spouses are supposed to be a pain in the rear when you're expecting."

"Actually, she's been great. Last night, she finally got to feel the baby move. The look on her face was priceless."

Wanda envisioned the scene. She knew how excited Lex was about Amanda's pregnancy. It showed every time she saw them together. And she also found new excuses to come into the office, usually bearing flowers or some other small gift. It was too cute. "I'm surprised she hasn't been by for lunch."

"She was going to. But she had to pick up a load of hay, because the guys are busy with other things." It had been a very unhappy Lex who left the house that morning. She had planned on taking Lorrie to school, Amanda to work, and run a few errands around town before lunch. But the man she bought the hay from called her, and the order had to be picked up today. She'd already sent the men out on other errands, and was stuck picking up the hay herself.

"That's a shame. I always enjoy seeing her."

Amanda finished her bottle of water and stood. "She has a good time coming here, too. Guess I'll finish up what I was doing, so I can grab Lorrie. We're meeting Charlie for lunch."

"That's great." Wanda stood and rinsed out her coffee cup. "Why don't you bring her over Saturday to play with Allison? We're planning on baking cookies."

"If you think she won't be too much trouble. You're a brave woman for cooking with two little girls."

Wanda followed Amanda out of the kitchen. "Brave has nothing to do with it. I'm going to enlist Dirk into helping. It's always fun watching him with the kids."

"All right." Amanda headed toward her office. She took the papers from her printer tray and sat behind the desk to look them over.

Ever since her mother had embezzled money from them a few years ago, Amanda had started running annual credit reports at the beginning of each year. She read over Lex's first. It had surprised her at first, seeing how clean her partner's credit was. Then she realized that Lex had rarely used her credit cards. When she did, she always paid them off within a few months. Something caught her eye. "That can't be right." Everything was clear, except—"Why has Kirk Trumbull put a lien on the ranch?" She picked up her phone receiver then paused. It wasn't something she should tell Lex on the phone. Instead, she dialed another number. She asked Charlie to pick up Lorrie at daycare, before she grabbed her purse and hurried home.

WITH A HEAVY thud, another bale of hay flew off the flatbed trailer. Lex placed her hands on her hips and stretched until several of her vertebrae popped. She groaned and took her hat off, wiping her forehead on the sleeve of her shirt. The trailer was still almost halfway full. She usually had Roy and a couple of the other men take care of it, but they were busy doing repairs to the bunkhouse after a particularly nasty ice storm had blown through. It was the second bout of bad weather they'd had since Christmas.

She placed her hat on her head. The work wasn't going to get done while she stood around. She wanted to finish so she could clean up before Amanda and Lorrie got home. She picked up another bale and tossed it, singing along with the truck stereo that was blasting through the open windows.

Amanda parked her Xterra beside the house and followed the loud music. She turned the corner of the barn and watched Lex work. Although she was wearing a long-sleeved denim shirt, Amanda could still see the muscles working along her back. The snug cut of Lex's jeans also caught her eye, and she stood quietly and enjoyed the scene.

Lex could feel someone watching her. She stopped what she was doing and turned around. Amanda was standing next to the barn, watching her every move. "Hey, there." Lex jumped down and met Amanda halfway. "What's up?"

"Hi." Amanda wiped a dab of straw from Lex's cheek. "How can you look so good, even when you're hot and sweaty?"

"Must be your eyesight. Because I know I'm a mess." Lex removed her gloves and leaned carefully so she wouldn't get Amanda dirty and kissed her. "I'm not complaining, but why are you here? Not to see me unload hay, I'd imagine."

"Unfortunately, no. Although it is a perk." Amanda took Lex by the hand, led her over to a bale, and sat. "There's something I need to tell you."

Lex felt her heartbeat quicken. "What's wrong? Is Lorrie all right?" She glanced at Amanda's stomach. "Is it the baby?"

"No, no." Amanda held Lex's hand close to her chest. "Everyone is fine. I'm sorry, I seem to be making a mess of this."

"Please, tell me."

Amanda exhaled heavily to settle herself. "I was doing our yearly credit checks, and found something that just didn't seem right."

"Don't tell me your mother has been at it again. We haven't heard from her in a couple of years." Lex removed her hat and wiped her sweaty brow with her shirt sleeve.

"No, nothing from her. But, for some reason, Kirk Trumbull has had a lien placed on the ranch."

Lex jumped to her feet. "What? Why would Hubert's lawyer do something like that? And how is that possible?" She began to pace back and forth.

"I don't know. Have you heard anything from him?"

"No, of course not." Lex stopped and tossed her gloves to the ground. "I'm going to go kill that son of a bitch."

Amanda stood and grabbed her by the belt. "No, you're not. We will drive into town and find out what's going on." She waited until Lex had calmed before releasing her. "Let's go on up to the house so you can get cleaned up."

"But—"

"Please don't argue with me. I'm tired, and I've got a headache that would fell a moose."

The look on Amanda's face made Lex realize how rash she had been. She took Amanda's hand from her belt. "I'm sorry. Maybe you should stay home and get some rest."

"No, I'd rather be with you." Amanda tugged her toward the house. "But I won't mind putting my feet up until you're ready to go." She knew Lex's temper could get her into trouble. Amanda hoped that if she were there, she'd be able to keep her calmer.

THE DINGY OFFICE smelled like cheap cigars and old perspiration, and the lighting was dismal, at best. The greenish pall on Amanda's face wasn't a surprise. Lex considered asking her to wait in the truck, but she knew it wouldn't do any good. "Are you going to be all right?"

"I think so." Amanda glanced at her lover. "If he gets too obnoxious, I'll throw up on him."

Lex squeezed her hand before releasing it. "If you need to, we're out of here. He's not worth it."

Heavy footsteps broke into their conversation. A corpulent man, panting and sweaty, stood less than ten feet from them. "What do you want?"

"I think I should be asking you that, Trumbull." Lex closed the distance between them and he stepped away several steps. "Why did you put a lien on my ranch? I don't owe you anything."

"No, but your brother does. He hasn't paid me a cent of his court costs." Kirk turned and went to his desk, not caring whether she followed or not. Stacks of old magazines and newspapers littered the desktop, along with file folders.

Lex tipped the only visitor's chair and dumped the trash that covered it. She took off her coat and placed it over the seat for Amanda. "Here, sweetheart. I don't want you to catch anything." She gave Kirk a nasty look as she stood close to the desk with her arms crossed over her chest. "Drop the lien."

He sat in an old, cloth covered desk chair. Threadbare in most places, darkly stained stuffing peeked out from multiple holes. The furniture creaked in complaint at his heavy body, but amazingly didn't collapse. "Hell, no. It's the only way I can get my money." Trumbull seemed to have noticed Amanda's appearance. "Well, well. Ain't you something." He smirked at Lex. "How'd you manage that one?"

"None of your damned business." Lex placed her hands on his desk. "Hubert has nothing to do with the ranch. If you want money from him, that's your problem."

"I'd say it's your problem, too." He opened the top right desk drawer, brought out a file, and tossed it on the desk by her hands. "I've got signed affidavits from him that show he's part owner. I am well within my rights."

Lex took the file and checked the papers. "Who's this judge? I've never heard of him."

"He's a younger guy who took over when Judge Packer retired. Hubert signed those affidavits years ago, and the judge thought they were more than enough proof to issue the lien."

"You know this is total bullshit." Lex threw the folder onto the desk, narrowly missing him. "Hell, you were there when Judge Packer threw out Hubert's claim to the ranch. It's got to be a matter of record."

Kirk settled in his chair. "Maybe. But it could take months to get this taken care of in court." He nodded in Amanda's direction. "It's not good for a broad in her condition to be under stress, you know. And something like this can be pretty stressful."

"Bastard!" Lex lunged across the desk at him.

He scooted out of her reach and laughed. "Watch it. You don't want to add assault charges, do you?"

Amanda wasn't in the mood to bail her partner out of jail. She stood and took Lex by the arm. "Lex, this isn't getting us anywhere. Let's go." Her head was pounding and she was feeling sick to her stomach. "Please?"

"You'd better listen to her, Walters." He stood, but kept the desk between them. "Take me to court if you want. But I'll file enough motions to keep you busy for years, if I have to. I have nothing better to do."

Lex started around the desk, but Amanda's hold on her arm tightened. She thought about jerking free, but one look at her lover's face changed her mind. "What's wrong?"

"It's nothing. I've got a little headache."

The argument with the sleazy lawyer was quickly forgotten. Lex grabbed her coat and put her arm around Amanda's shoulders. "Come on. Let's get you out of here." She solicitously led her lover away. "The bastard isn't worth it." She looked at him before she opened the front door. "This isn't over, Trumbull. I'll take care of you, later."

"Looking forward to it." His words followed them from the office.

Amanda was pale and perspiring. Her head was pounding, her

hands shook and, for a moment, she felt as if she would faint right there on the sidewalk. She was glad for Lex's supporting arm around her shoulders. Black spots dotted her vision. "I- I don't—" Her knees buckled and only Lex's strong hold kept her up.

"Amanda?" Lex half-carried her lover to a nearby bench. She knelt at her feet. "I'm calling an ambulance." She dug in her coat pocket for her cell, but Amanda stopped her. "What?"

"I'll be okay in a minute. Let me catch my breath." She dropped her head onto Lex's shoulder and closed her eyes. The headache didn't fade, but at least her nausea was better.

Lex put her arms around Amanda and stroked her hair. She didn't know if the action was for Amanda's sake or her own. Her own hands were trembling, and the fear of something happening to Amanda or the baby weighed heavily on her mind. As much as she hated to bow to anyone, her wife and child were more important than anything. She'd check with her lawyer later to see what her options were about handling the lien.

Amanda raised her head and looked into her lover's worried eyes. "I'm okay."

"Are you sure? Because I can take you to the hospital." Lex put one arm underneath Amanda's legs and the other around her shoulders. She started to rise, but was stopped by a hand on her arm.

"Don't you dare pick me up. You'll hurt yourself."

"But—"

"No." Amanda brushed her fingertips across Lex's cheek. "But I wouldn't mind if you brought the truck around. I'm still a little shaky."

Lex kissed her lightly on the lips. "You got it." She quickly stood. "Don't go anywhere. I'll be right back." She took off around the corner at a jog.

Amanda opened her mouth to tell her not to hurry, but Lex was out of sight before she could say anything. She was going to have to have a little talk with her wife. If Lex was this panicky now, she didn't think she'd be able to handle her when she finally went into labor.

"I TOLD YOU this wasn't necessary." Amanda sat on the examining room table, glad she was finally able to change from the dreaded gown. She gave Lex, who was wisely on the other side of the room, a disgusted look. Earlier, when Amanda had gotten into the truck, Lex informed her that she had an emergency appointment with her obstetrician. Two hours later, here she was. If looks could kill, there would only be a charred spot where Lex stood. "I'm feeling better."

Lex turned away from the window. She'd take Amanda's anger at her anytime, as long as she knew she was all right. But it was probably going to be a very chilly ride home, no matter what. "You're still pale, sweetheart. How's your headache?"

Amanda lied. "Not as bad."

The door opened and Dr. Vaughn stepped into the room. She noticed the distance between the couple and pursed her lips to keep from laughing. Over-protective spouses were not new to her. "Lex, why don't you join us over here?" She considered offering her protection, but didn't think Amanda was in the mood for levity.

Lex bravely took her place next to her wife, and was pleasantly surprised when her hand was grasped and held tightly. "Is Amanda okay?"

"That's what we're going to try and find out." The doctor sat on a rolling stool and moved closer to them. "Amanda, how long have you been getting these headaches?"

"A couple of weeks, I guess." Amanda did her best to ignore the look she knew she was getting from Lex. "But today was the first time it's been that bad."

Dr. Vaughn wrote something on the chart. "Your blood pressure is elevated, which I believe is the leading cause of the headaches. The blood sample we took is to check your total serum protein and I'd also like to schedule you for a glucose tolerance test next week, to be safe." She stood and gave Amanda a no-nonsense look. "I'll know more after the tests, but it's imperative you lower your stress." She turned to Lex. "That means you, too."

"Whatever it takes." Lex willed her heart rate to slow. The last thing she needed was to pass out in the doctor's office. "Is there anything else I can do?"

The doctor patted her on the arm. "Calm down. As far as I can tell, everything is going to be fine. Amanda, get more rest and drink plenty of fluids. You're slightly dehydrated."

"More fluids? I pee constantly, as it is."

"Sorry, doctor's orders." Dr. Vaughn scribbled something on a note pad and handed it to Lex. "Give this to Charlotte up front and she can schedule the test." She started to leave the room. "Amanda? Don't be too hard on her. Lex was right in having you come in."

Amanda waited until the doctor left, before she allowed Lex to help her down from the table. "Don't let it go to your head."

"What?"

"What she said. Just because you were right this time, doesn't mean you can hover more than you already are." She put her arm around Lex and leaned into her. "But if you want to take me home and give me another long massage, I'm all yours."

Lex did her best not to gloat. It would only make things harder on her later. "I like the sound of that." She escorted Amanda from the office, relieved that she wasn't in as much trouble as she had feared.

AFTER RETURNING FROM the doctor's office for the second time in as many weeks, Amanda was beside herself. The news hadn't been good. She was inconsolable, although Lex tried her best to bring her out of her funk.

The drive home had been tense, and now that they were in the house, Lex tried again. "But, it's not as bad as it could have been." She followed behind Amanda until they were in the kitchen.

"Not as bad?" Amanda opened a cabinet and brought out a glass, slamming the door shut. "How can you say that?" She opened the refrigerator, took out the carton of low-acid orange juice, and poured it into the glass. Replacing the carton, she slammed the appliance's door. She turned her angry eyes to Lex. "It practically amounts to house arrest."

Lex considered taking Amanda into her arms in an attempt to calm her. When she took a step forward, the glare she received caused her to rethink the notion. "I know it feels like that now, but the doctor is concerned for you. And so am I."

Amanda's glucose tolerance test came back as borderline. Dr. Vaughn explained to them how the baby was large for its gestational age and it was too soon for the intensity of the false labor pains she was already beginning to feel. Amanda would have to stop working until after the baby was born. Because of her family history, or, at least, her sister's first delivery nightmare, the doctor ordered Amanda on limited bed rest. It hadn't been a complete surprise to Amanda, but she still felt like she was being imprisoned. "It's too soon for this. I don't want to be stuck out here with nothing to do. I'll go nuts."

The comment stung. Lex thought Amanda liked having the ranch as their home. "Do you want us to get a house in town? Or maybe stay with your grandparents?" She waited until Amanda sat at the table. "What do you want?"

"No, that's not what I meant." Amanda looked into the glass of juice as if hoping to find the answer there. "I want to be able to enjoy this."

Lex knelt next to her chair and cautiously put her hand on Amanda's stomach. "You can. We will. Don't think of this as a bad thing, sweetheart. We can spend this time together, learning how the baby grows."

Amanda raised her head and gazed into her lover's eyes. "Together, huh?"

"Yep. You don't think I'm going to let you have all the fun, do you?" Lex took Amanda's hand and held it to her chest. "This is a magical time, and I plan on sharing every single minute with you."

"Keep reminding me of that, will you? And please don't let my bitchiness run you off." Amanda used her free hand to cup Lex's face. The stories she had heard from other women about their spouse's lack of support had worried her. But she should have known better than to think Lex would fall into that category. She was truly blessed to have such an understanding partner.

"Never. You're stuck with me. Besides, bed rest can be a good thing, you know. I'll be there to keep you company." Her lascivious grin had the desired effect. Amanda's laughter was music to her ears.

"I think the operative word there is rest, Slim. And if you're in bed with me, the last thing on my mind will be rest." She felt the burden lift from her shoulders, and now the thought of spending the next three months at home didn't seem so bad.

Chapter
Twenty-Nine

LEX STOMPED ALONG the sidewalk, her hands itching to throttle someone. They were shoved in the pockets of her duster and her hat was low over her eyes. The meeting with her lawyer didn't go as she had hoped, but she knew it would be in bad form to strangle the bearer of the bad news.

Melvin Taft contacted her after an unsuccessful meeting with the judge. The new magistrate was not impressed with the particulars of the case. He refused to rule on the validity of Kirk Trumbull's claim, saying the two parties would have to come to an understanding on their own. Mel related his feelings that Judge Stewart was homophobic, and that Trumbull had used that to his advantage. The only way to remove the lien was for Kirk to voluntarily remove it, which wasn't going to happen, or to pay him. That option didn't sit well with Lex, either. But a drawn-out court battle would have too many adverse effects on her family, and it was something she was determined to avoid.

"Damned jackass." Lex was on her way to the sleazy lawyer's office. The itemized bill Trumbull had presented Melvin with was outrageous. "Five dollars for a freakin' pen. Where the hell did he buy it? A government auction?" She was so angry over the news, she didn't see the body she slammed into until it was too late. Lex suddenly found herself sitting on the sidewalk.

"Watch it!" Hubert rubbed his shoulder. He considered kicking his sister for the fun of it. But she got to her feet before he could move. "What the hell's your problem?"

Lex dusted off her backside and readjusted her hat. "Besides you?" She looked around and saw several people watching them. "I'm almost glad I ran into you. We need to talk."

Her words sounded foreboding, but he'd be damned if he let her know it rattled him. "Make an appointment. I don't have time to mess with you."

"You'll make the time, brother." Lex leaned closer and lowered her voice. "Because you don't want to cross me right now."

"I'm so scared." But he backed up a step. He was bigger than she was, but the glint in her eyes made him uncomfortable. "Is that a threat?"

Lex's smile didn't reach her eyes. "Maybe. Where's your new office?" She knew as well as everyone else that his other place had been closed down shortly after he left for prison.

He gestured behind her. "About a block that way." Hubert grabbed her arm. "Come on. We might as well get this over with. I have things to do, you know."

"Keep your damned hands to yourself." Lex shook him off and walked beside her brother. His attitude only increased her ire, and she was hard-pressed to keep from slamming him into a wall and taking her frustrations out on him. When they stopped in front of a run-down storefront, she couldn't help but chuckle. "This is it?"

Hubert fussed with the lock until he was finally able to kick the door open. "Shut up. It's only temporary until my new place is ready." He had to use his shoulder to push the door open enough to step inside.

The musty air tickled Lex's nose and she fought the urge to sneeze. A lamp was on near the back of the room, its dim light casting eerie shadows in the cluttered space. Boxes, newspapers, and books were strewn everywhere. She had to sidestep a broken chair in order to follow him to his desk. "Nice place."

"Fuck you." Hubert sat behind the scarred desk, almost toppling out of the rickety chair. He shoved an old pizza box off the top in a pitiful attempt to make his space appear more professional. "The maid hasn't been in yet."

"Whatever." Lex considered cleaning off a chair but changed her mind. She didn't plan to be here long. She decided to get straight to the point. Amanda was waiting for her at the Cauble's, where she'd dropped her off earlier. "You need to pay your lawyer."

He carefully leaned back in his chair. "Why? The sorry bastard didn't do his job. I don't owe him shit."

"Wrong." She put her hands on her hips so she wouldn't be tempted to strangle him. "You owe him close to fifteen thousand dollars."

"What's it to you? It's none of your damned business."

Lex kicked a pile of empty food containers out of her way and moved closer to the desk. "It became my business when he decided to come after me for the money."

Hubert laughed. "Big fucking deal. Do you think I care?"

"You should." Lex started around the side of the desk, which caused him to slide quickly out of the way. "Because if I have to settle your debt, I plan on taking it out of your worthless hide."

He moved casually to keep the desk between them. "Like you could." He saw her tense and knew things were about to get out of hand. "Wait." Hubert gestured around the room. "As if you couldn't tell, I'm not exactly swimming in dough right now." He needed a plan, and soon. Hubert knew his sister wasn't bluffing. An idea blossomed in his head. "How about this. You pay Kirk, and I'll get a second mortgage on my house to pay you back." No need to tell her he already had a second mortgage and was behind on his house payments.

Something sounded fishy. Lex hadn't expected him to go along with her quite so easily. But it was more than she hoped for. "Give me something in writing before I leave."

"Sure, no problem." He dropped into his chair and had to yank several times before the desk drawer opened. He took out a piece of paper, but couldn't find a pen.

Lex sighed and took a pen out of her coat pocket. "Here."

Hubert jerked it out of her hand and stared at it. The pen was hand-carved wood and had her name engraved across the barrel. "Full of yourself, aren't you?"

"It was a gift."

He grunted, but used it to scribble several lines on the paper. With a flourish, he signed the document and handed it and the pen to her. "There. Happy?"

"Not until I get the money from you, I'm not." Lex read the paper then folded it and tucked it away. "I want a bank draft by the end of next week."

"Fine. I'll mail it to you." He stood. "Now get out. I've got stuff to do."

Lex smirked. "Hopefully, cleaning this dump up is first on your list." She tipped her hat. "Nice doing business with you, bro."

Hubert watched as she picked her way toward the door and left. "Good riddance, bitch." He looked around the room and nodded to himself. If things went right, he wouldn't have to worry about the office.

THE COFFEE SEEMED tasteless to Amanda, so she put the cup down in disgust and sighed. Not even the cheery kitchen could bring her out of her funk. "I might as well give up coffee altogether. Decaf's nasty. And I know I'll pay for it later." She pushed away from the table and went to the refrigerator for a glass of milk instead.

Lois stood and took both mugs to the sink and rinsed them. "I have to agree with you. I don't care what they say, I can tell the difference."

Talking about coffee somehow brought Amanda's thoughts to the one person who was never far from her mind. "I wish Lex would get here." She edged next to Lois and glanced out the window. "I can't wait to hear what she found out at the lawyer's office."

"I'm sure she'll be here as soon as she can. Why don't we go into the den and relax?" Lois put her arm around Amanda's shoulders as they left the kitchen. She had taken it upon herself to keep her company, since Anna Leigh and Jacob had left earlier to help a friend.

Amanda wanted to scream at Lois' attempt to keep her occupied. The woman meant well, but it made her feel as if she had a babysitter. Next time, she decided, she would bug Lex until she allowed her to go along. "I don't want to relax. I'm already bored to tears." But she lowered herself into the comfy chair nearest the fireplace. "It's bad enough that I've had to quit working."

"Are you regretting your decision to get pregnant?"

"No." Amanda rubbed her stomach and smiled as the baby kicked. "This is the most amazing thing in the world. I never thought I'd have this."

Lois wasn't exactly sure what Amanda meant by that. "A baby?"

"A family. Growing up, I never thought about the whole 'getting married, having kids' thing. I figured I'd leave that up to Jeannie. Then I met Lex, and everything changed." Amanda stood and went to the window to look out. "From the moment I looked into her eyes, I knew I wanted to spend the rest of my life with her." She brightened as Lex's truck pulled into the driveway. "She's here." Amanda started to go to the front door to meet Lex, but quickly remembered she was supposed to be resting. She went to her chair and tried to look innocent.

The door opened and Lex stuck her head into the living room. "There y'all are." She took off her hat and draped her coat over an empty chair. "Hey, Lois."

"Hello, Lex. Amanda was talking about you."

Lex sat on the edge of Amanda's chair and kissed her cheek. "Not all bad, I hope."

Amanda closed her eyes at the touch of her lover's lips. "Nope. I was telling Lois how easy it was to fall in love with you."

"Oh." Lex felt a blush heat her face. She quickly recovered, however. "Hope you told her how you practically threw yourself at me." She jumped when Amanda swatted her leg. "Ow."

"Serves you right." Amanda left her hand on Lex's thigh. "How'd it go at the lawyer's?"

It was the one subject she didn't want to go into, but Lex knew Amanda wouldn't let it go until she found out. "Not too well. Melvin told me the only way to remove the lien is for Trumbull to revoke it or for me to pay what's owed."

"That's not right! You shouldn't have to pay for your stupid brother. He's not worth it." The thought of Hubert getting away without paying for his legal fees made Amanda so mad she could barely see. "Can you have him arrested for fraud or something?"

Lex could feel Amanda shaking. "Calm down, sweetheart. It's going to be all right."

"But he—"

"Will pay, believe me." Lex couldn't keep the smirk off her face.

Amanda knew the look. Her partner definitely had something up her sleeve. "What?"

As much as she wanted to hear what Lex was going to say, Lois forced herself to leave the room. It was a private matter between the two of them, and if they wanted anyone else to know, they'd share.

Out of the corner of her eye, Lex noticed Lois' departure. To keep Amanda from getting a crick in her neck, Lex slid off the arm of the chair. She moved to the sofa, not surprised when Amanda joined her.

"Are you going to tell me or do I have to guess?" Amanda picked up Lex's hand and began to trace her fingers across the top. Her hands were strong and callused, and had always fascinated her.

Lex enjoyed the attention for a moment then mentally shook herself to get to the subject. "I caught Hubert on the street, right after I had spoken to Melvin."

Amanda raised her head. "You didn't stomp him, did you? Although the jerk deserves it."

"No, I was actually fairly civil, believe it or not."

"Then you're a better woman than I am," Amanda grumbled. "I'd have kicked his ass."

Lex didn't doubt that for a moment. The thought of her wife taking Hubert down brought a smile to her face. "As much as I'd enjoy the sight, I'm afraid it wouldn't do us any good."

"I know. But I can dream, can't I?"

"Yep."

"Okay. I think I'm over it. What happened?" Amanda rested against Lex's side. She couldn't believe how tired she was. She fought off a yawn. "Go ahead."

Lex put her arm around Amanda's shoulders. "We went to his office. Or at least a little hole in the wall he's using. It's nasty." A poke in her ribs got her attention. "We had a nice chat," another poke told her she wasn't believed, "and we came to an understanding. Since I'm stuck paying the bill, I authorized Melvin to take care of it. Hubert's getting a second mortgage on his house and is going to pay me next week."

"How did you get him to agree to that?" A thought occurred to Amanda. "You didn't have him pinned to the wall or something, did you?"

"No, although that would have been fun."

Amanda closed her eyes. Lex's voice always soothed her. As tired as she was, it wouldn't take much for her to doze off. "If he's going to mortgage his house, why doesn't he pay the lien?"

It was a valid question, and one Lex had already thought of. "Because I don't trust him. I don't want to lose the ranch and it would be safer for me to pay the bill, and then try to get the money out of his worthless hide."

"Makes sense." Amanda yawned again. "Sorry."

"Don't be." Lex kissed Amanda's head. "Nap time?"

"No." She sounded like a petulant child, but Amanda didn't care. "I don't want to nap. I want to stay here with you." But her body betrayed her by relaxing against her lover.

"Uh-huh." Lex stood, bringing Amanda up with her. "How about we both go upstairs? I could use a nap, too."

Amanda allowed Lex to guide her out of the den and up the stairs. "I don't believe you, but I'm too tired to call you on it." She stumbled at the top of the stairs, thankful for her partner's firm grasp. She felt Lex's arm tighten around her shoulders. "Don't even think it."

"What?" Lex opened the door to the guest room.

"You were about to pick me up. I could tell."

"I wasn't—"

Amanda tugged on Lex's arm. "You were, too." She sat on the edge of the bed. When Lex removed her shoes, she opened her mouth to argue.

"Ssh." Lex lifted Amanda's legs and helped her get comfortable. She covered her with a quilt, before taking her own boots off and climbing beside her.

"You don't have to coddle me." But Amanda was grateful for the attention. Her eyes closed in relief when Lex tucked an arm around her.

"We can argue about it later." Lex had to smile as soft snores answered her. She kissed Amanda's cheek. "Rest well, sweetheart." Everything was finally settling down, and Lex couldn't be happier.

Chapter
Thirty

LOS ANGELES IN February was wonderful, compared to where she had been. The winter chill in Paris had seeped into her bones, and Elizabeth Cauble couldn't wait to get to her leased bungalow on the beach and soak in the sun. But she had a few things to attend to before she enjoyed her return to the States.

The sleek sports car cut through the freeway traffic with ease. Elizabeth considered hiring a driver, but after being chauffeured around Europe, she longed to be behind the wheel again. The rented Mercedes SL500 was perfect for her needs. She had the top down and felt freer than she had in years. Her red scarf held her perfectly coiffed hair in place, and her designer sunglasses kept the bright California sun out of her eyes.

She took the next exit, cutting in front of several cars as she swerved across two lanes of traffic. Elizabeth waved behind her at the indignant honking. It's what they deserved for getting in her way. Twenty minutes later, she double-parked the Mercedes in front of an upscale building. She didn't bother to lock it. After all, this was Beverly Hills.

Elizabeth glided into the store as if she were royalty and was granting favor with her subjects. The art gallery was decorated with sparsely scattered paintings, yet reeked of pretentiousness. When no one greeted her, she crossed her arms over her chest and cleared her throat loudly.

The room echoed, but otherwise remained silent.

"Excuse me!" Elizabeth bellowed in her most commanding voice. Her nose lifted slightly in the air as she waited impatiently.

The click-clack of high heels against the polished marble floor moved closer, until a diminutive brown-haired woman pulled up short in astonishment. "Mrs. Cauble?" Her dark brown eyes blinked nervously. "What a pleasant surprise."

"I'm sure it is." Elizabeth haughtily glared at her. She strode by the clerk on her way to the office. "Delilah, I'm going to check the books."

The clerk followed along, struggling to keep up. "Darla, ma'am."

"No, I rather like Delilah better. Come along." Elizabeth snapped her fingers. "I want to see how you've been handling things in my absence."

"Yes, ma'am."

It took Elizabeth only an hour to see that her gallery thrived under the young woman's care. She knew it had been doing well. Along with the money she had absconded with years previously, the funds directly deposited in her overseas bank account kept her living comfortably. She closed the accounting program on the computer and spun her chair around to focus on Darla. "It appears you've been doing quite well, my dear. I don't recall my daughter handling the gallery any better."

"Thank you, ma'am." Darla felt a kernel of pride at her employer's remarks. "Oh! By the way, I hear that congratulations are in order."

"I beg your pardon?"

Darla didn't see the look of consternation that crossed Elizabeth's face. "You know, your daughter's wedding? I wish I could be there. I suppose that's why you've returned to the United States, isn't it?"

Elizabeth couldn't believe what she was hearing. Her daughter, getting married? She knew it was only a matter of time before Amanda came to her senses and dumped that ill-mannered, uneducated, no-good Lexington Walters. It was bad enough she had to cavort with a woman, but to be with someone so obviously beneath her station was unacceptable. "Of course. It's only proper that I attend. Amanda wouldn't want it any other way."

"Amanda?" Darla shrugged. "I guess she will be glad to see you, too. But I was talking about Jeannie. She was so excited the last time I spoke with her on the phone." Jeannie and Darla had known each other since college. It was Jeannie who hired her to work in the gallery, and once she had become pregnant with her first child, she turned over the managerial duties to Darla.

"Jeanne Louise? That vegetable? Who'd marry someone who can't even swallow her own drool?"

The vehemence in Elizabeth's voice unnerved Darla. "Um, Mrs. Cauble? Surely you realize Jeannie has fully recovered from her stroke. I figured you kept in touch with her, even though you'd been in Europe all this time."

Elizabeth recovered from her surprise quickly. "No, I'm afraid not. The last time I heard anything about my daughter, she was in an assisted care facility. I've been quite busy in Paris."

"Oh."

"No matter." Elizabeth rose and waved her hand in the air dismissively. "When and where are the nuptials?"

Darla's face went blank. "Huh?" She wished the woman would speak English. She barely understood her half the time.

"The wedding, Delilah. What date has been set?"

"You don't know?"

Elizabeth sighed dramatically. "I believe we have already established that." When the young woman didn't answer, she snapped her fingers in front of Darla's face.

Darla blinked. "I'm sorry. The wedding is set for next week. You know, Valentine's Day?"

"How droll." Elizabeth tucked her purse beneath her arm and walked out of the office. "It appears I will be making another trip."

Darla scurried behind her. "Mrs. Cauble?"

"Yes?" Elizabeth stopped. She had so much to do and chatting with this silly girl was only wasting her time. "What is it?"

"Would you mind giving Jeannie something for me?" Darla rushed to the office and reappeared, carrying an envelope in her hand. "I have been meaning to mail this."

Elizabeth took the letter from her. "And what, pray tell, is this?"

"A gift card. For the baby."

"Baby? Oh, you mean my granddaughter?" Elizabeth tucked the envelope into her purse.

Darla shook her head. "It's for her son. She gave birth at Thanksgiving. Isn't it wonderful?"

Having a baby out of wedlock was not Elizabeth's idea of wonderful. She tried to keep an impassive look on her face. "I suppose. Now if you'll excuse me, I must be going. Since my dear Jeanne Louise has two young children, she'll need her mother." She turned and strode purposely out of the gallery. There were plans to make, and a trip to prepare for.

NO MATTER WHAT the temperature was, or how nicely the room was decorated, the obstetrician's exam room always felt cold and uncomfortable to Lex. And she wasn't the one who had to lie on the table with only a thin gown and a sheet for protection from the chill. She tightened her grip on Amanda's hand. Even though her partner was once again fully dressed, Lex still detected coolness in their joined hands. "Are you doing okay, sweetheart?"

"Better than you, I think." It never ceased to amuse Amanda at how nervous her usually confident wife became once they stepped through Dr. Vaughn's doors. "Relax. I'm feeling much better, I promise."

The door opened and Dr. Vaughn stepped inside as Amanda spoke. "You're right. The latest tests show everything is closer to normal range." She wrote something in Amanda's chart and placed it on the counter. She hoped her next news would bring her patient out of the funk she admitted to being in. "If things keep progressing this well, we may be able to reconsider the caesarean."

As happy as Lex was to hear the news, she was terrified of anything happening to her partner. "But will it be safe?"

"As safe as any delivery can be. But," here the doctor gave Amanda a severe look, "you have to promise to keep behaving yourself. No working, lots of rest, and absolutely no stress. If your blood pressure goes up again, I'll put you on total bed rest."

Lex answered for both of them. "We promise." She flinched when Amanda squeezed her hand particularly hard. "What?"

"You're not the one who has to do nothing all the time." Amanda pulled her hand away and attempted to cross her arms over her stomach. Not being able to do so comfortably made her even more upset. "This is so unfair."

Dr. Vaughn tried to gently reassure her. "You knew you'd have to make certain concessions when you decided to become pregnant."

"I know. But I didn't think I'd be forced to give up so much. And what about next week? My sister is getting married and she wants me to be her matron-of-honor."

"You can still participate, as long as you don't overdo it." The doctor patted her on the knee. "Don't think of this as a bad thing. You'll be begging for quiet once the baby arrives."

Amanda slipped her hand into Lex's. "I remember what we went through with Lorrie." She rested her head against her partner's arm. "I'm very lucky to have Lex. She had more sleepless nights than I did."

"I've enjoyed every minute of it." Lex was glad Amanda seemed more like herself. She never knew which one would make an appearance—happy, glad to be pregnant Amanda, or the woman whose glare could melt steel. Lex had been on the receiving end of that particular look more than once. She still hadn't figured out why. "So. Dr. Vaughn, is there anything special we can do to help Lorrie understand all this? She's felt the baby kick, but I think she's still confused."

Dr. Vaughn checked her watch. "I think I can help you with that. Let me find out something." She headed toward the door. "I'll be right back."

Lex exchanged confused looks with Amanda. "Was it something I said?"

The door opened and the doctor came in with a pleased look on her face. "Are you busy tomorrow afternoon?"

"Not that I know of." Amanda verified that by watching Lex shrug. "What's up?"

"I don't know why I didn't think of this before. We have a 'big brother, big sister' program and the next class is tomorrow afternoon. It's a puppet show that helps explain what a new baby means to the household. Afterward, I spend about fifteen minutes with each family so the child can hear the baby's heartbeat with a stethoscope. It goes a long way in making the big brother or sister feel more a part of the experience." The blank stare she was getting from Lex surprised her. "Trust me, it's a lot of fun."

"I'm not sure if I want her to have that much knowledge. Lorrie already outthinks me more than she should." Lex's proud look told she wasn't serious. "Are you sure she's not too young for it?"

Dr. Vaughn adjusted the white coat she wore and placed her hands in the pockets. "Not at all. We have several different classes. She'll be with kids her own age."

Amanda slid from the table less gracefully than she wanted. She welcomed Lex's steadying arm around her shoulders. "It sounds wonderful." She pulled her top over her stomach. "Would you mind giving Lex all the details? I've really, really got to go." She toddled out of the room as fast as her growing bulk would allow.

LEX HELD LORRIE'S hand after they left the truck. Amanda walked quietly beside them. She had been introspective all morning, and Lex wondered what was going on with her. Once inside the doctor's office, they were directed to a conference room at the end of the hall. Excited children's voices streamed through the open door. Lex struggled to keep Lorrie from racing inside. "Hang on there, lil' bit. No running indoors." Lorrie broke free and took off, leaving her parents behind.

Amanda couldn't help but laugh at the look on her partner's face. "She listens about as well as you do." She followed their daughter at a slower pace until they were inside the organized chaos of the room.

Six other young children were chatting excitedly with each other, some pointing to the elaborate puppet stage set up in one corner of the room. A man and a woman, both appearing to be in their mid-twenties, stood close by. They were dressed in black and the woman glanced up and noticed the latest arrivals. She brushed her red hair away from her face and her eyes widened when she recognized Lex and Amanda. She said something to her partner and walked across the room toward them.

"Oh, shit." Lex hoped there weren't any liquids nearby. What were the odds that Ashley Pendleton would be one of the puppeteers? She put her arm around Amanda and led her to the rear wall, where the other parents sat.

One of the women held out her hand but didn't bother standing. She was further along than Amanda, but appeared happy to see them. "Amanda? What a small world."

It took Amanda a moment to place her. "Laurie Roland?" It had been four years since she had sold them a house, but Amanda rarely forgot a face. She shook Laurie's hand before sitting next to her. "Where's Dan?"

"He's over there, getting me some juice." She pointed to another wall where a refreshment table had been set up.

"I think I'll go say hello. Excuse me, ladies." Lex nodded to Laurie and crossed the room. She had a feeling there was about to be a major gab session between the two pregnant women and she'd feel more comfortable talking with Dan.

Laurie laughed when Lex made her escape. "Is she as squeamish as Dan? I swear he turns white during every one of my exams."

"Worse." Amanda watched her daughter interact with a smaller girl, whose wispy blonde hair stuck out over her head. She pointed to the two girls. "It looks like our daughter Lorrie has already made a friend."

"Are you talking about that dark-haired little girl?" At Amanda's answering nod, Laurie chuckled. "She's with my Courtney. Oh look. Isn't that sweet?" Lorrie had taken Courtney's hand and led her close to the front of the stage. They sat next to each other and continued to chatter.

Amanda loved how open and friendly Lorrie was with other children. "Your daughter is beautiful, Laurie. How old is she?"

"Thank you. She's twenty-seven months, but hasn't seemed to have hit her terrible two's...yet. How about yours? I see that she's the spitting image of Lex." She leaned closer to Amanda and lowered her voice. "How did you manage it? Forgive me for saying so, but I can't picture Lex pregnant."

The loud laugh that unexpectedly erupted from Amanda caused them to be the center of attention for a moment, before everyone returned to their own conversations. "I'm sorry. But, you've got it so right. Lex would have to be sedated for nine months if she were pregnant."

"I can imagine. Well, no matter how she came to be, she's absolutely adorable." She noticed Amanda bristled when the female puppeteer approached Lex. "Do they know each other?"

"Not as well as that bi-, I mean woman, would like to." Even though Amanda would have liked nothing better than to yank the woman bald-headed, she stayed where she was to allow Lex to handle things. For now.

Lex felt a touch on her back and assumed it was Amanda. "Hey there, beautiful." She turned and realized it was Ashley. "Forget I said anything." She took a step away to keep the woman out of her personal space. The last thing she wanted was for Amanda to see their interaction and get bent out of shape. "Hey, Ashley. I didn't know you did puppets."

"That's because you didn't take the time to find out anything about me." Ashley stepped between Lex and Dan, turning her back on him to remove him from the conversation. "I see you're still with that fat gal. Don't you know you could do so much better?"

"I think you should leave." Lex's voice was soft, but the angry glint in her eyes spoke louder than her words.

Ashley ignored the warning and moved closer, her breasts almost brushing Lex's shirt. She had barely touched Lex, when her hand was grabbed and squeezed. "Let go. You're hurting me."

Lex leaned close so that her words wouldn't be overheard. "If you ever say anything about my wife again, you'll find out what hurt is. Get it through your thick skull, woman. I don't want anything to do with you. Back off, and go play with your puppets." She released her grip and stepped around Ashley. "Dan, why don't we go sit with our ladies and enjoy the show?"

Dan wasn't sure what had transpired, but was more than happy to follow Lex. The redhead had given him the creeps. "Sure."

Amanda waited until Lex got comfortable next to her before she took her hand and held it in her lap. Lex's heavy exhale concerned her. "Are you all right?"

"Yep. I don't think she'll bother us anymore."

"Good. I was wondering what we'd have to do to get it through her head." Amanda scooted closer while the room quieted down and the puppets came to life.

"CAN I BE on teebee?" Lorrie tapped the monitor with one hand, fascinated. She pointed to a rapidly moving image on the screen. "What's dat?"

Dr. Vaughn coughed to cover her laugh. "That's the baby's heart beating. Remember? It's that fast thumping sound."

Lorrie bounced her head. "Bum, bum, bum, bum." She slid off Lex's lap and climbed into the chair next to the table. She watched the doctor move the wand across Amanda's stomach. "Dat's dumpin?"

"Well, yes. We use this to help us see the baby. It also lets us hear the thumping." Dr. Vaughn took one of Lorrie's hands and helped her grip the wand. "Here, you can do it, too." She noticed Amanda squirming. "Are you doing all right?"

"My bladder's about to burst, but otherwise I'm doing great." The wand slid all across Amanda's stomach, which bounced while she laughed at the look of concentration on Lorrie's face. "Careful, sweetie. That tickles. And I don't think me laughing too much is a good thing right now." Then she squirmed some more. Her bladder was demanding attention.

Lex took up a position behind Lorrie, although she knew the doctor wouldn't let her fall. She was impressed by how patiently Dr. Vaughn answered all her daughter's questions. It affirmed in her mind their decision to use the doctor, who was new to the area.

Lorrie swiped her free hand through the gel on Amanda's belly. "Uck!" She made a fist, which caused it to squish between her fingers.

She turned and held out her hand to Lex. "Momma, help."

"Hang on, kiddo." Lex grabbed a towel and picked up Lorrie. She missed the tiny hand, which bypassed the towel and splatted against her cheek. "Ugh."

Dr. Vaughn took pity on Lex and took over the cleaning duties. Once she was finished, she helped Lorrie down to allow Lex a chance to wipe the gel off Amanda. "Come on, Lorrie. Let's go find some milk and cookies while your mommy gets dressed."

Amanda sat up after they left. She liked how down to earth Dr. Vaughn was. "We got lucky with her, didn't we?"

"Yep." Lex helped her with her blouse. "And the doctor's pretty cool, too." She waited until Amanda had pulled on her pants before she picked up her shoes. "I think Lorrie had a good time today." She knelt by Amanda's chair and slipped the comfortable shoes on her feet without a second thought.

Amanda studied Lex's head. Something shiny caught her eye. "Ooh."

"What?" Lex felt the top of her head, where Amanda tugged on a strand of hair. "Hey! Why are you pulling my hair?"

"I found your first gray." Amanda released the strand of silver.

"You did not!"

"Did too!" Amanda pulled on it again. "Right here."

Lex grabbed Amanda's hand. "Yank it out."

"No! I like it." Amanda tucked it down. "I think you'll look good with gray hair."

"I'm too young to be getting that old." Lex scratched her head. "I don't want to be old and gray before Lorrie starts school. They'll think I'm her grandma or something."

Amanda rolled her eyes. "One gray hair does not make you old, silly. Now help me up so I can run to the restroom and you can relieve Dr. Vaughn of our daughter."

Lex did as she was asked. While they walked out of the office, she rubbed the top of her head again. Maybe they'd stop by the drug store on the way home and pick up some hair color.

Chapter
Thirty-one

THE FIGURE IN the mirror had become unrecognizable to Amanda. She glared at her reflection. The vibrant blue dress fit her form a little too well for her taste. She tugged at the sides in an effort to make it look better. "I look like a blueberry."

Lex tucked in her navy blue dress shirt and buckled her belt. The black slacks she wore were a concession to the special day. She had promised Jeannie she'd "clean up," although she teasingly threatened to wear her old scruffy boots and her usual battered cowboy hat. Her sister-in-law hadn't been amused. She glanced at Amanda. "No, you don't."

"I most certainly do."

Lex fastened the buttons on her cuffs and moved to stand behind her lover at the mirror. She put her arms around Amanda and rested her chin on her shoulder. "You know, now that you mention it, you do remind me of something."

Amanda tensed. "What?" Lex's breath tickled her ear. She fought the urge to brush the maddening lips away. The gentle assault continued as Lex nibbled on her neck. She tapped the top of Lex's head. "Hello? You were saying?"

"Hmm?" It was always fun to tease Amanda, but Lex relented. "You look stunning. Seeing you standing there like that takes my breath away. I don't know how you manage it, but you keep getting more beautiful every day."

Although she didn't believe a word of what her partner said, the sentiment touched Amanda deeply. "You're so sweet." She tangled her fingers in Lex's hair and pulled her closer. "But I thought you said this dress reminded you of something."

"Yep. It sure does." Lex kissed the skin where Amanda's neck met her shoulder. "It reminds me how lucky I am to be married to you."

Amanda turned in her arms and gave Lex a heartfelt kiss. "I'm going to have to keep you." A knock on the door kept her from more in-depth exploration. "Someone has rotten timing."

Lex kissed the tip of her nose. "Nah. Another minute like this, and we'd be late for the ceremony."

The door opened and Jeannie came into the room. She noticed the way Lex was wrapped around Amanda. "Don't you two ever get enough?"

"Nope." But Lex loosened her hold and moved a step away from Amanda. "I guess you want some last minute instructions from your sister, huh?" She started to walk around Jeannie, who stopped her with a hand on her arm.

"Actually, I wanted to talk to you both." Jeannie adjusted her dress and sat gingerly on the edge of the bed. She had decided against a traditional wedding dress. Instead, she wore a simple, pale blue silk dress that came to just above her knees. She held a small jewelry box that she kept moving from one hand to the other.

Amanda noticed the gesture. She could tell that Jeannie was nervous about something, and she didn't think it was her impending nuptials. "Are you okay?"

"Yes. I mean, no. I mean, I think so." Jeannie gnawed at her lower lip. This was going to be a touchy subject, and she was still debating on whether it was a good idea or not. Unable to come up with a suitable opening, she wordlessly handed the jewelry box to her sister.

Lex stepped behind Amanda and peered over her shoulder. "What's that?"

"I don't know." Amanda opened the box and saw two gold rings nestled in green satin. "Jeannie?"

"Okay, let me explain." Jeannie stood. "These are mine and Frank's rings. I don't know what you're going to tell Lorrie when she gets older, but I thought—"

Amanda snapped the lid shut. "You thought she might like them?" She handed the box to Lex.

Jeannie lowered her eyes. She knew it had been a stupid idea. Her voice was barely audible. "I know she's your daughter now. But I only thought she'd like to have something of her father's, when she's older." She was surprised when she felt her sister pull her into an embrace.

"That's an incredibly thoughtful thing to do, Sis." Amanda knew how hard it was for Jeannie to give up that final link to Frank. "Lex and I discussed this when we adopted Lorrie. When she's old enough, we plan on letting her know who her father is. And we'd like to tell her how brave and selfless her real mom is, too."

"I'd like that." Jeannie wiped a tear from her cheek. "I guess I'd better get out there. Gramma is probably tearing the house up looking for me."

Amanda grasped her hand. "I'll go with you. It's almost time for the ceremony to start." She followed Jeannie out of the room.

Lex studied the velvet-covered box she held. The aching loss was almost as strong today as it had been three years ago. She missed the robust man who had so easily befriended her. "Don't worry, Frank. I promise I'll keep a close eye on both your girls." She placed the box into her overnight bag and left the room.

WHILE AMANDA RUSHED to one last bathroom break, Lex was in the kitchen struggling to keep Lorrie from removing her dress. The pale yellow dress flared out around her knees, due to the lacy petticoats beneath it. The lace itched, and Lorrie wanted no part of it. "Hold still, lil' bit. Your bow came untied." Before she could move her hand away, Lorrie had pulled the bow loose again.

"No!" Lorrie started to swing the ends of the bow around. "Don't want dis."

"I know, but it'll only be for a little while, then you can get into your play clothes." Lex tied the ribbon and caught the little girl's hands before she could do any more damage. "Lorrie, stop."

Lorrie jerked her hands away. "No!" She stomped her foot for good measure. Her new black patent-leather shoes clacked loudly on the tile floor. She pulled at the frilly dress Jeannie had picked out for her. "Momma, dis no good." She shook one foot. "Hurts."

"I know it's not comfortable, sweetheart. You won't have to wear it long, I promise. As soon as the ceremony is finished we'll go upstairs and change." If Lorrie wasn't in the wedding party, Lex would have dressed her in something more appropriate. As it was, she argued for days about Jeannie's choice of clothing.

Instead of having Lorrie be the flower girl, Jeannie and Rodney decided to keep things simple and have her carry the rings. Lorrie had been very excited about her participation until she saw what she was going to have to wear. Even at three, she was extremely opinionated about her clothes. Amanda swore it was Lex's fault, even though she'd never expressed her views on fashion around their daughter.

Amanda stepped into the room. She wished for a camera when she saw her partner trying to reason with their daughter. "Do you need any help, Momma?"

Lex stood and dusted off the knee of her slacks. "No, I think we have it handled." She took Amanda's hands in hers and kissed her lightly on the lips. "Are you doing okay?"

"I'm fine. But this had better be a short ceremony. Otherwise, I'm afraid I'll embarrass myself by running off to the bathroom...again." Both turned when they heard a mysterious thump. "Lorrie!"

"Dere." Lorrie stepped away from the trash can with a satisfied look on her face. Her feet were bare and she was on the verge of pulling her dress over her head when Lex interrupted her.

"Lorrie, no." Lex dipped one hand into the trash and grimaced when her hand found the shoes. She pulled them out slowly. Coffee grounds covered the leather. "I can't believe you did that." Something unidentifiable dripped from one of the shoes. "Ugh."

Amanda had to cover her mouth to keep from laughing. The look on Lex's face was priceless. She cleared her throat before speaking. "I don't think those are salvageable."

Lex took them to the sink. "No kidding." She placed the shoes on a paper towel and washed her hands. "Now what are we going to do? She can't go barefoot."

"Oh, I don't know. I think it would be cute." Amanda held up her hand before Lex could say anything. "I'm kidding. What other shoes does she have here?"

"Her boots and I think a pair of sneakers." Lex exhaled heavily when she heard a happy yelp come from Lorrie. The child was now dancing in place, wearing only her white tights and underwear. The dress was hanging half in, half out, of the trash. "Dammit!"

Amanda grabbed Lex's arm as she walked by. "Honey, wait." She could tell Lex was close to her breaking point. "Since Lorrie's boots are here, I'm assuming her jeans are too?"

"Yeah. Martha told me she wanted to dress like me this morning, so she wore her cowboy outfit." Now that she was over the original shock, watching Lorrie dance gleefully around the kitchen did seem quite amusing. "Looks like the ring bearer is going to be more casual than everyone else." She kissed Amanda's cheek. "We'll be down in a few minutes." Lex held out her hand. "Lorrie, come on. Time to get dressed."

They were almost out of the room when Amanda called out to her. "Don't forget her belt and hat. We might as well go all the way."

That got a laugh out of Lex. She couldn't wait to see the look on Jeannie's face when she saw Lorrie. It would serve her right, for trying to make Lorrie wear something so uncomfortable.

Fifteen minutes later, everyone was in their place outside. Lex walked slowly toward the minister, with Amanda's hand tucked in the crook of her arm. In front of them Lorrie strutted proudly, her western hat bobbing with each step. Her jeans were neatly pressed, and the shirt she wore was a bright yellow. Even her boots gleamed in the early afternoon sunshine.

Lex placed a kiss on Amanda's cheek before kneeling to whisper something in Lorrie's ear. She must have been satisfied by her daughter's answer, because she kissed Lorrie on the nose before sitting in the front row.

The murmuring crowd silenced as the string quartet began to play the traditional wedding march. All heads turned to see Michael escort Jeannie toward her future husband, who stood nervously in place. Rodney's face was pale. It took his younger brother, Jared, poking him in the arm to make him blink and attempt to relax.

All was going smoothly until it was time for Lorrie to give up the rings. When the minister held out his hand, she tucked the pillow close to her and shook her head. "No. Mine."

Everyone laughed, but the minister didn't feel like arguing with a three-year-old. "Young lady, you've done a commendable job. Now it's time to relinquish the rings and sit." He reached for the satin pillow to which the rings were tied.

"Mine!" Lorrie jumped away.

Rodney waved off Lex, who started to stand. He knelt in front of the little girl. "Hi, Lorrie."

She wrinkled her nose and looked at him for a long moment. "Hi." Lorrie gave him a bashful smile.

He leaned closer and lowered his voice. "Are you ready for this to be over? It's kind of boring, isn't it?"

"Yep."

"Well, if you'll give the nice man the rings, we can finish all this boring stuff and go have cake."

Lorrie seemed to consider his request. "Otay." She didn't like the minister so she gave the pillow to Rodney. "Dere."

"Thank you, Lorrie." He stood and handed the rings to the reverend. "I think we're ready to finish this up." Rodney took his place beside Jeannie again. They exchanged vows, and the entire gathering was relieved when the happy couple went down the aisle together.

THE MILLING CROWD was a perfect place to hide. Although she didn't think the Ladies Auxiliary Hall was appropriate for the festivities, Elizabeth had no problem blending in with the other people in the room. The circle of women she had joined were all dressed in their Sunday finery and barely gave her a moment's notice. Most of them were her own age and, without knowing it, their chatter provided her with a detailed description of the wedding ceremony she missed.

Elizabeth was still seething over the loss of that particular milestone in her daughter's life. Not because she wanted to be there for Jeannie. No, she believed it was her inalienable right as the mother of the bride to be an integral part of the ceremony. *I would have done so, anyway, if it had been in a church, like a proper wedding.*

One of the women waved her drink around to punctuate her point. "Mind you, I have no problem with young children having a small part in a wedding. But you think they would give that young one better manners," a particularly snotty woman shared. "Allowing their daughter to throw such a fit. It's not proper."

The lady next to her rolled her eyes. "Mona Lennon! I thought she was precious. And I don't remember your own grandchildren being very well behaved at that age."

"Hrumph. Mine are angels, compared to that heathen. I mean, seriously, Shirley. What she was wearing was totally inappropriate."

"Get over yourself, Mona. You're jealous because Lois was the one who did most of the planning. I would think it's the mother's right, being so heavily involved. Lois did a beautiful job."

There was another thorn in her side. Elizabeth was hard-pressed to keep an outraged look off her face. She knew all about Lois. The interloper had snagged her husband away from her. It didn't matter to Elizabeth that they had been divorced for nearly a year before he remarried. Michael was hers and no court order could change that. She could be silent no more. "She's not the real mother though, is she? Does anyone know why the bride's own mother wasn't present?"

Mona snorted. "That psycho?" She leaned in closer to Elizabeth. "I heard she was locked up in a loony bin somewhere."

Elizabeth was about to defend herself when she heard a commotion across the room. Rodney was dancing in place to the music, holding a young girl on his shoulders. The child had both hands tangled in his hair and was chattering happily. She wondered who the little girl was, until she saw her daughter Jeannie pull on her legs. *Could that be?* Yes, she was the right age. Elizabeth felt a small stirring of pride at how beautiful her granddaughter had become. Although she would have to talk to Jeannie about how to dress her more becomingly. *That western outfit! Disgusting! Jeannie can't truly be well if she let her daughter dress like that worthless dirt farmer of Amanda's.*

Shirley noticed where Elizabeth's attention had shifted. "Isn't she adorable? I think she looks so much like her mother."

"That she does." Even from her distant vantage point, Elizabeth could see that.

In the kitchen, matronly ladies moved about at a frenetic pace, loaded with platters of hors d'oeuvres and ingredients for punch. They bustled about with almost military precision as they prepared refreshments for the guests. Amanda, bored beyond belief, sat in a corner out of the way. She had tried to help with the preparations earlier, only to be directed to a chair by her grandmother. Every time she tried to get up several of the women had clucked their disapproval, until she surrendered and plopped into the seat they assigned her.

"Are you all right, dearest?" Anna Leigh noticed the expression on Amanda's face and mistook it for weariness. She sat next to her and in concern, placed a hand on her granddaughter's arm. "Perhaps I should take you home."

Amanda hated feeling so useless. "Please don't. I'm fine." The baby moved, causing her to groan and stand. "Well, I was. Save my seat, will you? My daughter has made her presence known and demands attention." She moved slowly through the door, grumbling under her breath. "I'm so sick and tired of racing to the bathroom every five minutes." She caressed her stomach while she waddled to the restroom. "Would you please give your poor mommy a break?"

Another shift in her baby's position made her quicken her steps. "Gee, thanks."

In the circle of women, Elizabeth gasped when she saw Amanda's condition. "Oh, my."

Shirley mistook her expression. "Isn't she beautiful? Pregnancy does suit her."

"Yes, it does." Elizabeth felt vindicated. *It's obvious I've missed many things in my children's lives recently. Apparently, Amanda has had a change of heart and has dumped that woman and found herself a husband. It's about time.* Now she had two daughters she could be proud of.

Another's entrance into the hall deflated Elizabeth's happiness.

Lex strode into the room purposely, stopping along the way to shake hands with several people before gesturing toward the dance floor. She was almost there when Lorrie spotted her.

"Momma!" Lorrie squirmed until Rodney helped her to the floor. She ran to Lex and held out her arms.

"Hello there, lil' bit. Have you been good?" Lex scooped her up and swung her around, as her daughter squealed her delight.

Elizabeth had heard enough. She pushed through the crowd until she was close enough to the pair to be seen. "Put my granddaughter down immediately, you bitch!"

Lex almost dropped Lorrie but regained her equilibrium quickly. "Watch your language around my daughter, Elizabeth. What are you doing here?"

"Protecting what's mine." Elizabeth moved closer. "Now hand her to me." A curious crowd began to form around them.

Amanda had heard the clamor when she came out of the bathroom. In moments, she was at Lex's side. "Mother? What are you doing here?"

Elizabeth spun around. "Please don't worry yourself, dear. I'm only trying to remove this unwelcome visitor before she causes a scene."

Jeannie and Rodney were soon flanking Lex and Amanda. Jeannie had told him more than he cared to know about this woman. During Jeannie's rehabilitation, she had told him how Elizabeth had disowned her when she became incapacitated, and about her mother's unhealthy obsession with Amanda. "Mrs. Cauble, perhaps you should leave." He was gratified that Martha had stayed at the Cauble's with Teddy. He didn't want this unstable woman anywhere near his son.

"I'm not going anywhere until this is resolved. How can you stand here while she puts her perverted hands on my granddaughter?"

Lex took a step away before passing Lorrie over to Rodney. She wanted her hands free in case Elizabeth did something rash. "As you can see, you're not welcome here. Get out before I have the pleasure of throwing you out."

"You wouldn't dare!" Elizabeth looked at Amanda. "Surely you're not going to stand there and let her speak to me that way?"

Amanda entwined her arm with Lex's. "I am. And if I wasn't in this condition, I'd help her. Go home. This is a family event and you're not welcome."

Elizabeth turned to Jeannie. "Is that true? Don't you want your own mother here?"

"You haven't been my mother for years, Elizabeth." Jeannie put her arm around her sister in a show of support. "Please leave."

Lorrie didn't understand what was going on. She wriggled in Rodney's grasp until he had no choice but to let her down. Frightened over the adult's angry voices, she stood behind Lex and wrapped her arms around her leg. "Momma?" She pointed to Elizabeth. "Who's 'dat?"

It suddenly dawned on Elizabeth what Lorrie said. "Momma? That's impossible."

Michael quickly joined the group. He took Elizabeth's arm in a firm grasp. "Let's go, Elizabeth. You have no right to be here."

She jerked ineffectually at his hold. "Release me at once. I have every right. This is my family."

The excitement was becoming too much for Amanda. Her heart was pounding and she could feel the pressure building in her head. She swayed and would have fallen if not for the grip she had on Lex. "You don't have a family. Please don't ruin this day for Jeannie." She faltered and was relieved to have Lex's support.

"Sweetheart?" Lex forgot all about Elizabeth when she felt Amanda sag against her. Although she wanted nothing more than to throw her mother-in-law out of the building, her wife was her first concern. "Let me take you home." Without another thought, she turned her back on Elizabeth and carefully led Amanda away from the excitement.

Lorrie, who had started to follow her parents, glared at Elizabeth. She pointed a bold finger in the agitated woman's direction. "Bad." Then, afraid she'd be left behind, she quickened her pace and grabbed hold of Lex's pants leg.

Michael waited until they were out of earshot. He pulled Elizabeth in the opposite direction, toward the back door. "Let's go. You've caused enough trouble for one day."

"Let me go this instant! You can't treat me this way." Elizabeth's voice continued to rise as they left the building. "This isn't over, not by a long shot."

Jeannie watched them leave. She could feel the room's attention centered on the drama that played itself out. "Well, wasn't that exciting? Come on, everyone. Let's dance." She took Rodney's hand and led him to the dance floor, earnestly hoping her sister was all right.

Chapter
Thirty-two

THE WEEKS FOLLOWING the wedding were uneventful. Lex spent most of her time close to the ranch house, concerned about Amanda. Her partner had been uncharacteristically quiet after the wedding, even though Elizabeth had made herself scarce.

At the moment, Lex was searching for her missing daughter. Lorrie's disappearance was completely her fault. She had gone inside the house earlier and forgotten to make certain the latch closed on the back door. When she returned downstairs, the back door was wide open and Lorrie was nowhere in sight. Lex had to find her before Amanda woke from her nap. She had Martha checking the house for the missing tot.

Lex stepped inside the horse barn. Nothing seemed out of place. "Lorrie?" She didn't think her daughter was strong enough to open the door, but she wanted to make sure. "Lorrie? Are you in here?"

She checked every stall, but there was no sign of her. A quick check of the tack room door showed it was locked. Lex headed through the back and toward the hay barn.

The side door to the barn was partially open and Lex took that as a sign that Lorrie could be there. There wasn't much inside that could hurt a small child, thankfully. The sweet smell of hay tickled Lex's nose as she crossed the threshold. "Lorrie!" A far off rustle alerted her to the child's presence. "Come on out, kiddo."

High pitched giggling was the only answer.

Lex moved deeper into the barn. The hay muted the sounds, so it was impossible to tell where Lorrie was hiding. "Lorrie, I'm not playing around. Where are you?"

Soft footfalls above surprised her. There was only one way to get upstairs and that was by ladder. With her heart pounding, Lex jogged to the ladder and climbed as quickly as she could. As she reached the top, she saw a blur duck behind a bale of hay. "Lorrie! Stop running around." Lex hoisted herself up and went to where her daughter was hiding. As she reached the bale, Lorrie laughed and took off running again. "Damn it! Lorrie, get back here."

"Get me, Momma." Lorrie giggled and ran toward the ladder.

"Wait!" Lex chased after her. The twelve foot drop to the barn floor was getting too close.

Lorrie continued to run. It was fun being chased by her momma. She turned and saw Lex getting closer. "Yay! Get me!" She didn't notice how close to the edge she had become.

"No!" Lex dove toward Lorrie, stretching out as far as she could reach. She was barely able to get her fingers around a tiny arm, as Lorrie tumbled from the loft.

"Momma!" Lorrie squealed in pain and surprise. She swung through the air, crying. "Momma!"

Lex slowly lifted Lorrie into the loft. "It's okay, sweetheart. You're safe." She pulled the screaming child into her arms. "Sssh."

Lorrie's cries grew in intensity. "Momma, hurts!"

"Let me see." Lex noticed the discoloration on Lorrie's lower arm where she had grabbed her. "I'm so sorry, baby." She touched Lorrie's elbow, which sent the little girl into renewed screams. After a closer look, it was obvious that something was wrong. "Damn." As carefully as possible, Lex tucked Lorrie against her chest and cautiously made her way down the ladder.

THE EMERGENCY ROOM doctor wrote in the chart before closing it. His dark eyes blinked behind the wire rim glasses he wore. "It's actually a very common injury among children, Ms. Walters." He had seen dozens of cases of "nursemaid's elbow", where the child's elbow becomes dislocated. It was a quick fix to pop the joint into place. "She'll be good as new in a day or so."

Once her arm had been taken care of, the sudden relief from pain mixed with the mild sedative caused Lorrie to fall asleep. She lay peacefully snuggled against Lex, who rocked her gently. "Will she have any problems with the arm when she's older?"

"Probably not. At her age the joint is mainly cartilage, so there should be no lingering effects." He showed her out of the examination room. "She'll have forgotten about it long before you do."

"You've got that right." Lex adjusted Lorrie in her arms and held out her hand. "Thank you." After shaking his hand, she maneuvered her way through the people milling in the hall and was met by Martha.

"Everything okay?" Martha brushed her hand lightly over Lorrie's hair. "Poor little tyke looks tuckered out."

Lex blinked away her tears. Now that the emergency was over, the shock of what could have happened to Lorrie hit her. "Yeah." She kissed her daughter's hair. "Thanks for driving us in."

"That's my job." Martha knew the look. She held out her hands. "Why don't you let me take her, so you can give Amanda a call?" It had taken all Martha's considerable negotiation skills to keep Amanda at home instead of coming to the emergency room. Only the promise of a phone call immediately after seeing the doctor appeased her.

"Good idea." Lex was loath to give up her daughter, but it would have been too hard to juggle Lorrie and talk on the phone at the same time. She reluctantly passed the sleeping child to Martha. "I'll be right back."

Since she had left her cell phone at home, Lex headed for the bank of payphones close to the waiting room. She fished changed out of her pocket and placed the call. Amanda answered on the first ring. "She's fine."

"Was it broken?" Amanda was still peeved she was stuck at home. "Are they putting it in a cast?"

Lex turned so she could watch Martha with Lorrie. "No. He called it 'nursemaid's elbow,' and said it was pretty common. I did it to her when I grabbed her arm." The knowledge of being the one to cause Lorrie pain made Lex feel physically ill. "It's all my fault."

"Lex, you can't think that way. If it hadn't been for you she could have fallen out of the loft."

"Yeah, right. And if I'd made sure the damned door was closed right, she wouldn't have gotten out at all." Lex slammed her hand against the wall in disgust. "Listen. I've got some paperwork to finish and then we'll be on our way home. Is there anything I can get you?"

"Just the two of you. Hurry home."

After promising to return as soon as possible, Lex returned to relieve Martha of Lorrie. She held her daughter carefully, although Lorrie never stirred. "You ready to get out of here?"

"Sounds good." Martha placed a steadying arm around them as they left the emergency room. Neither noticed the woman who had walked in.

ELIZABETH CAUBLE WAS surprised to see the trio, and was extremely curious as to why they had been there. She had come into the hospital to get a physician's referral. As a condition of her release, Elizabeth had to keep in touch with a psychiatrist at least once a month. Since she planned on being in Somerville for a while, she needed to get the name of a local doctor. There was no way she'd return to the hospital they'd locked her away in for over two years. She hurried to the admitting station. "Excuse me, but I'm looking for my granddaughter. She was brought in a short time ago."

The nurse raised her head. Her nametag identified her as Kelly. "What's her name, ma'am?"

"I think it was my daughter-in-law that brought her in. Lexington Walters?" Elizabeth had no idea what last name Lorrie would be listed under. Rivers? Cauble? There were too many variables.

"Oh yes." Kelly's fingers tapped quickly on the computer keys. "I'm sorry, they've already checked out. You must have barely missed them."

In an acting performance that would have made the Academy proud, Elizabeth put a shaky hand to her mouth. "Oh dear. And I promised I would be here."

Kelly nodded sympathetically. "That's all right, ma'am. According to the records, she only had a minor elbow dislocation. She'll be fine. Maybe if you hurry you can catch them before they leave."

Elizabeth fought to keep the satisfied look from her face. "I'll do that, thank you." She tapped the counter with a red-tipped finger and strolled from the emergency room, her earlier quest forgotten.

IT WAS THE most annoying feeling in the world, causing Amanda to open her eyes and grimace. Half-asleep, she rolled out of bed and staggered to the bathroom. She hated these middle of the night excursions. It seemed she had barely gotten to sleep, when the baby pressed against her bladder and made her get up again.

Blissful moments later, Amanda stumbled into the bedroom and climbed into bed. She then realized the other side of the bed was empty and, judging by the coolness of the sheets, had been for some time. "Dammit, Lex." After heaving herself into a sitting position, she got out of bed again and stepped into the hall.

Muted light spilled from Lorrie's bedroom. The nightlight gave up enough illumination so Amanda could see her partner's form slouched in the corner rocking chair. She stepped quietly into the room until she was next to the chair. With the lightest of touches, she stroked Lex's face.

Lex jerked awake. "What's wrong?" She looked around the room, her vision lingering on a peacefully sleeping Lorrie.

"Nothing's wrong. I woke up and you weren't there." Amanda didn't bother to struggle when Lex pulled her onto her lap. It wouldn't have done any good. So she sat and enjoyed the feeling of her partner's arms around her. "I'm going to squish you."

"Yeah, right." Lex kissed Amanda's neck. "What are you doing up?"

Amanda was too busy luxuriating in the feelings Lex's touch brought. She tilted her head back and closed her eyes. "Did you say something?"

Lex's hands moved to rest against Amanda's stomach. "Junior wouldn't let you sleep, huh?"

"No. She seems to think it's fun to dance on my bladder at two in the morning. Stop trying to change the subject. What are you doing in here? Did Lorrie have a bad dream? She looks like she's sleeping fine to me."

"She is. I came in to check on her and I guess I fell asleep." Lex tried to fight off a yawn but failed.

Amanda grabbed one of Lex's hands and stood. "Come on. You'll sleep a lot better in our bed and so will I." With a tug, she brought Lex to her feet and pulled her from the room.

Once they were both comfortably settled in bed, Amanda could tell that Lex was troubled by something. "Want to talk about it?"

Flat on her back with her hands behind her head, Lex stared at the ceiling. "About what?"

"You've been brooding since you got home this afternoon."

"No I haven't."

Amanda yanked Lex's hair. "Have too."

"Have not."

"Have too." Amanda chuckled. "I think we've spent too much time with our daughter. We're beginning to sound like her."

Lex couldn't help herself. "Are not." She laughed when her arm was swatted. "Hey!"

"You're a brat." But Amanda relented and instead wriggled until she was lying as close as she could. "Are you still upset about what happened today?"

"Yeah." Lex rolled onto her side and propped her head up on her hand. "She could have been seriously hurt or worse today. If I hadn't caught her—"

"But you did. And she's going to be fine." Amanda took Lex's free hand and laid it on her stomach. "I was scared to death and I wasn't even there when it happened." The baby kicked. "You're a great momma, Lex. Our kids are probably going to turn us gray before our time, but I won't regret a minute as long as you're here with me."

With a heavy sigh, Lex lay down on her stomach but didn't lose touch with Amanda. "I love you."

"I love you, too." Amanda tucked the covers around her wife.

Less than an hour later, Lorrie's cries woke them both. Lex was almost to the door before Amanda could open her eyes. "I'll get her." She crossed the hallway and flicked on Lorrie's light. "What's wrong, lil' bit?"

"Momma!" Lorrie sat up and rubbed her eyes with her good hand. "I'm scared."

Lex scooped her out of bed and held her close. "Bad dream?"

"Uh-huh." Lorrie sniffled and tucked her head beneath Lex's chin. "I falled." The soothing touch on her back calmed her, as Lex carried her into the master bedroom.

"It was only a bad dream, sweetheart. You're okay." Lex crawled into bed, keeping Lorrie between her and Amanda.

Amanda turned on her side and brushed the hair out of her daughter's eyes. "Your momma's right, honey. Why don't you go to sleep, and we'll be right here, okay?"

"Otay." Lorrie rolled until she was up against Amanda. Her eyes closed almost immediately.

Lex leaned over and kissed Lorrie on top of the head before settling behind her. "Sleep well, Lorrie." She thrust the feelings of guilt down, knowing she'd be in for more sleepless nights.

SOFT CRYING WOKE Amanda. She could tell it was early morning, as the barely risen sun painted the bedroom in muted tones of gray. She rolled over slightly to see tears glistening off Lorrie's cheeks. "What's the matter, sweetie?" She brushed at the dampness in an attempt to sooth her daughter.

"Hurts," Lorrie sniffled. She cradled her arm against her body.

Amanda turned again, and grabbed the bottle of baby aspirin from her nightstand. She placed one in Lorrie's mouth. "Chew this up, it'll make you feel better." Once Lorrie swallowed the medication, Amanda carefully held her close. It was then she noticed the other side of the bed was empty. There were no lights on that she could see. "I wonder where she's gotten off to so early?" Deciding to look for her wayward spouse later, she rubbed Lorrie's back to sooth her.

The next time she opened her eyes, the room was naturally well-lit, and still Lex was nowhere to be seen. She kissed the sleeping child's head and eased off the bed. Her bladder was making itself known, as usual. After adjusting her pillow to take her place, she toddled to the bathroom.

Once Lorrie was awake, she followed Amanda downstairs in anticipation of a promised breakfast of oatmeal. "Where's Momma?"

"I don't know, honey. We'll find her after we eat. How's that sound?"

"Otay." Lorrie climbed into her chair and waited patiently as her mommy placed water on the stove to boil. She took the cup of juice Amanda placed in front of her and drank. "Good."

Amanda was about to join her, when she heard rhythmic thumping outside. She peered through the kitchen window. "What on earth is she up to?" She started to leave the kitchen. "Lorrie, be a good girl. Mommy will be right back."

"Otay." Lorrie concentrated on her juice, while tracing the cartoon character placemat in front of her.

The noise became louder when Amanda opened the back door. She wrapped her arms around herself to ward off the morning chill. The sight that greeted her caused her to wrinkle her brow in confusion. Behind the house, small wooden posts were nestled in holes around the yard. The fence would enclose a large area, effectively keeping Lorrie from straying again. Her partner was in one corner, with her back to the house.

Even with the light frost that covered the ground, Lex's dark tee shirt was already damp with perspiration. Her long-sleeved denim shirt hung on a nearby post. She slammed the posthole digging tool into the ground then raised a clump of damp grass and mud. The implement was almost as tall as she, and the double wooden handles opened outward as she raised it from the hole she dug. Small dual spades would pinch together and remove a load of dirt. After dropping the dirt to the side of the hole she made, she repeated the action. Freckles danced around her, yipping and using one paw to dig at the pile of dirt.

"Freckles, stop that." Lex rested one arm against the tool, removed the baseball cap she wore and wiped her brow on one shoulder. She looked around at her handiwork, proud with how far she'd come. If she kept at it, she'd be finished by early evening. Only the sound of Amanda's voice kept her from beginning again.

"Lex?" Amanda moved forward, until she stood on the bottom step. "What are you doing?"

"Making sure what happened yesterday won't happen again." Lex left the digger in the hole and walked to where her partner stood. "What time is it?"

Amanda brushed a smudge of dirt from Lex's cheek. "A little after nine. How long have you been out here?"

"A while."

From what Amanda could see, it was obvious that Lex had been working longer than she admitted. Almost all of the posts were set, where there hadn't been any the night before. "It's kind of short, isn't it?"

Lex shrugged and turned to study her handiwork. "Not for a picket fence. Four feet is tall enough. Any higher, and it would be hard to see over."

"Why a picket fence?"

"Because, knowing your daughter, she'd climb over a chain link. And a six-foot privacy fence is too ugly, and it would ruin the view from the house." Lex brushed at the dirt on her jeans.

"Makes sense, I guess." Amanda huffed indignantly. "Hey, wait a minute. My daughter?"

"Yep. I remember the stories your family told about you growing up."

Amanda put her hands on her hips. "It wasn't that bad."

"Does the phrase, 'fell asleep in the old oak in the backyard' ring any bells?"

"Okay. But I was only — "

Lex interrupted her. "Five. And Jacob said it was the only time your grandmother ever spanked you. He said you scared her to death."

"Fine. That one time. It's not like I — "

"Stowed away on a train bound for Houston?" Lex found her mouth covered by Amanda's hand, and her eyes twinkled merrily.

"Enough. But when Lorrie starts roping Freckles, she's your daughter." Amanda looked at where the fence would soon be. "Will it get painted, too?"

"Huh?" Lex twisted her body to look at the yard.

Amanda draped her arms over Lex's shoulders and rested her chin on her head. "A white picket fence? Pretty domestic, isn't it?"

"Never thought of it that way, but I guess you're right." Lex turned and had to tilt her face up to receive Amanda's kiss.

They were interrupted when an old four-door truck, hauling a flatbed trailer, stopped outside the posts. Roy opened the driver's side door and hopped out, followed by three other men. "Hey, boss. Here's the rest of the wood. You want us to get started?"

"We'll finish this conversation later," Lex promised her wife, before she left to give instructions to the hired hands.

Amanda sighed and went inside the house, looking forward to seeing the finished product.

HUBERT TOSSED ANOTHER box into the trunk of his rental car. He couldn't believe how lucky he'd been. His sister hadn't bothered him for weeks and he was sure she had forgotten all about their arrangement. But he knew his luck wouldn't hold. It never did where she was concerned. The woman was relentless in finding new ways to harass him. He went into the house and looked through each room. Other than the broken down furniture, the only thing he was leaving behind were piles of trash. "Don't say I never gave you nothing, Lex."

He slammed the front door behind him and didn't bother to lock it. He didn't care what happened to the house. Not anymore. Hubert was in debt up to his neck and the two mortgages he had on the house guaranteed that he'd never break free. It was definitely time for a change of scenery. He climbed into the car then took an envelope out of his interior jacket pocket. It was addressed to his sister and inside was a note thanking her for taking the old house off his hands.

It hadn't been hard to get a fake driver's license for one of his old girlfriends from Austin, whom he'd sweet-talked into passing for Lex. When it was time for the mortgage closing, she flashed her fake identification and forged Lex's signature on the loan papers. There was no other way he could have gotten a loan. The local banks were on to him, but the mortgage companies that advertise on the Internet had no idea they were dealing with an unscrupulous deadbeat. However, "Lex's" credit was stellar and the mortgage companies were more than happy to accept her as his "cosigner".

He kissed the envelope. Revenge was so sweet. "Thanks, Sis. Not only have you paid off my legal debts, you get to pay off my mortgage, too. That should set you back some, bitch." He chuckled and dropped the key in before sealing it closed. A quick run by the post office on his way out of town and he'd leave this sorry place behind him for good.

TO ELIZABETH'S EYES the small, albeit neatly-kept, house was not much larger than a cracker box. She found it hard to believe anyone lived in such squalor, especially her ex-husband Michael. After seeing what Somerville had to offer, she knew he'd have to lower his standards. But the address she found in the telephone directory appeared beneath even him. "I wouldn't allow a dog to live in this dump." She stepped from her leased car and headed primly up the walk. After a tug on her glove, Elizabeth rang the doorbell.

The door opened and a surprised Lois stood silently with her mouth hanging open slightly.

Elizabeth tucked her handbag beneath one arm. "Well? Aren't you going to invite me inside?"

Lois frowned before she stepped away. "I suppose so." Her ingrained good manners took the most inopportune times to slip out. She led her uninvited guest to the living room. "Can I get you something to drink?"

"Tea would be nice." Elizabeth perched daintily on the edge of a wing-backed chair. "Thank you." She gave her hostess a civil smile.

"Of course." Lois left the room, more confused than ever. She hurriedly put the tea service together and brought it into the living room. There was no way she trusted Elizabeth Cauble any further than she could throw her, and she was loathe to leave her unsupervised in her home. Once the tea had been poured, she took her own place on a floral-patterned sofa. "This is a surprise. What brings you by?"

Elizabeth took a sip of her tea and nodded her appreciation. The woman was a hick but she could at least make decent tea. "This is purely a social call. I thought since I would be settling down here in Somerville to be closer to my family, you and I should get to know each other better."

Tea almost went through Lois' nose and she coughed and sputtered for over a minute. "You're not saying you want to be friends, are you?"

"Heavens no. But since we have our family in common, it is practical, don't you think?"

"Uh, well. I'm not sure." Lois was not prepared for a reasonable Elizabeth, although what she said did make sense.

With a slight clatter, Elizabeth placed her cup and saucer on the coffee table that was between them. "I've realized, belatedly I'm afraid, that I've allowed my family to slip away from me. I miss my daughters and I'm hoping it's not too late to reconnect with them." She sniffled and removed a lace handkerchief from her purse, dabbing at her eyes. "I want to be more involved with my grandchildren. Is that so wrong?"

"Of course not."

Elizabeth continued on as if she hadn't heard Lois' reply. "I feel like such a failure. When I found out that little Lorraine had been taken to the hospital, I was beside myself with worry."

Lois scooted forward and patted Elizabeth awkwardly on the knee. "There, there. Everything turned out fine. I think Lex took it harder than Lorrie did."

"But her poor little arm." Elizabeth hid her face with her hand as if to disguise her tears.

"Well, I happen to think it could have been so much worse. And Lex certainly didn't mean to dislocate her arm."

The front door opened and they were interrupted by Michael's accusing voice. "Elizabeth? What the hell are you doing in our house?" He stormed over to where his ex-wife sat and reached for her arm.

"Michael, wait." Lois stood and stopped him. "It's not what you think."

"I seriously doubt that." He shook off Lois' touch and yanked Elizabeth to her feet. "I don't know what scheme you've cooked up this time, but you leave Lois out of it."

Elizabeth struggled helplessly against his grip. "Please, Michael. I only —"

"Shut up. I'm not going to fall for any of your games." He opened the door and shoved her out onto the steps. "Stay away from my family, Elizabeth. Your bullshit isn't going to work around here anymore." Not waiting for her to respond, Michael slammed the door closed.

After one last look at the door, Elizabeth straightened her jacket and readjusted her gloves. "We'll see about that, Michael. I haven't even gotten started yet." She picked up her dignity and left as regally as she came.

Once in her car, she made another decision. "Perhaps I've gone about this all wrong." She started the vehicle and drove across town, another idea blooming. It took her less than ten minutes to find her goal. Another house, even smaller than the previous one, appeared Spartan but neat. Had she not followed Jeannie earlier in the week Elizabeth would have thought she had the wrong address. The driveway was empty, but she could see lights on inside. With a satisfied smile, Elizabeth climbed out of her car and headed up the walk.

JEANNIE LIGHTLY RUBBED her son's back. He had been fussing ever since her mother arrived and she couldn't help but wonder if he could sense something was wrong. "Mother, please. You don't know what you're talking about."

"And you do? Jeanne Louise, you're the one who gave her baby away. I don't think you should have an opinion one way or another. Whatever made you do such a thing?"

"I had no choice!" When her son began to cry, Jeannie lowered her voice. "I had lost my husband and I couldn't do anything for myself. Lex and Amanda were there for me when you weren't."

Elizabeth took a deep breath and released it slowly. "I wasn't given a chance. That woman has poisoned my whole family against me. Because of her—"

Jeannie quickly cut her off in mid-tirade. "Because of Lex, Amanda is happier than she's ever been. Lorrie is thriving and I couldn't ask for a better person to raise her." Another quick dig popped out of her mouth before she could stop it. "And, if anything happens to me and Rodney, we've made arrangements for them to take care of Teddy, too."

"What?" Elizabeth jumped to her feet, her purse hitting the floor with a loud thump. "Have you lost your mind? That pervert has no right to be near my grandchildren!" She took several steps toward Jeannie, who stood and tucked her son even closer to her chest.

"That's enough, Mother."

"No, I don't think so. You have no right to make any kind of decisions where my grandchildren are concerned. I should take them both and raise them properly." Elizabeth held out her hands. "Give him to me. You obviously can't be trusted."

Jeannie turned away slightly to keep Teddy away from her mother. "Get out of my house." When her mother came closer, Jeannie reached for the telephone. "Don't make me call the police."

"You wouldn't dare."

"Try me."

It was obvious that Elizabeth wasn't going to get her way. She picked up her handbag and stiffened her spine proudly. "There's no need to be nasty, Jeanne Louise. I was only trying to help you. It's quite apparent you have no intention of listening to reason. Perhaps I've wasted my time."

"That's the first thing you've gotten right today." Jeannie strode purposely toward the front door and opened it. "Please don't come back, Mother. I have nothing else to say to you."

Elizabeth breezed by Jeannie, her head held high. "We'll see about that." She sniffed haughtily as she left the house.

THE DISCUSSION HAD been going on for over an hour and yet nothing had been resolved. Lex and Amanda were alone in the kitchen, since Lorrie was spending the day with Martha at the cottage. Lex had been unsuccessful in getting Amanda to regain her composure. The phone call from Jeannie, telling them about

Elizabeth's visit, had sent Amanda into a rage, which turned into tears soon after. She sat at the table with her head resting on her arms. Nothing Lex said could allay Amanda's fears.

"Sweetheart, please. You need to calm down." Lex touched Amanda's back in an effort to comfort her.

Amanda raised her head and glared at her. "Don't tell me what I need to do. You obviously aren't taking this very seriously." She stood as quickly as her bulky body would allow and left the room in a huff.

"Damn." Lex followed her to the den, where she saw Amanda staring out the front window. "Hey."

Not bothering to turn around, Amanda continued to look across the front lawn, not actually seeing anything. "How do we know she's not up to something?"

Lex walked up behind her and put her hands on Amanda's shoulders. "I'm not going to let her near you, I promise."

"You can't stop her." Amanda rested her cheek on one of Lex's hands. She felt defeated, as if nothing they did would matter. "No one can. She's always done whatever she wants to and we haven't been able to do a damned thing."

There weren't any words Lex could find to refute that statement. Instead she stepped closer and put her arms around Amanda. They stood quietly for several minutes, until the phone rang. Lex kissed Amanda's cheek. "Guess I'd better get that."

"Don't." Amanda nestled against her. It was the only place she felt safe. "Please hold me."

"I'll never stop," Lex whispered in her ear. She rocked Amanda in her arms, determined to keep Elizabeth away from her family, no matter what it took.

Chapter
Thirty-three

FOR OVER TWO weeks, everyone in the family had made a point of staying vigilant and keeping an eye on Elizabeth. Charlie had his deputies watch for her while they were out on their rounds, but she went about her business as if nothing was wrong.

He sat in his office, reading over the latest reports from his men. The woman was maddening. She knew she was being watched but didn't seem to be bothered by it. In fact, Elizabeth waved or spoke to whichever officer came upon her. Charlie closed the folder and threw it across his desk. "Damn woman!"

"Everything okay, boss?" Jeremy came in and sat in the chair across from Charlie. He knew from his own experience while watching her how aggravating Elizabeth could be.

"No." Charlie scratched his head. "Are you absolutely positive she hasn't done anything wrong? Jaywalked, littered, picked her nose in public?" When he had first become sheriff, Charlie had been amazed at the inane laws that were still on the books. Picking your nose in public was one of his favorites, as was the law that forbade anyone to serve a drink to a horse in a saloon. On Sunday.

Jeremy laughed at the mental picture of Elizabeth Cauble being caught for something so ridiculous. "No, I'm afraid not. And believe me, we watched her for any infraction."

"I know. Thanks, Jeremy." Charlie leaned back in his chair and rested his hands across his stomach. "I'm getting too old for this crap. You know, you'd make a great sheriff."

"Uh-uh. I'm perfectly happy letting you have all the glory." Although he did aspire to go higher in the department, Jeremy was in no hurry to see Charlie leave.

With a heavy sigh, the sheriff scooted his chair away from his desk and stood. He was feeling too old. It was time to retire while he could still enjoy his family. "You might want to reconsider. I'd be glad to put in a good word for you with the city council."

"You're not serious?"

"Damn right I am." Charlie took his hat from the hook near the door and placed it on his head. "Hold down the fort. I'm going to take a quick drive around and then head on home."

Jeremy stood. "No problem, Charlie. I'll see you tomorrow." He watched the sheriff leave, thinking about their brief conversation.

AMANDA WAS COMFORTABLY ensconced on the sofa in the den, watching a television program Lex had recorded for her earlier. Several loud thumps overhead caused her to close her eyes and grumble. Lorrie had been rambunctious all day. It was the biggest reason she was now upstairs playing with Freckles.

Another heavy thump and then a high-pitched squeal, made Amanda regret sending Lex to Martha's after lunch. She had been hovering nearby for the last couple of weeks and Amanda finally got to her breaking point. When Martha decided it was time to clean out her kitchen cabinets, Amanda didn't have to think twice about volunteering Lex to help.

Freckles' barking caused Amanda to close her eyes and count to twenty. It didn't help. The sudden silence from upstairs worried her. She was about to get up to check on them when she heard careful footsteps coming down the stairs.

Five minutes later, Lorrie and Freckles burst into the room. "Mommy, look. Fleckles is funny."

The happy dog bounced to where Amanda sat and jumped on the couch next to her. She reeked of Lex's cologne and was wearing what appeared to be a necklace.

"Lorrie, what is Freckles wearing?" Amanda tried to catch her, but the dog bounded out of reach.

"She gots pretty." Lorrie came around the sofa. "Smells pretty, too."

Even though Amanda had always loved the perfume Lex wore, having it reek from their dog was almost more than she could handle. There was no way she'd be able to give Freckles a bath without help. She picked up the cordless phone and hit the speed dial for Martha's house. "Martha, is Lex real busy?"

"No, honey. We're finished. I've been keeping her over here to give you some peace. Is everything all right?"

"Not exactly. Lorrie covered Freckles in Lex's cologne and I need her to come home and give her a bath. Obsession and dog do not go together, believe me." Amanda rubbed her nose in a feeble attempt to relieve her sinuses.

The humor in the situation didn't escape Martha, who covered the mouthpiece with her hand and spoke to Lex. Before she could finish her sentence, the sound of her front door slamming could be made out. "She's on her way."

"So I gathered." Amanda heard their back door open and close. Her wife apparently ran the entire way. "She's here. Thanks, Martha."

"Anytime, sweetie."

Freckles heard Lex come in the house and jumped from the sofa to race from the room. Lorrie was fast on her heels. "Fleckles, wait for me." In her excitement to greet her momma, Lorrie accidentally ran into an end table and knocked the lamp off onto the floor. The glass base broke, causing shards of glass to go everywhere. "Mommy!"

Lex ran the rest of the way down the hall until she was in the living room. "Lorrie, stay still." She scooped up Freckles, tucked her under one arm, and walked cautiously to where her daughter stood. Squatting carefully, Lex opened her free arm and waited for Lorrie to climb up. She stood slowly, carried Freckles to the office, and closed the door. Then she took Lorrie to the couch where Amanda sat. "Stay here with Mommy, while I clean up the broken glass."

Lorrie trembled as she snuggled into the comfort of her mother's arms. "Otay."

It didn't take long for Lex to clean up the mess. Giving Freckles a bath was a more difficult chore. Not because the dog didn't want to get wet, but because she thought it was playtime as soon as her feet hit the water. By the time Freckles was clean, Lex's shirt and jeans were completely drenched. She went upstairs, changed her clothes, then joined her family in the den.

Lorrie was lying beside Amanda, sound asleep. Lex sat on the floor in front of them and rested her head against Amanda's legs. "Freckles is clean, finally. I left her in our room until she's completely dry."

"Good." Amanda ran her fingers through Lex's hair. The motion relaxed them both. "I'm sorry I was so grumpy this morning."

"You have nothing to apologize for. I know I've been a little over-protective lately." Lex closed her eyes as Amanda's fingers began a deep scalp massage. "Damn, that feels good."

They sat quietly for several minutes, both enjoying the peace. Finally, Lex turned slightly and removed Amanda's slippers. She began to rub her feet, smiling at the low moans of pleasure from her lover. "I was thinking."

"Mmm?" At the moment, Amanda would have agreed to anything, as long as the massage continued.

"Why don't I take Lorrie to daycare tomorrow? Give you a chance to kick back and take it easy."

"That's all I do now, is take it easy. I'm not allowed to do a damned thing." Amanda stretched her legs out as Lex's hands began to caress her calves. "Oh, yeah. I'll give you exactly ten years to quit doing that."

Lex raised her head and winked. "If you'll go upstairs, I'll do even better than that."

"Don't tease."

"I'm not." Lex stood and hefted Lorrie into her arms. "I'll put this one down for her nap, then I'll give you an even better massage." She left the room, smiling as she heard Amanda following close behind.

THE NEXT DAY, Elizabeth left the motel where she was staying and decided to drive around to become more familiar with the town. She'd spent the last couple of weeks keeping a low profile, although it had been fun to tease the local law enforcement. She was parked at a light when she recognized the large, green truck which lumbered by. "What is that woman doing? I thought for certain she would be at her ranch at this time of day." Her curiosity getting the best of her, Elizabeth turned at the light and followed at a discreet distance.

It wasn't hard to keep Lex in sight. Even in a town as rural as Somerville, where every other vehicle was a truck, Lex's was easy to spot, due to the ranch brand on the doors. When she parked in the lot of the Methodist church, Elizabeth couldn't have been more surprised. She watched as Lex took Lorrie inside. It was only then she noticed the sign which told of the daycare facilities at the church. "I see."

After a few minutes, Lex returned alone. She got into her truck and left, never noticing Elizabeth's car parked close by.

Elizabeth tapped the steering wheel as she considered her options. An idea came to her, so simple she didn't know why she hadn't thought of it before. A quick shopping trip was in order. She had things to do, and plans to make.

BARELY TWO HOURS later, Elizabeth parked her car as close to the church entrance as possible. She went inside and smiled at the heavyset young woman sitting behind the desk. "Good afternoon."

The woman looked up from the magazine she was reading and pursed her lips. "Yes? May I help you?"

"Of course." Elizabeth removed a paper from her purse and handed it to the woman, whose nametag showed her name was Katie. "My name is Elizabeth Cauble. I'm Lorrie's grandmother."

Katie took the folded sheet of paper and looked it over. "Lorrie?" She'd only been at the church for a week, and had no idea which child Elizabeth was talking about. "Oh. Lorrie Walters."

Walters? Dear Lord, how dare they change my *granddaughter's name! Well, that will be remedied soon enough.* "Yes, right. Something has come up, and they've asked me to take little Lorrie to her doctor's appointment this afternoon. I'm sure the note speaks for itself."

"I suppose." Katie pushed her glasses up on her nose and read the paper again, this time more carefully. "I'll have to see some identification, to be safe."

"Oh, I understand completely. I wouldn't expect anything less, as far as my granddaughter's safety is concerned." Elizabeth removed her wallet from her purse and showed her driver's license to Katie.

After assuring herself that Elizabeth was who she claimed to be, Katie stood. "If you'll wait right here, I'll go get her."

Elizabeth couldn't keep a smile of triumph from her face. "You do that." She crossed her arms and waited until Katie returned, with Lorrie in tow. "There's my girl."

Lorrie took one look at Elizabeth and balked. "No! Bad!"

"No, dear. It will be fine." Elizabeth reached for Lorrie, but Katie paused.

"I don't think she wants to go with you." Katie wasn't so certain letting Elizabeth take the child was such a good idea. "Maybe I should call her mother, to make sure."

Elizabeth took another step forward. "You can, if you like. But my granddaughter is only throwing a tantrum because she doesn't like to go to the doctor, and I'm usually the one who takes her. She'll be fine." She took Lorrie by the arm. "Come along, Lorrie. We have an appointment to keep."

"No!" Lorrie tried to squirm out of her grasp. "Don't wanna."

"See here, young lady. I won't tolerate that sort of behavior." Elizabeth jerked her forward. "Let's go."

"Mrs. Cauble, wait." Katie picked up the phone. "Let me call Ms. Walters. I'm sure she can calm her daughter."

"No, don't! You can't reach her right now." Elizabeth struggled to come up with something. "She's in a very important meeting at the moment. That's the reason I have to take my granddaughter." She pulled Lorrie closer to the door. "Trust me, this happens a lot. Once we're in the car, she'll settle down."

Katie shrugged her shoulders. It's not like she got paid much for this job. Certainly not enough to go to so much trouble. And if the girl's mother was in a meeting, she didn't want to be the one to disturb her. "Well, all right." She knelt by Lorrie. "You be a good girl for your grandmother."

"No!" Lorrie struggled to break free.

Elizabeth practically dragged her from the church. "Behave. I'll most definitely have to teach you better manners."

Lorrie continued to scream and balk as she was taken to the car. "I want momma!"

"Too bad. You'll do much better with me." Elizabeth buckled her into the car seat she had purchased earlier. "Once we're at the motel, we'll see about getting the next flight to California. Private school will do you a world of good." She started the car and left the parking lot, pleased with her plans.

Inside the church, worried about her decision, Katie watched through the front door. She became even more concerned when she saw how Elizabeth struggled to get Lorrie into the car.

"What's going on?" Another woman came into the office and

stood next to Katie.

"I think I may have screwed up," Katie confessed. She turned and had trouble looking her boss, Delores, in the eye. "What's the policy for family members picking up children?"

Delores had been running the preschool for years, and didn't like the tone in employee's voice. "Why?"

"A little girl's grandmother came in, and I don't think the girl wanted to go with her. But she had proper identification."

"Was she on the approved list?"

Katie frowned. "What list? No one ever said—"

Delores pushed by her and opened the bottom drawer of the desk. "What was the child's name?"

"Um, Lorrie. Lorrie Walters." Katie looked over Delores shoulder as the older woman flipped through the files. "What's that?"

"Her file. Any time someone comes in and wants to pick up a child and you don't know who they are, you have to bring out the file and check for instructions." Delores used her index finger to follow the information on the page. "Damn!"

"What?"

Delores picked up the phone. "Only the parents are authorized, unless they call and tell us otherwise." She dialed the contact number on the paper. "This is not good."

BUSINESS SLOWED AT the diner. The lunch crowd was thinning out, and only a few stragglers were left. Lex sat at the counter, working on her third cup of coffee. The newspaper that rested beside her empty plate had kept her occupied for quite a while, but now that she was finished with her meal, Lex was bored.

Francine came by with the coffee pot. "Another refill?"

"Nope. I've been goofing off long enough." Lex took out her wallet and laid several bills on the counter. "Has Monty been in today? I was supposed to meet him about some horses he had for sale."

The waitress picked up the ticket and cash, and was about to give Lex her change, when she was waved off. "Thanks, hon." She pocketed the generous tip and winked at her benefactor. "Actually, I haven't seen him around in a couple of days."

"Damn. Guess we'll get together some other time." Lex folded the paper up neatly and set it on the next barstool. As she stood, her cell phone rang. "Hello?" She only had to listen for a moment before understanding that something was very wrong. "I'm on my way." Lex raced out of the diner, almost knocking down a man as he came inside. She muttered an apology but didn't slow down.

She was in the truck in seconds, with her cell phone tucked between her ear and shoulder. "How long ago did they leave? What was she driving?" Lex didn't bother to buckle her seatbelt as she started the vehicle. "What idiot let that woman leave with my daughter?" She slammed the truck into reverse and wheeled away from the diner. "I am calm, Delores."

A horn blasted to the left of her, making Lex realize she ran a red light. "Do you know which direction she went?" The truck fishtailed as she turned the corner. "Dammit! No, not you. I'm on my way. Call the sheriff." Lex tossed the cell phone into the seat beside her.

The streets were fairly deserted, so Lex felt comfortable speeding up. As she headed toward an intersection, the light began to change. She gunned the engine and raced through, ignoring the siren that soon followed. The flashing lights she saw in her rear view mirror were merely an annoyance, and the congested intersection ahead was the only reason she stopped. Lex slammed her hands on the steering wheel. "Get out of my way, dammit!"

Jeremy had been surprised by the vision of Lex's truck racing by, until he heard the bulletin come across the radio. He got out of his car and walked toward the truck. Once he reached the window, he tapped on it. "Lex, I need to talk to you."

She rolled the window down. "I don't have time, Jeremy. Write me a ticket if you want, but that crazy bitch—"

"I know." The radio on his belt crackled.

Another officer's voice came through loud and clear. "This is Oscar. The suspect passed me, going west on Fillmore. I think she's heading toward the Sunset Lodge motel."

Jeremy clicked the mike that was positioned on his lapel. "That sounds about right, Oscar. From our recent surveillance, it's where she's been staying. Are you still in your personal car?"

"Yeah. Do you want me to follow her?"

"Only from a distance. I don't want her spooked." Jeremy knocked on the truck's door. "Don't worry, Lex. We'll get her back." He jogged to his car.

Lex looked in her side mirror. "Not without me, you're not." She glanced to the right, and drove her truck onto the sidewalk. There was no way she'd sit back and let them go after Elizabeth without her.

THE MOTEL WHERE she had been staying was billed as the nicest in town. To Elizabeth, it was still a dump. She did consider it fortuitous that she was able to park right in front of her room, instead of having to go through a lobby. Especially now that she was saddled with a screaming child. She took Lorrie out of the safety seat. "Would you shut up? I've had about all I can stand of your whining."

"No! I want my momma!" Lorrie kicked at Elizabeth, who dragged her out of the car and into the room. "Momma!"

Elizabeth pushed her into the bathroom and closed the door.

"Stay in there until you calm down, you ungrateful little brat. I've got plans to make, and your nasty little attitude isn't helping." She picked up the room phone and was about to dial out when she heard sirens in the distance. "That's impossible."

She went to the window and peeked through the curtains. There were several cars in the parking lot, but nothing stirred. "I think I'll go see what's happening." She opened the door and raised her voice, to be heard over Lorrie's pounding of the bathroom door. "Grandmother will be back soon, dear. Be good." Elizabeth walked calmly to the end of the building and looked around the corner. She saw several police cars, and realized her plan was unraveling. "Damn! Will nothing go my way?" She hurried to the room and grabbed her purse. A fast retreat seemed the best course of action.

It wasn't hard to leave unnoticed. Elizabeth used the parked vehicles as cover, and watched in amusement as several deputies ran into the motel's office. "Idiots." She knew there was a car rental office across the street, and decided it was time to get a new vehicle.

MARTHA HUNG UP the phone and closed her eyes. Charlie had told her everything he knew, including how Lex was out somewhere "in vigilante mode". He promised he'd call as soon as he knew anything. She only hoped it would be good news. The thought of telling Amanda what was happening worried her. The last few weeks had been rough on the pregnant woman, and Martha feared the toll this would take on her health.

The day-to-day stresses of living with an energetic three-year-old were wearing Amanda down, no matter how she tried to convince everyone to the contrary. Her blood pressure was up, and it was almost impossible for her to get any rest.

"Who was that on the phone?" Amanda came into the kitchen and sat at the table. Her feet and back were taking turns at which hurt the most. "Is Lex on her way home?"

Martha turned from the counter and tried to paste a smile on her face. "No, that was Charlie. I haven't heard from Lexie today." She hoped she could get away with the little white lie. Unable to keep still, she poured a glass of milk and placed it in front of Amanda, then sat next to her.

"That's sweet he still calls you during the day." Amanda took a sip and savored the feel of the cold beverage sliding down her throat. "Oh, that's good." A strong kick from her unborn child caused her to wince. "Someone's active today." She placed her palm on her stomach. "I think she misses her sister. Lorrie's been talking to the baby a lot lately."

The mention of Lorrie brought tears to Martha's eyes. "Oh, that sweet angel." She turned her head away.

"Martha?" Amanda touched her on the back. "What's the matter?"

"Nothing." But Martha sniffled and wiped her face with the ever-present dishcloth.

That was more than enough to alarm Amanda. "It wasn't a social call from Charlie, was it?" She waited until Martha turned around. "Is it Lex? Oh, God. Not Lorrie? Please tell me what's happening."

Martha took Amanda's hands in hers and tried to impart all the strength she had into their connection. "As far as we know, she's fine. But your mother took Lorrie from the daycare."

"Oh no." Amanda's heart began to pound. "When? Where's Lex?"

"A little over an hour ago. But they called Lexie immediately, and the entire sheriff's department is looking for her." Martha rubbed her thumbs across Amanda's knuckles. "Evidently, Lexie is out looking for her, too."

Amanda lurched to her feet. "I've got to get to town. What if something happens? I need to be there." She started to leave the kitchen, when a sudden cramp seized her and caused her to double over. "Oh, God."

LEX WAS IN a panic. Although she knew approximately where the motel was, she made several wrong turns in her haste to get there. The truck skidded through a patch of water, and she was barely able to keep it on the road. With a curse, Lex turned onto Fillmore Street.

She could see the flashing lights of several sheriffs' department cars, and was so focused on them she didn't see the person who ran in front of her truck until it was too late. She slammed the brakes and turned the wheel sharply, but the vehicle was still moving fast when it hit the body. The airbag deployed, causing Lex's head to snap with enough force for her to see stars. A thin trickle of blood ran from one nostril, although she was too stunned to realize it.

Once her vision cleared, Lex got out of the truck and stumbled to the front, where she saw the crumpled form of Elizabeth Cauble partially under the vehicle. She dropped to her knees and fought the urge to throw up. Blood was beginning to pool around the unconscious woman's head, and her left leg was twisted at an unnatural angle. Lex was about to check for a pulse when a deputy knelt beside her.

"You'd better not touch her, Lex. I saw what happened, and an ambulance is on the way." Russell put his hand on her arm and turned her to face him. "How about you? Are you okay?"

Still in shock, Lex continued to stare at Elizabeth's motionless body. "It happened so fast. She came out of nowhere."

"I know. There was no way you could have avoided her. She ran from between two cars. I didn't even see her until I heard—"

"Heard me hit her. Yeah." Lex rubbed her face with one hand.

Russell helped Lex to her feet as several firemen moved in. They stood nearby while the men worked to save Elizabeth's life. "Come on. I'm going to have to get your statement."

Lex brushed his hand away. "Later. Have you found my daughter?"

"I'm not sure. We've got guys searching the area, but—" Russell was speaking to an empty space, as Lex ran toward the motel.

Her boots pounded against the pavement of the parking lot, and Lex's lungs began to burn from the lack of oxygen while she ran as fast as she could. As she got closer, she saw Jeremy open one of the rooms and go inside. Lex headed toward him, fighting off the men who tried to stop her.

Oscar grabbed her arm. "You can't go in there, Lex. We have to secure the area."

"Back off, Oscar." Lex jerked away and shoved him, which brought three other deputies over to subdue her. "Dammit, let go of me." She kicked one of the men, and elbowed another in the ribs.

Wayne, one of the older deputies, brought out his heavy flashlight and slammed it into the middle of her back, dropping Lex to her knees. He'd never liked the woman, his animosity going all the way to high school. Not convinced that Lex was under control, he pulled it back to swing again, but had it taken away by Oscar.

"Hold it." Oscar knelt beside Lex, who had her head bowed and was breathing heavily. "You okay?"

Lex slowly got to her feet. "Yeah." She gave Wayne a dirty look. "Touch me again and I'll shove that flashlight up your ass." Her attention moved to the motel room door, when Jeremy came out, carrying a hysterical Lorrie. Lex pushed through the group of deputies and took Lorrie into her arms. "It's okay, sweetheart. I'm here." She quickly checked her daughter over, to assure herself she was all right.

A fireman started to take Lorrie, but the look on Lex's face caused him to take his hand away. "Ma'am, we need to take her to the hospital, to be sure."

"I'll do it." Lex cradled Lorrie to her chest, stroking her hair and whispering words of comfort. In moments, the exhausted child was asleep in her arms.

Charlie, finally arriving on the scene, moved through the crowd. "Lex, I'll take you." He put his arm around her waist and led her to his car. "I don't want you to get any more upset, but Amanda's there."

Someone had taken the child seat Charlie kept in his trunk and placed it in the backseat of his squad car. Lex buckled Lorrie in and sat beside her. "What do you mean she's there? How'd she know to—"

"She didn't. Martha brought her in." Charlie started the car and eased it through the crowded parking lot.

Lex leaned over the seat and grabbed his shoulder. "What?

Dammit, Charlie, what's going on?"

He flipped on the siren and sped through the streets. "She collapsed. I don't know all the particulars yet." Charlie glanced at her reflection in the rear view mirror. "The doctors were checking her out when I left."

"God no." Lex ignored the tears falling down her cheeks as she struggled to keep from completely losing her composure.

Chapter
Thirty-four

VOICES AND MACHINERY came together in a frenetic symphony, as the emergency room doctors and nurses worked together. Their focus was on a frail form, which was barely recognizable beneath their hands.

One leg was immobilized in an air cast. Elizabeth's left arm hung limply from the table, dried blood covering her painted red nails.

"I'm not getting a pulse," a nurse announced, her gloves stained with blood.

The doctor looked at a monitor, where a long tone and flat lines verified what he already knew. "We've done all we can do." He raised his eyes to the clock on the wall. "Time of death, four twenty-six."

THE HOSPITAL STAFF tried to take Lorrie from her, but Lex wouldn't let go. She sat on the edge of the stretcher with Lorrie in her lap. The last thing she wanted was for her daughter to be alone around strangers.

Lorrie clung to Lex fearfully, and only allowed the physician the barest contact. She tucked her head against her mother's chest and whimpered as the doctor listened to her lungs.

"She seems fine, Ms. Walters. I don't see any indications of abuse." The doctor removed his stethoscope and let it hang freely from his neck. He snapped off his gloves and tossed them in the nearby trash. "You may want to have her pediatrician give her a more thorough exam though."

"I'll do that." Lex looked down at the child in her arms. "Are we done here?"

He nodded. "Give us a call if you need anything else."

"Thanks." Lex stood and left the room, anxious to find Amanda. When she saw Charlie leaving the elevator, she picked up her pace to meet him. "Did you find out anything?"

He lightly grasped her arm and guided Lex to the elevator. "She's upstairs and the doctor's with her."

They rode the elevator in silence, both too caught up in their thoughts to speak. Lorrie dozed off during the ride, her day finally catching up to her.

When the doors opened, they were quickly met by Martha. Her reddened eyes spoke volumes. "I'm so glad you're here."

"How is she?" Lex wanted to brush by her, but Martha placed her hands against her hips.

"Dr. Vaughn is still in there." Martha touched Lorrie's head. "How's this little angel doing?"

Lex swallowed hard and bit her lip. "The doc said she's fine, only exhausted." Her legs shook when the day's events finally hit her. Only Charlie's strong grip kept Lex from falling.

He guided her to a chair in the nearby waiting room. "Might as well take a seat. There's no telling how long the doctor will be in with Amanda." He sat on one side of her, while Martha took the other.

"I should be in there with her." Lex was about to stand again when Lorrie opened her eyes.

"Momma?" Lorrie touched Lex's cheek. "I wanna go home."

Lex blinked the tears out of her eyes. "I know, baby. We will later." She turned her head and kissed Lorrie's palm. "How are you feeling?"

"Love you, Momma." Lorrie giggled when Lex nibbled on her fingers. The earlier terrors had already begun to fade from her memory.

The door to Amanda's room opened and Dr. Vaughn stepped out. She brushed one hand through her hair and glanced around. When she saw Lex, she took a deep breath and went to stand in front of her. "I'm glad you're here."

Lex quickly stood. "How is she?"

"I'm not going to lie to you, it could have become very serious." Dr. Vaughn held up her hand to stop Lex from replying. "Thankfully, your mother got her here quickly, and we were able to stop the contractions."

"Contractions? You mean she went into labor?" Without being aware of it, Lex allowed Martha to take Lorrie, who went willingly into her arms. When her hands began to shake, she tucked them into her pockets. "Is the baby okay?"

Dr. Vaughn finally smiled. "They're both fine. But I'm going to have to insist she stay here with us until the baby's born. Her blood pressure worries me, and if we don't get it under control, I don't see any way she can deliver this baby without a caesarean." At Lex's pale look she patted her arm in reassurance. "I plan on doing everything I can to make this as smooth a delivery as possible. Let's cross that bridge when we come to it."

"All right." Lex exhaled heavily. "Can I see her now?"

"She was resting when I left, but as long as you don't upset her, I think it'll be okay."

"Thanks." Although she felt like hugging the doctor over the positive news, Lex settled for shaking her hand. She gave her a bashful smile and hurried to Amanda's room, where she stood at the door for a moment, before straightening her shoulders and going inside.

CHARLIE WAS LEFT by himself while Martha took Lorrie to the bathroom. He stood, stretched, and was caught off guard when he heard Wayne's voice behind him. "What are you doing here? You're supposed to be guarding Elizabeth Cauble. I don't want that woman to have any opportunity to get loose."

"Uh, well. That's kind of what I came up here to talk to you about." Wayne looked around to verify they were alone. "She didn't make it."

"What?"

"Yeah. The doctors tried, but they told me that even if she'd lived, her brain was so messed up she'd be a vegetable for the rest of her life."

It sounded like poetic justice to Charlie. "Too bad."

Wayne didn't seem to be in agreement. "I guess. So do you want me to do it?"

"Do what? Notify the family? No, I'll take care of that."

Wayne hitched up his duty belt and settled it more comfortably on his hips. "Okay, but that's not what I'm talking about. I meant I'll be glad to bring in Walters."

"Excuse me? What exactly do you mean by that?"

"Well, vehicular homicide isn't something you can write a ticket for."

Charlie glared at him. "That's the last time I want to hear you utter that phrase, boy. Russell saw the entire thing and he told me there was no way in hell Lex could have avoided hitting her. So get that thought out of your head."

"But—"

"No buts. You go on to the station and write your report. I'll be here for a while, so turn it in to Jeremy when you're finished."

Properly chastised, Wayne shrugged his shoulders and stomped away. He wasn't about to argue with the sheriff. He got into the elevator and jabbed the button to take him to the first floor.

With a shake of his head, Charlie watched him leave. "Kids." He turned when he felt a presence behind him.

Martha had returned, with Michael and Lois in tow. She still held a restless Lorrie. "Look who I found."

Michael grasped Charlie's hand. "We got here as soon as we heard from Martha." He was alarmed by how shaken Charlie appeared. "Are you okay? Has something happened to Amanda?"

"No, no. Lex is still in with her, so I'm sure she's fine." Charlie debated on whether to talk to Michael in private, but realized they'd end up telling Martha and Lois, anyway. "I hate to be so blunt, but do you know who would be your ex-wife's next of kin?"

Michael frowned. "I don't know. Her family pretty much washed their hands of her years ago. I guess it'd be me or the girls. Why? Is she screaming for bail already?" Martha had given him the entire story of the kidnapping.

"I'm afraid she won't be doing any more screaming. She's dead."

All three of them spoke at once. "What?"

Charlie didn't want to get into all the details. "She was hit by a truck when she tried to get away from the motel. She died earlier in the emergency room."

"She's dead?" As many times as he had wished death upon his ex-wife, it still came as a complete shock to Michael. "Has anyone told Amanda?"

"No. I just found out. I was about to call you."

Lois took Michael's hand. "Maybe we should keep this from her, for now. She doesn't need the added stress."

Her husband agreed. "I should tell Jeannie though. And I've got to see about making arrangements, I guess."

Martha put her arm around him. "There'll be time enough for that later. I'll help you if you like."

"Thanks." Michael traded looks with Charlie. "I'm going to go see Jeannie. Let Amanda know we'll be back."

"Sure."

"Are you going to tell Lex?"

Charlie paled, knowing what the news would do to Lex, who felt wholly responsible for the accident. No matter how many times he'd already told her it couldn't have been avoided, she continued to feel guilty. "Uh, no. Not right away. Let her focus on Amanda."

LEX STOOD INSIDE the door of Amanda's room and stared at the figure asleep in the bed. Her lover looked more peaceful than she'd seen her in weeks. She decided to keep most of the details of Lorrie's abduction quiet, at least for now. Lex only hoped Amanda wouldn't ask too many questions. She moved slowly to the bed and wasn't surprised to see her partner's eyes open. "Hey, sweetheart." Lex took Amanda's hand and kissed the knuckles. "How're you doing?"

Tears dampened Amanda's eyes. "Much better now." When Lex sat beside her, Amanda squeezed her hand, as if to reassure herself Lex was there. "What happened?"

Lex swallowed heavily. "Your mom picked Lorrie up at the church, saying she was supposed to take Lorrie to the doctor. She took her to her motel, and locked her in the bathroom. We still don't know why she did that."

"But Lorrie's okay, right? She didn't hurt her, did she?"

"No, I don't think so. Lorrie kept crying but I think it was because she didn't know your mother, more than anything else. She's with Martha now."

Amanda noticed a few crimson spots on Lex's shirt. "Is that blood?"

Lex looked down at her chest. "Uh, yeah. It's nothing." Her eyes rose when Amanda touched her chin.

"Is it yours?" At Lex's nod, Amanda looked at her more carefully. She could see some swelling and bruising on Lex's face. "Who hit you?"

Lex blanched. In her relief at getting Lorrie back, she'd put the accident in the back of her mind. The last she heard, Elizabeth had been rushed to the emergency room. She didn't even know if charges would be filed against her for the accident. "It's not important."

"It is to me."

"I'm fine." Lex fussed with the blanket covering Amanda, then placed her hand on her stomach. "How's Junior treating you?"

Amanda shook her head at the name. "Our daughter is going to come into this world answering to that name, if we're not careful. We should think of something else."

"Okay. I promise we'll find something before she's born. Although I think Junior is a fine name."

"You would." Amanda swatted her. "I guess Dr. Vaughn talked to you, huh?"

"Yep." Lex played with Amanda's hair. "Looks like you'll be having room service for a while."

"I'd rather be home with you and Lorrie. Think you can break me out?"

Lex shook her head. "Not a chance, sweetheart. But I'm going to be right here with you until our daughter is born."

"But Lex, it's going to be weeks! I don't want to be stuck here for that long." Amanda felt like ripping the intravenous tube from her hand and climbing out of bed. "Please talk to the doctor? I'll go crazy stuck in here. There's got to be some kind of compromise we can work out." She fought back a yawn. With all the excitement, she was completely worn out.

"I'll see what I can do, okay? Until then, why don't you try to get some rest?"

"I've been resting." Amanda's eyes closed against her will. Her lips barely moved, but her words were clear. "Don't leave me."

"Never." Lex kissed her lightly on the lips. "I love you." She brushed her fingers along Amanda's cheek. "Sleep well, love. I'll be here when you wake up." Lex hooked her foot around the leg of a nearby chair and dragged it over. Without releasing Amanda's hand, she sat and tried to get comfortable.

A LIGHT TOUCH on her shoulder jarred Lex out of a deep sleep. She struggled to stay upright in the chair and glared at the intruder. "What?" A quick glance at the bed showed her partner still sound asleep.

The nurse smiled kindly at her and spoke in a low voice. "I'm sorry to disturb you. I've got to get Ms. Walters' vitals and then the doctor will be in to do an exam. I'm afraid you'll have to leave."

"I'm not leaving." Lex stood slowly as various aches made themselves known. "I promised her."

Amanda yawned as she woke. "It's okay. Why don't you grab something to eat?"

"But—"

"I'll be fine." Amanda squeezed Lex's hand and pulled her closer. She was rewarded with a kiss. When they broke apart she lowered her voice. "Bring me a chocolate shake?"

Lex glanced at the nurse, who had found something beyond the window very interesting. "Sure." She dropped another quick kiss on Amanda's lips and left the room.

Out in the hall she almost ran into Jeannie, who immediately engulfed her in a fierce embrace. Lex looked at Rodney, who gave her a reassuring smile. They were alone, as they had left Teddy with her grandparents. "It's okay."

Jeannie stepped away and wiped at her eyes. "How is she?"

"Doing good. I've been sent on a quest for a chocolate shake." Lex tucked her hands into her back pockets. "You should be able to go in to see her after they finish all their tests and stuff."

Rodney appeared anxious and he gestured down the hall with a tilt of his head. "I'll run down and get a shake from the cafeteria, if you'd like." He knew Jeannie wanted to talk to Lex alone, and it gave him a perfect excuse to leave.

"Sure." Lex reached for her wallet but he waved her off.

"Don't worry about it." He squeezed Jeannie's arm. "I'll be back in a flash."

Lex watched him leave before turning her attention to her sister-in-law. Jeannie's eyes were puffy and red. "Are you all right?"

A heavy sigh was Jeannie's answer. She sniffled and pasted on the best smile she could muster. "I will be. It's going to take a little time though. Even though she was a thorn in everyone's side, she was still my mother." In her grief, Jeannie hadn't listened when she was asked to keep Elizabeth's death a secret.

The past tense Jeannie used while referring to her mother caused Lex to pale and stumble until she hit the wall. "Was? She's dead?"

"Yes. I thought you knew." Jeannie didn't understand Lex's reaction. She knew there was no love lost between the two. "She passed away a few hours ago in the emergency room."

"No." Lex felt lightheaded. "I'm so sorry." Bile rose in her throat.

"Excuse me." She stumbled past Jeannie and rushed down the hall toward the restroom.

Stunned, Jeannie watched Lex go. She didn't hear Martha come up beside her.

"Where's Lexie going? Is everything all right with Amanda?" Martha had feared the worst when she noticed Lex's abrupt exit.

"I don't know." Jeannie turned to Martha. "According to Lex, Amanda's doing okay. But she seemed upset when I mentioned Mother."

Martha cupped Jeannie's elbow with her hand. "What do you mean?"

Tears welled in the younger woman's eyes. "I can't believe she's gone." She gave a watery smile. "I always thought Mother was too tough to die."

"You told her?"

"I thought she already knew." Jeannie shrugged her shoulders. "It's not like they got along or anything."

Martha released her arm. "I'm sorry, honey. I know it's a terrible shock to you." She was torn between giving Jeannie comfort and checking on Lex. Her maternal instincts quickly won out. "I'm going to go check on Lexie. I'll be back in a few minutes."

LEX CUPPED ANOTHER handful of cold water and splashed it over her face. She raised her head and studied her reflection in the mirror, the haggard face almost unrecognizable. Her stomach had been empty and the dry heaves had left her weak. She rested her elbows on the marble countertop and buried her face in her hands.

The bathroom door opened and the shuffle of soft-soled shoes echoed in the otherwise empty room. Martha put her arm around Lex's waist, offering her silent support. They stood there for several minutes, until Martha finally spoke. "I'm sorry you had to hear about it that way, honey."

"Does Amanda know?" Lex still hadn't raised her head.

"No, not yet. We thought it would be best to wait until the doctor says it's okay." Martha rubbed Lex's back. "Michael offered to speak to her."

Lex raised and turned to face her. "No, let me. It's my fault and I think I should be the one to tell her."

"You can't blame yourself. The deputy who witnessed the accident told Charlie she ran right out in front of you. There was no way you could have avoided her." Martha shook her head. "God forgive me for saying this, but I can't muster up any sympathy for that woman. But I'm sorry for what this is doing to you."

Her stomach rebelling, Lex spun and raced to the nearest bathroom stall. She dropped to her knees and began to retch again violently.

Martha came in behind her and lifted Lex's hair away from her face. After Lex was finished, she helped her to her feet and wiped her face with a damp paper towel. "It's going to be okay, baby. Don't tear yourself up over this."

Lex took the towel away and exhaled heavily. "I don't see how I can't. This is going to devastate Amanda, and things will never be the same." She went to the sink and washed her face. After rinsing her mouth out, she blotted her face with a dry towel and leaned against the counter.

"No, they won't. All you can do is put this mess behind you and move on." Martha pulled Lex into her arms. "Have faith, Lexie. I truly believe it will work out."

"I hope so." Lex held on to Martha as if her life depended on it. She had no idea how she would tell Amanda that she was the cause of Elizabeth's untimely death.

AMANDA WORE AN extremely satisfied look on her face when Lex came into her room. "Hi. The doctor gave me permission to leave tomorrow."

"That's great, sweetheart." Lex tried to make her smile sincere, but her heart wasn't into it.

"What's wrong? I thought you'd be happy."

Lex swallowed heavily and nodded. She sat on the edge of Amanda's bed. "I am." She took one of Amanda's hands into her own. "I, uh, have something I need to tell you."

"Is it Lorrie? Is she okay?" Amanda shook her head. "I thought you said she was all right."

"No, she's fine." Lex lowered her eyes to study the blanket. "It's about your mother."

Amanda frowned. "What has she done, now? I thought she'd be in custody. Did she escape?"

Lex shook her head. "No." She looked into her lover's eyes. "There was an accident."

"What kind of accident?" Amanda read the intense sorrow on Lex's face and it scared her. "Lex?"

"I'm so sorry. She's gone, sweetheart. They did everything they could for her."

The frown on Amanda's face grew and she shook her head slowly. "No. That's not possible." She started to breathe heavily. "It's another one of her tricks."

"I'm afraid not, love." Lex brought their linked hands to her chest. "She was trying to get away from the deputies and ran out in the middle of the street." Here she inhaled deeply to gather her courage. "It happened so fast." Lex blinked away the tears that filled her eyes. "I never saw her. One minute I was driving along, the next," she lowered her head, "the next second she jumped out right in front of me."

The words slowly registered to Amanda. "You hit her with your truck?"

"I couldn't stop. I tried." Lex felt her heart break when Amanda pulled her hand away.

"You killed my mother?"

Lex reached for her but was rebuffed. "I swear, Amanda. I did everything I could to avoid her. I'm so…so, sorry. Please forgive me."

Amanda closed her eyes and raised a shaky hand to cover her mouth. The moment felt so surreal. "I think I need some time alone."

Her head bowed, Lex swallowed a sob. "I understand." She tripped over a chair as she backed out of the room. "I'll be right outside, if you need me." She stumbled through the door, her grief at what she'd done overwhelming her.

MICHAEL HANDED HIS daughter another tissue. He'd been with Amanda for the past couple of hours, holding her hand. Jeannie had left earlier, promising to return with dinner, although none of them had felt like eating.

Amanda blew her nose. "Thanks." She dropped the used tissue on the mounting pile in her lap. She couldn't remember when she'd cried so much. "It's hard to believe she's gone."

"I know. I keep expecting her to barge in here any minute, making some ludicrous demand."

She smiled at his comment. "She was something, wasn't she?"

"Yeah." Michael rubbed her knuckles with his thumb. He felt it was time to broach another subject with her. "Lex is devastated, you know. She's taken the responsibility entirely on her own shoulders."

"She would." Amanda watched their hands then raised her eyes to his. "It's not her fault. If it hadn't been Lex, it would have probably been someone else. It was just a shock, you know? I needed some time to come to grips with the whole situation."

He tightened his grasp for a moment before standing. "Let me go get her."

"Thanks."

Moments after Michael left, the door opened slowly. Lex stepped inside the room but stood close to the door. "Hey."

The grief-stricken expression on her partner's face was more than Amanda could bear. She held out her hand and in seconds Lex dropped to her knees beside her.

"I'm so sorry." Lex held Amanda's hand to her cheek. Her tears quickly dampened their fingers.

"Shh." Amanda pulled Lex to her and tucked her head to her chest. She used her free hand to stroke her lover's head. "It's going to be all right." Amanda hadn't been as upset with Lex as she was with herself. At the news of her mother's death, all she could think about was the relief of knowing they'd never be bothered by Elizabeth again. It was her guilt at that revelation that engulfed Amanda, and she knew it would be a long time before she would be able to forgive herself.

Chapter
Thirty-five

AMANDA SLAPPED THE fake leather arm of the wheelchair. "This is ridiculous, Lex. I'm perfectly capable of walking." Lex ignored her outburst and continued to push her toward the front pew of the sparsely filled church. "I mean it. I've been cooped up in the house for two days. Even the doctor said I was fine." She turned so she could look up into the still face of her partner. "Are you even listening to me?"

"I heard every word you said." Lex lowered her face until her lips were almost touching Amanda's ear. "But I also heard Dr. Vaughn say you were to stay off your feet. So please try to relax." She left a quick kiss on Amanda's cheek before standing tall once again. She didn't miss the heavy sigh that answered her, but elected to stay quiet and continue the short trek. This was one gathering Lex was not looking forward to. Even though Amanda had insisted she didn't blame her for Elizabeth's death, Lex knew her sentiment would not be shared by Elizabeth's family. Today would be the first time she would meet the rest of the Kingston clan.

The front pews had been taken over by the family and their spouses. Morris, Christina and their partners were on the far end, a conspicuous space between them and a severe looking matron, Paula Kingston. The oldest of the clan, Paula's bleached hair was pulled into a tight bun and her face was pinched in perpetual disapproval.

Anna Leigh and Jacob were at home, taking care of Lorrie and Teddy. Lex parked the wheelchair beside the opposite pew, where Michael, Lois, Jeannie and Rodney sat. She started to go sit behind them, but Michael motioned to the space next to him, on the end nearest Amanda. Lex looked as if she'd disregard his gesture, until her partner took her hand. With the part she played in the current situation weighing heavily on her mind, she didn't feel comfortable taking a position with the family. But with Amanda's insistent tug, she pushed her reservations deep down and took the offered seat. The squeeze on her hand made her discomfort less stifling.

Michael leaned into her and spoke softly. "How are you holding up?"

A halfhearted shrug was her answer. Lex was saved from any other conversation when the minister stepped to the podium. "Good morning. Thank you all for coming. We're here to celebrate the life of Elizabeth Kingston-Cauble." He droned on for thirty minutes, extolling the life of the woman most had come to loathe.

Michael turned his head and snuck a glance at Paula, who dabbed at her eyes with a handkerchief. He nudged Lex, who had also noticed Paula's apparent grief. "She's almost as good an actress as her sister was. Believe me, there was no love lost between the two of them."

His comment caught Lex off guard. She wasn't sure what to think, so she kept silent.

At the minister's request, Paula stood and made her way to the podium. She made a show of straightening her black dress before speaking. The heavy nylon material stretched tightly over her thick form. "Thank you, Reverend." After a deep breath, she removed a folded paper from her purse. "My sister," she paused and looked out over the small congregation, "my best friend, left us all too soon. She was cut down in the prime of her life." She glared at Michael, who had to clear his throat to cover his snort of derision. "She was a special woman, whose gifts of love and charity were spread among us all."

"Speaking of spreading, isn't she laying it on a little thick?" Michael's whispered comment elicited an elbow to the ribs from Lois.

Unable to help herself Lex chuckled, but quickly covered her actions with a fake cough. Her hand was squeezed harder and she pasted a solemn look on her face. She whispered her apologies to Amanda.

Paula was able to finish her eulogy without any more interruptions. Without further ado, she picked up the expensive Grecian bronze urn that held her sister's remains, and paraded to her seat.

The minister returned to the podium, flustered by her actions. He'd never seen anyone take the remains during a service. "Um, yes. I suppose we are finished. Unless anyone has something they'd like to say?" A heavy silence answered him. "Well, then. Thank you all for coming."

Everyone stood and some began to mill about. Michael, Lois, Jeannie and Rodney all stood around Amanda's chair. Jeannie touched her sister's shoulder. "How are you doing?"

"Better than Lex." Amanda watched as her lover spoke to Morris and Christina. "I tried to get her to skip the services, but she wouldn't."

"She's not still feeling guilty about Mother is she?"

Amanda shook her head. "She says she isn't, but I know better." She tugged on her sister's hand. "Could we go somewhere alone and talk?"

"Sure." Jeannie took command of the wheelchair and wheeled

Amanda into the outer vestibule. "What's up?"

"We haven't had much time together since this happened." Amanda looked around to make sure they were alone. "Are you doing all right?"

Jeannie guided Amanda near a bench so she could sit also. "I'm okay. I was more worried about you."

"We're funny, huh?" Amanda played with the hem of her black sweater. "If I say something, will you promise not to get mad?"

The tone in her voice worried Jeannie, who covered Amanda's hands with her own. "Hey. I know we haven't always seen eye to eye on everything, but you never have to worry about that. You can tell me anything."

Amanda stared at their hands, unable to look her sister in the eye. "When I found out, you know, about mother." She took a shaky breath. "Oh God, this is so hard to say."

"You don't have to —"

"I was glad." Amanda's voice cracked. "When I heard our mother was dead, all I could think about was how she wouldn't be plotting against us anymore." She raised her head, tears threatening to fall from her eyes. "I'm horrible, aren't I?"

"No!" Jeannie lowered her voice. "No, honey. Not at all. To tell you the truth, I wasn't too upset either. She's given our family a lot more trouble and heartache than anything else. And she's never been much of a mom to either of us. How does Lex feel about it?"

"Um, I don't know. We've kind of tiptoed around the subject. I know she feels guilty, so I didn't want to add to it."

Jeannie shook her head. "You're as stubborn as she is. What am I going to do with you two?"

The shuffling of feet silenced them both. Lex stepped into the antechamber, apparently looking for her wife. "Is everything all right?"

Jeannie squeezed Amanda's hands before standing. "Yes. I thought it would be better for Mandy to be out here, away from the crowd." She leaned over and whispered in her sister's ear. "Talk to her." She gave Lex a hug and kissed her cheek. "I'll see you two at the house."

Once Jeannie left Lex sat next to Amanda. "How are you holding up?"

"I've been better," Amanda admitted, brushing a stray tear from her cheek.

"Do you want to skip going to Jeannie's? I'm sure the family will understand if you're not there."

Amanda seriously considered asking Lex to take her home so she wouldn't have to face the Kingstons. She'd never gotten along with her mother's family, especially after Paula and her mother banished Morris. But as distasteful as it was, she felt she needed to at least make an appearance. "I doubt it, very seriously. My aunt isn't the understanding kind."

"Your dad doesn't have much use for her, I've noticed." Lex began to push Amanda's chair out of the church.

"That's putting it mildly."

They reached Martha's Explorer, which she had insisted they drive, instead of the Xterra. Martha decided Amanda's SUV was too rough-riding, and wouldn't take no for an answer. Lex unlocked the doors and helped Amanda get seated. She folded the wheelchair and placed it carefully in the back before coming around and getting in behind the wheel. She was about to start the vehicle when Amanda touched her arm.

"Can we sit here for a little while? I'm in no hurry."

"Sure."

Amanda turned slightly so she could see Lex's face. "This has been hell for you, I know."

Lex bit her lip and nodded, but didn't say anything.

"I can't even begin to think what you've gone through this past week." Amanda touched Lex's cheek. "When I found out that Mother had taken Lorrie, I completely lost it. But I knew you'd make everything okay."

"I'm so sorry about your mother. It—"

"Shh." Amanda covered Lex's mouth with her fingers. "Don't you dare apologize for something that wasn't your fault." She inhaled, then exhaled heavily. "As much as I hate to admit it, when I heard what had happened, I couldn't help but be glad."

"What?"

"Yeah. Imagine that." Amanda lowered her eyes. "God forgive me, but I was actually thankful my mother was dead."

Lex tipped her head back and closed her eyes. She reached for Amanda's hand and held it tight. "That's what has been bothering me, too."

"Yeah?"

"Yep. I kept wondering if I meant to do it. I know I tried to stop but what if, deep down, I didn't? Because I sure as hell wasn't upset she was gone. Only that I was the one who caused it." Lex raised their joined hands and kissed Amanda's knuckles. With her lover's admission, the pressure that had been building in her chest for days finally lessened.

PAULA KINGSTON STALKED through the small house, ignoring the condolences of those around her. She was a woman on a mission and nothing would keep her from finding a certain person. She peered into the kitchen and saw her quarry. A satisfied smirk crossed her pinched features. "There you are."

Standing between Michael and Lois, Lex looked up. A look of dread raced across her face when she realized who had spoken. She placed her coffee cup on the table, before it fell from her nerveless fingers.

Michael nudged Lex aside. "Hello, Paula. Is there something I can do for you?"

"No, I believe you've done more than enough. But I would like to speak to your friend, here." The predatory smile she gave Lex was anything but friendly.

Before her father-in-law could intervene again, Lex straightened her shoulders and stepped by him. "Why don't we go out on the back porch, where we won't be disturbed?" She wasn't about to let Paula cause a scene which would get back to Amanda. Lex opened the back door. "After you." Once the door was closed behind them, she turned to the older woman. "What can I do for you, Ms. Kingston?"

The casual attitude from Lex incensed Paula. "Considering you murdered my sister, I think you've done more than enough, don't you agree?"

"Actually, it was an accident." With nonchalance she didn't feel, Lex leaned against the wall and crossed her arms over her chest. "But I'm sure you've already read the police report."

"Of course I have. It's the only way I could learn the truth."

"The truth, Ms. Kingston, is that your sister kidnapped our daughter. If she hadn't been running away from the police, she'd still be alive today." Lex hadn't been prepared for the slap, which caused her head to slam against the wall.

"How dare you!"

The back door opened and Michael stood in front of Lex. "Paula! Have you lost your mind?"

Paula puffed up indignantly and pointed at Lex, who was rubbing her sore cheek. "This...this...woman, seems to be proud of what she's done."

"No, ma'am. As much as I didn't care for your sister, I would have never wanted to cause her harm." Lex only hoped she could get away with the white lie.

Michael put his arm around Lex. "Elizabeth was lucky it was Lex driving that truck and not me. I might have backed up and hit her again." He pointed a finger in Paula's face. "This is the last we'll hear of this, Paula. You're not going to bully us around like you do your own family." He started to lead Lex into the house, when she stopped.

"Ms. Kingston, believe me, I'm truly sorry for your loss." Lex lowered her voice. "But, if you so much as look at Amanda wrong and upset her, I won't be responsible for my actions." She followed Michael inside, leaving the eldest Kingston seething on the back porch.

Once inside, Lex brushed off Michael's concern as he offered to get her ice for her face. "Don't worry, I barely feel it." She almost rolled her eyes at the look on Lois' face.

"Lex, honestly. Come over here to the sink and at least let me put a cool cloth on you." Lois grabbed her arm and pulled her across the room. She ignored Lex's mutterings, and in moments had a damp towel against her reddened cheek. "Now hush."

"Yes, ma'am." Lex accepted the mothering in the spirit in which it was given. As she quietly allowed Lois' gentle ministration, she couldn't help but overhear a conversation Michael was having with another member of the family.

"You know, Michael, as much as Paula thrives on ceremony, I was surprised to find out she had Elizabeth cremated. I had been expecting an open casket, with a several-day viewing." The man who spoke was several years older than Michael and had been introduced earlier as a second-cousin.

"Well, Simon, it wasn't Paula's call. I was still listed as her next-of-kin, and decided it would be easier on the family this way." Michael lowered his voice, but could still be heard. "I thought she might as well get used to the heat."

Jeannie's voice from the doorway caught everyone's attention. "Lex, there you are. Amanda's been looking for you." She came into the room, giving Paula a nasty look when her aunt stormed through the room, muttering under her breath. "What bit her in the butt?"

Michael shook his head. "You don't want to know." He watched as Lex left the room in a hurry. "Is your sister okay?"

"Oh sure. I think she was tired of fending off the attentions of Great-Aunt Marnie. She keeps trying to touch Mandy's stomach, so she can tell her what sex the baby is."

Lois joined them. "Didn't anyone tell Marnie we already know?"

"Well, yeah. Several times as a matter of fact. But you have no idea how stubborn that woman is." Jeannie linked arms with the couple. "How old is she anyway? At least ninety, right?"

"She's got to be pushing a hundred by now. I think she was closing in on seventy when you were born." Michael nudged his daughter. "At least she hasn't asked Amanda to name the baby after your Great Uncle Bertram, has she?" At Jeannie's answering nod, he sighed. "We'd better go save Marnie."

Lex searched through several rooms, until she heard her partner's exasperated voice. She nudged her way into the crowded sitting room, where Amanda's wheelchair took up residence in one corner.

"Look, Aunt Marnie. We already know we're having a girl, remember? Jeannie told you earlier." Amanda held out her hands to keep the old woman's claw-like hands away from her.

Marnie's fingernails were close to an inch long and painted mulberry, and they clacked together when she reached toward her grand-niece. "Now honey, you know I've never been wrong. I can tell you—" Her hands were grasped in a firm, but gentle grasp.

Lex knelt next to the elderly woman. "Mrs. Dardenryple, that's kind of you to offer. I've heard from everyone in the family how on-target your predictions are." She tried not to grimace as the sharp digits poked into her palms. "But you told us earlier that Amanda is going to have a little girl, remember?"

The old woman frowned slightly. "Of course I did." Marnie pulled her hands free and patted Lex's cheek. "You're a cute one. But don't be trying to pull the wool over old Marnie's eyes. I can see that you're not with child."

"Um, right." Lex's eyes widened as she frantically thought of what to say next. To her relief, another family member came to the rescue.

Morris placed his arm around Marnie's frail shoulders and led her away. "There you are, sweetheart. I've been looking all over for you. Kevin has a cup of tea with your name on it." The crowd, which had been enjoying the show, followed the pair, leaving Lex and Amanda alone.

When Lex's head bumped against her, Amanda ran her fingers through her lover's hair. "Nice timing."

"Your Great-Aunt needs to be declawed before someone gets hurt." Lex turned to look into Amanda's eyes. "She's a character, that's for sure."

"Oh, yeah. When we were little, Dad used to threaten to send us to live with her if we didn't behave. He never followed through, though."

The thought of a small Amanda being chased by Marnie gave Lex the chills. "That'd be enough to scare me."

Michael's voice could be heard in the next room. "Paula, stop." Michael tried to keep the heavy woman from entering the sitting room but she bullied past him.

"Shut up, you little toad. I've had about all I can stand of you." Paula stood in the doorway glaring at Lex. "There you are."

Lex stood, positioning herself protectively in front of Amanda. "Yep. Here I am." She was tired of putting up with the likes of Elizabeth, and now her shrewish sister Paula. "What do you want now?"

The tone in Lex's voice should have warned Paula she was about to bite off more than she could chew but she ignored it. "I think you owe me, and this entire family, an apology."

"Excuse me?" Amanda started to rise from her chair, but Lex's hand on her shoulder stopped her.

"Ms. Kingston," Lex put her hands on her hips, "Paula. I don't owe you a damned thing."

Paula's face reddened. "My sister—"

"Was not a nice woman," Lex finished for her. "She plotted and schemed until her husband lost everything. Once she was through with him, in some warped effort to control her daughter, she tried to poison me, almost killing Amanda instead." She held up her hand to stop Paula from interrupting. "She burned down my house, with Amanda inside, escaped from a mental institution, embezzled from us, and last but not least, kidnapped her own granddaughter." Lex stepped forward, causing Paula to move away. "So don't give me some sob story about poor Elizabeth and expect me to cower and beg for your forgiveness. Because it's not going to happen."

"You hateful bitch." Paula looked around the room at the congregated family members. "Are you all going to stand here and let her get away with this?" She pointed at Lex. "She's the one who killed Elizabeth!"

An elderly man, who had stood silently by, shuffled forward. "Paula, that's quite enough." He took a surprisingly strong grip on her arm. "You've caused enough of a scene. It's time for you to take your Aunt Marnie and me home." He allowed her to leave the room on her own before turning to Lex and holding out his hand. "I'm Bertram, Marnie's husband. You take good care of our little Amanda there, you hear?"

"Yes, sir." Lex shook his hand. He was strong for his age, which had to be at least ninety. "If there's anything I can do for you, Mr. Dardenryple—"

"We're fine, young lady." He gave Amanda a wink and left the room as quietly as he had entered it.

Lex watched the rest of the family, ready to do battle if she had to. She was met with either warm smiles, or accepting nods, as they filed out of the room.

"That went, um, well, I guess." Amanda sat in the wheelchair and rubbed her stomach. "Your Momma was pretty cool, Junior. You should have seen her." She smiled at Lex when she turned around.

"Yeah?"

Amanda nodded. "Definitely." She held out her hand, which was quickly taken. "Ready to take me home, Slim? I think I've had about all of this I can stand."

Lex bent and kissed her. "You got it."

Chapter
Thirty-six

THE HEAVY OAK desk was cluttered with paper and Lex added to it by tossing another envelope onto one of the piles. "I hate paying bills." She picked up another, not recognizing the return address. One quick swipe with the letter opener gave her easy access to the contents. She unfolded the yellow sheet and scanned it. "What the hell?"

It was a notice from a mortgage company, warning her she would soon be in default—on a property inside the city limits of Somerville. The address was familiar and Lex realized with a sinking feeling it was Hubert's house. "Damn." She picked up the phone and dialed a number from memory, feeling her blood pressure rise as the recording announced the number was no longer in service. "I'm going to kill that son of a bitch." With everything that had been happening, she had forgotten the deal she had made with her brother.

She picked up the phone and dialed the number on the notice. "Hello? I need to speak to someone about a letter I received. Thanks." While she was on hold, Lex opened another envelope. It was a past-due notice from the electric company, warning that the power would be shut off at Hubert's. "Sorry bastard. He must have skipped town." A confused voice brought her back to the call. She apologized to the woman and gave her the account number.

"Yes, Ms. Walters. We show here you co-signed the loan for Hubert Walters."

"When was I supposed to have done this?" Lex opened two more letters, both disconnect notices for the house in town. Somehow, all of Hubert's mail had been forwarded to the ranch. "Dammit!" At the huff of indignation on the other end of the line, she quickly apologized again.

"As I was saying, since we are unable to reach Mr. Walters, the loan has defaulted to you. Either pay the amount due, or we'll take custody of the property in question."

Lex closed her eyes and silently counted to ten. "Fine. Take the damned house. Anything else?"

"No, ma'am. We'll send you a letter, stating we've begun

foreclosure proceedings. Have a nice day."

"Yeah." Lex slammed down the receiver and glared at the phone. "If I ever see Hubert again, I'll castrate the son of a bitch with a rusty spoon." She checked the rest of the bills, satisfied that there would be no more surprises.

A rustling from the doorway caught Lex's attention. She looked up and noticed a tousled head peep over the top of the desk. All of her anger quickly deflated when she saw the innocent face of her daughter. "Hey, lil' bit. Have a good nap?" She'd left Lorrie on the couch, where she had nodded off while watching a favorite video.

"Yep." Still about halfway asleep, Lorrie stumbled around the desk and crawled onto Lex's lap. "I'm thirsty."

"Well then," Lex stood and settled her daughter against one hip, "let's go see what we can get into." She headed toward the kitchen, reminding herself to call Lois and see how Amanda was faring.

Since Dr. Vaughn only allowed Amanda out of the hospital with the stipulation she would stay close by, they accepted the offer to stay with Michael and Lois. They took over the spare room, and the house being only one story meant Amanda didn't have to worry about stairs.

Lex volunteered to take Lorrie for the day, since she had to handle a few things out at the ranch. She was almost to the kitchen when the flap to the pet door swung open, and an excited Freckles raced into the house. The radio collar allowed the dog to go in and out, but kept the door locked to keep Lorrie inside. They'd found out the hard way how easy it was for her to slip through.

"Fleckles!" Lorrie slid out of Lex's arms and hugged her pet. "Eew. Momma, Fleckles smell yucky."

"Now what?" Lex sniffed the air, then noticed several new dark spots on the terrier's white coat. "Someone must have been rolling in the stables again." She sighed when Lorrie began to wrestle the dog. "Great. Now both of you get a bath." She wondered if she could get away with bathing them both at the same time. A smirk crossed her lips. It probably wouldn't be wise, because if Amanda found out Lex would be the one in the doghouse. "Okay, kiddo. Let's get you and your buddy cleaned up, then we'll have a snack before we go see your mommy."

SHORT, LOUD RAPS on the front door woke Amanda. She opened her eyes and looked around the unfamiliar surroundings before realizing where she was. The clean living room was warm, and she was hunkered on the sofa, tucked in one corner while her feet were stretched across the cushions. There was also a soft afghan across her legs that hadn't been there before. The knocking continued, so she struggled to her feet to answer the door.

Amanda opened the door, wishing she hadn't. "Aunt Paula. What are you doing here?"

"I've come to take care of something my sister obviously couldn't," the matron huffed. Paula was dressed in a form-fitting navy dress, similar to the one she wore to the funeral. Her purse hung from her arm, and she peered at her niece through black-framed glasses. "Well? Am I to stand here all day?"

With an aggrieved sigh, Amanda held the door open and escorted Paula into the living room. She sat on the sofa and gestured to a nearby chair. "Forgive me for not playing hostess, but I'm supposed to stay off my feet."

Paula lowered her bulk into a floral print wingback chair. "I can see. You know, your mother talked to me at length at what a disappointment you'd been to her."

"What else is new?"

"You've got a sharp tongue on you, girl. No wonder poor Elizabeth was at her wits end." Paula leaned forward to make her point. "Now listen to me. It's about time you quit behaving inappropriately and find yourself a nice man and settle down."

"Aunt Paula—"

"I realize it will be harder since you're in that condition. But you're young and reasonably attractive. Once you lose that weight, I'm sure you'll catch some young man's eye."

Amanda balled her hands into fists and fought the urge to throw something into her aunt's smug face. "That's enough."

But Paula was only getting started. "You can't possibly be happy, taking up with her. She murdered your own mother! You've betrayed the family and tarnished your mother's memory."

"Excuse me?" As hard as it was, Amanda stayed seated. "You have no right to talk to me that way! I love Lex and she loves me. Nothing in my life concerns you, or your precious family."

The front door opened and Lois stepped inside, her arms full of grocery bags. "Amanda? Is everything all right? I heard—" she stopped when she saw who else was sitting in her living room.

A small blur raced by her. "Mommy!"

Amanda opened her arms and greeted Lorrie. "Hello, honey."

"I think this is all of them, Lois." Lex came inside, also loaded down with several bags. She almost ran into Lois, who was frozen in place.

Paula turned in her seat to take in the newcomers. "Good afternoon, Lois." She pointedly ignored Lex.

"What the hell is going on here?" Lex placed her bags on the floor and stepped farther into the room. "Amanda, are you okay?" She went to take her partner's outstretched hand.

Tension weighed heavily in the room. Lois was torn between calling Michael at work or standing close by in case a referee was needed. She looked on helplessly until a subtle nod from Lex calmed her. "I think I'll get these groceries put away."

Amanda kissed Lorrie on the head. "Why don't you go with Mimi? Maybe she'll give you milk and cookies."

"Yep. Me help Mimi." Lorrie gave her mommy one last hug and hurried after Lois.

Lex waited until Lorrie and Lois had left before she turned to Paula. "Is there some reason you're here?"

"You're a nasty one, aren't you?" Paula sat taller in her seat. "Before you so rudely interrupted, I was having a private conversation with my niece. Now if you'll excuse us—"

"Lady, there's no excuse for the likes of you."

Paula pursed her lips, looking frighteningly like her sister. "You're as uncouth as Elizabeth described. But if you insist on butting in, fine. Amanda and I were discussing how it was time for her to straighten up and behave in a proper manner."

"No, you were trying to tell me how to live my life," Amanda sputtered. She gasped as a sharp pain lanced through her stomach.

Lex dropped to her knees beside her. "Sweetheart?" She began to panic when Amanda moaned and wrapped her arms around her belly. "The baby?"

"Oh, God." Amanda bit her lip and leaned as far forward as she could. "I think we'd better call the doctor."

"It's going to be okay." Lex got to her feet and yelled for Lois, who rushed into the room. "I'm going to take Amanda to the hospital. Could you—"

Lois kept Lorrie by her side. "Don't you worry about about a thing." She put her hand on Lorrie's head. "Would you like to stay with me and make some more cookies?"

Torn between her parents and the thought of fresh goodies, Lorrie stuck her finger in her mouth. "Momma?"

"Oh for heaven's sake." Paula stood and fussed with her purse.

"Not one word," Lex warned her. She squatted next to Lorrie. "I have to take your Mommy to the doctor, lil' bit. Can you stay here with Mimi and be a good girl?"

Lorrie gave her a bashful grin. "Yep. We makes cookies."

"Great." Lex kissed her forehead and straightened up. She went to help Amanda to her feet. "Can you walk?"

Amanda put her arm around Lex and leaned into her. "As long as you're here with me."

Paula grabbed Amanda's arm. "You can't be seriously thinking of going with her?"

"Let go of me."

Lex wrapped her fingers around Paula's wrist and squeezed until she let go of Amanda. "Touch her again and I'll wring your damned neck."

"You shouldn't be allowed behind the wheel. For all we know, you'll kill Amanda and the baby, too." Paula rubbed her sore wrist.

Amanda turned on her. "Aunt Paula, go home. You're not wanted, or needed here." She allowed Lex to help her out of the house.

"Why, the nerve!" Paula blinked in shock at her niece's words. She turned to Lois. "Can you believe that?"

Lois gave her a smug look. "She's right. Why don't you slither under your rock, wherever it is? Our family is doing very well without you." She held the door open wide. "Goodbye."

Paula puffed up and sniffed. "Fine. I have a plane to catch this evening anyway." She raised her head high as she crossed the threshold.

Lois watched from the door as Lex and Amanda drove away. She felt a tiny hand tangle in her slacks. "Why don't we call your Gampi and see if he'd like some cookies, sweetie?"

"Yum. Gampi likes cookies." Lorrie wrapped her hand around Lois' finger and tugged her in the direction of the kitchen.

LEX SLAMMED THE heel of her hand on the middle of the steering wheel, blowing the horn. The old man on the tractor ignored her and continued to drive slowly in the middle of the street. "Would you get off the damned road? What the hell is he doing on a residential street, anyway?"

"Honey, calm down. I'm fine." Amanda's own panic had lessened when she realized it was only labor pains she felt. She braced one hand on the roof of the Explorer as Lex whipped around the tractor.

"Dumbass." Lex barely slowed at the stop sign before taking off again. She spared a glance at Amanda. "You okay?"

Amanda nodded. "You don't have to hurry. We have plenty of time." She felt another strong contraction and then a warm wetness. "Oops. Um, Lex?"

"Huh?" Lex stopped at a red light and turned her head toward Amanda. "What's the matter?"

"I think my water broke."

"Shit!" After a quick look both ways, Lex raced through the intersection. "Should we call the doctor again? Maybe I should have called an ambulance. Damn. I knew I should have—"

"Honey, please. It's all right." Amanda inhaled sharply. "Ooh. That was a good one." She kept one hand on her stomach, as if to sooth her unborn child.

"What?" Lex kept looking from the road, to Amanda, and back again. "Please don't have the baby yet. I haven't finished reading the book on delivery." She hit the horn again as she came upon another traffic light. "Come on, idiot! Move!"

Amanda tried to keep from laughing. "Lex, it's a red light. People are supposed to stop."

"Not today." Lex growled and stuck her head out the window. "Would you go already? The damned light's green!" she yelled, hitting the horn again. When the car ahead started to move, Lex swerved around it and sped through the intersection. "Ha!" She drove several blocks without any interference, and was feeling quite proud of herself.

"Lex."

No answer.

"Honey?" Amanda still couldn't get her lover's attention. She was sure it would be something funny to tell their grandchildren, but right now, she was beginning to get a little irritated. "Lex!"

"Hm?"

"You missed the street." Amanda pointed to their right. "It was a block earlier."

"Damn." Lex checked her mirrors, and seeing the coast clear, executed a perfect U-turn. "Why didn't you say something?"

"I tried. You weren't listening." Amanda breathed a sigh of relief when the hospital came into view. She wasn't surprised when they ended up in the emergency entrance.

Lex parked the Explorer and jumped out. With the engine still running, she hurried around to the passenger side and opened Amanda's door. "Oh, wait." She held up her hands and started walking backward. "Don't go anywhere. I'll be right back." Before Amanda could speak, she raced into the hospital. Seconds later, Lex came running out, pushing a wheelchair. "Here." She helped Amanda into the chair and started toward the hospital doors.

A stern looking nurse met them at the door. "I told you I would have an orderly assist you," she chastised Lex. "You're not authorized to bring in a patient."

"I didn't have time to wait. Can't you see that my wife is in labor?" Lex jumped away when she was slapped away from the chair by the nurse. "Hey."

"Young lady, I'll take it from here. You have to move your car."

Lex almost ran into the automatic door before it hissed completely open. "I'm not leaving her."

Dr. Vaughn stood at the admitting desk, trying to keep from laughing. She'd already been at the hospital, checking on another patient, when Lex's frantic phone call had come in. "Lex, calm down. Amanda, how are you doing?"

Amanda shook her head. "Better than she is, I think. My water broke about five minutes ago."

"You are ready, aren't you?" The doctor patted Amanda's hand before looking at Lex again. "Lex, we're going to get Amanda settled first. Take care of what you need to, then Nurse Harvey will bring you in."

"But—" Lex was loathe to leave Amanda's side.

Amanda winced as another contraction hit. "I'll be fine." She held out her hand and brought Lex close, pulling her down for a quick kiss. "But I think our daughter is getting impatient. So hurry."

"Okay." Lex kissed her again. "I love you."

"Love you, too." Amanda waved to her as she was wheeled away.

LEX HAD RETURNED from parking the SUV when she saw Dr. Vaughn hurrying toward her. "What's wrong? Is Amanda okay?"

"We've got a slight change in plans. Amanda's fine, but she's being prepped for surgery." Dr. Vaughn had to grab one of Lex's arms to keep her steady. "We've already given her the epidural, but I don't trust her blood pressure, so we're going to do a cesarean. I thought you might want to come with me and get scrubbed up."

"Uh, yeah. Right." The thought of being present while they cut into Amanda made Lex feel lightheaded. But she refused to give in to her fear. "Lead on, doc."

After changing and being briefed on what to expect, Lex followed Dr. Vaughn into the operating room. She swallowed heavily and took her place next to Amanda's head. "Hi, sweetheart."

Amanda rolled her eyes upward. "I'm glad to see you."

"I wouldn't miss this for the world." Lex brushed her fingers across Amanda's forehead. "Looks like you're all set."

"Yeah. The epidural they gave me has done wonders. You know, even though I didn't want to go this route, once those labor pains set in, I changed my mind."

Lex was relieved as well. She hadn't been looking forward to seeing her lover in pain, no matter what the circumstances were. A quick glance down Amanda's body shifted her nerves into high gear. Sterile cloths were draped across her entire form, except for her stomach, which was now a lovely orange color. It was then that Lex realized she'd have a perfect view, and the thought caused black spots to float across her vision.

Dr. Vaughn noticed her discomfort. "Lex? Are you going to be okay in here?"

"Yep. Fine. No problem." Lex nodded nervously, much to the amusement of her wife.

"Honey? Hey, it's not much different from seeing a calf born."

Lex shook her head. "It's very different. You're no cow."

The entire room broke into chuckles over that statement, and even Amanda giggled. "Well, thanks for that vote of confidence."

Once everyone had settled down, the doctor made the initial incision. Lex kept her eyes on Amanda's face, gratified to see she was in no pain. "Doing okay?"

"Yeah." She wrinkled her nose. "That's weird."

"What?"

"I can feel it, sort of."

The doctor overheard their conversation. "It's not painful, is it?"

Amanda tilted her head slightly as she considered her answer. "No. More like it's disconnected. Like how it feels when someone touches the outside of your shoe. You know it's there, but you can't feel it."

"Perfect." The doctor continued, speaking in low tones to her staff.

Lex concentrated on her wife, whose eyes never left hers. "I love you, Amanda." She had no idea how much time had passed, but looked up in surprise when the doctor spoke out loud again.

"Here she is, ladies." Dr. Vaughn brought their daughter out into the world. Small and red, her tiny face was scrunched in displeasure at her new surroundings. She kicked and opened her mouth, showing off her lungs with a loud squall.

With her own head raised slightly by Lex, Amanda was able to see. "She's beautiful."

Tears of joy spilled from Lex's eyes. She'd never seen such an amazing sight in her life. She watched as the nurse took their baby across the room to the warmer, then turned her attention to her wife. "You did good, Mommy."

While the doctor began closing the incision, the nurse completed her tasks and brought the baby to the new parents. She offered her to Lex, who accepted the precious bundle with awe.

Lex held their daughter close to Amanda's head, the baby still crying loudly. "I don't think she's very pleased with us right now."

The nurse watched the new family bond. No matter how many births she witnessed, it never ceased to put a smile on her face. "Have you decided on a name?"

Amanda looked at her daughter, then met her wife's eyes. "Melanie." She didn't miss the joyful look that crossed Lex's face, even with the mask she wore. Naming the baby after Lex's grandmother was something she had hoped to do. "Right?"

For a long moment, Lex couldn't speak. Then she decided to add to the new tradition. "Melanie Leigh."

Chapter
Thirty-seven

THE ENTIRE FAMILY stood by patiently in the waiting room for any news of the impending birth. Martha, who arrived with the Caubles, hadn't stopped pacing. Her soft shoes squeaked with each step on the clean tile. She considered it very lucky that she had been shopping with Anna Leigh when they received the call from Lois, telling them Amanda had gone into labor.

Michael met her in the middle and held out his arms. "Would you care to dance?"

She curtsied. "Perhaps another time, kind sir." She shared a laugh with him then they joined the rest of the group. "How long has it been? Shouldn't we have heard something by now?"

"I think it's been about five minutes from the last time you asked." Anna Leigh handed Martha a paper cup full of coffee. "I know this sounds ridiculous, but why not have a little of this to calm your nerves?"

Jeannie snorted. "Like she needs caffeine." She sat beside Travis, since her husband Rodney was home with their baby and Lorrie.

Charlie came into the room, jingling a set of keys. "Any word?"

"Not yet," Jacob answered. "We were enjoying the show your wife was putting on." He gestured to the keys. "Got it unlocked, I see."

"Sure did." Upon pulling into the hospital parking lot, Charlie noticed his wife's SUV — parked sideways with one tire up on the curb and running. With the doors locked. Not for the first time, he was glad he carried an extra set on his own keychain. "I guess I should give Lex points for remembering to lock the truck."

Martha came up and gave him a hug. "Don't you be giving her any grief. She had more important things on her mind."

Charlie decided now wouldn't be the time to mention to her the "mess" he noticed in the passenger seat. He was going to owe Jeremy big time for handling that little detail for him.

The door of the obstetrics hall opened, and a frazzled but proud Lex came in. Still dressed in her green hospital scrubs, she was immediately surrounded by the group. She had a hard time understanding all the voices that chimed in at once.

"How is Amanda?" "Was it a girl?" "Is the baby okay?" "How much does she weigh?" "Does she have any hair?" And the funniest question, by an overexcited Jeannie, "Who does she look like?"

"Hold on, everybody." Lex had to raise her voice to be heard. The silence was immediate, as if someone had flipped a switch. "Amanda's great and our daughter is perfect." She was embraced by Anna Leigh and Martha at the same time. "Whoa. Easy, ladies, there's plenty of me to go around."

Martha was the first to recover her voice. "Details, please. Give us all the particulars."

Lex couldn't keep the wide grin off her face. "Um, sure." She held out her hands, spaced a foot and a half apart. "She's about yay big, red and wrinkly, and the biggest little attitude I've ever seen."

Anna Leigh shook her head at Lex's high spirits. "That's not exactly the details we want, Lexington. Specifics would be nice."

"Oh. Well, she's six pounds, eight ounces, and almost seventeen inches long. Better?"

"Much." Anna Leigh turned to her husband, who was standing behind her. "Isn't it marvelous, darling? We have another great-grandchild to spoil."

His grin was almost as large as Lex's. "Best news I've had all day. But why don't we allow Lex a chance to sit down?"

The crowd parted, although Lex stood in place, practically bouncing on the balls of her feet. "Thanks. I don't have time, though. I want to get back to Amanda." She started to leave then turned around. "Oh yeah. If y'all will give her a little time, she should be ready for visitors." With a quick glance at her watch, she spun on her heels and hurried back to Amanda, fearing she'd miss something important in those precious moments.

Martha rolled her eyes. "I'm going to thump her good when I see her again. That darned brat forgot to tell us what they named the baby."

AMANDA WATCHED IN amazement as her daughter nursed against her breast. The newborn's tiny mouth worked furiously. She brushed her fingertip along Melanie's cheek. The overwhelming awe Amanda felt was like nothing she had known before. She raised her head when the door opened and her wayward spouse poked her head inside. "Did you find everyone?"

"Yep." Lex was still so excited, she didn't think her feet touched the floor as she moved to stand beside the bed. With a shaky hand, she lightly cupped Melanie's head. "She takes after her mommy." Her eyes rose to take in Amanda's face. She leaned over carefully and kissed her. "I love you."

"I love you, too." The baby stopped nursing, so Amanda pulled her away from her body. She had to tug slightly to get Melanie to release the nipple. When she did, the infant squeaked her protest. "Looks like she takes after you, also."

Lex grinned proudly as she lifted Melanie away. "She knows a good thing when she sees it." She kissed the top of the baby's head and gently rubbed her back. While Amanda covered up, she said, "You don't have to do that on my account, sweetheart."

"No, but I have a feeling we're soon going to have a roomful of visitors."

"Only if you feel like it." Lex cradled Melanie close to her chest. "Besides, I'm not ready to share you two with the rest of the world."

Amanda watched with joy as Lex bonded with their daughter. The nightmares she had before the baby was born, that Lex wouldn't have anything to do with her, were totally unfounded. "I know what you mean. I like it being only us."

There was a light rap on the door before it cracked open. "Hello," Anna Leigh's voice called, "is it all right for us to come in?"

Amanda mouthed to Lex that she told her so. "Sure. Come on in."

Anna Leigh, Jacob and Travis moved slowly into the room. Their eyes focused on the small bundle in Lex's arms. Anna Leigh was the first to find her voice. "Oh my. She's precious." She stepped closer to Lex, who reluctantly handed the baby to her. "Thank you, Lexington." Anna Leigh placed her lips on the pale fuzz that covered the baby's head. She sent a concerned look to her granddaughter. "How are you faring, dearest?"

"Much better than I thought I would." Amanda tugged the bedcovers higher. Since she had recently breastfed Melanie, she still wasn't comfortable sharing her personal space, even with her family.

Jacob stood next to his wife and peered at the sleepy infant. "Mandy, I do believe she has your nose."

"That's what Lex keeps telling me. I'm not so sure, though." Amanda secretly hoped the baby's eyes stayed blue, so that she'd share that characteristic with Lex. "I've already discovered that she has Lex's appetite."

Travis came to the bed and brushed Amanda's hand. "Are you sure you're up to company? You seem pale."

His concern touched her. "I'm okay. But I'm curious. How did you three manage to be the first ones in?"

Jacob held out one arm in an exaggerated pose of strength. "We won the arm-wrestling contest. And believe me, Martha's a lot stronger than she looks."

Lex did a double take. "What?" Although she wanted to, she forced herself not to take her daughter from Anna Leigh's loving arms. She hated to share.

"My husband is pulling your leg. It was Jeannie's idea. She

thought it would be more fair if we visited according to seniority."

Amanda squeezed Travis' hand. "It sounds like a great solution." She cleared her throat to catch Lex's attention. Her lover came to stand next to her. "I take it you didn't tell them what we named her?"

All eyes turned to Lex, who blushed at the oversight. "I, um, can't remember."

"That's right. You took off before we had a chance to find out." Travis put his arm over Lex's shoulders. "Not that we blame you."

Lex got over her embarrassment and happily accepted the baby from Anna Leigh. "I'm sorry about that, folks." She looked to Amanda, who nodded. "Since Amanda didn't like my idea—"

"Junior? Please!" Amanda rolled her eyes. "That's evil."

"Amanda, Junior," Lex corrected. She shrugged her shoulders. "Anyway, Amanda came up with the perfect name."

"We came up with it."

Anna Leigh gave them both a stern look. "Are you going to tell us before she goes to college? Or are we going to have to find out by reading her diploma?"

Amanda took over, knowing how Lex tended to get sidetracked whenever she was excited about something. "We wanted to give her a name that meant a lot to us, so I thought that Melanie would be the perfect choice."

"And, since she has two amazing great-grandmothers," Lex piped in, "Leigh was the obvious decision for her middle name."

The room became silent as their words soaked in. Travis was vaguely aware of the dampness around his eyes, and wiped at them hastily. "I think Lanie would have been extremely proud, girls."

Anna Leigh watched as Lex handed the baby to Amanda. "I don't," she raised a trembling hand to her mouth, "I don't know what to say."

Jacob pulled her close. "Melanie Leigh Walters. It has a nice ring to it."

Chapter
Thirty-eight

THE RUN-DOWN motel was long past its glory days. Even at its prime, over fifty years ago, it had been less than stellar. Now there were too many layers of paint peeled away in places, and the neon sign had long-ago grown dark. There were a dozen rooms, six on each side of a gravel lot, and all but three were vacant.

A black, four-door Mazda compact sat in front of the last room. The rear passenger window was partially lowered at an uneven angle, stuck in the same position for years. Three of the bald tires were without hubcaps. The radio antenna was bent in the middle, and the body was scarred with deep scratches and dents.

From the alley behind the building ran a wild-eyed teenaged boy. His jeans were stained and torn, and his tee shirt hung loosely on his lanky body. He looked behind himself and swore out loud when he heard heavy footsteps coming his way. In a panic, he removed a small plastic bag from his front pocket and tossed it into the old car, before racing through the parking lot and across the street.

A panting police officer gave chase. Sweat dripped down his face and into his eyes. Parts of his knit uniform shirt were dark with perspiration. He paused long enough to announce his location through the radio clipped to his shoulder, then sprinted after the teenager. Within moments, the motel lot was quiet once again.

Inside a room, Hubert Walters was propped against an old wooden headboard. There was an empty pizza carton next to his leg. He scratched at his beard, which he had grown to help hide his identity. He didn't know if his sister had filed any criminal charges against him, but he wasn't about to take any unnecessary chances. His week-old beard was liberally peppered with gray.

He jabbed at the remote control which was bolted onto the nightstand. The television screen hissed loudly and mocked him with only snow for a picture. "Damned piece of shit." He gave up, and in his anger threw his dinner box across the room.

Hubert looked around at his surroundings in disgust. The only furniture in the room was the nightstand, bed and television. His suitcase sat open on the floor next to the dank and mildewed bathroom, and he decided it was time to move on.

Within half an hour, he had gathered his meager belongings and tossed the suitcase into the trunk of the cheap car. It took several tries before the trunk lid would stay closed. After he turned in his room key, he squeezed his bulk into the car. He pumped the accelerator several times before turning the key and prayed silently until the wreck sputtered to life.

As he backed out of the parking space, the car jarred to a stop with a crunch. "Dammit, what now?" He looked in the rearview mirror and saw the trash dumpster he had ran into. "Son of a bitch." With another curse, he put the car into drive and scattered gravel as he spun out of the motel parking lot.

LONG MILES OF the Oklahoma highway put Hubert in a trancelike state. He blinked tiredly at the white stripes as he tried to stay awake. The radio in his car was broken and he was beginning to regret his decision to head toward Kansas. Flashing lights in his rearview mirror startled him, and he glanced down at the speedometer. No, he wasn't speeding. With an aggrieved sigh, he edged toward the shoulder of the road.

State Trooper Richard Johnson stepped out of his vehicle and adjusted his belt. He pushed his hat further down on his forehead and carefully walked toward the old car. With his hand on the butt of his gun, he tapped on the driver's window.

Hubert swallowed his nerves and struggled with the crank. The window only went halfway down before stopping.

"Sir, could you roll down your window the rest of the way?"

"I can't. It's broken." Hubert tapped his fingers on the steering wheel. He started to sweat. The cop's wary attitude was making him nervous.

Trooper Johnson noticed his discomfort. "Sir, could you please step outside your vehicle?" He took two steps away and unsnapped his holster.

"Shit." Hubert struggled with his seatbelt and had to bump his shoulder against the door to open it. He almost fell from the car, but righted himself and climbed out slowly. "Is there a problem? I didn't think I was speeding."

"No, sir, you were not. But you do have a broken right taillight."

Hubert shook his head. "Well, hell. You stopped me for that? This is bullshit." He started to put his hands on his hips, when the officer reached for his gun.

"Sir, keep your hands away from your body." The trooper took several more steps back and kept his hand on his gun when Hubert didn't comply.

Hubert raised his hands. "Give me a fucking break. I haven't done anything wrong!"

"Get on your knees and lock your fingers together behind your head." The officer waited until Hubert complied, then handcuffed him. He brought Hubert to his feet and stood him next to the old car. He pushed him face first against the trunk. After a careful search of his pockets, the trooper found Hubert's wallet. He was looking at the ID when he noticed a small bag of white powder resting on the back seat of the car. "Sir, I'm going to have to search your car."

"Whatever." The dust on the car made its way into Hubert's nose, causing him to sneeze. One side of his face was now gray from the trunk. He was lifted away from his car, led to the police car and helped into the back seat. "I haven't done anything wrong! What the fuck is your problem?" The door slammed in his face, and he watched in disbelief as the officer took a small plastic baggie from his car. "Hey! That's not mine! You planted that!"

The trooper came to the car and put the bag away. He typed Hubert's information into his computer, and smiled when he found out his new passenger was not only out of state, but on parole. "Mr. Walters, I'd advise you not to say anything else at this time." He went on to Mirandize Hubert. "Do you understand your rights, sir?"

Hubert kicked the seat in front of him. "This is total bullshit! I'm being railroaded!" He continued to yell and curse as the trooper drove down the highway.

THE HOSPITAL WAS quiet due to the late hour. Martha moved silently down the hall until she came upon Amanda's room. She opened the door slowly and shook her head at the scene before her.

Lex was slouched in a rocking chair by the window, her head tilted and her eyes closed. Her hands were linked and resting on her stomach and light snores escaped from her mouth. She had changed to the same clothes she had on when she brought Amanda to the hospital, her shirt heavily wrinkled and no longer tucked in.

Martha went to Lex and shook her shoulder. She kept her voice low, so as not to disturb Amanda. "Lexie, wake up."

"Hmm?" Lex's eyes stayed closed, but not for long. They popped open when Martha pinched her arm. "What?"

"You need to get some sleep." Martha's nose twitched. "And a shower, too."

Lex blinked a few times. "I was asleep."

"You know I meant in a bed, you rotten kid." But Martha belied her comment with a tender touch on Lex's cheek. "Honey, you're not going to be any good to your family if you're dead on your feet."

"I know, but—"

Martha took one of Lex's hands and pulled her to her feet. "No buts. Amanda's probably going to sleep until morning, so you have plenty of time to go to Lois and Michael's."

"Okay." Lex watched Amanda sleep. "I'll be out in a second."

"Good girl." Martha strutted from the room, extremely proud of herself.

After the door closed behind Martha, Lex stood beside Amanda's bed and watched as she slept. Her whispered words could barely be heard in the room. "Martha's dragging me out of here, sweetheart. But I'll be back as soon as I can, okay?" She kissed Amanda's forehead and left the room before Martha could return to fuss at her.

Out in the hallway, Martha tapped her foot. "You didn't wake her, did you?"

"Of course not." Lex took one last look at the door. "I can always get cleaned up and be here before she knows I'm gone."

"You'll do no such thing." Martha took her arm and practically dragged Lex away. "You need to go. Little Lorrie has missed you something awful."

Lex pulled up. "Damn. I should have gone to get her." She headed toward the nursery. "Let me take a quick run to see how Melanie is first."

Martha had to hurry to keep up with her. "Would you slow down? Not all of us were graced with giraffe legs."

THE FOLLOWING MORNING, Lex showered and dressed, leaving her blue western shirt unbuttoned. She stood in front of the bathroom mirror and fluffed her wet hair with a towel. Still trying to get fully awake, she brought the towel away from her head and leaned closer to the mirror. Several shiny hairs near her temple caught her attention. "I don't believe this." She was about to yank them from her head when she heard the door handle rattle.

"Momma, lemme in." Lorrie pounded on the door for good measure. "Pease?"

Lex draped the towel around her neck and hastily buttoned her shirt before she opened the door. She staggered when Lorrie wrapped herself around her legs. "Hey there, lil' bit." Lex scooped up her daughter and accepted a sloppy kiss. "How's my girl? Have you been good?"

"Yep. Where's Mommy?"

There was no need to make up any story since they'd been preparing Lorrie for the time when the baby would be born. "She's at the hospital."

"Does Mommy gots owie?"

"Um, no. Well, kind of, I guess." Lex took Lorrie into the room Lois had given them and sat on the bed. "Remember we told you how Mommy had a baby in her tummy?"

"Yep." Lorrie wriggled until she was comfortable on Lex's lap.

Lex used her fingers to comb through her daughter's unruly hair. "Well, it was time for the baby to come, so we took mommy to the hospital to see the doctor."

Lorrie seemed to think about what Lex told her. She rested her head on her momma's cheek. "I want my Mommy."

"I know, sweetheart. How about after we have breakfast, we go see her? I bet she'll be glad to see you."

"Otay." Now that her curiosity had been sated, Lorrie was ready for action. She climbed off Lex's lap and tugged at her momma's hand. "Can we eats like hosses?"

Lex allowed herself to be dragged from the room. Amanda had teased her about the only breakfast food she could cook without burning. Oatmeal before it was microwaved looked like horse feed, or so Amanda said. It quickly became Lorrie's favorite, which pleased Lex to no end. "Sure thing, lil' bit." Lex picked her up, which caused Lorrie to squeal. "Then you can tell your Mommy all about it." She hoisted her daughter onto her shoulders and did a slow lope to the kitchen.

VOICES MINGLED TOGETHER in the open room, as several officers and suspects argued amongst themselves. Hubert sat next to a crowded desk with his head in his hands. He raised his head when a short man in uniform dropped into the rolling leather chair across from him.

"Mr. Walters, are you aware of the conditions of your parole?" Officer Griffith flicked through the faxed sheets he'd received moments ago.

"Yeah, I guess." In actuality, Hubert had no idea, other than the weekly reports he was required to make to his parole officer. "When do I pay my ticket and get the hell out of here? I've got places I need to be."

Griffith placed the papers on his desk. "Don't worry. You'll be going, soon enough. Your parole has been revoked and you're facing charges in Texas, as well as here."

"Revoked? What the hell does that mean?"

"Rescinded, repealed, cancelled. Take your pick."

Hubert slapped his hand against his thigh. "I know what the word means, goddamn it. I'm not an idiot." He thought for a moment. "I need to call my lawyer."

The officer turned the phone around to face him. "That's the first sensible thing you've said since you were brought in here. Don't take all day." He opened the bottom drawer of his desk and flipped through several file folders before taking out a form. "I've got plenty of paperwork to keep me busy."

"Jackass," Hubert mumbled under his breath. He jabbed the

buttons on the phone, and waited impatiently for an answer. "Come on, damn it. Pick up the phone." He bounced his knee nervously. "Hey, Kirk. I need a little help."

"Now what? I'm not going to be a part of any more of your schemes, Hubert. I almost lost my license over that last fiasco. So if that's what you're calling about—"

"No, nothing like that." Hubert cut him off before he could go into a full rant. "Would you shut up? I'm in trouble and I need a lawyer."

A heavy sigh escaped from Kirk. "What else is new? Where are you anyway? Your sister called me a couple of days ago, ready to rip my head off."

"Forget about her, damn it. You've got to come up here and take care of some things."

"Up where?"

Hubert glanced at the cop, who was ignoring him. "Oklahoma. They've got me on some trumped-up possession charges."

"You've got to be kidding me. You crossed state lines? Damn it, Hubert, that's against the conditions of your parole. Wait. Did you say possession? What have you gotten into now?"

"It's not mine, dumbass. Someone planted it in my car. But these bozos won't listen to me. So you've got to get your ass in gear and take care of it. I'm not about to go to jail."

Officer Griffith chuckled. "Want to bet?" He cleared his throat and continued to type after Hubert glared at him.

Hubert sighed and returned his attention to Kirk. "What? I missed what you said."

"I'm not driving all the way up to Oklahoma, Hubert. I'm not even licensed to practice law outside of Texas. So you'll have to find a lawyer there."

"What the hell do I pay you for, then?"

"You haven't, remember? You told me to get it from your sister, who, by the way, has filed charges against me. I'll be lucky to keep myself out of jail, asshole. So go to hell." Kirk hung up without letting Hubert answer him.

"Fuck!" Hubert hit his leg with the receiver. "Son of a bitch."

The cop turned in his chair to look at him. "Problem?" He seemed to enjoy Hubert's discomfort.

"No. I mean, yeah. My lawyer can't make it. You got one I can talk to?"

"They'll appoint you one, Mr. Walters." Griffith pushed the paper across the desk and held out a pen. "Read this over and sign it."

Hubert took the pen and scribbled his name across the bottom of the page. "Now what?"

"I'll take you to the holding cell, until your counsel arrives." He stood and gestured for Hubert to do the same. "Do you have any family to notify?"

For a second, Hubert considered calling Lex, but quickly decided against it. He had a feeling she wouldn't help him, family or not. "No, I've got nobody." He walked ahead of the cop, trying to figure out how his life had gotten out of hand so quickly.

THE MATERNITY WING of the hospital wing was bustling with activity as Lex and Lorrie walked toward Amanda's room. In one hand, Lex carried a small teddy bear with a balloon attached, which Lorrie helped pick out. Her other hand was held firmly by her daughter, who clutched a page out of a coloring book, which she had colored for her mommy.

Lorrie's eyes grew wide when a woman pushing a cart of books and snacks rolled by them. She'd never seen so many goodies before. "Momma, what's dat?"

Lex was saved by a voice from behind them. "That's something the nice lady takes to all the rooms, so folks will have snacks and stuff to read." Martha stepped around them. "Good morning, girls."

"Mada!" Lorrie released Lex's hand and practically leaped into Martha's arms. She waved the paper in Martha's face. "I made dis for Mommy."

Martha noticed the date and Lorrie's name on the bottom of the page, printed neatly by Lex. "It's beautiful, honey." She was pleased to see that her nagging worked. Lex's eyes were clear and the exhaustion from the previous day was gone. "You look much better today, Lexie."

"Thanks to you." Lex kissed Martha's cheek. "One of these days I'll learn not to argue with you."

"Uh-huh. It'll snow in July before that happens." Martha turned and continued toward Amanda's room, leaving Lex sputtering in the hall.

Lorrie squirmed in Martha's arms as they stepped into Amanda's room. "Mommy!" She tried to get down, but Martha held firm.

"Hold on there, sweetie, we have to be careful. Your Mommy's pretty tender right now."

Amanda held out her arms when Martha cautiously helped Lorrie onto the bed. "Hi, baby. I've missed you." She kissed the top of her daughter's head.

Lex came into the room and placed the balloon-wielding bear on a side table. She took her place on the other side of the bed and kissed Amanda's cheek. "You're looking great, sweetheart."

"I doubt that, but thanks." Amanda self-consciously brushed her hair down with her hand. "I'd kill for a bath."

Lex leaned close and whispered in her ear, "I'll give you a sponge bath, later." She kissed Amanda's ear before straightening up. "Love you."

"Love you, too." Amanda noticed the paper Lorrie was holding. "What's that?"

Lorrie stared at the paper before thrusting it in Amanda's face. "I clorled dis for you."

"It's beautiful." She raised her eyes to Lex. "I'm glad you went home and got some rest." She had been surprised to wake up and find herself alone, but had a feeling Martha had sent her partner away.

"It wasn't my idea." Lex pointed to Martha. "She made me."

"Good."

They all turned toward the door when a nurse came in, carrying a fussing Melanie. "I believe it's someone's lunchtime." She handed the baby to Amanda. "How are you doing?"

"Sore, but tired of lying around."

Lorrie oooh'd in surprise when she saw the infant. "Mommy? Who's dat?"

"This is your baby sister, sweetie. Her name's Melanie." Amanda pulled the baby's blanket away enough so that her arm was showing. "Would you like to touch her?"

"I can?"

Lex moved to stand behind Lorrie. "Yep. Be real easy." She lightly touched Lorrie's arm with her fingers. "Like that."

"Otay." Lorrie held out her hand cautiously and touched Melanie's arm. "Soft. Likes Teddy is." Emboldened by Amanda's smile, she rubbed her as if the infant were a pet. "I likes the baby."

Melanie, tired of the attention, began to cry, which scared Lorrie. "Mommy?"

"It's okay, lil' bit." Lex covered Melanie's arm and kissed Lorrie on the head. "Melanie's still getting used to us. And I think she's hungry."

"Oh." Lorrie tugged on the baby's blanket. "S'okay, Melly. Momma gets you sumpin' to eats." She turned to Lex. "Momma?"

Lex tried to keep from laughing at her daughter's plea. "Actually, kiddo, that's something your Mommy is going to have to do. Right, Mommy?"

"Right." Amanda started to pull down her top, before realizing Martha was standing nearby. She wasn't too comfortable nursing in front of anyone besides Lex. "Um — "

Martha waved her hand. "Say no more. I think I'll go check out the gift shop."

"Mada, I goes?" Lorrie loved spending time with her parents, but she loved running around a lot more. Since the baby wouldn't play with her, she'd find something else to do.

"Sure, honey." Martha helped her from the bed. "We'll be back in a little while. I've got to spend some time with my favorite girl."

As soon as the room quieted, Amanda held one hand out to Lex.

"Come here. I think this is going to be a two-person job."

Lex eased Amanda far enough up so Lex could sit partially behind her. "How's this?"

"Perfect." Amanda opened her top and guided Melanie to her breast. Not much encouragement was needed, as the infant quickly latched on to her nipple and fed hungrily. "I still say she's got your appetite."

Lex chuckled as she lightly stroked the baby's head with her thumb. "You seem to bring that out in us." She became quiet as she thought about how different her life had become. If someone would have told her ten years ago that she'd be sitting on a hospital bed with her wife and newborn child, she'd have laughed in their face. Now, she couldn't remember what it felt like to be alone. Amanda had brought so much into her life. She kissed Amanda's temple. "I love you."

Amanda turned her head slightly. She could see the moisture pooling in her lover's eyes. "You've made my life worth living, Lex. I love you, too." They shared a sweet, tender kiss, both looking forward to the rest of their lives.

Other Carrie Carr titles published by
Yellow Rose Books

LEX AND AMANDA SERIES

Destiny's Bridge - Rancher Lexington (Lex) Walters pulls young Amanda Cauble from a raging creek and the two women quickly develop a strong bond of friendship. Overcoming severe weather, cattle thieves, and their own fears, their friendship deepens into a strong and lasting love.

Faith's Crossing - Lexington Walters and Amanda Cauble withstood raging floods, cattle rustlers and other obstacles to be together...but can they handle Amanda's parents? When Amanda decides to move to Texas for good, she goes back to her parents' home in California to get the rest of her things, taking the rancher with her.

Hope's Path - Someone is determined to ruin Lex. Efforts to destroy her ranch lead to attempts on her life. Lex and Amanda desperately try to find out who hates Lex so much that they are willing to ruin the lives of everyone in their path. Can they survive long enough to find out who's responsible? And will their love survive when they find out who it is?

Love's Journey - Lex and Amanda embark on a new journey as Lexington rediscovers the love her mother's family has for her, and Amanda begins to build her relationship with her father. Meanwhile, attacks on the two young women grow more violent and deadly as someone tries to tear apart the love they share.

Strength of the Heart - Lex and Amanda are caught up in the planning of their upcoming nuptials while trying to ger the ranch house rebuilt. But an arrest, a brushfire, and the death of someone close to her forces Lex to try and work through feelings of guilt and anger. Is Amanda's love strong enough to help her, or will Lex's own personal demons tear them apart?

The Way Things Should Be - In this, the sixth novel, Amanda begins to feel her own biological clock ticking while her sister prepares for the birth of her first child. Lex is busy with trying to keep her hands on some newly acquired land, as well trying to get along with a new member of her family. Everything comes to a head, and a tragedy brings pain - and hope - to them all.

SOMETHING TO BE THANKFUL FOR

Randi Meyers is at a crossroads in her life. She's got no girlfriend, bad knees, and her fill of loneliness. The one thing she does have in her favor is a veterinarian job in Fort Worth, Texas, but even that isn't going as well as she hoped. Her supervisor is cold-hearted and dumps long hours of work on her. Even if she did want a girlfriend, she has little time to look.

When a distant uncle dies, Randi returns to her hometown of Woodbridge, Texas, to attend the funeral. During the graveside services, she wanders away from the crowd and is beseeched by a young boy to follow him into the woods to help his injured sister. After coming upon an unconscious woman, the boy disappears. Randi brings the woman to the hospital and finds out that her name is Kay Newcombe.

Randi is intrigued by Kay. Who is this unusual woman? Where did her little brother disappear to? And why does Randi feel compelled to help her? Despite living in different cities, a tentative friendship forms, but Randi is hesitant. Can she trust her newfound friend? How much of her life and feelings can Randi reveal? And what secrets is Kay keeping from her? Together, Randi and Kay must unravel these questions, trust one another, and find the answers in order to protect themselves from outside threats — and discover what they mean to one another.

ISBN 1-932300-04-X
978-1-323300-04-8

DIVING INTO THE TURN

Diving Into the Turn is set in the fast-paced Texas rodeo world. Riding bulls in the rodeo is the only life Shelby Fisher has ever known. She thinks she's happy drifting from place to place in her tiny trailer, engaging in one night stands, and living from one rodeo paycheck to another – until the day she meets barrel racer Rebecca Starrett. Rebecca comes from a solid, middle-class background and owns her horse. She's had money and support that Shelby has never had. Shelby and Rebecca take an instant dislike to each other, but there's something about Rebecca that draws the silent and angry bull rider to her. Suddenly, Shelby's life feels emptier, and she can't figure out why. Gradually, Rebecca attempts to win Shelby over, and a shaky friendship starts to grow into something more.

Against a backdrop of mysterious accidents that happen at the rodeo grounds, their attraction to one another is tested. When Shelby is implicated as the culprit to what's been happening will Rebecca stand by her side?

ISBN 978- 1-932300-54-3

FORTHCOMING TITLES
published by Yellow Rose Books

Blue Collar Lesbian Erotica
Edited by Pat Cronin and Verda Foster

We don't all live in million dollar homes and drive fancy sports cars. We don't all live the life portrayed on television or in some of our books. Most of us live average lives in average homes and average circumstances. So why not have stories about us?

Blue Collar Lesbian Erotica is a collection of stories about the average lesbian in hot, steamy encounters in not-so-average places. Okay, sometimes the women are lawyers or actresses, but the sex doesn't always take place where you would expect: taxi cabs, convents, back yard tents.

This anthology goes outside the norm and provides a collection of stories you won't see anywhere else.

Available July 2008

Love's Redemption
by Helen Macpherson

Ten years ago talented Lauren Wheatley was on the verge of golfing greatness. As the world's number one amateur, she stood on the cusp of entry to the women's professional tour. However in a quirk of fate, she imploded in spectacular fashion, during a tournament that would have signaled her immediate entry into the professional ranks. She walked away and never played golf again.

Jo Ashby is a reporter narrating and producing the "Where Are They Now?" series, a program focusing on well-known people who have left fame behind, instead opting for a different direction in life. Her subject for the final program is the enigmatic Lauren Wheatley who, despite Jo's best efforts, evades her attempts at an interview.

Jo travels to the pristine wilderness of Tasmania to confront Lauren. However, instead of confrontation, she is captured by the beauty of the surrounding land and the woman herself. Coupled with this beauty lies a greater story behind the fragile facade of Lauren's life.Can Jo break through the barriers Lauren has shielded herself with, and conquer the riddle that is Lauren Wheatley? Can Jo reconcile her professional requirements, yet face her own demons and, once and for all, put them to rest?

Set against the backdrop of the Tasmanian wilderness, *Love's Redemption* follows the rocky lives of two headstrong women, affirming that sometimes the phrase "and they lived happily ever after" is often more fairytale than fact.

Available November 2008

ANOTHER YELLOW ROSE TITLE
You may also enjoy:

Second Verse
by Jane Vollbrecht

It's been two years since Gail Larsen, editor for Outrageous Press, has so much as held hands with anyone. Her isolation is self-imposed, due to the guilt she feels over an accident involving her beloved Marissa. Then a special editing assignment throws Gail together with Connie Martin, one of the leading ladies of lesbian fiction. Gail is at first amused by Connie's pit-bull personality in a Pekinese body, but amusement turns to attraction, and attraction to heart-wrenching torment.

Following an intense month working with Connie on her soon-to-be-released book, another opportunity comes Gail's way. Her lifelong friend, Penny Skramstaad, asks her to come to their hometown of Plainfield, Minnesota, to help clean out Penny's parents' house. For more than thirty years, Gail has harbored an unanswered longing for Penny. When Gail and Penny go to the homecoming dance at Plainfield High, old ghosts re-emerge, and Gail and Penny are forced to finally confront them.

With Connie on one side and Penny on the other, Gail fears she's trapped between two women — one she'll never have and one she doesn't want.

As Gail comes to know the truths about both Connie and Penny, she also comes to know herself, perhaps much better than she ever thought she might. One thing she's sure of: she wants a partner who will dance with her for the rest of her life. Can she find someone who'll last through the Second Verse?

ISBN 978-1-932300-94-9

OTHER YELLOW ROSE PUBLICATIONS

About the Author

Carrie Carr is a true Texan, having lived in the state her entire life. She makes her home in the Dallas/Ft. Worth metroplex with her wife, Jan. She's done just about everything from wrangling longhorn cattle and buffalo, to programming burglar and fire alarm systems. Her time is spent writing, traveling, and trying to keep up with their two dogs - a Chihuahua/Boston Terrier-mix named Nugget, and a Rat Terrier named Cher. Carrie's website is www.CarrieLCarr.com. She can be reached at cbzeer@yahoo.com.

VISIT US ONLINE AT
www.regalcrest.biz

At the Regal Crest Website You'll Find

- The latest news about forthcoming titles and new releases

- Our complete backlist of romance, mystery, thriller and adventure titles

- Information about your favorite authors

- Current bestsellers

Regal Crest titles are available from all progressive booksellers and online at StarCrossed Productions, (www.scp-inc.biz) and also at www.amazon.com, www.bamm.com, www.barnesandnoble.com, and many others.

Printed in the United States
141729LV00003B/65/P